S0-BTZ-218

DESIRE'S BETRAYAL

Marlee settled her glittering blue gaze upon him. "You're leaving, and I want you to know . . . I would deem it a great honor, my lord, if you would make me your wife in every sense of the word."

Lark bolted out of the chair. "Marlee! Do you know what you are asking?"

"Yes, my lord," she said, stepping closer and wantonly wrapping her arms around his neck.

He could not resist her. With a groan, he pulled her into him, claiming her full, tempting lips in a fiery kiss of aching need and pent-up passion.

"You've asked for this, my love, remember that," she heard him murmur at her mouth.

Lark knew, in the back of his mind, that he should admit the truth to her, that he should do the honorable thing and leave. But he'd never felt this way before . . . and as he undid the back of her silver gown, Lark knew he didn't give a damn about honor. All he wanted was Marlee—and a fleeting moment of happiness to last the rest of his years.

DANA RANSOM'S RED-HOT HEARTFIRES!

ALEXANDRA'S ECSTASY (2773, $3.75)

Alexandra had known Tucker for all her seventeen years, but all at once she realized her childhood friend was the man capable of tempting her to leave innocence behind!

LIAR'S PROMISE (2881, $4.25)

Kathryn Mallory's sincere questions about her father's ship to the disreputable Captain Brady Rogan were met with mocking indifference. Then he noticed her trim waist, angelic face and Kathryn won the wrong kind of attention!

LOVE'S GLORIOUS GAMBLE (2497, $3.75)

Nothing could match the true thrill that coursed through Gloria Daniels when she first spotted the gambler, Sterling Caulder. Experiencing his embrace, feeling his lips against hers would be a risk, but she was willing to chance it all!

WILD, SAVAGE LOVE (3055, $4.25)

Evangeline, set free from Indians, discovered liberty had its price to pay when her uncle sold her into marriage to Royce Tanner. Dreaming of her return to the people she loved, she vowed never to submit to her husband's caress.

WILD WYOMING LOVE (3427, $4.25)

Lucille Blessing had no time for the new marshal Sam Zachary. His mocking and arrogant manner grated her nerves, yet she longed to ease the tension she knew he held inside. She knew that if he wanted her, she could never say no!

Available wherever paperbacks are sold, or order direct from the Publisher. Send cover price plus 50¢ per copy for mailing and handling to Zebra Books, Dept. 3586, 475 Park Avenue South, New York, N.Y. 10016. Residents of New York, New Jersey and Pennsylvania must include sales tax. DO NOT SEND CASH.

LYNETTE VINET
PASSION'S DEEP SPELL

ZEBRA BOOKS
KENSINGTON PUBLISHING CORP.

For my Daddy,
Joseph Charles Slaughter
1919-1991

ZEBRA BOOKS

are published by

Kensington Publishing Corp.
475 Park Avenue South
New York, NY 10016

Copyright © 1991 by Lynette Vinet

All rights reserved. No part of this book may be reproduced in any form or by any means without the prior written consent of the Publisher, excepting brief quotes used in reviews.

If you purchased this book without a cover you should be aware that this book is stolen property. It was reported as "unsold and destroyed" to the Publisher and neither the Author nor the Publisher has received any payment for this "stripped book."

First printing: November, 1991

Printed in the United States of America

Whoever has a mind to abundance of trouble,
Let him furnish himself with a ship and a
woman.
— Mary Evelyn
A Voyage to Maryland;
Or, The Ladies' Dressing-Room

Chapter One

The Cornish Coast of England
1725

"I now pronounce you husband and wife."

The magistrate smiled at the bride and groom, his job completed with those few words. The wedding ceremony was over, seemingly finished before it had begun. Marlee Stafford found herself embraced by Hollins Carpenter, the man who stood next to her and who had placed a ruby and gold filigree ring upon her third finger not five minutes ago. Hollins kissed her forehead in a polite but distant manner. "My best wishes to you, Lady Arden," he addressed her by her new name.

"Thank you, Mr. Carpenter." Marlee's answer was automatic as she was somewhat dazed to realize she was a married woman. Only that morning she'd gone shopping in the village with her Aunt Clementina and two cousins; the purpose of the trip was to buy material to make a proper wedding gown. And now she would be unable to use the fine white silk she'd carefully chosen for her wedding in one month's time to Lord Richard Arden. Hollins Carpenter was at the house upon their return, and his news took her completely by surprise.

"Lord Arden requests the marriage ceremony be performed by proxy today, my dear." Carpenter, who was Marlee's solicitor as well as Richard Arden's, had told her this startling news in as gentle a voice as he could summon. "He's aware your Uncle Jack has already made some arrangements for the ceremony, but . . ." And here Carpenter glanced down at the wooden floor in her aunt's home, seeming to trace every nick in its polished surface before he looked up again to settle his spectacles upon his nose. "The baron has been abed lately and fears traveling might deter his hasty recovery. He has appointed me to be your proxy groom. I do hope you don't mind."

Mind? Certainly Marlee minded. It wasn't everyday she'd be married, especially not to someone she'd never met. Tales about Lord Richard Arden, Baron of Montclair, abounded throughout Cornwall. Some people considered him to be the devil himself with his black hair and devilishly dark eyes. Rampant rumors circulated about his drinking, the large amounts of time he spent at the gaming tables. Tongues wagged that he'd sired half a dozen children without benefit of clergy. Indeed, Arden was a rogue of the highest order and she was going to marry him. She must marry him because only a rogue would have her.

For more than a fleeting second Marlee did wonder if Lord Richard was truly ill. Perhaps he feigned poor health as an excuse to marry her and lay claim to her fortune without making her a true wife, without meet-

8

ing her face to face. So much had happened in such a short time, beginning with Arden's sudden marriage proposal and now ending with a hasty wedding. Marlee couldn't help but be suspicious of Arden's motives. It was a well-known fact that his ancestral home Montclair had fallen into disrepair. Carpenter had already confided to her that Arden needed Marlee's wealth to pay his creditors.

Carpenter had convinced Marlee that the marriage would solve a great many problems for herself and Lord Arden. Marlee could see the wisdom behind Carpenter's suggestion, but no matter the circumstances for such an alliance, Marlee wouldn't allow Arden to use her fortune without making her his wife in every sense of the word. She might only be the daughter of a tin miner, but she did possess some pride and wouldn't allow a rogue like Richard Arden to deny her the chance to be a proper wife.

With a determined smile on her beautiful face and a slight inclination of her dark head, she placed her hand on Mr. Carpenter's arm. "You've looked after my interests since my father's death and I know you wouldn't play me false. Since Lord Richard trusts you so well, I will be most pleased to have you stand in for him during the ceremony. I hope when I meet Lord Richard I shall find him in good health." She purposely flashed the solicitor a dazzling smile. Her cheeks dimpled prettily with the effort, causing her sapphire-colored eyes to glow like the sky on a sunny afternoon.

Hurriedly she changed into an ice blue gown which was fashioned from the finest silk and pulled her dark tresses away from her face with a white ribbon. Within

9

minutes she stood before the magistrate in Jack and Clementina's McBride's small parlor and placed her trembling hand in Mr. Carpenter's steadying clasp.

Her aunt and uncle with their daughters in attendance watched as Marlee Stafford became Lady Arden, Baroness of Montclair.

Carpenter swallowed and patted her hand during the ceremony but not once did he look at her directly until the moment he kissed her forehead at the ceremony's end.

In the background Clementina sniffed and wiped at her eyes with a lace kerchief. Marlee sighed, knowing the woman wasn't crying because she'd miss her niece though it would be nice to think so. Finally, after eight years of caring for her sister's child, Clementina would be free of Marlee. No, the tears were joyous ones because Marlee, the orphaned but wealthy relation, had married into the aristocracy. Clementina's mercenary heart must be weighing the advantages of having a relation with noble connections, now that her daughters Daphne and Barbara were of marriageable age. Marlee would be able to introduce them to eligible and wealthy young men, giving Clementina the hope that her girls would marry well.

"Such a happy day this is," Clementina spoke aloud and noisily blew her nose. "We've a baroness in the family. It was worth all the trouble that lying Tim Lee caused with his nasty comments about Marlee's virtue."

A blush suffused Marlee's cheeks. How dare her aunt mention such a thing now, especially with the magistrate nearby. He'd no doubt gossip about all that was said and done in the McBride household today.

She could just hear all the wagging tongues, but soon she'd leave the village and go to live in her husband's home, putting all of the nasty and untrue rumors firmly behind her.

Thankfully, her Uncle Jack was more tactful and kinder than his wife. He shyly kissed Marlee's cheek. "I wish the best for you, dear girl. We all do. Be happy in your new life." Gesturing toward his daughters, he urged them forward. "Girls, come wish your cousin Marlee happiness."

Barbara, Marlee's younger cousin, rushed toward her and clasped her hand. She peered at the ring on Marlee's finger. "How beautiful it is, and how lucky you are! Oh, I do wish you good things, Marlee. May I come visit you at Montclair? I should like that ever so much."

"Yes, I believe I'll have need of a friendly and familiar face." Marlee warmly regarded Barbara. Out of all the McBrides, she liked Barbara the best. They were friends as well as cousins, and she knew she'd miss Barbara when the time came for her to depart with Mr. Carpenter for Montclair. However, she doubted she'd miss Daphne much—if at all. That sentiment was brought home when Daphne casually sauntered near and barely gave a glance at Marlee's outstretched hand.

"Isn't it a beautiful ring?" Barbara gushed to her sister, her chestnut-colored curls bouncing upon her forehead in enthusiasm.

"As rings go, I suppose it will do," Daphne laconically proclaimed and didn't give the ring an extra look.

Hollins Carpenter turned from his conversation with the magistrate and Jack. He smiled indulgently

11

at Daphne. "If I may say something about Lady Arden's ring, Miss McBride."

Daphne shrugged, pretending a disinterest which Marlee guessed Daphne didn't feel.

"Lady Arden's wedding ring," Carpenter interjected with a bright-eyed stare which caused his plain face to seem surprisingly animated, "is over three hundred years old. It was worn by the first Lady Arden and has graced the finger of each subsequent baroness. The craftsmanship is unequaled, the ruby is the most dazzling of any comparable jewel in England. Lord Arden is indeed fortunate to have such a gracious and lovely wife as Lady Marlee to wear it. I'm certain that one day some lucky gentleman will present a similar wedding ring to you."

For just a second something like adoration behind the spectacles flickered in the depths of Carpenter's eyes for the blond-haired Daphne. Marlee noticed it, but Daphne, too caught up in her envy for Marlee, didn't. "Personally, I'd prefer a much larger stone," was Daphne's cutting remark. "Marlee, for all her wealth, is fortunate to marry at all, considering that no decent young men darkened our doorstep after her reputation was ruined. Everyone knows that Richard Arden only wants her for her money."

"Daphne!" Barbara clutched her milky-white throat. "You shouldn't say such terrible things, not today of all days."

"Well, it's true and you well know it, Barbara McBride."

Clementina suddenly intervened by clapping her hands. "Girls, bid the magistrate farewell and go wash for supper. I'm certain Mr. Car-

12

penter has things to discuss with Marlee."

Marlee was grateful that for once Clementina had silenced Daphne. However, she guessed the magistrate would rush to tell everyone about Daphne's remarks and, once again, the silly story about her fall from grace would be bandied in the village.

Minutes later, Marlee found herself sitting on a hard-backed chair in the parlor before a small tea table while Mr. Carpenter sat across from her. On the table he'd placed an official-looking document.

"I never believed the rumors," he offered kindly and adjusted his spectacles.

"Thank you for saying that, Mr. Carpenter. "I wish others didn't. People can be quite cruel, you know."

"You're a baroness now, my lady. What others think and say can no longer harm you."

"I doubt, sir, just as I doubt that I shall ever get used to being addressed as "my lady." Such a title is rather daunting to a tin miner's daughter."

"Lady Arden," Carpenter intoned in a deep and serious voice with a demeanor to match. "You *are* Lady Marlee Arden, Baroness of Montclair and wife to a powerful man. The tin miner's daughter is no longer."

Marlee laughed out loud. "Oh, piddle, Mr. Carpenter. You know perfectly well that in my heart I am William Stafford's daughter and descended from peasant stock. It was my father's good business sense which allowed him to own the mines instead of working in them like his father and grandfather before him. Otherwise, I doubt a powerful and well-bred man as Richard Arden would wed me for myself. We're both aware he married me for my fortune."

"Yes, well . . ."

"Mr. Carpenter, you're turning red with embarrassment. Please don't be embarrassed for me. After all, you are the one who informed my husband about my less than promising matrimonial circumstances. I'm well aware my marriage isn't a love match, but I hope to change that after I arrive at Montclair and meet my husband. I have high expectations for the future."

"Yes, my lady, as do I." Hollins sighed and reached for a quill with a suddenly unsteady hand. Marlee couldn't dislike the man, even if he had arranged a marriage between two of his clients to bail her groom out of financial difficulties. Arden might prosper financially, but she'd prosper, too, in the scheme of things. She'd have a husband and a home, no longer existing as an unwanted relation.

It seemed her large fortune was all that mattered to some people, her groom included, she admitted glumly to herself. Arden was as mercenary as Clementina and Jack who had wanted her to live with them after Marlee's father's death. Poor, little orphan girl, Clementina had said with misty eyes at William Stafford's funeral. There must be something she could do for her only sister's child.

It turned out there was.

William had turned her guardianship over to the McBrides in his will. Marlee had thought her aunt and uncle had truly wanted her — they seemed so pleased to have her — until Mr. Carpenter told them a small stipend would be paid each month for her care. Clementina had declared it wasn't enough, that poor Jack would have to slave away forever as a bank clerk when an heiress lived under their very roof. Their daughters wouldn't have the fine silks and satins which a girl as

14

wealthy as Marlee could easily afford. Surely, they should be paid more for Marlee's care. But Hollins resisted, adamant in following William's will to the letter.

Each month when the small stipend arrived, Marlee endured her aunt's hateful gazes, the stinging silences. Every day Marlee prayed that she'd grow up fast and leave the McBrides. They didn't abuse her but she wasn't wanted either, and that knowledge hurt as much as any slap or heated retort would have.

When she was seventeen, Tim Lee, the son of the local minister, entered her life. He was a good-looking lad of nineteen and intent upon following in his father's footsteps. Marlee was friendly with Tim, finding him to be a nice enough person but not truly encouraging his attentions to her when he suddenly expressed more than a passing interest in her. Whenever Tim appeared at the house, she'd dutifully sit with him in the garden under the watchful eye of Clementina. Her aunt wished for a marriage as a way of getting her niece out of the house. But when Tim proposed to Marlee, she refused. There was nothing about Tim that would cause her to want to spend the rest of her life as a pastor's wife. She gently told him she was unworthy of his affections, and he should seek a bride elsewhere.

Tim took her refusal in good stride, or so Marlee had thought. Two weeks later, Marlee had nearly forgotten the proposal when rumors started circulating about her virtue. It seemed Tim Lee had confided to a dear friend that Marlee refused to marry him because she found herself unworthy. The friend, perhaps with a bit of exaggeration on Tim's part, put his own connotation on Marlee's "unworthiness."

Reverend Lee paid an unexpected visit to the McBrides to declare that he'd not welcome a "Jezebel" into his family and was deeply relieved that Tim had the good sense not to call upon Marlee again.

Weeks later Tim married a preacher's daughter from Devon, but the damage to Marlee's reputation had already been done. People whispered behind their hands whenever Marlee went to the village, causing her distress and unease. As far as Clementina was concerned, the worst happened when no young men with money or connections called upon the two McBride sisters. It seemed Daphne and Barbara would remain spinsters — and all because Marlee had rejected a suitor.

Now, with Marlee's marriage to Lord Arden, she could make up for her cousins lack of suitors. She could present the two girls with an opportunity to enter polite circles so they might attract wealthy husbands. She felt she did owe the McBrides something for her care, and perhaps her arranged marriage to a dissolute aristocrat would make up for any inconvenience they'd suffered. Evidently her fall from grace didn't matter to Richard Arden. He'd married her anyway.

"My lady." Mr. Carpenter's voice drew Marlee from her reverie. She blinked and discovered he was holding the quill out to her. "The papers are in order. All that is required is your signature."

"I'm sorry. My mind was wandering." She smiled apologetically and glanced to the spot where he pointed on the parchment before her. "What am I supposed to sign?"

For a moment Carpenter appeared almost sheepish, even hesitant. "This document turns over your inheritance to Lord Arden, if you wish. Your father wanted you to decide the matter of your fortune's disposal for yourself."

This was news to Marlee. She hadn't known about such a stipulation in her father's will until this moment and was disbelieving. "You mean I have a choice in the matter?"

"Well . . . yes—you do."

"Why didn't you inform me about this before now, Mr. Carpenter?" Marlee felt anger and dismay rising within her to have been purposely left in the dark by Mr. Carpenter, a man whom she thought she could trust. No doubt he had feared that if she'd known about the document, she'd have reneged on the marriage contract. Evidently her father had drafted the document to protect her interests by allowing her the choice in turning her fortune over to her husband. Her dear, sweet father was looking after her in death, even if living people weren't.

"I admit I should have told you." Carpenter's forehead broke out in droplets of perspiration. He glanced at his watch fob and some seconds passed before he looked directly at her. "Accept my apology for this oversight, however, I trusted you would feel duty bound to turn your assets over to your husband and hoped you'd regard the document as a mere formality."

Was Carpenter daft? she wondered. Signing such a document was not a "mere formality" as far as Marlee was concerned. With a few strokes of the quill, she'd be turning over her entire fortune to a dissolute aristo-

17

crat, a man who was known far and wide as a debauched rake. Once she signed the paper she had no idea how she'd be treated by her new husband. When she was living under his roof, she'd be at his mercy with no leverage against poor treatment. She'd been willing to put her body and fortune into his hands and hope for the best. She realized there was little else she could do but sign the document since she was legally married. And she would sign—in her own good time. Let Carpenter and her errant baron of a husband stew in their own juices until she was ready. A long wait would serve them right and teach them that she wasn't a stringed puppet.

It was apparent from the way Carpenter eyed her that he hoped she'd sign the document. Even now, he was pushing the quill nearer to her hand. Marlee took it. Carpenter sighed in apparent relief while Marlee held the quill between her fingers and silently read the document. It was as Mr. Carpenter had told her. If she signed, her fortune was entrusted to her husband, but if not . . .

"What happens if I don't sign, sir?"

Her question clearly took Carpenter unawares. "But—you must. Lord Richard married you only—"

"To claim my fortune," she finished the sentence for him. "Yes, I've been reminded about that a number of times today. But this has come as more than a surprise to me and I don't want to be rushed. You can understand, can't you?" She placed the quill on the table.

"Yes," Carpenter countered with a grimace because he understood only too well. Lady Marlee Arden was going to assure herself a place at Montclair by not signing immediately. He'd not intended to dupe the

18

young woman, because he was fond of her, at least as fond of her as a solicitor could be of a client. But Arden's interests meant a lot to him, too. He'd served the Ardens for a number of years and felt duty bound to extricate young Richard out of his latest financial mess. By doing so, he'd also helped Marlee Stafford obtain a husband and a position that few young women in her class could hope to achieve. He already knew that Richard would insist upon an annulment if Marlee didn't agree to turn her money over to her husband.

Yet Carpenter sensed her hesitancy and decided that delaying the signature might not be a bad idea. Considering the tragedy he'd left behind at Montclair, Marlee might be a widow before she was given the chance to be a proper wife. Once again he looked at his watch. "Since you're unwilling to sign, my lady, I must leave. Lord Arden awaits me."

Marlee rose when Hollins did. A puzzled expression puckered her forehead when he rolled the document and placed it in his jacket pocket. He started for the door and her voice halted him. "Mr. Carpenter, I'll pack only a few things and will be ready to leave shortly. Please be seated and wait."

"I should like to wait, my lady, but the day grows short and I promised Lord Arden I'd hurry back."

"But surely you're going to escort me to Montclair. Morning will be soon enough to leave."

"I—I can't. I must hurry back. When Lord Richard is well, he'll send a carriage for you. Now, I really must go."

With a quickness Marlee didn't know Hollins possessed, he scooted from the room and out of the house like a cat who'd spotted a dog. She stood in stunned silence, not feeling anything, barely thinking until the shocking reality of what had just happened hit her like a toppling house.

She'd been abandoned.

A cry of dismay tore from her throat. She'd been foolish to marry Richard Arden. He must have known about the document all along and played his cards that once he'd married her, she'd have no choice but to sign. But she hadn't signed and that was the problem.

Carpenter must have been under orders to leave her at the McBrides if she didn't entrust her fortune to the baron. She'd bet that her husband would allow her to rot here before he did the honorable thing and sent for her. He'd bestowed his name and title upon her but she was nothing to him other than a means to an end. But so was he.

More than anything she wanted a home and a husband. Even a rakish mate was preferable to remaining with her aunt and uncle in a remote village where she had as much chance of finding a husband as capturing a rainbow with her bare hands. And if it meant turning over her assets to the mercenary cad she'd married . . .

"I'll sign my fortune away," she hissed under her breath at the closed front door, "but Richard Arden won't be rid of me so easily."

And with that invective hanging in the air, Marlee rushed to her room and began preparations for her trip to Montclair.

Chapter Two

Lark Arden sat in silent disbelief in the large library at Montclair. The dusty tomes lining the shelves hadn't been perused in years. Lark thought that the last person to touch the vellumed volumes had probably been his grandfather. Most certainly his cousin, Richard, hadn't spent any time reading to enrich his mind, what little of one he'd possessed when he wasn't out whoring or gambling away the family fortune. Because of the cobwebs hanging from the corners of the high ceilings and the musty scent permeating the air, Lark surmised that no servants had cleaned or opened the room since his grandfather's death years ago.

He now knew Hollins Carpenter had told him the truth about Lord Richard Arden, the late Baron of Montclair. The man had been penniless.

"Damn the deceitful bounder!" Lark muttered, his exasperation clear in the way he rose from his chair to savagely pull back the dark green drapes and to throw open the window. Golden sunshine tumbled into the room, highlighting the overall neglect.

Simon Oliver, Lark's childhood friend, gazed in

consternation at Lark and repositioned himself in a large chair, upholstered in a plaid fabric which was so faded it was difficult to determine the original colors. "Don't speak ill of the dead, Lark. Your cousin is gone and can't defend his actions."

Turning from the window, Lark's ebony hair fell across his forehead and nearly obscured his blacker than pitch-colored eyes. Within the depths of those eyes burned red-tipped flames so angry was he by the unexpected turn of events at Montclair. "For heavens sake, man, Richard was a ne'er-do-well and knew it. If I'd have known the true state of affairs here, I'd never have left Virginia," Lark admitted before hurriedly amending, "Yes, I'd have come here if only to strangle my cousin and the inept solicitor in his employ."

"You don't mean that," Simon said with a calmness that soon transferred itself to Lark. "You've suffered a great shock. You know you wouldn't have harmed your unfortunate cousin, though I admit he must have been quite a rakish bastard from the tales I've heard about him."

"Yes, yes, he was." Lark pulled off his brown velvet jacket and threw it onto the back of his chair. The startling white of his ruffled shirt enhanced the remnants of his tan. It had been a long time since he'd been out in the open seas, working alongside his crew in the scorching sun of the Caribbean. He missed the sound of the waves crashing against the hull, longed for the warm sea breezes against his bare skin. He ached once again to see the night sky, filled with billions of twinkling stars and a moon so bright it caused the ship to be bathed in silver. Lark had planned to experience these things again, to feel the swelling surge of the sea

22

beneath his feet as he undertook the most important mission of his life.

But Richard Arden had destroyed his plans, his hopes, his mission. Damn Richard for spending Lark's own inheritance! Damn Hollins Carpenter for letting him!

Lark folded his arms across his chest and addressed the fair-haired Simon, a man who was as different from Lark in both temperament and looks. In all of the years Lark had known Simon, he'd never seen Simon lose his temper. "I wish now I had claimed my money years ago, after Grandfather died. I'm sorry my father couldn't make peace with him, that I listened to him when he ordered me not to use the money. At the time, I didn't need it; Arden's Grove didn't need it."

He thought with longing of the large plantation along the banks of the James River, not far from Williamsburg. He wondered how his mother fared in running it without him. But she'd run it when he was off to sea, hunting down pirates, and she'd taken charge after his return when he was so ill and near death. During his recovery, he learned the overseer had planted only tobacco, depleting the once rich and fertile soil, making a quick profit and absconding with the money. Lark had put all of his available cash into recouping his losses. Nothing was left to outfit a ship and crew. He didn't blame his mother for the plantation's calamity; she'd been under duress because of his father's death. But Lark did blame someone else, a conniving and despicable human being—the pirate Manuel Silva—a man whom Lark intended to hunt down and kill.

"I wish I could lend you the money," Lark heard Simon say, "but my father keeps a tight rein on my funds until I turn twenty-five in six months' time. If you could wait until then . . ."

"I appreciate the offer, friend, but time is a luxury I can ill afford these days."

"Yes, I know."

"If only Richard wouldn't have taken out the wildest stallion in the stables and been thrown by the blasted animal on the day of our arrival. God! Do you realize the odds of such a thing happening? I think I'm cursed, I truly believe I am. So many terrible things have happened over the last few months—" Lark broke off, unable to think about the horrible things he'd endured, unable to dwell upon the unthinkable which must have befallen the helpless young woman who'd been entrusted to his care. "Somehow I have to get the money I need to outfit a proper ship and crew," he spoke determinedly but grew quiet when the housekeeper and only servant, Mrs. Mortimer, appeared in the doorway.

"I've brought you tea, my lord," she said and entered the room with a silver tray and tea service atop it. She was a plump woman with gray hair and the largest pair of green eyes Lark had ever seen. Her dark brown dress was made of sturdy gingham and the white cap she wore was immaculately clean. Though she bobbed a curtsy to Lark after she poured the tea, her demeanor was stiff and frozen, a clear indication to Lark that she didn't like him or care to address him in the same manner as Richard Arden. And why should she like him? To her, he was a usurper, a stranger who had inherited Richard's title and Montclair upon

24

Richard's untimely demise. Lark recalled how diligently she'd nursed Richard after the accident, how she'd stayed by his bedside and called him her "lamb." She'd taken care of Richard when he was a child, and no matter his faults, Mrs. Mortimer remembered him as a sweet-faced little boy and not the reckless man he had become. Even now, two days after Richard's death, the woman's eyes were still red-rimmed.

Lark, too, was aggrieved by Richard's death but not because he'd cared about him. The two men had never met until the day Lark arrived in Cornwall, the day Richard met with his fatal fall. To Lark's consternation, Carpenter had taken off for God knew where and left a delusional Richard. Richard lingered in agony for five days with a back injury and mumbled some gibberish about a wealthy bride. Lark and Simon, with the help of Mrs. Mortimer, had done all they could for Richard, who refused a doctor. But Lark doubted a physician could have helped Richard. His injuries were too extensive.

Shortly after Carpenter returned, Richard took a turn for the worse.

Wanting to leave Cornwall as soon as possible, Lark requested his inheritance from Hollins Carpenter who was forced to admit the truth. There was no money—no money at all. Richard had spent his own fortune and pilfered Lark's. Carpenter admitted he didn't know that Richard's gaming debts were so great. Lark's grandfather, the old baron, had entrusted Lark's inheritance to Richard upon his death. Carpenter had no control over the money, but if it was any consolation, Montclair and the title were now Lark's. Perhaps he could sell the estate?

Even now to think about selling this moldy, decaying crypt of a house offered Lark little hope of raising enough money for his mission. With the house and grounds in such deplorable shape, little chance existed in attracting a buyer. "I don't know what I'm going to do, Simon," Lark solemnly intoned. "The fates have conspired against me."

A knock discreetly sounded on the library door and Lark gruffly ordered the person inside. Hollins Carpenter entered with a frown that caused his spectacles to dangle on the tip of his long, thin nose. He carried a piece of parchment. "Forgive me, my lord, but I wish a word with you alone."

Lark couldn't get used to being addressed in such a way by Hollins or Mrs. Mortimer. He gestured the solicitor to a chair. "You may speak freely in front of Mr. Oliver."

"If that is your wish, my lord."

The man, whom Lark appraised as about forty, appeared uneasy as he sat down. His face was flushed and he raked a hand through his graying hair. "There's a matter I must speak of, my lord, something I've neglected."

Lark flexed his broad shoulders. "Good God, man, don't tell me any more bad news about my inheritance."

Mr. Carpenter swallowed hard, seemingly cowed by Lark's superior build and strength. "Uh, no, my lord, but perhaps my news might affect you indirectly."

"How is that?" Lark toyed with a letter opener, not taking his gaze from the solicitor.

"I failed to mention to you that your cousin had married," Carpenter hurriedly spoke. "The day after

26

Richard's accident I journeyed to the young lady's home at his request. He was very ill but still he wished to marry the woman who had accepted his suit. The ceremony was performed by proxy and was somewhat of a surprise to her. You see, she and her family didn't expect me to arrive, but Richard. Well, of course, I couldn't tell them he was injured and might not survive. In fact, I believed he would be all right, as did he. Otherwise, a marriage wouldn't have been necessary."

"Yes," Lark noted sourly. "A dead man couldn't be a bridegroom."

"Exactly."

"Go on."

"Well, Miss Stafford, or rather Lady Arden now, expressed her desire to come to Montclair, but I thought it was best to make a hasty retreat before answering her. I had to see how things were with Richard first, to learn what he wished to do. Now there is little reason for her to come here at all, except I received this missive today." Carpenter held out the letter to Lark. "Your cousin's bride informs me she will soon be arriving at Montclair. I'm amiss as to what I should do. Her husband isn't here to greet her."

Quickly scanning the very feminine penmanship, Lark raised a quizzical eyebrow. "Why tell me about any of this, Carpenter? You're Richard's solicitor."

"Yes, yes, but you must realize, my lord, Marlee Stafford, er, Lady Arden, believes herself to be married to a healthy young man who is still living. Her aunt and uncle wanted her to marry Richard for the title and estate. They're rather common people, but Lady Arden inherited a large fortune from her father. She may not be an aristocrat by birth but by marriage,

27

she is your cousin's widow. And now you're the Baron of Montclair, while she believes herself to be the baroness. This unfortunate situation places both of us in uncomfortable positions."

"You're in an uncomfortable position, not I," was Lark's blunt comment to Carpenter. "Tell me about Marlee Stafford."

"Lady Arden," Hollins reminded Lark, "is an heiress, the daughter of a common laborer who managed to own a tin mine and made a fortune. She has lived with her aunt and uncle for eight years, but from what I've seen of the girl, she's never fit in very well with them. Different, I suppose you'd say, much too pretty and bright."

"Why did Richard choose to marry a common wench or need I ask?"

Hollins sighed. "Her fortune, my lord, is too great to be overlooked. I admit I informed Richard about Marlee. I knew he was having a terrible time financially, and she was unable to find a husband because of the gossip about her—reputation."

"Ah, I take it Lady Arden was too free with her favors."

"I can't say, but no decent young men offered for her. I suppose her wealth was too strong for Richard to resist. And I doubt her lack of reputation meant anything to him while his title and lands overpowered the McBride family. Thus, the aunt and uncle accepted his suit. I will say her father must have anticipated some problems with her fortune for he made a stipulation that after his daughter's marriage the money would pass to her husband only upon her signature on the necessary paperwork."

Lark tapped his fingers on the parchment. "Has she signed yet?"

"No, my lord."

"I see, Mr. Carpenter."

"Do you, my lord? I trust you do. I hope when Lady Arden arrives she won't be too upset over her husband's death. But she shouldn't be since she never met him in the flesh."

"A most unfortunate and distressing situation for the young woman," Lark proclaimed and rose from his chair. He walked across the room to the window and gazed down at the rocks and pounding surf on the beach below him.

"Yes, my lord," Carpenter hastily agreed. "Your cousin was many things, and not all of them pleasant, but he didn't deserve such a cruel and painful end. Lady Arden doesn't deserve never to have a beginning."

"Quite right, Carpenter."

"Then I trust I have your permission to explain to the young woman about your cousin's death." Carpenter looked expectantly at Lark but a minute passed without an answer. Even Simon raised a quizzical eyebrow at the lengthy silence. "My lord?" Carpenter queried with a furrowed brow to Lark's back. "Did you hear me?"

Lark was quiet for a few more seconds. Then he turned to face Carpenter and Simon with a serious but detached demeanor. "My hearing is unimpaired, I assure you. Gentlemen, I believe my money problem is solved, but only if I have your fullest cooperation." His gaze encompassed Simon and Hollins

29

Carpenter.

"You have mine, my lord," Hollins readily assured Lark but Simon remained silent.

Taking his place behind the large desk which had once belonged to his grandfather, Lark took a deep controlling breath. He didn't like what he planned to do, in fact he hated it, but there was only one way to reclaim what Richard had stolen from him, only one path opened to get the money he needed to fulfill his mission. He said confidently, "When Lady Arden arrives at Montclair, she shall meet her husband and be more than willing to sign away her fortune."

Hollins slowly stood up, a puzzled expression on his plain face. "I don't understand, my lord. Richard Arden is dead."

"Ah, Carpenter, must I explain it to you? Am I not Lord Arden, Baron of Montclair?"

"Yes, most assuredly you are, my lord."

"And didn't Miss Stafford marry Lord Arden, Baron of Montclair?"

Before Hollins could respond, Simon jumped to his feet and interrupted. "Yes, Lark, but she didn't marry *you!* I don't like where this plan of yours is headed."

Lark laughed but it wasn't a merry sound that echoed in the library. "You know me too well, Simon, and you know how desperate I am."

"Dammit! You can't mean to deceive this young woman, tell me I'm wrong."

"You aren't wrong."

The deadly earnestness in Lark's voice caused Simon to wince. "I won't support you in this sordid deception, nor will I help you. You can't trample on the young lady's feelings and get away with it."

"With your assistance, I can. Believe me, I detest what I plan to do but I haven't any other choice. Don't desert me, Simon. I've always counted upon our friendship. I must have your help and Carpenter's support if this plan is to work."

Lark suddenly looked very tired to Simon, not resembling the robust young man of minutes ago. He'd recovered from his illness, or at least Simon had believed the recovery to be complete, but now Simon worried that his friend might suffer a relapse if he didn't help him. The pain, worry, and anxiety which Lark had suffered the last few months had nearly killed him, and Simon didn't wish to be the cause of further distress to Lark, not if he could prevent it. But what Lark planned was monstrous and totally out of character for him. Yet Simon hadn't been with him when he'd been hunting down pirates, blowing ships and men to pieces. Somehow the experiences had changed Lark from a concerned and well-intentioned individual to a cold and calculating man. Perhaps if he no longer had to worry about finances, then things would set themselves aright and the Lark of old would return.

"I'll help you in any way you wish," Simon reluctantly assured Lark before he left the room, "but I don't condone the method."

"I should like to know what is happening here," Hollins peevishly put in when he and Lark were alone.

"Then I shall explain it to you," was Lark's chilly retort, his dark eyes moving away from the door which had just closed behind Simon to Hollins. "Mr. Carpenter, my ne'er-do-well cousin spent my inheritance. Even if you didn't control the purse strings, you should have stopped him. I hold you responsible for what happened, and I will reclaim what is rightfully mine through Richard's widow."

Carpenter grimaced, not seeming to care for Lark's critical remark. "How shall you accomplish that, my lord?"

"Quite simply. When Richard's wife arrives, she shall not be informed of his death. I shall pose as Richard until she signs over her fortune. Then I'll take what is due me. I'll find a ship and outfit it with a crew. After I am gone, I'll leave you to the duty of telling her the truth as you're so adept at breaking bad news."

Carpenter's face paled and his mouth trembled. "My lord, I can't allow you to do this. Lady Arden is an innocent, totally blameless for Richard's mistakes and you mustn't use her—"

"My cousin was a rogue," Lark bitingly observed and came to stand intimidatingly over the man. "Miss Stafford's lack of reputation, which I'm certain must have some validity, would have appealed to Richard. I have no qualms about assuming his identity to get my hands on his bride's fortune. All I want is what is due me. She will keep the house and land, she can call herself a baroness, a countess, or a queen for all I care. But this woman is my last hope of getting the money I need. I shall use her in any way I choose, Carpenter. Any way."

Hollins understood the implication behind Lark's words. "Not in that way, my lord."

"Don't cross me," Lark warned. "The sooner she signs the papers, the sooner I'll be on my way and you can explain to her ladyship that I coerced you into deceiving her. Then you won't need to tell her how you, her trusted solicitor, allowed her departed spouse to spend my inheritance with your knowledge. If she were to somehow learn the truth, it might cause her to find someone more trustworthy to look after her fortune. I'm certain you'd miss your large retainer fee. Are we in agreement, Carpenter?"

"Yes, my lord," he answered stiffly and was sufficiently moved by Lark's threat not to argue further. "Is there anything else?"

Lark retreated to lean against the edge of the desk. "Inform Mrs. Mortimer of our plans. I expect you can force the woman to keep her mouth shut during the time I am in residence. Tell her not to admit any unexpected visitors, also."

"Mrs. Mortimer is getting on in years and fears losing her post, my lord. She'll do as I ask."

Lark gave a curt nod and started for the door, intent upon going upstairs to rest. "Good, Carpenter. Do whatever you must to gain her silence."

"I trust the outcome of so much deception shall not result in a hollow victory for you, my lord."

Carpenter's words caused Lark to pause. He managed a thin smile that barely warmed his eyes. "At this stage of my life, any victory is welcomed."

33

Chapter Three

As the carriage precariously climbed the steep hill upon which Marlee's new home sat, a vicious wind blew in from the ocean. Swirling, purple clouds dipped low from the sky to threateningly graze the four-corner towers of the gray stone manor house.

With the imminent storm and the restless wind stirring the unkempt grounds, Montclair resembled a once elegant and wealthy woman reduced to an ugly, begging hag. Large pieces of mortar had broken from the roofline and a chimney looked ready to topple. Marlee noticed a window in one of the towers was broken. The overall impression was one of neglect.

"Oh, my," Barbara voiced Marlee's own thoughts and craned her neck from the carriage window to get a better view. "Montclair isn't what I expected." She managed an encouraging smile. "Perhaps the interior makes up for the facade."

"I assume the inside will be as horrible to behold," Marlee responded with more than a hint of disgust in her tone. To think that Lord Arden's excessive vices had caused the house's ruination angered her. Apparently, he possessed little pride to allow this to happen to a once grand and gracious home.

"Be thankful Daphne caught a cold and Mother stayed home to nurse her. I can just imagine what their comments would be."

Marlee nodded, indeed grateful that only Barbara had accompanied her to Montclair. She didn't think she could have endured Clementina's sour company or Daphne's constant complaints for the long journey. As it was, she was apprehensive about meeting Richard Arden, and more than a little frightened to imagine what he'd think of her. She'd written to Mr. Carpenter over a week ago to inform her husband of her imminent arrival. She also felt certain that Arden's palms were itching in anticipation to control her fortune.

Seeing the poor condition of Montclair, Marlee now knew she'd turn her fortune over to her husband. She aimed to restore Montclair to its former glory, confident her money was all that was needed, but she'd be damned if a notorious rogue like Richard Arden would do her out of any more of her father's hard-earned money to support his lechery and gaming habits. Somehow she'd tame him and become the true mistress of his home and maybe, his heart.

The weather-battered doors to the house swung open just as the rain started and the carriage jerked to a halt. Inside the doorway a plump woman with a white cap atop her head dropped a curtsy. "I'm Mrs. Mortimer, the housekeeper, my lady. Welcome to Montclair." Immediately the old lady began helping Marlee and Barbara out of their cloaks and issued an order to the driver to carry their trunks up the broad staircase.

"I ain't no lackey," the man grumbled under the weight of one of the trunks. "Why can't a man servant lend a hand?"

"Go on with you," Mrs. Mortimer urged, silencing the man with an imperious look. Marlee flashed the housekeeper a questioning glance of her own but surmised the reason no other servant came forward when the woman began dragging the largest of Marlee's trunks into the vestibule; Mrs. Mortimer was the only servant.

"Let me help you," Marlee volunteered, quite used to doing things for herself.

"Oh, no, my lady," Mrs. Mortimer protested, genuinely horrified at Marlee's suggestion. "I can manage with the driver's help. Please wait in the parlor while I fetch — Lord Arden. He's in the library with Mr. Carpenter and a friend."

They followed Mrs. Mortimer out of the lofty hall where high above them were clerestory windows which allowed sunshine into that portion of the house on a clear day — but with the rainstorm outside, the only light was the large, flickering candle that the housekeeper took from a wall sconce.

Trembling with uncertainty, Marlee sat beside Barbara on a divan that was in need of new stuffing. Luckily, a fire blazed in the hearth and dispelled the icy chill in the parlor, but nothing melted the feeling of dread that wrapped cold fingers around Marlee's soul. "You're shaking," Barbara noted and wrapped her warm mittened hands around Marlee's own.

"I'm being a silly goose, I know, but when Lord Arden walks into this room, my life will forever change."

"It already has," Barbara said wisely. "Now make the best of things, just like Papa says."

"What happens if I can't or my husband won't? I've never been married and have no idea how to keep my husband happy or to manage a house as large as Montclair. Goodness! Mrs. Mortimer is the only servant here, I'd wager."

"Then there's your answer. Your first chore as the baroness is to find adequate help. I predict that Mrs. Mortimer will be delighted to aid you in that endeavor. The poor lady seems much too overworked. As far as making your husband happy"—and here Barbara blushed—"I can't offer any advice."

Marlee worriedly bit at her lower lip. "Suppose he's an ogre, a beastly man? I've heard such awful stories about him that I believe them. From the look of things, he's a disreputable and lazy rake."

"I'm certain Lord Arden is a fine man. You know how people gossip." Despite her encouraging words, Barbara patted Marlee's hand in grim acceptance.

They waited in companionable silence. The only sounds were the pelting of rain outside and the howling winds. Though a slice of trepidation slid down Marlee's backside, she did wonder if Arden would find her acceptable. She'd piled her dark brown hair atop her head, as befitted a married woman. The gown she'd carefully chosen that morning was a deep blue satin, simply cut, with a square bodice that was edged with embroidered pink roses. It was her best dress but she realized it probably paled among the elaborate and jewel-encrusted clothes worn by aristocratic women, women with whom her new husband had no doubt dallied if the rumors were to be believed.

Never one to worry about her appearance too much, she accepted the compliments about her beauty in good measure. However, the men who had complimented her were common men, totally unlike the polished dandy she'd married. She felt drab and as unattractive as a field mouse. No matter how Montclair had fallen, she was out of place here among the portraits of impressive Arden ancestors who gazed down from the walls. She didn't belong and would never belong because she wasn't of aristocratic birth.

Her ancestors had been poor Cornish men and women, eking a living from the land, whether by farming or mining tin. It was only through her father's intelligence that her family had prospered. In fact, her father had barely been able to read but he'd made certain his daughter was well educated by engaging the best tutors. Marlee had loved her father with all of her heart. No man could ever take his place in her life, certainly not a rogue like Richard Arden.

The minutes ticked away. She fidgeted in her seat. Why hadn't Arden put in an appearance by now? Wasn't he curious about her? One would think he'd be eager to inspect her, to woo her into signing over her fortune to him. Instead it seemed he was purposely keeping her waiting and she grew annoyed at the slight.

She fingered the fraying damask on the divan then set to examining the faded draperies on the floor-to-ceiling windows.

"What are you doing?" Barbara asked and joined her by the window where the rain beat mercilessly and showed no sign of abating.

"I'm deciding how to redo this room. It's deplorable. I think blue would show up nicely for the chairs—the same shade as my gown, I think. Don't you agree?" Marlee didn't wait for Barbara's answer but went to inspect a high-backed wing chair. Taking a handful of her gown in her hand, she placed the material upon the chair cushion as a sample, totally unaware that her lace-edged petticoat and white-stockinged legs were all too visible to the two handsome men who watched from the doorway. "I think this color will do nicely. What do you say?" she asked Barbara.

"I'd say you're a very fetching sight, my lady," the taller and darker of the two men responded.

Both girls turned in unison, their faces blazing. Marlee was so stunned that she tripped over her own feet and fell backward into the chair she'd been appraising. Her gown twisted around her calves, preventing her from moving. Tongue-tied over her clumsiness, she wasn't certain what to say to the black-haired man who suddenly loomed over her and extended a hand to her. He was so very tall and broad of shoulder that she was forced to stretch her neck to see his face.

Ebony eyes, darker than the heavens on a cloudless night, raked her from the top of her head to the tips of her kid slippers. A few strands of black wavy hair fell carelessly but attractively upon his forehead and skimmed his black-winged brows. A superbly molded nose was a clear indication of his aristocratic heritage as was his well-formed mouth that slashed into a disarming smile to reveal a beautiful set of teeth.

Attired in a brown velvet jacket over a cream-colored shirt, he wore buff-colored trousers and brown

39

boots. With each movement of his upper body Marlee feared his wide shoulders would rip open the expensive material. She felt incredibly tiny as he stood over her, suddenly fragile and more than dismayed to meet her new husband in such an unladylike and less than aristocratic position. But his hand was outstretched to her, and she shyly took it, finding not the smooth, soft skin she'd expected but a hand which was tough and strong, callused, too, and surprisingly gentle.

"Forgive me," Marlee began and blushed a violent shade of scarlet as she attempted to untangle her skirts. With Barbara's assistance she managed to set her gown aright and once again stood on her two feet. After she'd put herself in order she was all too aware of his dark eyes dancing with amusement. He was silently laughing at her. How foolish and clumsy she must look to him!

"There's nothing to forgive," he kindly returned. "I startled you and do apologize. I trust you're Lady Marlee." At her curt nod, he bowed and kissed her hand. "I'm Lord Arden, Baron of Montclair."

How she wished he'd have introduced himself as Richard, her husband. It was his formal introduction which dispelled any absurd fantasies she held of having a true marriage. They'd share the same home but would exist as polite strangers, and evidently her husband wanted their relationship to remain on such terms. But, of course, he would. In his eyes she wasn't his equal and she must remember that fact. He'd married her sight unseen—only for her money—so she knew where his interests lay. But he was nothing like she imagined he'd be. She'd heard he was handsome, but not this heart-stirringly handsome, not so hand-some that she gazed at his tanned face in rapturous awe. When she realized she was gaping at him like a lovestruck imbecile, she quickly withdrew her hand from his.

"I trust you're in good health, sir. Mr. Carpenter advised me that you had been ill." Arden looked in bloody good health to Marlee, sustaining her earlier belief that he'd not been sick at all.

"My recovery is complete, my lady. I thank you for asking."

The other gentleman cleared his throat at this point and Arden turned to introduce him to Marlee. "May I present my best friend, Simon Oliver."

Marlee dropped a curtsy and gave her hand to the blond-haired man. She found she immediately liked Simon Oliver. There was something in his face, something in the set of his jaw which gave her the impression that he was a dependable sort of person, a loyal friend, someone who wasn't wild or impetuous. Already she sensed he was totally different from her errant husband. Simon paid her a nice compliment, but Marlee immediately saw that his interest wasn't in her but Barbara. Taking Barbara by the arm, she moved her nearer to Simon. "This is Miss Barbara McBride. We are cousins."

Both men responded warmly to Barbara who curt-sied beautifully. "I hope you don't mind my bringing Barbara along, my lord. I assumed she would be welcome," Marlee said with a bit of defiance in her tone. Arden wouldn't dare not allow Barbara to stay at Montclair, not when Montclair was Marlee's home now as well as his.

A delighted smile split Arden's sensuous lips. "Your cousin is most welcome."

"Thank you. You're most generous with your hospitality."

"Montclair is your home too, my lady. You may do as you will."

This was an unexpected turn of events. Marlee was a bit put off by Arden's willingness to allow her free rein. A strange warmth suffused her at his words, at the sudden smile he threw her way. Perhaps — perhaps things might work out for the best. Maybe he truly was going to settle down and be a proper husband. However, the warm glow dissipated a second later when Arden said to her, "Mr. Carpenter is in the library and is eager to speak with you. Do you wish to speak with Carpenter now about anything or would you and Miss McBride prefer to rest first?"

Of course "anything" was her money. Marlee heaved a ragged and defeated sigh. She forced herself to remember he didn't want her for any other reason than her money and was now eager to have her sign her fortune away to him. Why else would Carpenter be at Montclair? No doubt he was waiting in the library with quill in hand, ready to dip it in the ink pot for her. Well, let him wait, Marlee decided defiantly. Let them all wait! She belonged at Montclair and would take her good time in signing anything. "We should like to rest," she said to Arden with a sweetness which belied her true feelings. "The journey was long and tiring."

A shard of triumph gleamed in her eyes at Arden's momentary look of disappointment, but in a flash he was smiling charmingly again. "Mrs. Mortimer will show you to your rooms. As soon as you're both rested, please join us for a late supper."

"Thank you, my lord," was her polite reply.

Mrs. Mortimer appeared, followed by the surly carriage driver who disappeared into the rain outside. Marlee couldn't help but notice the odd expression on Mrs. Mortimer's plump face when Arden told her to escort them upstairs. The old woman curtsied stiffly and turned her back to him in what seemed a clear gesture of disdain. Moments later when the three women were trodding down the threadbare carpet in a long, dark corridor, Mrs. Mortimer turned kindly eyes upon Marlee. "If there's anything you want, my lady, you or Miss McBride, just ring for me. Might take me awhile to answer but I'll come, never fear."

"I appreciate your kindness, ma'am. In fact I realize you need some help, so I shall speak to Lord Arden about hiring a decent staff. Rest assured, I intend to make changes at Montclair." Marlee had hoped her reassuring statement would bring a bright smile to the old lady's face. Instead the woman bit down upon her lower lip, almost as if she fought the urge to cry. She flushed and looked guiltily away.

"Oh, my lady, if only you knew the changes that have been wrought already."

Marlee barely had time to ponder Mrs. Mortimer's strange words before she was led into a bedroom. As the housekeeper carefully lighted a number of candles to illuminate the room, Marlee and Barbara gasped at the scene before them.

"How utterly lovely," Barbara commented, but Marlee found herself unable to speak.

Before her on a dais stood the largest and most

elaborately carved bed she'd ever beheld. Fashioned from a sturdy oak, the bed's massive posts, complete with green and gold hangings, nearly touched the ceiling. Ensconced in two corners of the room were double wardrobes, crafted from the same wood; on an opposite wall was a delicately etched looking glass above a dressing table. A Persian carpet, so extravagantly beautiful that it resembled a painting and so thick that Marlee feared to tread upon it, lest she drown in its softness, covered the floor.

Had she entered a princess' chamber from a fairy tale? Was this bewitching room truly hers? She'd never expected anything this lovely or so richly appointed. But she'd never been in a mansion which resembled a castle or had a clear idea of how the aristocracy lived. If this room was any indication of how Montclair had been in the past, then indeed, Montclair must have been magnificent.

"Is this my room?" she found herself asking Mrs. Mortimer, still unable to believe such a splendid room could possibly be meant for her.

"Yes, my lady. I hope all meets with your approval."

"Oh, it does! This is a very fine room." And that was an understatement.

A wisp of a smile appeared on Mrs. Mortimer's face as she lit the last candle. "This room belonged to Lady Helena, the old baroness. I served her a number of years. She was a fine lady and pretty like you, your ladyship. Ah, the times we had before a ball in the old days. Lady Helena would be primping and prancing before yon mirror hours before the musicians struck up. The baron, Lord Michael that is, would pace the hall and poke his head round the door, raising a fuss for her to hurry and decide on a gown. What a pair they were!" She chuckled heartily. "Then after the ball, they'd come upstairs with their arms wrapped around each other and lock themselves away in here.

"No one heard nary a peep out of them, sometimes not for a day and a half, which some people who stayed over said was rude, but I knew the baron and his lady had eyes for only each other. Made no difference if the house was filled to overflowing with fancy guests; they didn't come out of this room until they were ready. It was like that until the day my lady died. And then Lord Michael had a falling out with his son, and nothing was the same at Montclair—ever again."

The old woman's eyes misted and she rapidly blinked away her tears. "There I go woolgathering again. My husband always said 'tis a sign of aging."

"Oh, no, I don't believe that," Marlee said with understanding. "I know how wonderful it is to relive happier times."

"Ah, my lady, you're kind, how very good you are."

"Now what about Barbara's room?" Marlee asked, seeing how awestruck her cousin was and feeling the very same way. She doubted she'd ever believe this room was truly meant for her. She might be the new baroness but at heart she was still a tin miner's daughter.

"Oh, forgive me, Miss Barbara. Follow me." Taking up her candle, Mrs. Mortimer gestured to Barbara, but Marlee's voice momentarily halted them before she'd properly phrased her question.

"Does Lord Arden sleep in this room, Mrs. Mortimer?"

"No, my lady. *He* sleeps in the state bedchamber on

the opposite side of the house."

Marlee grimaced at the swift riposte and couldn't stop her face from coloring to realize what she'd asked. Mrs. Mortimer was a housekeeper and knew her place. The very vehemence expressed in her reply left no doubt in Marlee's mind that something as personal as Lord Arden's sleeping arrangements wouldn't be discussed with the new baroness.

Marlee bit down on her lower lip, wondering what sort of a dolt Mrs. Mortimer must think her. But she had no one to ask about the sleeping arrangements. She couldn't very well walk up to her new husband and inquire if he'd be sharing a bed with her. Maybe Lord Michael had stayed in the same room as Lady Helena because he had loved her, but Marlee didn't think Richard Arden would consider sharing a connubial bed with his new bride. Lord Richard didn't love his wife, and that was that. Still, might he not want children—legitimate ones?

The door to the room closed behind the housekeeper and Barbara. Marlee stood in the candlelit bedroom which was almost too beautiful to touch and uncertainty engulfed her. She was a baroness but what did the title mean? What did it mean to be Lord Arden's wife? She was woefully ignorant of what her new positions entailed. At that moment she wished she'd accepted Tim Lee's marriage proposal. Being a minister's wife didn't seem so terrible now.

There was a man downstairs who was her husband, a man who had seen what a clumsy goose she was. Her fortune had bought him but she realized no amount of money would keep the man from wandering, if he wished to chase a skirt or two he would. The dazzling smile he'd shot Barbara during the introductions hadn't gone unnoticed by Marlee. It was only now that she was alone did she put a name to how she'd felt when he'd welcomed her cousin to Montclair.

Jealous. She'd been jealous of the way he'd looked at Barbara, a way he hadn't reserved for his bride.

A loud clap of thunder caused her to jump, and she chastised herself for her nervousness and distracted musings. Of course Arden would be taken with Barbara, as any man would be with a pretty female. And many men had told her that she, Marlee Stafford, was pretty, too. So, why did it suddenly seem so important for Arden to find her attractive?

"Because you've already started to fall under his spell, you idiot," she mumbled aloud in disgust.

She couldn't put out of her mind that her new husband possessed a godlike physique, that his face was endearingly rugged and well formed, or forget how perfectly smooth his lips had looked or how they felt like warm velvet on her skin when he'd kissed her hand earlier. How difficult life would be for her, now that she was married to such a man. But she wouldn't fall under Arden's spell as gossip claimed many other women had done. Somehow she'd put a stop to her own feelings where he was concerned.

Arden wanted her only for her money, nothing else, and she must remember that he was mercenary at heart. He might try to charm her, and perhaps he would succeed somewhat. There was no denying he was an unusually handsome man, and she was human enough to be susceptible to flattery. But she mustn't forget it was her hefty purse which had brought her to Montclair, not her looks. Arden wouldn't forget,

47

either.

And she wouldn't forget that as Lord Arden's wife, she owed him obedience and respect and she'd give him children, if he so wished. But never would she give her heart to the rogue.

It was all that was left to her.

Chapter Four

As the storm raged unceasingly outside, Marlee sat in the protective warmth of Montclair's library before Hollins Carpenter. His smile seemed a bit forced to Marlee, but as always, he exuded a politeness with which she couldn't fault. She longed to dislike the man but she didn't. In his own efficient way, Carpenter had seen to the varied wants of his clients and made her a baroness in the process.

However, she'd been seated before him for ten minutes and he hadn't brought out the paperwork for her to sign. In fact, he hadn't mentioned anything at all about it, concentrating instead on social amenities and inquiring about Daphne's health. Marlee couldn't help but wonder what Hollins Carpenter was about.

"I do hope you'll be happy here, Lady Arden," he said to her.

"I trust I shall be," she responded and was more than a bit surprised when he rose from his chair to usher her to the doorway. "Is our conversation at an end?"

"Yes, my lady. Supper awaits and Lord Arden gave explicit instructions that we were to dine promptly at seven. I promised him that I'd keep you only a few minutes."

"But . . . but what about the document? Shouldn't I sign it now? I thought that's why you wished to see me."

Behind his spectacles, Carpenter blinked steadily. "Whenever you're ready to sign, my lady, send for me."

And that was all he said to her.

They joined Lord Arden in the dining room where Simon had already engaged Barbara in conversation, and where it seemed everyone was waiting for Marlee's appearance before being seated. Arden came forward from the shadows of the room and offered his black-clad arm to her. Marlee absently took it, feeling a bit confused from her encounter with Carpenter. She didn't know why the man hadn't pressed her to sign away her fortune as she'd expected, why suddenly the very reason for her marriage didn't seem as important. But then she gazed into Arden's handsome face and suddenly forgot the document. Instead she noticed the fiery amber gleam in his eyes and realized that he possessed the most adorable cleft in his chin. She was mesmerized by him, unable to concentrate on anything but him.

"You look beautiful tonight, my lady. Very beautiful."

His compliment took her unaware and she blushed, stumbling over her own words as she mumbled an indistinct remark. God! He must believe her to possess a speech impediment as well as being a clumsy bumpkin. What was there about this man that always left her feeling completely vulnerable, that caused her to forget her own good sense?

The group sat down to eat at the longest table Marlee had ever seen. According to tradition, Arden was seated at the head of the table and the mistress of the house at the opposite end—and that was where he had seated her. A large golden candelabra, glittering with lighted candles, sat in the center of the table and obscured Marlee's view of her husband while Mrs. Mortimer hobbled around the table to serve a delicious crab stew and biscuits, warm from the oven.

After everyone had eaten, Simon and Barbara withdrew to the far end of the parlor, engrossed in each other's company. Mr. Carpenter bade a good night and retired to a guest room. Marlee waited uncertainly beside Arden. Her flushed cheeks matched the color of a pink satin rose on her gown. When Arden touched her hand, she giggled like a nervous school girl.

"I trust your room is to your liking, my lady."

"Oh, yes, my room is quite nice." It was better than nice but she decided not to make too much over it. She must stop acting like a bumpkin whenever he as much as looked at her or touched her. Perhaps she'd do well to adopt a worldly air with her sophisticated husband. She didn't want him to think she was too provincial. "It shall do quite well," she told him with a blasé flutter of her pink and white silk fan.

The large ornate clock in the vestibule chimed the hour, breaking into their conversation. Arden smiled apologetically at her. "I hadn't realized it was so late. You must be tired. I'll escort you to your room."

She wasn't tired at all, but Marlee didn't dare object, especially not when Simon and Barbara rose and wandered toward the stairway. "I believe the long journey has undone the ladies," Simon observed and threw an assessing glance at Arden.

"Yes, I believe we all need a good rest," Lark noted grimly but smiled pleasantly when they reached Marlee's chamber door. "I'll send Mrs. Mortimer to help you prepare for bed." Before she could respond, Lark planted a very proper kiss on Marlee's hand and made his way down the long hallway toward the other end of the house.

Simon exhaled audibly and led Barbara to her own door before politely bowing and withdrawing to a room farther down the hall. No sooner had Marlee closed her door than Barbara tapped upon it. She rushed into the room and twirled, her satin skirt resembling a summer peach. "Oh, Marlee," she gushed with such enthusiasm and prettiness that Marlee instantly knew what she was about to say. "I'm in love, quite head over heels about Simon! Isn't he the most handsome man you've ever seen?"

Simon was handsome but not as handsome as Arden. "Yes," Marlee agreed. "I believe he is an honest and decent man. I wonder why he and Richard are friends." That comment slipped out without Marlee's awareness and when she realized what she'd said, she amended, "I'm certain Lord Arden has a great many good qualities. I must watch what I say about my husband. He is a stranger to me."

"Lord Arden is taken with you, Marlee. I can see the way he looks at you."

Marlee hadn't noticed. She couldn't hope that his compliments and smiles could hold anything more than politeness. Yet he'd told her she looked beautiful and his smile had been more than warm, his eyes more than bright. But she wouldn't put too much stock in such things. No doubt he'd looked that way at other women before her. Still she longed to believe that he might find her the smallest bit attractive.

"My lady," came Mrs. Mortimer's voice from the doorway. "Are you ready to undress?"

The old lady began undoing the back of Marlee's gown and soon she was properly attired in her white lace night rail, her hair loosened and hanging to her waist. After Mrs. Mortimer left to ready Barbara's night clothes, Barbara kissed Marlee on the cheek and smiled encouragingly. "I know your wedding night will be wonderful." Then she swiftly departed and Marlee was left alone, standing in the center of the room—waiting.

Her wedding night. She'd forgotten that fact in all the hubbub of her arrival, her first meeting with Arden. But now a clammy fear clutched her heart. How would she deal with Arden when he came to her to claim his husbandly rights? What would it be like to lie in his arms, to taste his kisses, to be completely possessed by such a rogue? Her head swam with the seductive images revolving in her brain and she moaned aloud. She was so inexperienced, not woman enough for such a worldly man. But then she clutched the bedpost to steady herself as a frightening thought assailed her. What would she do if he didn't come to her?

She'd barely had time to dwell upon such a possibility when a knock sounded on her door and Arden's voice came through the door panel. "My lady, 'tis your husband."

Husband. He'd said husband. Marlee's heart pounded like a dozen steeds rushing through the countryside. "Come in, my lord," she called in a small, tight voice.

The door opened. Arden waited in the doorway, still wearing his formal black evening attire. For a few seconds he looked at her, really looked at her. His gaze was bold and streaked appraisingly up and down her slender form where the night rail hugged her curves. The transparent material did little to disguise her womanly attributes in the waning candlelight, but Marlee was unaware of the seductive picture she presented.

When he moved toward her, her breath caught in her throat. With a few strides, his powerful body separated the gap between them, almost as if a magnet drew him to her.

He's come to claim me! her mind cried and she was suddenly more than eager to experience his kiss, his arms around her. Gazing up at him with trepidation on her face, the uncertainty of her own inexperience gnawed at her. She doubted she'd be able to make this man happy and she wanted to make him happy. Sometimes he looked at her with such sadness that she knew a terrible torment ate away at him. But now there was another emotion on his face, something so heart-stirringly primitive that she shivered with fear and anticipation of the unknown.

She made a formal curtsy. "My lord."

He gently took her by her arms and pulled her up. "Don't curtsy to me. I want no homage from you, Marlee."

"What—what do you want?" She could barely speak, barely breathe.

"You know what I want, you know."

His mouth, burning with the heat of a hundred suns, descended upon hers. Her lips opened to him, drinking in the moistness of the warm assault like a dewy rosebud after a rainstorm, opening and blossoming beneath the golden rays. The blood streamed through her veins with quicksilver speed, beating out a wild, sweet cadence in every nerve of her being. He pressed her against him, the obvious bulge in his trousers a blatant signal of his desire. *He wants me, he wants me, he wants me,* her heart joyfully sang.

"Ah, Marlee," he breathed beneath her lips and broke the kiss. "You're so lovely, so enchanting. So—sweet." His voice suddenly sounded like a tortured growl. Marlee could feel his heated gaze upon her though her eyes were closed. She opened them to find herself staring into orbs so black that they resembled the heavens on a dark night, a night without a pinpoint of light in the velvet firmament. His expression was blank, utterly devoid of emotion.

A shiver, not from desire or passion, slid down

her back when suddenly he grinned at her. "Forgive me, my dear, but I fear your charms have undone me for the moment. I shall leave you to your rest." He kissed her forehead and released her.

Luckily Marlee grabbed onto the bedpost for support or she'd have fallen like a rag doll at his feet. Dimly she wondered what she'd done to cause him to act this way. One second he was kissing her like he truly wanted her, and then he was pushing her away without the least hint of regret. What had she done? What hadn't she done? She didn't know, just didn't know how to please a man like Richard Arden. "My—my lord—what?" She also didn't know what to ask.

He didn't bother turning around to look at her as he made his way to the door. "Sleep well, Marlee. I shall see you in the morning." His strong hand pulled open the door and closed it with a resounding thud behind him.

She waited by the bed for what seemed an eternity. Her mind whirled with images of the passion she'd seen on his face, the memory of the kiss which so completely destroyed her senses. Never had she imagined a kiss could be filled with so much fire and longing, and now she felt unfulfilled and bereft. She had wanted Arden to keep kissing her, to hold her in his arms forever. She had wanted him to love her, to make her his wife—and now he was gone. He'd left her confused, humiliated, and disappointed. But soon her disappointment gave way to something else—something akin to anger.

"The bloody bounder!" she hissed under her

breath. Regaining the use of her legs, she went to the dressing table and grabbing a thick, silver hairbrush within her slender hand, she hurled it with uncharacteristic force against the oaken door. "Play games with me, will you! How dare you, Richard Arden! How dare you stir my passions and then run away like the cowardly rogue you are. I'll not have it. I'll just not have it!"

But Marlee wasn't certain what she would have. She only knew as she plopped herself on her bed and gritted her teeth that she wouldn't allow Richard Arden to use her. He'd come to her to make her his wife, and then left her before performing his husbandly duty. Was he playing some sort of perverse game with her? Was he dangling before her the fleshly pleasures which awaited her in his arms if she signed the document of her own volition? And if she did sign, would he willingly bed her? Did he believe he could make her a slave to her own base desires?

Yes. She was inexperienced but something wild and hot had flared between them and she wouldn't deny what she'd felt for him. Yet if Arden thought to tantalize her with his kiss as a way of bringing her to heel, he was mistaken. Oh, she'd sign the document and be done with it, but all in her own good time. First, her husband must learn a lesson about women—about her. That kiss had taught Marlee a great deal about herself, and she knew that with Arden as a lover, she'd enjoy marriage very much. But if he thought to make her a slave to passion, he was mistaken.

"Before I'm through with you, my dear husband,"

she whispered to the ornately scrolled ceiling, "you'll beg me to love you. Then we'll see who is slave to whom." And with that, she blew out the candle and plotted how to tame a rogue.

Chapter Five

The following morning Mrs. Mortimer appeared at Marlee's door with a small silver tray, filled with a freshly baked cinnamon muffin and a cup of hot tea. As Marlee ate, the old lady pulled a gray and white day dress from the wardrobe and laid it across Marlee's bed. "I hope the gown meets with your approval, my lady," Mrs. Mortimer said and smoothed down the wrinkles in the bodice.

Marlee assured her it did, unused to being addressed so formally and knowing it would do little good to ask the housekeeper to address her any other way. After Marlee finished eating, Mrs. Mortimer proceeded to brush Marlee's hair into a becoming bun atop her head, but Marlee's mind wasn't on her hair or her gown at the moment. She wondered about her husband and what would be his reaction to her after their burning kiss last night. Her face still felt warm just to think about how she'd responded to him.

"Have you seen my husband this morning?" she

casually questioned the housekeeper after she'd changed into her dress. For just a second Mrs. Mortimer stopped working her fingers on the buttons at the back of the gown before dutifully continuing with her chore.

"You mean himself, Lord Arden," the old woman ground out through clenched teeth.

Who else did the woman think she meant? Sometimes Marlee wondered if Mrs. Mortimer might be addled. She'd met her only the previous day and had immediately liked her, but there was something malevolent in the woman's attitude whenever Arden was near or whenever Marlee mentioned him. Marlee puzzled over this, sensing something wasn't right but couldn't discern what might be wrong. "Of course I mean Lord Arden," Marlee said with a smile. "I wondered if he'd eaten yet."

"Aye, he has and off he went."

"Do you know where he's gone?" Marlee felt slightly disappointed to discover Richard wasn't in the house and that she might not see him that morning.

"No idea, my lady," Mrs. Mortimer replied stiffly and shook out Marlee's skirts. "His lordship tells me nothing, and *I* don't want to know what he's about." She hobbled over toward the table where the tray was set and gingerly picked it up. "Now if you're finished with me, Lady Marlee, I have to help Miss Barbara dress, then see to me chores in the kitchen."

"Mrs. Mortimer, will you be free sometime this afternoon?"

"What have you in mind, my lady?" The large green eyes settled tiredly upon Marlee, almost as if she expected another task to be doled out to her.

"I'd like your assistance in interviewing people from the village. Montclair needs a competent staff of servants, and I trust you'll help me choose the best qualified people. Do you think you might know anyone who'd be interested in working at Montclair? If so, I'd appreciate your sending word to them." Marlee could tell her words eased the old lady's fears and her burdens when a large grateful smile spread across the woman's lined and weary face.

"Oh, my, that would be grand!" she exclaimed in breathless surprise. "Aye, I know just the people who would welcome the chance to work at Montclair. I'll send word with me nephew who lives in the village. He always comes on a Wednesday to see how I'm faring. In fact, my lady, he would be a good stable lad, if you'd consider hiring him. 'Tis been a long time since the stables were cleaned out, and I know other members of me family who'd like to work here—and would do you proud—if you'd consider taking them on, that is."

Marlee laughed at Mrs. Mortimer's enthusiasm. This was the first time she'd seen the old woman really smile. "I'll be happy to interview all of them."

Half an hour later, Marlee threw on her white

shawl and headed downstairs. Montclair was such a dark, dingy house with little natural light allowed inside because of the heavy drapes on all of the windows. She could visualize how the house would look, how elegant and grand it would be, once she finished redoing it. And it would be so nice to have her husband's involvement in the refurbishings. She couldn't help giggling to herself to imagine her swarthy and broad-shouldered husband surrounded by mountains of colored fabrics and tapestries as he dutifully helped her in the choosing. In fact she realized that attaining Richard's help in the redecorating was the first step in taming him—and that was a project she truly relished.

In the vestibule she found herself face to face with Hollins Carpenter and grew annoyed to find him still at Montclair, however, she knew why he stayed on. No doubt he'd remain in residence until she signed her fortune away. "Have you seen my husband this morning?" she inquired.

"Yes, my lady."

"Where is he?"

"He—uh—he had business to attend to." Hollins blinked steadily behind his spectacles, but Marlee guessed he was hedging, not willing to tell her where her husband had gone. The rogue had probably ridden into the village to take up his dubious ways again. Anger suffused her face to think he was still up to his old tricks, but Hollins hurriedly put her worry to rest when he said, "Mr. Oliver is with him, my lady." This was Carpenter's way of saying that Simon was a steadying influence upon Arden.

Marlee breathed a relieved sigh. "Then he is in good hands, as Montclair shall soon be. I shall conduct interviews this afternoon to find adequate help. Mrs. Mortimer's family members might be interested in working here."

For a second, Marlee thought Hollins's face was about to explode. His cheeks puffed out and turned from their usually pale color to apple red. "Oh, Lady Marlee, I can arrange for help. Don't trouble yourself," he hastily declared.

"For heavens sakes, Mr. Carpenter, you look ready to die of apoplexy. I'm capable of hiring a competent staff. Mrs. Mortimer has agreed to help me."

"I'm certain you are quite capable, but shouldn't you wait and consult Lord Arden?"

"I see no need to trouble him with such mundane matters. I am mistress here now *and* Lady Arden, as you have reminded me a number of times. I'm certain I can engage a staff of able and capable workers."

"But there will be strangers at Montclair, my lady." Carpenter's countenance suddenly paled. Marlee thought he looked positively frightened at the thought.

"They won't be strangers for long," she assured him, totally baffled by the man's uneasiness. "Have I your help if I need it?"

Carpenter swallowed hard and inclined his head

in what Marlee took to be a nod. "Strange man," she mumbled under her breath as Carpenter excused himself and headed for the library. Going into the drawing room, she found Barbara sitting on the divan and sipping tea from a dainty damask tea cup.

"Mrs. Mortimer makes the most delicious tea," Barbara uttered after bidding Marlee a good morning. "This is my third cup. And her cinnamon muffins melt in the mouth. She is so efficient, considering she has no help."

"I'm going to interview people today for positions here, but when I told Mr. Carpenter about what I plan to do, he looked ready to have a fit," Marlee confessed worriedly to Barbara. "He thought I should consult Lord Arden first, and now, I wonder if I should. After all, Carpenter knows Richard and his tastes. I don't want to offend Richard, but I must assert myself and take over the household matters."

"Hmmm, I'm not certain why hiring a staff would bother Lord Arden. I tend to think that Mr. Carpenter sometimes anticipates problems where none exist."

"I understand that Simon is gone off somewhere with Lord Arden." Marlee glanced out of the floor-to-ceiling window, not expecting to see Arden on the grounds but her heart beat hard as if she did, or would have liked to see him. "Do you know where they went?"

"No," Barbara admitted glumly. "I had hoped Simon would take me for a carriage ride this afternoon since the rain has stopped. There's precious little to do here for amusement."

That was true, but Marlee didn't mind. Somehow the quiet and serenity of Montclair had seeped into her soul. More than anything she wanted to remain as mistress of the estate and somehow find a place for herself in Arden's affections.

"I've cooked and cleaned for all me fifty years, my lady, and if I do say so meself, I'm a fine one with a rag and a broom. You'd not see a speck of dust at Montclair if you hire me on." The pleasant-faced woman who sat stiff-backed in the large chair before Marlee shifted uncomfortably but continued in an earnest voice, "Me sister Rose Mortimer can swear on the good book about me housekeepin'. And me son would make a fine stable lad for you." Her tone became low and almost imploring. "Life has been hard since me husband passed on last year. The farming t'ain't been good with just me and Denney to do the plowing. Me husband was a strong fellow until he got sick."

Marlee appraised Mary Carter, finding her to be a candid woman. Her hair had once been brown but was now streaked with silver. Her large green eyes, so much like Mrs. Mortimer's, clouded with tears but there was something strong and vital about the woman, an honesty about her which appealed to Marlee.

Marlee had no doubt that Mary would be a fine addition to Montclair, as would Denney, her fourteen-year-old son, whom Marlee had already interviewed and who now sat near the library window with his cap clutched in his grimy hand. Marlee could tell the mother and son were in need of jobs by the shabby clothes they wore and a good meal by the thin look of them—and she intended to remedy their unfortunate situation very soon.

Already that afternoon she'd interviewed and hired a gardener, a woman to help in the kitchen, and an upstairs maid—all relatives of Mrs. Mortimer. When Mrs. Mortimer had told Marlee that she had family eager to work at Montclair, the woman hadn't lied.

"I believe both of you shall do very nicely. I'll have Mrs. Mortimer show you to your quarters and ready a warm plate of stew for you. It's nearly supper time." Marlee felt her insides light up at Mary's reaction.

"Oh, thank you, my lady! You're so good and kind. Me Denney thinks so, too, don't you, lad?" Mary rose from her chair and clapped her hands in delight as she cast a beaming smile in her son's direction. The boy bobbed his head eagerly.

"I'll work hard for you, my lady, I swear I will," Denney assured Marlee.

"I'm certain that with your help, Montclair shall be efficiently run." Marlee rose from her chair and called to Mrs. Mortimer who waited outside the library door and told her to take Mary and Denney to the servants' wing.

For some reason Marlee noted that Mrs. Mortimer cast sidelong glances at the door. "Is something wrong?" Marlee queried.

"It's Mr. Carpenter, my lady," she admitted with a sniff of disdain. "He's pacing the halls, not too thrilled about your hiring a staff, I think."

"Why ever should that bother him?"

"You'd best ask him, my lady. Or your husband," Mrs. Mortimer whispered so low under her breath that Marlee scarcely heard her.

Her husband. Marlee's heart jolted at the thought of him. She hadn't seen him all day. Where was Arden? Was he in the village, carousing with tavern wenches? She didn't want to think about such a thing, in fact she didn't have time to dwell upon Arden's vices when she heard Carpenter's voice in the hallway. "My lord, please don't go into the library now . . ."

"Why ever not?" came Arden's crisp retort and Marlee heard the impatient clicking of his boot heels on the marbled floor as he headed in her direction.

"Because Lady Marlee—is hiring a staff." But Carpenter's response came too late. Already Arden waited in the doorway when Marlee turned from the others to gaze upon him.

Her heart fluttered like a dowager's fan to see him again. The corners of her mouth started to turn into a pleased smile but the welcome faded from her eyes at his appearance. Standing there with a riding crop in hand, his dark hair windblown and ruffled, Arden looked like the devil himself. It wasn't so much the fact that he was dressed entirely in black or that his usually shiny boots were now caked with wet sand that caused her uneasiness. In a corner of her mind, Marlee thought the clothes suited him more than the properly attired dandy she'd come to expect. There was something else, something more disturbing.

It was his eyes.

They glowed hot, almost like black pearls drenched in blazing sunlight. Her pulses beat hard as his sweltering gaze settled upon her. "What is going on here?" he asked in a silky controlled tone of voice, but Marlee noticed the displeasure concealed beneath the polished facade.

She curtsied as she'd been trained to do by Clementina, not out of a sense of deference but because she was so nervous at taking the household duties into her own hands she didn't know how else to react. After all, Montclair was his home, not hers. Not really. Not yet.

"I've hired a staff, my lord." And that was the simple truth of the matter. If he didn't like it, she couldn't help his feelings, but she wouldn't apologize — not in front of the help.

He looked about to explode, and she braced herself for an outburst. Instead, his demeanor and stance relaxed. He nodded in what she perceived was a dismissal. "I'd appreciate some privacy.

I have things to discuss with Carpenter."

"Yes, my lord." Marlee hurried her charges out of the room, conscious of his onyx gaze upon her back. When she'd closed the door behind Arden and Carpenter, she spotted Simon and Barbara at the far end of the hallway. She'd have fled in their direction, but Mary Carter's voice rooted her to the spot as the woman and her son followed after Mrs. Mortimer to the kitchen.

"Rose, that didn't look like Lord Arden. 'Tis been some time since I last saw him, but he looks different somehow, I can't explain it but—"

"Hush, Mary!" Mrs. Mortimer demanded and Marlee saw her take her sister roughly by the arm, pulling her along beside her.

"Me mum's right, Aunt Rose," Denney insisted. "That man t'ain't Lord Arden, not Lord Richard. I know—I saw his lordship just a few weeks back when I visited and—"

"Quiet the both of you! Now keep your silly ramblings to yourselves and come fill your bellies and mouths with me stew." Mrs. Mortimer's voice became low then drifted away to nothing.

A draft suddenly rushed through the hallway and Marlee's skin chilled at what she'd heard, or rather what she'd seen. It wasn't what Mary and Denney said about Arden that bothered her, it was the way Mrs. Mortimer reacted. The housekeeper had practically used force on the both of them as she whisked them off to the kitchen. Why had she done that? Was it to silence them, to keep her from overhearing. But why?

The man in the library with Hollins Carpenter was Richard Arden, Baron of Montclair, her husband. There was no good reason for servants' silly prattle to unnerve her. It was only when Barbara and Simon called to her to join them for tea in the parlor did she forget what she'd overheard. Yet for the rest of the afternoon, a vague uneasiness settled upon her.

"I've found the perfect ship, Carpenter. She's strong of timber and sleek of hull. With the proper rigging and crew, I shall soon be able to sail after Manuel Silva." Lark finished gazing out of the window and with his arms folded resolutely across his broad chest, he turned to Hollins. "I've been interviewing able-bodied crew men from the village."

"Is that wise, my lord? I mean, suppose someone becomes suspicious—"

"No one knows who I am, Carpenter," Lark ground out. "The men meet on the beach and know me only as Captain Lark. No one suspects I'm impersonating Richard. And as for your being so concerned about my deception"—Lark impaled the solicitor with a black look—"then explain why Lady Arden was hiring a staff, why strangers were allowed into Montclair. You know very well we agreed that no one would be admitted to the house while I'm here."

Sweat popped out upon Carpenter's forehead. "Er, well, I had no control over the matter, my lord. Lady Marlee informed me what she was going to do, and you weren't here to change her mind. I couldn't very well forbid her from hiring a staff, that would have seemed odd to her. As it is, Mrs. Mortimer is more than upset and I fear she may eventually break down and admit the truth to your wife—I mean, Lady Marlee. You must understand what a delicate position you've placed me in, sir. I hate lying to her."

Lark hated lying to Marlee, also, but he'd never admit that aloud. He'd chosen the perfect ship and was now hiring on a capable crew. All he needed was the money. And Marlee still hadn't signed the document. He repressed a sigh to think about his cousin's widow. Everything would be so damned simple if Marlee had turned out to be an ugly and mean-spirited woman. But she wasn't.

Marlee was more beautiful than he could have imagined. Even now, he could visualize the way tiny golden sparkles danced within the centers of her sapphire eyes. Worst of all, he could still recall how her lips had tasted when he'd kissed her. They'd been sweet like cinnamon, warm and soft as velvet. He'd wanted to make love to her but had pulled away from her, because he'd considered himself to be an honorable man. He wouldn't bed her only to attain her purse.

But he wasn't a man of honor any longer—not now—not when he was deluding her into thinking

71

he was her husband. And Marlee wasn't virtuous, though she gave the impression that she was an innocent. Any woman as beautiful and wealthy as Marlee shouldn't have had to marry a man she'd never met. This thought led Lark to attribute his own behavior by giving credence to the story Carpenter had told him about Marlee.

For all her seeming innocence, she wasn't virtuous. If she had been, Richard wouldn't have married her in the first place. So, why not woo Marlee into signing the document? Why shouldn't he bed her and enjoy bedding her to get what he wanted? She'd appeared more than eager for his touch and kiss the night before—a clear indication to Lark that Lady Marlee Arden must be what Richard had thought she was—a wanton.

"Carpenter, inform Mrs. Mortimer that Lady Marlee and I shall dine alone tonight in the dining room," Lark brusquely ordered and headed for the door. "And make certain we're not disturbed."

The gown Marlee chose to wear that night was one of her most colorful. Dressed in the cream silk creation, Marlee's delicate coloring was enhanced by the orange and green embroidery. The vivid colors caused her cheeks to glow, the pale yellow silk tabby petticoat highlighted the matching slippers on her feet. When she glided into the candlelit dining room that night, it seemed to Lark that she was the sun personified.

She stopped short when he came to take her arm. "Am I early, my lord? Barbara and Simon haven't come down yet."

"You're on time, my dear. The others are eating in their rooms tonight. I informed Mrs. Mortimer that we are to dine alone."

"Just the two of us?" Her voice became small and hesitant.

"If you'd rather not—" He appeared disconcerted.

"Oh, no, this is fine, my lord," Marlee hurriedly assured him, because this was very fine indeed, dining alone with her husband. She started to take her place at the end of the long table when Arden gently nudged her forward, leading her to the chair beside his own, as if he truly wanted her there.

More than anything in the world, Marlee wanted to be near him, literally ached for her husband to care for her. But she was wise enough to realize he didn't, not now at least, but perhaps in the future. She was willing to wait; she'd wait forever.

When he took the liberty of filling her crystal goblet with a rich red port, her fascinated gaze rested on his strong and capable hands. Everything about Arden fascinated her. Tonight, as always, she was struck at his handsomeness. Attired in a wine-colored jacket which was fashioned from a soft velvet and lined in a black silk material that matched his trousers, he looked exceedingly wonderful. His hair was slicked back into a queue and emphasized his rugged and masculine features. Marlee found herself memorizing each and every line on his face.

"My lady, is something wrong?" he asked her in a surprisingly husky voice that sent shivers of primitive delight down her spinal column. "You've not stopped staring at me. You may tell me if my costume is amiss. I won't fault you for your honesty, I promise you."

"Forgive me, I'm sorry, but—" she stopped herself, feeling a blush start at her hairline and spread across her entire face and neck at what she was about to say. But she couldn't help herself and plodded on daringly as she burst out, "You're so handsome, my lord, that I can't help but stare." There she'd been honest with him and said what was on her mind but couldn't speak what was in her heart.

He stared hard at her, and seemed startled himself, almost as if he hadn't expected such an admission. Finally, he laughed aloud, but she knew from the joyous quality of his tone that he wasn't offended or thought her a simpleton, either. "How delightful you are, Marlee, utterly and completely delightful."

No one had ever called her "delightful" and because Arden was the first to compliment her in such a way, his words touched her heart. "I believe in being honest, my lord."

Lifting his glass of port, he solemnly toasted her. "To you, Marlee. I wish others could share your honesty."

He sounded so sad that Marlee felt tears spring

to her eyes and was grateful she didn't have to say anything because Mary Carter entered the room and served their stew. When Mrs. Mortimer later appeared to take their plates away, Marlee cleared her throat. "I hope you don't mind that I've hired a staff without asking your permission."

Leaning back in his chair, the candlelight clearly emphasized the rugged planes of his face. "Montclair is your home, I told you that already. You may do whatever you wish here."

"Thank you, my lord. I should like to start refurbishing the house as soon as possible. Mrs. Mortimer assures me that there are competent carpenters in the village to take care of any structural damage. Also, the furnishings shall also need to be recovered and new drapes placed on every window."

"I'm certain you're up to the challenge."

"Yes, but, but," and here she wasn't too certain she wanted to be honest, frightened he'd put her in her place by refusing her since their marriage wasn't a love match.

"What is it, Marlee?"

She bit at her lower lip and hesitantly raised her eyes from the white lace napkin in her lap to guilelessly meet his perplexed stare. "I would deem it an honor, my lord, if you'd agree to help me. Montclair will always be your home, and I should like to make choices that please you, and since I don't know your tastes . . ."

Arden took a deep controlling breath and sipped his port. It seemed a very long time before he spoke, and by the time he did, she was clutching at the napkin, frightened she'd been too forward. His gaze settled upon her, enveloping her in heat. "Everything about you pleases me, my lady. I'll help you in any way I can."

She wanted to cry aloud her happiness. This was the first indication that Arden was beginning to accept her, to truly think of her as mistress of Montclair. Soon, she hoped, he'd come to want her as his wife. Because the warmth in his eyes expressed his desire, perhaps he was beginning to care for her, but for now she settled for his help with the house. Redoing Montclair was the first step in taming Arden. "Thank you, my lord," she stated simply but her heart sang with joy.

He rose and gallantly extended his arm to her. "Would you care for a stroll on the terrace? There's a full moon tonight."

In a trance, she nodded and placed her hand on his arm, not caring about the moon but wanting only to touch him. If Arden had issued an invitation to hell, she'd have gladly risen and followed him, so mesmerized was she.

From the flagstoned terrace, they gazed down at the black abyss of sea below them. The darkness was obliterated by a silver moonlit patch upon the rolling surface. Thunderous waves echoed in the night, pounding the rocky cliffs and dampening their faces with a fine sea mist. The night air was charged with awesome energy and something else—something which left

Marlee's knees feeling weaker than sea kelp.

She shivered from the coolness of the night, more than surprised to suddenly feel Arden's hands on her shoulders as he placed his jacket about her. Now she trembled but not from any chill and discovered herself to be warmer than she'd ever been in her life.

"The sea is a powerful force of nature and must be respected," she heard him say over the sound of her heart hammering in her ears. "There's nothing greater in God's universe, nothing more magnificent. I miss it so."

Marlee noticed he wasn't looking at her, or apparently aware of her. It seemed his vision was on a far distant point. "Have you sailed often?"

"What?" Arden glanced at her, her voice pulling him from his reverie.

"You sound as if you've been on many voyages. I had no idea you sailed. I mean all of the tales I've heard—" she broke off, unwilling to discuss his reputation.

"I can imagine the horrible things you've heard about Lord Richard Arden," he said, and she swore she noticed a gleam of amusement in his eyes. "But, I assure you, what you've heard has nothing to do with *me*."

"Forgive me, my lord, I shouldn't have said anything. Gossip hurts, believe me. I know firsthand how painful such loose talk can be. But I do wonder if you've ever sailed to distant places and, if so, I should like to hear about them. I've never been anywhere but my village — and here."

"No where else?"

She shook her head. "But I should like to see distant ports and visit all of the countries I've heard about. Have you been to America?"

"Er, why, yes, I have."

"Where in America?" Marlee asked, her eyes bright and glittering like starlight.

"Virginia, Williamsburg to be exact."

"Oh, how exciting! Did you see any savages? I've read about the heathens."

"Well, I've seen an Indian or two in my time."

"Were they very fierce?"

"Not the ones I've seen."

"Oh." Marlee sounded disappointed. To overcome the boredom of her everyday life, she'd read stories concerning savage attacks upon unsuspecting settlers and envisioned warrior chieftains prepared for battle. Suddenly America seemed as dull as the small village she'd left, and she sensed she amused Arden with her schoolgirl questions. "Have you ever encountered any pirates then?"

The change in his attitude was immediate. His expression darkened and his fingers dug into her shoulders until she winced. "Richard — please — you're hurting me."

"I'm sorry," he hastily offered when he realized what he'd done and loosened the pressure but still he held onto her.

"Have I said anything to offend you? If so, I do apologize but I don't know what I've done. You must forgive my country-bumpkin musings, sometimes I don't realize what I'm saying. You're so different from me, so noble and aristocratic, while I'm—a nobody—"

"Never say such a thing again, Marlee!" The vehemence behind his words startled her. "You're a baroness, you belong at Montclair. And even if you weren't a baroness, you'd still be yourself."

"And what am I?" she asked, not daring to move away from him, barely able to speak.

His hands moved from her shoulders to her waist and he drew her nearer to him, so close that in a second their bodies were touching and she could feel his heart beating. With his black gaze roaming her face, she saw the hunger in his eyes and wondered if he knew how much in love with him she was. "You're a damned desirable and beautiful woman, Marlee. And I want to kiss you like I kissed you last night. You stir up something in me, something like a strong current each time I look at you—"

"Kiss me," she begged and wantonly pulled his head closer to hers until his lips were a hairsbreadth from her own. "Kiss me like that again."

His mouth came down upon hers, bruising in its intensity, but Marlee felt only ecstasy. She met his kiss with a passion she didn't know she possessed, with a sweet yearning that flowed through her body like melted honey. When his tongue invaded her mouth and met hers, she moaned in absolute surrender. She belonged to Arden, her baron, the man with whom she'd fallen in love the first moment she set eyes upon him. Marlee literally ached for him, her body heating with each sweep of his hands across her back and down her buttocks to come upward and caress her swelling breasts. She knew now that he desired her, maybe not loved her yet, but in time he would. She'd make certain he would love her in time. At that moment she made her decision about her fortune.

"Ah, Marlee, Marlee, you're so beautiful," he murmured and skimmed her neck with kisses. "I want you so much, I need you so much—"

"I know," she whispered and allowed his mouth full rein upon her face and neck, giving her body to him to feast upon. "I need you, too, my darling. I never thought you would want me this way. I never thought I could feel this way. Tomorrow, I'll sign my fortune over to you. Everything I have shall be yours because I love you, Richard. I love you."

She began kissing him again until she realized that he was no longer returning her ardor. He'd loosened his hold upon her, and she'd been so dazed that she hadn't noticed. Opening her eyes, she found he was staring intently at her, almost as if he was warring within himself. Finally, his hands dropped away from her until one hand took her elbow. "The hour is late. I'll escort you upstairs, my lady."

As he started to lead her into the house, she turned to him with bafflement and pain etched upon her face. "What have I done, Richard? Tell me what I've done wrong."

"Nothing, my lady."

How formal he sounded, how frozen he looked. A cold fear swept into Marlee's heart. Somehow she'd lost him, but how could she lose someone who'd never really belonged to her in the first place? She was confused and hurt and so angered by his sudden withdrawal from her that she wanted to scream. In desperation she swung about when they reached the upstairs hallway and pulled off his jacket to throw it at him. "If I've done nothing wrong, my lord, then you have! I don't understand you, I don't. Did you trifle with me to gain my fortune? Is that what this is about?" Tears clouded her eyes and blurred her vision. "I should have known you didn't want me—but my—money. She took a deep sustaining breath. "Don't worry, my lord, I shall sign the paper in the morning. I do it not for you but for Montclair. At least I live up to the bargain I made."

He started to touch her, but she backed away. "Sometimes I think I hate you."

"Hate me then!" he thundered and grabbed her wrist. "I'd rather suffer your hatred than your love."

"I—do—hate you. I do!" She struggled to free herself but he was stronger. In an instant he'd swept her into his arms and pinned her against the wall until all the breath and fight left her body. Then his lips found hers and branded her mouth

81

with a kiss that left her clutching at his shoulders.

"Forgive me, Marlee," he said softly against her cheek. "But know that I could never hate *you*. No matter what happens in the future, believe I never wished you ill."

Before she could reply, he let her go and bounded down the stairs to disappear into the night.

Chapter Six

"The color for the draperies is most becoming, Marlee. I think your taste is excellent. I'm certain Lord Arden is very pleased with your choices." Barbara held up a swatch of velvet, a deep rose color, that was to be used on the windows in the dining room. Bolts of multicolored silks and satins were strewn upon the garden room floor, clear reminders of the recent renovation which had been undertaken.

With a disinterested air, Marlee fingered the materials. "I suppose the restoration will be finished sooner than I wish, and then what shall I do with my time?"

Marlee sounded so forlorn that Barbara turned her attention to her cousin. She gave her a quick hug about the shoulders. "You can devote yourself to your husband."

"Hah! Stop humoring me, Barbara. You know very well that the man hasn't spoken to me in over a week—and I don't care if I ever speak to him again. The notorious rake! He lulled me, positively lulled me into believing he might come to care for me, and what do I do but fall into his trap and tell him I'll sign away my fortune. I believe I'm the biggest fool alive!"

Barbara sighed. "You always intended to turn your money over to him, Marlee."

"Yes, but I—never intended to love him." Tears choked her and she turned her face away, grateful she had an unencumbered view of the beach and sea from the garden room window. Sunlight drenched the coast in warm, golden splotches, even touching her face with a tentative yellow finger through the wavy glass.

She'd signed the document exactly seven days before, in the presence of Mr. Carpenter, Simon—and the baron. Somehow she couldn't think of him as her husband any longer. Now he was simply "the baron," a man who had married her to claim her fortune and a man who'd never love her. One would think, since she'd turned everything to his control, that he'd express some gratitude to her. Except for the formal pleasantries one would bestow upon a guest, he'd said nothing to her after the kiss in the hall. And that's what she was, she reasoned; she was a paying guest at Montclair.

Oh, he allowed her free rein, she could do anything she wanted and he didn't seem to care. She saw very little of him and envied Barbara for the time Simon spent with her. How Marlee wished the baron would laugh with her, touch her, kiss her—

"I must go for a walk!" Marlee burst out and startled Barbara. She had to get out of the house or go mad with her own thoughts.

"Wait until I get my wrap, and I'll join you," Barbara offered.

"No, no, I want to be alone." Marlee patted Barbara's hand and smiled gently. "I need to think."

Barbara worried her lower lip. "I understand. Please be careful on the beach. Sometimes the rocks are slippery."

"It seems you know about the rocks?"

"Well, yes, Simon and I have gone for many walks."

"In the moonlight?"

"Yes," Barbara admitted with a dreamy expression on her face. "The beach is beautiful at night."

Marlee remembered how lovely the night had been when she stood within the baron's arms on the terrace. But she dismissed the memory, so pained by it that she hurriedly rushed into the back vestibule and retrieved a heavy gray shawl from the cloak hook. The color matched her day gown and her sorrowful mood, which was fine because Marlee doubted she'd ever feel lighthearted again.

Crude stone steps which were cut into the cliff fell from the back of the estate to the beach below. Marlee had never walked the beach before, her time having been taken up with coordinating the workmen who would soon descend upon Montclair. She hadn't approached the baron about colors or materials to suit his taste and she wouldn't. She'd burn in hell before she'd asked him anything. Montclair would shine with her handiwork and hang the baron's taste!

At the base of the cliffs, she removed her shoes and stockings, allowing the warm sand to spill across her bare feet. She felt wild and daring, more than exhilarated by the stiff sea breezes that tangled within the depths of her hair and wrapped her skirts around her legs. For the first time in her life, she was free—or as free as possible under the circumstances—and able to do whatever she wished.

Like an eager child, Marlee ran down the deserted stretch of beach until she grew breathless and her legs ached. Stopping by a large rock, she threw herself down beside it, basking in the noon sun. Soon she felt as warm as buttered toast. A great sleepiness began to overtake her, and she started to doze. She dreamed she heard the baron's voice in the distance and would have given herself up further to sleep, but the loud cawing of a nearby gull woke her.

For a few seconds, she was disoriented, even imagining she saw a large dark ship, wallowing in the waves before her. Her head cleared and the ship was still there. Then she heard voices on the opposite side of the rock, men's voices. Soundlessly, Marlee rose and climbed up the rock until she was able to peer over it. About fifty feet away were a group of men, many of whom looked in good need of a washing and proper clothing. Within their midst, stood the baron and Marlee's heart seemed to cease beating.

Once again, he wore only black. His booted feet were firmly planted in the sand and from the loud tone of his voice, he was issuing orders to the clustered men and pointing to large wooden crates. Marlee saw some of the men lug the crates to one of two longboats before rowing to the ship, waiting in the bay.

What was happening?

"Holcombe," Arden shouted to one of the men. "Where's Mr. Oliver?"

"On board ship, Captain. He's seeing to the repair of the hull."

"Then take some men and go help him. I won't tolerate any slacking off in my crew. All must be in readiness. We sail in two days' time." Arden fixed his attention on another group of men, so totally absorbed in the activity on the beach that if he'd have glanced upward, he'd have seen Marlee's shocked face staring back at him.

Her fingers gripped the cool stone as her head spun with the implications of what she saw and heard. Arden was the captain of the ship in the bay. No wonder he loved the sea and spoke fondly of it. He was getting ready to set sail in two days. He was leaving Cornwall, leaving her, and he hadn't told her. Did he hate her so much that he couldn't do her the courtesy of informing her that he was leaving? But why should he tell her anything, she who was a tin miner's daughter and not fit to bear the title of baroness. She meant nothing to him, nothing at all.

Still she remembered the way he'd kissed her. Deep within herself she knew that a man didn't embrace or kiss a woman in such a way if she repulsed him. She wouldn't let him get away without bidding her farewell—at the very least she deserved to be told goodbye—she deserved something other than his apathy.

Pulling herself up to the top of the rock, she stood upright and placed her hands on her hips. The wind was brisk now. Her hair tossed darkly about her face, her skirts clung wantonly to her thighs and the white lace hem of her chemise waved like a banner of surrender in the breeze. She resembled a wild, barefoot peasant girl.

"My lord!" she cried loudly and defiantly.

All activity stopped on the beach. The men looked up, their eyes agog at what they saw. "Lordy, who is that wench?" one of them near Arden asked.

Arden found he couldn't reply because he was surprised to see a woman there, a wildly beautiful woman. And realizing that the woman was Marlee took all thought and speech away.

"Hey, sweeting, what can I do for you? What can *we* do for you?" A leering sailor started forward, ready to claim the fetching sight atop the rock. When two other men made a move in Marlee's direction, Lark swung about with a vehement oath.

"Get your bloody carcasses to the ship and put your hands to work there! Now go, the lot of you!"

Lark's dark expression and voice caused the men to quickly scatter and head for the longboat. Lark moved toward the rock and seconds later, he stood before Marlee, gazing up at her. "My lady," he said with a restraint he didn't feel.

"There seems to be a great deal of activity here, my lord. Might I inquire what is happening?"

For a few seconds, Arden had the good grace to look sheepish. Then with an inscrutable expression, he said, "The ship is being loaded."

"I assume the ship is yours."

"Yes."

"I also assume that you're setting sail soon and didn't have the good grace to tell me."

"I was planning to inform you tonight, Marlee."

There was something soft and seductive in the way he said her name. Marlee's pulse quickened, her insides began to tremble as Arden's handsome face weaved a hypnotic spell about her again. And what was most disturbing to her was that he was unaware of the effect he had upon her. She must get away from him or risk complete humiliation if he realized she was succumbing to him. Gaining a foothold on a small jutting ledge on the rock, she started to scramble down, but Arden's arms reached out for her. In a blinding instant she was enfolded in his embrace, and he held her high above him.

Their gazes met and locked.

"You must be careful on these rocks," he gently said. "They're slippery."

She wanted to look away from him but hadn't the strength or will to resist. "I can manage."

"I know," he said and disarmed her with a smile. "I've discovered that about you."

Her hands involuntarily found their way to his shoulders. "You may put me down now, my lord."

"I've told you not to call me that, and besides, I don't want to put you down. I like holding you close to me."

Marlee groaned audibly. "Why must you say such a thing to me? Why must you torment me?"

"My wish isn't to cause you torment, my love. I want only your happiness."

"At what cost?" she bit out. "You've taken my fortune, and now plan to leave me. There's nothing left for me but torment. I can't see any hope of a true marriage between us."

Marlee was surprised that he didn't see fit to argue with her. Instead, he slid her body down the length of his until she was standing. He touched a wayward curl upon her cheek then caressed the spot with his fingertips. "Sometimes two people are given only a few moments of happiness, Marlee, and that's all they can hope for."

What was he telling her? Was he telling her anything at all? Why did she always feel there was some cryptic meaning behind his words? "You've taken everything from me and given me nothing in

return. What is it you want of me?" she cried and
started to pull away, but Arden kept a firm grip
upon her wrist. His lips sought and found hers,
quelling her words with the spark of his possession.

Marlee wanted to fight him, to punish him for
his dismissal of her feelings, but she was powerless
within his embrace and weakened by her own desire. A moan of surrender strangled in her throat.
"Let me go, please, Richard," she begged in a
husky voice and broke the kiss, frightened that if
she didn't resist, he'd claim her body and soul, that
he'd know how much she loved him. "There's no
need to pretend that you care for me; you now
control my fortune. I—I won't hold you to anything else."

Though her eyes were closed, she felt his gaze
upon her face. "I wish to God that you would hold
me close to your heart, Marlee. I wish—"

"Captain!" came the booming voice of a sailor
some yards away where he waited in a longboat.
"Begging your pardon, sir, but Mr. Simon needs
your help aboard ship."

"Damn!" Lark cursed under his breath.

"I'll return to the house," Marlee mumbled, more
than embarrassed to have been caught in such an
intimate exchange. She pulled away from him, but
their fingertips remained in contact for a few seconds longer before she drew them away.

"I must speak to you later," he told her and
there was something in his gaze that sent

a flash of warmth through her body.

Lark watched Marlee until she'd turned and practically ran down the beach. Minutes later he was standing on deck of the ship where Simon met him. "What was so blasted important that it couldn't wait?" Lark shot out irritably.

Simon folded his arms across his chest. "I saw what was happening on the beach between you and Marlee. I decided someone had to break up that tryst before it led to—something else."

"Back off, Simon. I don't need you playing watchdog."

"Oh, really? Then I'll play devil's advocate instead. What do you think would have happened if I hadn't intervened? I'd wager you'd have enticed that innocent girl into your bed and made her fall in love with you. Lark, you know good and well that you don't love Marlee. You know you can never marry her—"

"I know! I bloody well know that she can't belong to me, no matter what happens." Lark's hands raked through his tangled dark hair. For the first time since his altercation with Manuel Silva, there was true agony on his face. "I'm beginning to care for Marlee. Don't you think I know how futile my feelings are for her? Can't you see how I'm fighting myself not to love her? If she'd been shallow and vain, a wanton like I'd expected, all of this would have been so damned easy. But nothing is happening like I wished."

"You have your money now," Simon reminded

Lark. "The ship is ready to sail day after tomorrow. You have everything you wanted."

"Everything and nothing."

Simon laid a hand on Lark's shoulder. "I'm not going with you, my friend. I've asked Barbara to marry me."

Lark had expected as much. "Be happy, Simon. I'll miss you."

"I'll miss you, too, Lark. We've been friends a hell of a long time."

Lark managed a grin. "Yes, and you've never disappointed me. When I was away, you looked after Mother for me. Now, promise me that you'll see to Marlee. Make certain she's all right — after I'm gone — after she learns the truth about me."

"Are you going to tell her or is Carpenter?"

"I'll tell her," Lark decided. "I'll tell her tonight."

"Will you tell her about Lady Bettina?"

"No," Lark said and clasped the wooden railing until his fingers hurt. "Marlee need never learn about Bettina's kidnapping by Manuel Silva. She doesn't need to know about my betrothal to her. I believe it's best if Marlee thinks me a ne'er-do-well, a rake of the highest order. If I believe she hates me, then I can tolerate my marriage to Bettina. Knowing she loved me would be too much to bear."

"I want the silver and red dress for tonight, Mrs. Mortimer. Also, you shall serve us in my room."

"Us, my lady?" Mrs. Mortimer inquired of Marlee.

Marlee hung her shawl up on the wall peg, more than aware of Mrs. Mortimer's suspicious attitude, as she made her way into the kitchen. "His Lordship and myself, of course."

"I see, my lady." The color drained out of Mrs. Mortimer's face, and she looked like she might say something else.

"What is it?" Marlee asked.

The housekeeper gave a deferential curtsy. "Nothing, my lady. All shall be as you asked."

And all would be as Marlee wanted, she'd see to that. Arden had told her he wanted to speak to her later, and she now realized how much she loved him and would miss him. Whether he loved her no longer mattered to her. There was something about the way he'd held her earlier, the primitive fire in his kiss, which ignited a flame within Marlee.

Arden's loving her wasn't necessary. She wanted, craved, his possession of her body. She knew that if he sailed away, she'd miss him terribly until his return. She wanted him to miss her, too, to be so miserable without her that he'd hurry up and come home—to her.

The one way which she knew to make her husband desire her was to show him what he'd be leaving behind. Perhaps her money hadn't tamed him—she realized her money must be financing his voyage—but there was another way to tame a man. Before she was through expressing her love for Ar-

94

den, he'd never want to leave her again. And maybe, just maybe, a marriage based only on mutual physical attraction wasn't a bad way to begin.

Chapter Seven

"All is in readiness, my lady." Mrs. Mortimer completed the two table settings, then lighted the large white candle which stood between the gold-rimmed plates.

Marlee turned from the looking glass where her image reflected a silver gown, light and airy of material, with red rosettes on the full sleeves. The bodice was tight and much too low, as was the fashion. She'd originally hated the scandalous-looking creation after she'd bought it before leaving the village. It had been the only gown at the dressmaker's shop which wasn't sewn for an elderly matron, and she hadn't had the time to have her own dresses made before hurrying to Montclair. But now she was rather pleased at the way her full breasts strained upward and liked the way her already small waist appeared to be tinier. With her hair loose and fluffed about her face, Marlee decided she would appeal to Arden. She must appeal to him. Her heart was overflowing with love and desire for him.

She turned to Mrs. Mortimer. "My husband knows to come here after he's bathed and changed?"

"Yes, my lady. Lord Arden is aware he is to dine in here tonight."

"I shall serve him myself."

"Yes, my lady."

"Don't be so glum, Mrs. Mortimer. Smile for me, please."

"Yes, my lady." But the smile was nonexistent.

Mrs. Mortimer had hardly withdrawn when Arden tapped on Marlee's door. Marlee's heart beat hard and fast when she opened the door to him. A tender smile broke out upon her face because he seemed to be baffled at having been summoned to her room. "Come in," she sweetly invited.

"I've been told we're to dine in here tonight." Arden glanced at the table and then back at Marlee. "Are you ill, my lady?"

"Goodness, no!" She laughed up at him with sparkling eyes. "I'm very well—and I thought it might be nice to have an intimate supper—alone." She wanted to say more but couldn't when his large, warm hand took hers and brought it to his mouth for an endearing kiss.

"I quite agree with you," was his husky-voiced assessment.

Tingles of anticipation and desire streaked through her faster than a comet racing through the heavens. "Please be seated, my lord, and I'll serve your supper. You must be hungry."

"I am," he said, but she sensed he wasn't speaking about food for his eyes fastened on her mouth before straying to the lush, rounded mounds of her breasts. He smiled a lazy, crooked smile as he took his seat. "Outfitting a ship is not an easy task. I'm lucky to have found able-bodied men."

"Yes, good help is a wonderful thing to have." Marlee started serving the succulent beef that the cook had already cut into portions. She bent low over Arden when she placed his plate in front of him. Her breasts were so tightly laced that she feared they'd break loose of the stays she wore, but the beads of perspiration on her forehead had nothing to do with her attire. Suddenly she realized that his mouth was so near to her bosom that if he'd wished, he could have brought the pale, soft mounds to his lips—and she'd have willingly and wantonly allowed him to feast upon them.

"So is a beautiful woman." The heat of his words washed across her bare flesh like hot, licking flames.

"Your supper, my lord," came her voice in a breathy whisper as she pushed the plate near to him.

Instead of picking up the fork as she thought he'd do, he took her hand in his. "What have I done to warrant such personal attention?"

His touch caused a slow burning in her blood; her face flushed. Should she admit the truth to him about loving him, should she admit she'd miss him unbearably while he was away and would count the hours until his return? Ever honest, she realized she must. If he knew she eagerly awaited him, then maybe life would be different when he came home.

Marlee settled her glittering blue gaze upon him. "You're leaving, and I want you to know how much I've—come to care for you." Lowering her gaze, she nearly stumbled over her words so nervous was she. "I would deem it a great honor, my lord, if you would make me your wife in every sense of the word. I know I'm only a common person, but I swear to you that I love you, will love you forever." She bravely looked at him. "You don't have to love me in return. I know that a man of your background cannot love me and I dare not believe you ever shall—"

"Marlee! For God's sake do you know what you're asking?" Arden bolted out of the chair. His mouth was a white line in his tanned face.

"Yes, I know," she answered simply and molded her body against his, eager for his kiss upon her lips, in fact burning for it. "I'm asking—no, hoping—you will make love to me. I pray to God that you do."

"Be careful what you pray for, my love, you just may get it."

"I hope that I do, my lord."

With that, she wrapped her arms around his neck and wantonly pulled his head down until their lips met. It was a kiss filled with aching need and pent-up passion, exploding in an inferno of melting ecstasy. When his arms went around her and pulled her into him, Marlee knew she had won. "You've asked for this, my love, remember that," she heard

99

him say over the pounding of her heart. "I'm a man who can no longer resist you, sweet Marlee. Forgive me—"

"Shh, my darling. I don't want to speak or to think any longer. I want you to make love to me—now."

"Oh, Marlee, now is all I can give to you. Please don't hate me for wanting you."

"I can never hate you," she softly assured him, and at that moment she didn't believe she would ever feel anything for him but love.

With skillful hands, Lark undid the back of her silver gown, allowing it to fall like a pool of moonlight at Marlee's feet. Next, he removed her hoop petticoat and then her stays. Her breasts broke free of the restraint and Lark smothered a husky groan. Never in his life had he seen a more beautiful woman, and he'd seen and sampled many a lady's charms in his time. But there was something pure yet sensual about Marlee, a quality which stirred his blood from the very first moment he saw her. He needed her, wanted her, and no matter that his mission had brought him to Montclair and would cause his departure, he was determined to have her. For the first time in his life, he felt absolute tenderness, a melting of his senses. In the back of his mind he knew he should admit the truth to her, that he should do the honorable thing and leave. But he'd become engaged to Bettina out of honor and experienced no happiness because of it.

Now he didn't give a damn about honor. All he wanted was Marlee and a fleeting moment of happiness to last the rest of his years.

"You're so beautiful," Lark praised and cupped her breasts in the palms of his hands. Through the silky material of her chemise, he felt her nipples harden in response as his thumbs gently massaged them.

"I love when you touch me. I feel so alive—so quivery"

Her candor about her feelings amazed him. He couldn't help but smile. "And do you always feel quivery when a man touches you?"

She didn't realize he was teasing her. Her horrified expression lent credence to her true innocence. She stiffened imperceptibly but Lark felt her resistance. "No man but you has ever touched me. Please, I beg you not to believe the gossip."

"I don't," he hastily assured her with a fiery kiss upon her lips, but it wasn't until that moment that he truly discounted the story about her virtue. Her body relaxed against him and she placed her arms trustingly around his neck. He couldn't wait any longer for her, his loins ached with a fierce burning he'd never before experienced. Scooping her into his embrace, he lifted her off of her feet.

Marlee giggled in surprise. "What are you doing?"

"Carrying you to bed, sweetheart." Which is exactly what he did when he placed her in the center of the fluffy coverlet. He watched her for a moment. She appeared so beautiful in the candlelight, so seductive, with the transparent chemise doing little to hide her physical attributes. His tongue wanted to savor every luscious inch of her, to taste each curve and crevice of her body. He'd never hungered for a woman this much, and knew he must go slowly with her, but the fire curling through his loins caused him equal amounts of pain and pleasure.

"Are you supposed to undress, too?" she asked him with wide eyes which were softer than deep blue velvet. "I mean, is it customary for the man to undress?"

His deep laugh sent ripples of delight down her spinal column. Bending over, he kissed the tip of her nose. "Yes, my love, very customary."

With his gaze never leaving her, Lark stripped down to his trousers. His fingers stalled on the waist cord of his pants at her gasp. "Are all of the clothes removed?"

"Yes, of course. Didn't you know that?"

"No-o." Shaking her head, Marlee glanced down at her thin chemise. Her hands instinctively covered herself. "Must, must I undress entirely?"

"If you'd rather not, you don't have to, Marlee. But it would be very nice if you do." He kissed her with a sweet longing which left her breathless. "I think you'd like it very much, and if you're shy about it, I could assist you."

"Would you? I'm—afraid."

"Gladly, my love." His fingers itched to rip away the thin silk from her body. He removed his trousers, suddenly aware of the way Marlee's large, frightened eyes appraised his aroused manhood. There was curiosity in her gaze, too, but fearing she might withdraw from him, he quickly pulled down the cover and slid beneath it.

"Now, your turn," he invited and was more than relieved when she rose up on her knees to face him. Gently, he touched the white lace covering her breasts. "I don't bite, not unless you want me to." Lark flashed her a mesmerizing smile.

Marlee nodded, but he suspected his meaning was lost on her. Long dark strands of hair fell forward and covered her bosom. "Would your undressing me give you great pleasure?" she asked.

"Very great pleasure."

"Then undress me, my lord, and make me yours," she whispered. "I want to belong to you."

"Ah, Marlee, Marlee, you're mistress of my heart."

Tenderly, Lark pushed her chemise down until it rested at her small waist. His throat swelled, she was so beautiful, so perfectly formed. Her breasts were thrust upward, arching toward him, taunting him to take their globular fullness within his warm hands. He responded by bringing each nipple to his lips to suckle.

A wetness gathered within the very center of Marlee's womanhood. What Arden was doing to her felt so very wonderful that it seemed wicked to enjoy it. "Am I supposed to like this?" she asked, and her hands steadied on his broad shoulders to still the trembling which rocked through her.

His dark head moved from her breasts and he glanced up. "Don't you like this, sweet Marlee?"

"Oh, yes, very much," she breathed into his hair.

"Then enjoy it. There's nothing for you to be ashamed of, frightened about."

She swallowed convulsively. "Is there more?"

"Much more. Let me show you."

He guided her down onto the coverlet and removed the rest of the chemise. She lay there in complete surrender before him, vulnerable and so lovely that his heart contracted. His forefinger reached out and found the sensitive bud which was hidden within the lush folds of her body. Gently, he stroked the velvet nub, feeling himself become so hard and rigid that he feared he'd soon explode.

Something was happening to her. Marlee could no longer think, could barely speak. Her whole attention was fixed on the very center of her femininity where something within her was building to a fiery peak, threatening to overflow with molten heat. "What — what are you doing to me?" she asked in a low, breathy voice.

"What's the matter? Don't you like it? Should I stop?"

He stilled his finger and she arched her body to make contact with his fingertip. "Please don't stop. Don't ever stop. I — I just don't understand what's happening to me."

Her eyes were glazed with desire, and her voice was thick with passion. He knew it wouldn't be long until she found her release. "Lie still and enjoy, my love. Close your eyes and concentrate only on my finger within you, feel the pleasure it gives to you. Go on, Marlee, close your eyes."

Like an obedient child, she did as he commanded but was very much aware when he laid beside her to suckle one of her breasts. "I'm going to take you to paradise, my love," he promised with a spine-tingling tug upon her nipple.

Paradise meant heaven to Marlee, she'd heard a great deal about it from the minister's sermons each Sunday. But suddenly paradise took on a whole new meaning, and it was no longer a place within the clouds. It was here and now, a physical reality. With each silken stroke of Lark's finger, he brought her closer and closer to it.

She began to pant, writhing and arching toward the heavenly crescendo Lark promised. She wasn't certain what she was going to feel, but what she felt now was more wonderful, so stupefying, that no words could adequately explain the intense sensations gathering and spreading like sweet wildfire between her legs. A low moaning began in her throat. She was coming to an end that was also a dazzling beginning.

Marlee's release shook her to the very bane of her existence. Nothing and no one could have prepared her for the throbbing sensations centered within her womanly core. Like someone coming out of a daze, she opened her eyes to find Lark smiling down at her. He rose up on his knees and straddled her, his finger gently probing her body's crevice, opening her to him. It was then she felt his hardened manhood nudging the moist entrance between her legs and suddenly she understood what was about to happen and knew that she was created for this man to love.

She arched to meet his thrust but was unprepared for the sharp ache when her maidenhead tore. Instinctively she started to pull away, but he held her to him until the hard length of him stretched the tender walls. She moaned her pain and he kissed her. He kissed her until a flicker of pleasure darted through her and obliterated the pain.

With wondering eyes, she watched his face. He was more handsome, more manly, if that were possible, in the throes of passion. And his passion was for her.

Each taunting thrust took her to the summit. Grabbing onto his upper arms, Marlee's fingernails dug into the sinewy muscles. Her release was a heartbeat away, an eternity of waiting. Suddenly he went still and looked at her, his face a mask of pleasure. Once more, he thrust, and her name was torn from his lips.

Liquid warmth spewed inside of her, a throbbing which caused an exquisite explosion so intense that Marlee thought she'd die from the ecstasy of it.

Later, he held her in the crook of his arm, and her head nestled against his chest. "I never thought, never knew—" she began, but words seemed somehow inadequate to describe the sensations she'd felt.

"I know, I know," he said and kissed her until she was again clinging to him and aching for his possession. For the rest of the night, Marlee belonged to Lark body and soul. Near dawn, she drifted into a peaceful slumber.

Chapter Eight

Lark, however, didn't sleep. He couldn't. Guilt at what he'd done ate away at him like an acid, and he found all he could do was dully stare at the carved cherubs, naked and cavorting on the ceiling.

Marlee lay so trustingly in his arms. Every now and then she'd give a tiny sigh in her sleep, and he realized just how young and inexperienced she was. He'd taken advantage of her youth, her innocence, cruelly used her. Somehow he felt as if he'd just awakened from a torturous dream into a land of enchanted beauty. Never in his life had he felt so alive with a woman, or dared hope he'd find such happiness. But like all delusions of the mind and heart, happiness was a fleeting and gossamer thing. His short-lived happiness was about to end.

Quietly, he left the bed and dressed. He sat by the table and poured himself a large cup of port to fortify himself for what was to come. His gaze never left the sleeping young woman. Even now, after hours of unbridled lovemaking, his loins hardened at the sight of her. What was there about

Marlee that set her aside from the other women he'd known? God, if only he could have felt this same sensation for Bettina, maybe the forced betrothal wouldn't have seemed like the end of life itself for him.

He'd agreed to marry Bettina only to please his father. His father and Bettina's father had been great friends in their youth and both had wished to unite the two families through their children. Lark would have been married to Bettina now. Fate decreed otherwise when Manuel Silva captured the auburn-haired beauty off of Lark's ship after Lark had gone to Bermuda to bring her to Williamsburg. Lark knew he must find Silva soon and recapture Bettina—if she was still alive. He'd marry her out of a sense of honor. He owed her that much.

Lark shivered as an early morning rain gently beat upon the windowpanes. A chill settled over him, and he shivered not so much from the cold but from the thought of what awaited him in the future—his impending wedding if he found Bettina—and more imminently, Marlee's hatred when he told her the truth.

The moment of truth came sooner than Lark expected. Marlee stirred and rolled onto her back. Her beautifully formed breasts were bare. Lark wished he could make love to her again, just once more before he left her. Turning her head, she spotted him. A timid smile curved her lips and she sat up, immediately covering herself with the sheet.

"You're up and dressed already," she said more as a comment than a question. "I best get up and dress, too. I must look a mess."

"You look beautiful, wonderful," Lark hastily assured her and stifled the urge to sit beside her. He wanted to kiss her pretty mouth, to hold her and never release her. Instead, he resisted the inclination to touch her, but he impressed her delicate features upon his mind for later, when he needed to remember her.

"You look wonderful, too," she praised and dimpled. "You *are* wonderful."

He couldn't help groaning aloud when she took his hand and brought it to her lips. Her kiss felt like golden fire upon his flesh. "I love you so much, Richard. I shall love you forever."

"Marlee, stop!" he ground out and realized he'd startled her by the vehemence in his voice. He wasn't angry with her but with himself—so disappointed in himself that he wished to slither away and never face the light of day again.

"Have—have I been too bold?" she asked him and there were tears shining in her eyes. Instantly she withdrew her hand and held onto the sheet.

"It's not that, not anything you've done. God, Marlee, can't you see that I care for you? You've turned my life upside down."

"Is that so bad?" A delighted grin spread across her face, expressing her happiness and awe that he cared. "That's what I want, Richard, I've prayed for it—"

"Stop it, Marlee, no more, please."

"But I love you. I do." She started to get up, to reach out for him again, but he purposely backed away. "What is it, Richard? What have I done?"

"Stop calling me Richard for one," he said with such pain on his face that he noticed she immediately stiffened.

"Should I call you something else, *my lord?*" She sounded frosty. "I had thought that after last night you'd consider me as something more than a commoner."

"That's not it. You're making this very hard for me—and I deserve things to be hard, I deserve your hatred." Lark raked his hand through his hair. The agony in his eyes sent waves of fear spinning through Marlee, but he didn't realize this. All he knew was that he must confess his deception to her but he was unable to look at her. Instead his gaze found one of those infernal grinning cherubs on the ceiling. His attention was on the little carved statue the whole time he spoke. "First of all, Marlee, I am the Baron of Montclair, but I'm not Richard Arden. I'm Lark Arden, Richard's cousin, from Virginia. I've deceived you, Carpenter deceived you—"

He took a quick look her way and found her gaze was riveted on him. Never in his life had he seen another person's eyes grow so large. Swallowing a number of times, he thought his throat had closed up, but no, his voice came out surprisingly strong.

"I arrived at Montclair the same day that Richard had an accident. He died a few days later." He heard her audible gasp but continued, "You did marry Richard; never doubt that you're a baroness. But, well, I desperately needed to finance a voyage. My grandfather left me a trust, money which Richard illegally squandered. I arrived here to claim my fortune and found nothing. After I got over my frustration and anger, I learned about you, about your being an heiress. My only recourse was to pretend to be Richard, to woo you into signing the money away so I could take what was due me. And that's all I've taken, Marlee, only the amount that Richard owed me. The rest of the money is yours, Montclair and the title are yours—everything belongs to you."

He stopped, feeling a terrible weakness assail him. Whoever had said that confession was good for the soul had been wrong. Lark felt horrible, miserable. He didn't dare ask her forgiveness, but he'd like her to say something, anything. He'd settle for her aiming a candlestick at his head, gladly suffering the brunt of her rage.

Nearing the bed, he decided that she might be in shock, so still and quiet was she. "Marlee, are you all right?"

A trembling sigh coursed through her entire body. She looked at him but her eyes were a dull shade of blue, almost as if she didn't see him any longer. And he suddenly realized that for Marlee, he'd ceased to exist. He waited for what seemed like hours before she finally said anything, and when she did, it was spoken so softly that he barely heard the words, "Leave me alone."

The problem was he didn't want to leave her. He wanted to hold her again, to tell her that he loved her and would marry her. But he couldn't do any of that because he wasn't free to love her. "Marlee, I won't leave you like this — "

She suddenly rose up on the bed, resembling a wild-eyed specter with the white sheet wrapped around her. "I said go away! Leave me in peace, Lark Arden, or whoever you may be. Leave me alone!"

He was forced to leave when Mrs. Mortimer burst through the door and cast a venomous glance his way. "My lady, what is it?" the woman cried, but Lark somehow surmised that Mrs. Mortimer already knew what had happened — almost as if she'd expected it.

More than anything, he wanted to remain with Marlee, to somehow make amends for what he'd done to her, but there was nothing he could say or do to help her. All he recalled was the chilling sound of her cries of "Get out!" as he left the house.

Chapter Nine

"My lady, can I get you anything? Do anything for you?" Mrs. Mortimer's voice seemed to come from a far distance.

Marlee sat on the bed, her hands trembling with suppressed rage. She wanted to tear the bed sheets to shreds, to vent her fury upon something or someone, and the someone she had in mind was a deceitful cad with raven black hair and eyes so dark she could have drowned within their ebony depths. Someone named Lark Arden.

She shivered at the memory of it all, more than humiliated. The man had played her for a fool, had led her a merry dance so she'd sign away her fortune to him. Worst of all, she'd fallen in love with the bounder. What had she ever done to deserve such a fate as this?

"Lady Marlee, please, please say something," Mrs. Mortimer cajoled with a pat on Marlee's hand. "You're so quiet that I'm fearful. Should I fetch a doctor?"

Poor Mrs. Mortimer. She looked so distraught

and guilty—yes, that was it, Marlee decided. Mrs. Mortimer had known the truth and deceived her, too. The old woman dabbed at her eyes with the hem of her apron. "Forgive me, my lady," her voice broke and she sniffed. "I wanted to tell you all, but, but that Mr. Carpenter wouldn't let me. And that hateful man—"

"Lark Arden, you mean," Marlee burst out, needing to say his name aloud.

"Aye, him, my lady. He made me promise not to say a word, that I'd lose me post here if I opened me mouth about who he was. 'Tis been very hard for me since Lord Richard died. He was my lamb—not always a good man—but he was like the son I never had. Forgive me, I'm begging you, ma'am."

Despite the intense pain which ate away at Marlee's heart, she didn't hold Mrs. Mortimer responsible for what had happened. The woman was old and had gone along with the ruse only because she had feared being sent away from Montclair, losing her livelihood.

"I know you're sorry," Marlee told her. "I'm sorry, too, more than sorry. I should have known something was wrong, should have sensed it." But she hadn't sensed anything out of the way, too involved was she on winning her husband's affections—or rather Lark Arden's. God! how could she have been so dense?

"Can I be getting you something, my lady?" Mrs. Mortimer asked again, as if doing something for Marlee would allay her guilt.

Marlee merely shook her head, not truly wanting

anything but to be left alone, but instead of ordering Mrs. Mortimer out of the room, Marlee threw back the cover and bounded from the bed. Her face was stained pink as the memory of what had transpired between herself and Lark Arden in that very bed washed over her like buffeting waves. Before she'd made up her mind about what she was going to do, she was ordering Mrs. Mortimer to bring her the silver gown. Hurriedly, Marlee threw on her chemise and had the old lady pull the gown over her head. "But, my lady, you've not got on your petticoat and stays. You can't be thinking of running around without them."

"I don't have time for the blasted things," Marlee riposted, not the least concerned about her bad language. All she wanted was to track down Lark Arden before he sailed away for God only knew where. She had to see him again. She'd listened to his confession like a mute child, barely able to comprehend what he'd done to her, barely able to speak. But she had her wits about her now. Before Lark Arden sailed away — and as far as she was concerned he could sail straight to hell — she was going to tell him what she thought about him.

And the bounder better have the good grace to listen.

"Marlee, what's wrong? You look wild, and you're half dressed, too. What's happened?" Barbara eyed her cousin in concern, having nearly bumped into her in the hallway.

"I don't have time to talk now, Barbara. I'm going on the beach," Marlee cried over her shoulder and headed down the staircase like a silver tornado.

"But you aren't decently dressed!" Barbara called to no avail. Marlee didn't hear her.

On an impulse as she passed the library, Marlee flung open the door and found Hollins Carpenter. When he saw her, he flushed a vibrant shade of crimson and hastily rose to his feet. "Hatching any other plots I should know about?" she asked with such sarcasm in her tone that the man was left momentarily speechless.

"My lady, please."

"Go ahead, Mr. Carpenter, weasel your way out of this one. I should like to see you try."

With an unsteady hand, he pushed his spectacles upon his nose. "I beg your forgiveness and understanding, Lady Marlee. I never wanted you to be hurt, never dared believe Lark Arden would go to such lengths—"

Marlee's eyes widened, and this time she was the one who was crimson colored. "You know what happened—between us?"

"Yes. Arden admitted to me that he bedded, I mean, he told me what happened. He wants me to contact him if there is a child."

The breath rushed through her lips. She'd never considered that she might already be carrying a child. God willing, she wasn't. But what difference could a child make to him? Certainly, he wasn't willing to marry her or take responsibility for her or any child she conceived. If so, he wouldn't have rushed away. She wondered what was so important about this sailing trip that he must deceive her.

"Like hell you'll tell him, sir!"

"Lady Marlee!" Carpenter was aghast at her profanity.

She wagged a finger in his face. "Tell that bounder anything about me in the future, anything at all, and I'll do to you what you would have done to Mrs. Mortimer for breaking her silence. We shall part company, Mr. Carpenter, and I think you'll sorely miss the retainer fee I pay you."

"Yes, my lady." Carpenter was shaking, and Marlee felt some pity for him but not enough to apologize for what she'd just threatened. She'd meant every word of it. Now she must see to the cad who'd ruined her life and torn her heart to bits.

Without saying another word, Marlee marched from the library to the room off the kitchen. She grabbed her gray, woolen shawl and headed out the door, entirely aware of the baffled looks exchanged between the help. Mary Carter rushed forward as Marlee exited. "My lady, 'tis raining, you'll be catching your death outside!"

But Marlee took no notice of the woman. However, she couldn't ignore the small pellets of rain and pulled the shawl over her head as she headed onto the beach. She also couldn't ignore the thin silk slippers on her feet. Each step she took in the wet sand caused the shoes to sink and impeded her way. Taking them off, she carried them within the crook of her arm and continued down the beach, her eyes alert for sign of Lark's ship.

117

Nearing the rock she'd stood upon the previous day, she climbed to the top. The ship was in the same area it had been the day before but now the waves buffeted the hull. She needed to get to the ship and noticed a longboat, tied up at a small dock about a hundred feet away. She'd never been in a boat before, but she was so angry she'd have swum the distance to the ship. Somehow, she'd just have to figure out how to use the oars and hope for the best.

She started to scramble down from her perch, when she thought she heard her name being called. "Marlee, wait!" Turning toward the voice, she saw Simon bounding toward her, coming from the direction of the house. When he got to within a foot of her, she felt such disappointment that he, too, must have known about Lark Arden that she didn't know if she could look at him. "What are you doing here?" he asked in a rush. Droplets of rainwater dripped down his forehead, his blond hair was plastered to his head, and his clothes were soaked. "I went to the house to speak to Barbara and she said you'd rushed away like the devil was behind you."

"I've met the devil, and his name is Lark Arden." She couldn't help saying that and derived a bit of small comfort from Simon's sheepish look.

"Lark's sorry about what happened, Marlee. I'm sorry."

"Feeble apologies," she spat out and wiped the rainwater from her eyes.

Simon held out a hand to her as the rain intensified. "Here, let me help you down and take you back to the house before you slip and hurt yourself."

Ignoring his gesture, Marlee's face hardened. "The only place I'm going to is that ship to give Lark Arden a piece of my mind. I want him to know how he's hurt me—humiliated me—" Her voice broke. "I want him to know how much I hate him."

"You don't mean that."

"I do," she stubbornly insisted. "I need you to row me over there."

"That isn't a good idea. You'll say things to him that you don't mean. I think it's best that you give yourself time to think things through."

"Time so he can sail away you mean. Well, I won't. The despicable cad is going to hear what I have to say." She started to climb down from the rock, intent upon having Simon take her in the long-boat to the ship. Her mind was on what she'd say to Lark Arden, anticipating the moment when she could call him a cad to his face. She'd been at a loss for words when he confessed to her, but now words just seemed to fill up her brain until she felt ready to burst.

Simon's hand was within her grasp, and she was ready now to take it, but suddenly without warning, her heel slipped on the slippery ledge and she lost her balance. In an instant she found herself falling, waiting for Simon to steady her, but she realized he was farther away than she'd originally thought. She plummeted onto the sand at the same second her head hit a small rock at the base of the larger one. In the dim recesses of her brain, she heard Simon's voice beside her ear, crying for her to speak to him, to open her eyes. But all she felt was an intense pain and that was all she remembered before darkness overcame her.

"Marlee, wake up, are you all right?" Simon cradled the unconscious girl in his arms. The rain was now beating unmercifully down upon them. The blood from Marlee's cut on her forehead was dribbling down her left temple. She needed help. He picked her up, intent upon carrying her to the house, but Montclair was much too far away. The ship was closer, but it was due to sail in a few hours' time. Suppose she didn't regain consciousness until then — suppose Marlee was forced to remain on board?

A naughty grin spread across Simon's wet and handsome face. Marlee had wanted to go on board and see Lark anyway, he reasoned as he carried her to the longboat and laid her on the boat's bottom. He covered her with a blanket and began rowing to the large, dark ship in the bay. Now, she'd have the perfect opportunity to speak to him. In fact, they'd have months at sea to work out their differences.

Simon knew that Lark loved Marlee and would never be happy with Bettina. He wanted everyone to be as happy as he and Barbara were, so why not take the chance and put Marlee on the ship? Lark's and Marlee's happiness was worth the gamble.

Luckily, no one but Todd, a cabin boy, was about when he boarded with Marlee, hanging like a sack of grain over his shoulders. "Who's that?" the freckle-faced boy asked, curiosity glowing on his face.

"This is Captain Lark's lady, Todd. Is the captain in his cabin?"

"Naw, he be in the galley with the rest of the men."

Good, things were working out well, especially when Marlee gave a moan. She would soon be waking up, and what better place to open her eyes than in Lark's own cabin, in Lark's own bed?

Simon motioned the boy to follow him. Silently, the two made their way to the cabin where Simon deposited Marlee on Lark's bunk. Before fifteen minutes had passed, Simon had cleaned and dressed Marlee's cut. She was now moaning more often and regaining consciousness.

"I have to leave," Simon told Todd, "but I need you to look after Lady Marlee. See that she's warm and fed when she wants to eat. But under no circumstances are you to let her out of this room until the ship is a long distance away from here."

"Shouldn't I tell the captain?"

"Don't bother him, lad. Let's surprise him, shall we?"

Simon knew that Lark would be very busy for the next few hours and most probably wouldn't return to his cabin until long after the ship had left Cornwall. And then it would be too late for him to return Marlee to Montclair.

Simon couldn't help smiling to himself as he went to the galley to bid Lark farewell. One day, Lark would thank him for all of this — at least, he hoped so.

Chapter Ten

"Let me out! Open this door now!" Marlee pounded upon the thick wood door of the cabin but to no avail. No one seemed to hear her. Once again, as she had been doing for the last few hours, she rattled the latch only to find the door was still locked and not about to open. Stifling a curse, she found her way to the small porthole and looked out. Nothing but sea stretched before her.

A momentary dizziness washed over her, forcing her to sit upon the bunk. She held her head in her hands and fingered the white linen strip on her forehead that was tied at the back of her head. Simon, probably, had seen to the wound, and brought her aboard ship. But why would Simon do such an outrageous thing as to leave her here? He knew how much she hated Lark Arden, yet then again, she'd shouted to him to row her to the ship—but not at the expense of being kept a prisoner in a cabin.

Was this Lark's cabin? Glancing around the room, she saw that it was neatly furnished with only the barest essentials. A round-looking glass hung above a large chest of drawers, two chairs and a table were in the center of the room. In a corner was a sea chest with rolled maps on top of it, and standing beside it was a large, golden saber. The walled bunk on which she sat was comfortable enough, and the sheets were clean.

Her attention was diverted to a noise outside the door and once again, she shouted to be freed, but whoever was there paid her not the slightest bit of attention. Now her throat felt scratchy from her screams, another reason to hate Lark Arden. Where was he? Why hadn't he appeared before now? Though not certain of the time, she realized she must have been aboard the ship for some hours. Daylight was waning and shadows crept into the room. It was just like the hateful man to keep her waiting. When had he ever thought about her pain or pleasure?

A pink flush caressed her cheeks. Last night he'd thought about her pleasure, more than thought about it. His hands and lips, his body had driven her wild with wanton pleasure. "I won't think about any of that," she defiantly mumbled. Last night was over and gone as far as she was concerned and she refused to dwell upon any part of it. But the images wouldn't be dismissed so easily.

A pounding headache caused her to lie down. She'd rest until the cad showed up. He'd heed her demand to be returned to Montclair. It was the least he could do for her.

The wind was with them. With each billowing of the sails, *Her Ladyship,* as Lark had named the refurbished ship, left Cornwall farther and farther behind. There had been so much activity after the ship left port that Lark had had little time to consider his sins or even to think about Marlee. But now with the quiet of evening descending, a terrible loneliness cut through his soul. "God, if only life could sail as smoothly as this ship," he muttered to himself.

"Did you say somethin', sir?" Young Todd came forward, trudging a bucket of water behind him. Dipping a ladle into the water, he handed it to Lark.

"Nothing of importance, lad." Lark drank thirstily and gave the ladle back to Todd. "You've been kept busy since we left Cornwall."

"Aye, sir, I have. This ain't me first voyage. I was on another ship once, but t'wasn't much in the way of excitement. I'm lookin' for some adventure this time around, some fightin'. You think we'll come across some pirates before we reach New Providence?"

"Maybe."

Todd grinned. "I'm hopin' so. I want to feel me sword go through one of those infernal blackguards."

Lark felt he should tell the boy that killing was wrong, but what a hypocrite he'd be when the very purpose of this voyage was to kill a man. "Have the men eaten yet?" Lark purposely changed the subject.

"Aye, sir, everyone except you." He gave a long pause and watched Lark through narrowed eyes. "And your lady. I done promised Mr. Oliver to keep me mouth shut so you'd be surprised. But she's been doin' an awful lot o' bellowin', so she must be feelin' better after her bump on the head. I 'pect she must be hungry, but sir, I ain't too good at handlin' ladies—"

"What in the name of heaven are you jabbering about?" Lark's sudden outburst startled the boy, but in reality Lark was the one whose heart nearly jumped out of his chest. He grabbed the trembling Todd by the arm. "What lady?" he roughly demanded.

"The—one in—your cabin, sir. Mr. Oliver done said she was your lady, that she was a surprise and for me not to tell until we was a good ways out. Have I done wrong, Captain Lark? I didn't mean no harm."

Lark had already left the deck before Todd finished speaking. Taking two steps at a time, he was soon below deck and unbolting the cabin door. The lavender blue of dusk met his eyes when he rushed into the room. He could barely make out the familiar objects until his eyes adjusted to the dimness. At first, he saw nothing out of place, no one. But then he heard a rustling noise on the bunk and made out the shadowy outline of a woman's body. Moving closer, he stalled in his steps. Fear swept over him at the sight of Marlee turning over in her sleep, wearing a bandage on her head.

She'd been hurt. Damn Simon for not telling him!

"Marlee, Marlee, my love." Lark bent over her, his breath fanned the pale contour of her cheek; gently he touched the bandage. "It's me, my darling. It's Lark."

Her eyes opened and glowed an even deeper shade of blue in her pale face. "I know it's you, Lark Arden. Touch me again and I'll bite your fingers off."

He withdrew his hand, more than startled at her reaction. Finally, he grinned in relief and amusement to find she wasn't badly hurt. "From your spunky words, I can assume that your bump on the head hasn't robbed you of health."

"Assume nothing," she bit out and gingerly sat up. "I don't need your ministrations."

"What happened to you?"

Lark lounged against the wall with his arms nonchalantly folded across his chest, almost as if he discovered a woman in his bed everyday. And for all she knew about the man—which was precious little—he probably was used to that very thing. His casualness infuriated her; evidently he had no idea how much he'd hurt her. Yet, again, maybe he did know and didn't care. Well, she wouldn't care, either. "I slipped and fell on the beach."

"Climbing rocks again?"

Heat rose to her face at the suggestive quality in his voice. It was obvious that he was remembering the fiery kiss they'd shared on the very same rock from which she fell. She didn't want to remember that kiss or the way she'd wantonly given herself to him afterward. The memory was much too painful. "How I hurt myself isn't important, it's why I was on the beach in the first place."

Lark cocked an ebony-winged brow. "And that was?"

"To tell you what a bastard I think you are, to let you know how much I loathe you, Lark Arden—if that's your real name."

"Everyone is entitled to their opinion." His voice sounded light but he carefully withdrew into the room's shadows so Marlee wouldn't notice the pain on his face. He couldn't allow her to see how her words had stung him, though he deserved her hatred and must bear it for the time being. "My cabin boy said that Simon brought you aboard."

"Yes, and when I see him I'm going to make certain he knows how angry with him I am. But not half as angry as I am with you for keeping me here against my will. I've practically shouted until I'm hoarse, and you didn't lift a finger to let me out of here. You've kept me locked in here like I'm a thief or something—"

"Wait a second!" he shouted when she jumped from the bunk to land a small fist in the center of his chest. In one hand, he grabbed her two small wrists and kept them pinned against him. "First of all, I didn't have you locked in here, and secondly, I never knew you were here. Simon didn't tell me anything but farewell when he left the ship earlier. If I'd known that you were on board, I'd have made certain that Simon left with you. I don't have any reason to imprison you, Marlee. Please believe me that I have no use for you."

"Believe you, hah!" She struggled a bit but realizing Lark wasn't about to release her, she quieted. "I recall your using me—in a number of ways. I can't believe anything you say."

His heart turned over at the intense pain reflected in her eyes. Never had he willingly, knowingly caused such a gentle person as Marlee unhappiness. And knowing that he cared for this woman made her pain his own. But he could never tell her how much he did care and regretted what he'd done. She wouldn't believe him, and in her place, he wouldn't believe himself, either. In the end, it would be for the best that Marlee did hate him and believe he didn't care a whit about her. Otherwise, he'd be unable to go on with his life. " 'Tis the truth, my lady. I really have no use for a female on board, and most certainly not one like yourself."

"And what is wrong with me?" she shouted into his face.

"You're a lady, my dear."

"What's so terrible about that?" she persisted, undaunted by the amused smirk that turned up Lark's lips.

"Ladies don't get on well with a crew of men, men who have been at sea for months on end without a woman for company. So you see, being a lady is a handicap on board a ship. But as for being a woman who isn't a lady, well, that is another matter—a very enjoyable matter for all concerned.

You're useless to me as a lady, so I had no reason to lock you in. Understand, Marlee?"

"Not really," she admitted, growing more confused by the second but somehow feeling that Lark Arden was snubbing her. "Why is a lady different from a woman?"

"Ah, my innocent Marlee, I suppose I'll have to be frank with you." Lark decreased the pressure on her wrists and stroked her flesh with a whisper touch until Marlee noticed and shivered with pleasure. The previous night had taught him that Marlee responded to the slightest of touch, that in spite of her prim upbringing, she burned with fire. Here was a woman to fulfill all his dreams; here was a woman he could never claim for his own. "Do you remember what happened between us last night? Can you recall what I did to you?"

Marlee swallowed the painful lump in her throat. Tears burned her eyes, because she'd never be able to forget. "You're a—cad—for bringing it up."

"Well, that's what my men do to women, but I hasten to add that if they get their slimy hands upon you, my dear, you won't be pleasured and loved in the same tender way I loved you."

From Lark's serious and dark expression, she suddenly understood what Lark meant and gasped out loud. How awful, how horrible and demeaning. She must get off of this ship at once. "Take me back to Montclair. I insist you do."

"I can't."

"You're refusing me?"

"No, I can't take you back." He dropped her

hands, hating to break the contact with her warm flesh, but for his own sanity, he couldn't touch her again. "We're too far out at sea now, the tides prevent turning back to England."

"But — I want to go back!"

Lark smiled sorrowfully. "I want that, too, Marlee, but it seems Simon placed you here to force you to stay on board. He knew that I wouldn't be able to turn around; no matter what you think I didn't plan any of this. When we reach New Providence, I'll put you on a ship to England."

She absently toyed with the rosette on her gown. "When will that be?"

"Two months at the most."

"I can't stay here for two months with you!"

"Then I suppose you'll have to swim back. Two months aboard ship is all I can do for you. So, make the best of it."

Marlee stiffened her back. "Does making the best of it mean that I will be pawed by your crew?"

"I give you my word that you'll be quite safe as long as you stay in the cabin when I'm not with you to offer protection."

"I assume that I shall be safe from your lewd advances, too, Captain Arden?"

"Only if you want to be." For the space of a heartbeat, their gazes met before he turned away. "I'll have Todd bring our supper. Remain in the cabin until I return and let no one in but me. All right?"

"Aye, aye, Captain, whatever you say," she grumbled aloud, not caring for his high-handed attitude,

130

not wanting to be alone in the cabin without him, and disliking the fact that she was going to need Lark Arden if she wanted to survive this voyage.

A dismal sigh escaped her when she was alone. For two months she was going to have to share this cabin with Lark, to eat with him. To sleep with him? No, never that, she resolutely decided. He'd have to sleep on the floor and be glad of it. She'd make it to New Providence, wherever that was, and not worry one bit about Lark Arden while she did so.

Excitement churned through her despite her situation. She was going to see firsthand what a real sea voyage was like and discover just what her money had financed. Anything could happen on a ship, anything at all. She really wanted to go up on deck and look around but she couldn't do that right now—not without Lark. And no matter how much she detested him, Lark was her protector for the moment.

Her protector. Her lover. The thought rose unbidden in her mind.

No, Lark was nothing to her except a means to an end. As once he had used her, she now would use him—needed him, in fact, if she hoped to return to Montclair. And once she did get home again, she'd never give Lark Arden an extra thought.

"I'll be over him by then," she spoke to herself. "Maybe by living with him in close quarters, seeing him day in and day out, I'll finally be able to forget him and put all of this behind me. I *will* forget him," she fiercely vowed and pounded her fist in her vehemence.

But somehow part of herself wasn't so sure.

The meal passed pleasantly enough. Marlee discovered she was so hungry that she ate the salt pork and a baked potato without commenting on the bland taste. The wine, however, was excellent and after she'd imbibed two glasses, she found that she didn't seem to dislike Lark so much. In fact, she was quite curious about him.

"Where is this place we're going?" she asked and sipped delicately on her third glass of wine.

"In the Caribbean." Lark stretched his long legs out in front of him, seeming quite at home in the cabin.

"Shall we be there long?"

"*You* won't be there hardly any time at all. As soon as a ship is ready, you'll be returned to England."

"And will you stay there or go home to Virginia?"

"I hope my mission to New Providence will be over quickly, and yes, I do intend to return to Arden's Grove—my plantation," he informed her.

Marlee ran her index finger over the glass's smooth rim. "Somehow I can't envision you as a farmer."

His laugh, deep and sensual as velvet, enveloped her in its warmth. "I'm a planter, not a farmer. There's a difference."

"Tell me about Arden's Grove," she persisted, wanting to know about the place where Lark lived, hoping to see it through his eyes, because for some unfathomable reason she needed to know about him. Lark seemed happy to comply.

"Arden's Grove sits on the banks of the James River. We grow tobacco, very fine tobacco, as my mother is fond of reminding everyone for miles around." A flash of a smile highlighted Lark's face. "Mother is a remarkable woman, as was her mother before her. The plantation passed to Mother through my grandmother who'd married an Irish slave."

"An Irish slave, really? I've never heard of such a thing," Marlee blurted out.

Lark nodded. "My grandfather was captured at Drogheda by Cromwell's troops as a child and shipped to Bermuda where he worked as a slave until my grandmother married him. I'm certain there's an interesting story there, however, neither of my grandparents ever admitted how they happened to marry or how my grandfather attained his freedom. But they did start a most unusual tradition."

"Which is?" Despite her ambivalent feelings for Lark, Marlee couldn't help but be intrigued.

Lark poured himself another helping of wine and pushed his chair farther away from the table. He found himself enjoying his chat with Marlee; in fact, this was the first time they'd ever been alone without servants hovering nearby, except for the night in Marlee's room when he'd made love to her.

133

His blood fired at the memory, but he continued smoothly, "Grandfather was dirt poor and had nothing when he married my grandmother. To prove himself worthy of her, he somehow managed to attain a diamond wedding ring. Well, the story goes that she didn't believe the diamond was real but was a piece of glass. To prove her wrong, he marched her into the dining room where he took the ring from her finger and knowing that diamond cuts glass, he etched their initials into the windowpane. So, she had to believe the ring was real, as was his love for her. Now when anyone marries in the family, the prospective bridegroom must prove his worth by doing the very same thing.

"My father did it for my mother and won Grandfather's approval to marry her. But my mother's sister wasn't so lucky. Her intended *did* give her a piece of glass and was booted out of the house by my grandfather." Lark laughed heartily. "I would love to have seen that. Grandfather was such an imposing figure that I'd bet the man ran the entire distance to Jamestown."

Marlee giggled, feeling extremely light-headed and contented, an odd way to feel considering how much she hated Lark Arden. "Will you give your fiancée a diamond that cuts glass?" she asked, her eyes shining with a sapphire gleam.

Lark grew serious, unable to stop staring at her, but fearful she'd see the truth and realize how much he cared for her. Looking at her was painful, too hurtful. How could he admit to her that he'd already presented Bettina with a ring, a large diamond engagement ring which would definitely cut glass? "I need to go up on deck and watch," he told her and hastily rose from his chair.

Marlee's face fell at his abruptness. She'd forgotten who he was for a few minutes, and now remembered. This was the man who'd used her and taken her body, her heart, and her soul in one rapturous, fiery night. "Yes, do that," she replied without inflection.

For a second, it seemed that he hesitated. "Get some sleep, Marlee."

She nodded but narrowed her eyes, seeing his gaze was upon the bunk. "Where will you sleep?"

He pointed to the bunk. "There."

"But—but—you can't. I mean just because we spent the night—together once—doesn't give you liberty to expect me to sleep with you." She stood up, defiant and beautiful in her righteous indignation. "You're not my husband. I won't sleep with you!"

"Then don't," he said with a shrug of his shoulders. "But I sleep on the bunk." Without a further word, he went into the dimly lighted hallway, closing the cabin door behind him.

"Arrogant, pompous bully," she hissed under her breath. He really didn't care where she slept, maybe didn't care if she slept at all. Or did he think she'd be forced to share the bunk with him and endure his hands upon her during the night? The wanton images turned her legs to seaweed and she grew dizzy, not certain if the dizziness was from her head injury or too much wine. No matter. She was tired and needed to rest — but not in Lark's bed.

Pulling a quilt from the bottom of the bunk, she positioned herself into a chair and squirmed like a worm until she found a comfortable position. Throwing the blanket over her, she finally drifted into sleep. But when she woke to a bright sunshine-filled morning, she discovered that she was on the downy-filled bed and Lark was in the chair, snoring softly.

Chapter Eleven

Marlee had just started drinking her morning tea when Lark entered the cabin. He carried what appeared to be a man's shirt and breeches under one arm and a pair of worn boots in his hand. "I wish you'd think to knock," she irritably scolded him. "Suppose I wasn't dressed?"

"I've seen you without clothes," he drawled and a lecherous glint sparked in his eyes. "And undressing is exactly what I want you to do."

She nearly choked on the hot tea. "What—did you say?"

Lark handed her the clothes and boots. "These are for you. I can't have you parading around in that thin dress, as eye-catching as it is." His gaze lingered for a second too long on her full breasts which the tight bodice barely concealed. Clearing his throat, he went to the sea chest and took a map, unrolled it, and pretended an interest in coordinates he didn't feel. "The clothes belong to Todd and should fit you."

"But I've never worn breeches!" Marlee was horrified at the thought.

"There's a first time for everything," he succinctly observed and rerolled the map. "But if you want to go above with me for some air, you'll have to wear them. I don't want my men bothered by you."

"As if I *want* to bother them," she spat out. "I don't really want to be on this ship in the first place. I'm not certain why you're going to New Providence—I don't care, either. But I'd think you'd treat me like a lady instead of a deckhand until we get there."

"The clothes are to *keep* you a lady, my dear," he reiterated and malevolently grasped the hilt of a small sword which hung at his side. "I don't want to have to kill any of my men for leering or pawing at you. No one has the right to touch you."

Only you have the right, she thought and almost said this aloud, but she turned away so he wouldn't read the desire shining in her eyes. No matter what Lark had done to her, she still found him undeniably attractive. "Please leave so I can change."

"I'll be waiting on deck for you," he promised with a wink and left.

Marlee eyed the pale blue shirt and brown breeches in distaste. One month ago when she'd become the Baroness of Montclair she'd thought that she'd be dressed in the finest silks and satins, presiding over balls and parties with her husband, being introduced to England's aristocracy. Now, she didn't have a husband, was reduced to dressing like

138

a sailor without a tuppence in her pocket, and worst of all, she was dependent upon Lark Arden for her safety. She could almost imagine Clementina's shrill voice in her ear proclaiming, "How the mighty have fallen."

Marlee had to laugh as she began to undress. Wouldn't Clementina and Daphne be tickled to see her now?

The clothes, though snug, fit better than Marlee had expected, yet the boots were a bit too large for her small feet. After the shirt had been tucked neatly into the breeches, she found a comb and ran it quickly through her hair, fearful that if she dawdled for too long Lark wouldn't let her go on deck.

Coming onto the upper deck minutes later, Marlee squinted at the bright sunshine. Immediately she noticed Lark with his back to her, gazing out at the broad blue vista of calm ocean. A few of the men were diligently working until they noticed her. All stopped and stared. "Lordy, what a sight," one of the men said. " 'Tis a wench in breeches."

The other ribald comments drifted away when Lark turned and saw her. His mouth fell open at the sight of her, and he feared he'd done the wrong thing by ordering her to wear Todd's clothes. Instead of dispelling her natural beauty, the garments only seemed to enhance Marlee's figure. The gown had modestly covered her legs and hidden her beautifully rounded behind. But the pants fit her tightly, leaving very little to the imagination, and he knew what lecherous thoughts must be racing through many a man's head at the moment. Every

139

voluptuous curve Marlee possessed was apparent for all to see — for him to see. The shirt which had been big on Todd's slight frame fit Marlee snugly across the breasts and was more erotic and suggestive than the gown's low bodice had ever been.

Heaven help him. He was going to have a hard time protecting her from the crew, but an even worse time protecting her from himself.

Lark cleared his throat and took a large, commanding step toward her. Taking her arm in a gesture of protective ownership, he faced his men and raised his voice for all to hear. "Men, this is Lady Arden, my kinswoman. She is to be treated with respect and dignity. If any one of you so much as thinks of touching her, he'll answer to me and be lucky he doesn't find himself on the ocean's floor to feed the sharks." His eyes held a black warning. "Now get back to work and mind your manners."

Lark led her to a corner of the ship, away from the prying eyes of the crew. "You didn't take very long to dress," he said, his eyes now full of warmth. He liked the way her hair blew softly about her face and even caught a whiff of rosewater in the dark tresses.

"There wasn't much to change into," she said but wouldn't admit how much she liked the freedom which the pants provided. She didn't miss the hooped petticoats and stays one bit.

She leaned upon the thick wooden balustrade and breathed deeply of the fresh sea breezes. The only sounds were the shrieking of a gull overhead and the sloshing of the ship as it broke through the waves. For some moments, she was entirely at peace—more than contented because Lark was at her side. She didn't care if they never reached land.

"What are you thinking?" he asked with a husky trace to his voice.

Marlee discovered that Lark was watching her intently, and she liked the way he looked at her as much as she was unnerved by it. She should dislike what was happening. Yet, for some reason she didn't seem to mind being on a ship in the middle of the ocean with Lark. Though she did hate what he'd done to her, she doubted she could ever hate him when he looked at her in such a beguiling, heart-thumping fashion.

"I was thinking how everything has changed for me," she softly told him. "Because of you, my whole life is changed."

His expression grew somber. "I apologize again to you, but I've explained the reasons behind what I was forced to do."

"Not really. I'm still in the dark as to why this ship and so-called mission are so important to you that you'd lie to me to get the money. Why didn't you just ask for it, explain to me what Richard had done?"

"Would you have given me the money?"

"I don't know," she said.

"I took only what was due me," he insisted.

"You took more from me than that and you well know it!"

"Never forget that I took only what you offered me, Marlee. We both wanted what happened."

His eyes bored into her soul, and she trembled because he spoke the truth. She had wanted him, still wanted him, and this made her situation with Lark all the more distressing. "I wanted you because I thought we were married."

"I know, but the attraction is strong between us. I'll never want another woman as I want you, Marlee, never." Lark brought her against him, cradling her in his arms. She was very much aware of his lips upon her head. Somehow she believed him, aware that he suffered some painful emotion that she couldn't understand.

She relaxed against him, unable to resist him, drawn to him by an irresistible force that threatened to conquer her. She looked up at him. "If that's true, then why can't you admit you love me?"

It was the wrong thing for her to say. The color drained from his face. There was a hesitancy about him, almost as if he wanted to say what she ached to hear but couldn't. She felt him stiffen, and it was the long silence which followed that finally defeated her. He put her from him and grasped the balustrade with both hands.

Tears slipped onto her heart-shaped face of their own volition. "I would like to return to the cabin," she told him and tried to keep her voice from breaking.

"As you will." Lark called to Todd who hurried over to them. "Escort Lady Arden back to the cabin."

"Aye, sir," Todd quickly agreed and hurriedly followed after Marlee who nearly ran the length of the deck.

After that incident and for the next few weeks, Todd always accompanied Marlee for her walks. Lark was conveniently absent, but she always saw him on deck as he ordered the men about and helped with the rigging or steered the ship through the warm indigo waters. Those were the only times that she saw him, because he didn't sleep in the cabin and no longer took meals with her. He'd deserted her again, and she wasn't certain why.

One day, Todd was sitting next to her on a large, brown barrel while Marlee basked in the sun. Nothing could be seen on the horizon for miles. Todd sighed and absently scratched his red head. " 'Tis the most boring trip I've ever taken."

Marlee smiled indulgently at the young boy. Having spent so much time with him, she'd begun to like him. "Don't you have enough duties?" she asked him.

" 'Tain't that, my lady. I've got lots to do when I'm not watchin' over you for the captain. But I thought to have a real adventure, now that I'm a pirate hunter."

"A what?"

Todd's face became animated and he grinned broadly. "A pirate hunter. Captain Lark is one, the best one in the whole world. We're chasin' down sea pirates for the Crown—one blasted, nasty pirate in particular who blew up Captain Lark's ship and left him for dead a while back. We're goin' to

143

hunt him down and hang the bloke's head from a pike as a warnin' to other mean pirates. That's what we're goin' to do if we ever come across him."

This was the longest speech that Marlee ever remembered hearing from Todd. But it did explain Lark's obsession to get the money for a new ship. Somehow he had to redress the balance with this pirate.

Realizing how much the subject of pirates appealed to Todd, she knew he'd be eager to tell her anything she wanted to know about Lark and his plans. "Do you know how much longer we have until we reach New Providence?"

"Another few days." He sounded disappointed. "But we ain't run across no pirates yet, and I don't think we will."

"Ah, so you want to fight pirates, not just this particular one. By the way, what's this pirate's name?"

"Manuel Silva. Captain Lark said we'll know his ship because it's blue and black and he flies a flag with a vulture on it." Todd heaved a sigh. "But no one's seen it yet."

Marlee considered this information. Silva must be a Spaniard. "Don't despair, Todd," she said and ruffled his hair. "I'm certain you'll get your chance."

"No sign of Silva yet," Lark groused out loud and scanned the watery blue landscape. "Where could the bastard be?"

"I've no idea, sir," replied Douglas Holcombe, Lark's first mate and the only one of his crew who'd ever actively hunted pirates. "He's a slippery eel, well known for eluding authorities. I came up against him just once, about five years ago. The ship I was on was destroyed—I was lucky to be left alive. From what I've heard about the way he treats prisoners, they're better off dead."

Lark nodded, lucky to have found Holcombe in Cornwall. He'd been sharing his cabin since Marlee came on board. The young man had been in the Royal Navy at one time but was discharged because of the leg wound he'd received as a result of the fracas with Silva. He'd limp for the rest of his life, but that didn't stop him from wanting revenge upon the pirate. Lark wanted revenge, too, and would relish the sweet taste of it. But he couldn't stop a shiver at what Holcombe said about Silva's treatment of prisoners. Was Bettina still alive? Had she been ravished by the brutish Silva? If so, Lark prayed she was dead. He'd heard tales, too, about what Silva did to women prisoners and if she was alive, no doubt she'd already lost her mind.

"Todd told me that Lady Arden is ill," Holcombe noted and watched Lark's face for a reaction. He wasn't certain what the connection or true story was between Lark and Marlee Arden, but he knew a man in love when he saw one.

Lark made a sharp turn to face Holcombe. "What's wrong with her? Why didn't anyone tell me?"

"I'm telling you now, sir."

145

"Yes, fine. I'll go see how she is."

"Yes, sir, and if you wish to spend the night in your cabin with her, I won't be upset not to have you share mine."

Holcombe smiled knowingly at Lark. Lark wondered if everyone realized how much he cared for Marlee. Did the crew think she was anything more to him than a relation? He didn't care for the men talking about him behind his back or wondering why he didn't sleep in his own cabin. He hated their gossip to pass the time.

Maybe if they'd run across a pirate ship and actively get involved in a battle, then they'd have something else to think and worry about. He would, too. He was so aggravated with himself for constantly dwelling on Marlee, more than annoyed with Simon for having placed her on the ship in the first place. He'd welcome a sea battle, but he didn't really want one—not when Marlee was on board. Just to imagine the harm that might come to her was more than he could handle. He'd welcome the day they arrived in New Providence and he could send her home again.

He needed to pursue his life.

Lark knocked at the door and heard Marlee's weak, "Come in." She was lying on the bunk with her head turned away.

"I heard you weren't feeling well," he began. "What's wrong? Can I get you anything?"

"Nothing."

Turning her face to him, he noticed she was very pale. A thought as loud as thunder echoed in his ears. Suppose she was carrying his child? "Marlee, are you, are you"—he could hardly say the words—"sick because you're going to have my baby?"

Slowly, Marlee sat up, her dark hair spilled like black velvet across her shoulders. She eyed him in cold contempt. "I'm *not* carrying your child, I can assure you of that. And anyway, what difference would it make if I were? You don't love me and wouldn't marry me, either. So, you'll soon be free of me and can go about your pirate hunting—or whatever it is you do. Please don't worry about me."

"But I do worry."

Shrugging, she laid down again. "That's because you have a guilty conscience, not because you care about me."

Lark bent down, his mouth came so close to hers that she expected him to kiss her. But he didn't. Instead, he whispered so lowly that she strained to hear him. "I care more than you'll ever know, Marlee. And if you are carrying my baby, I'd make provisions for you and the child."

Her heart screamed only that he love her, but she didn't say that to him. "I have enough money to last the rest of my life. I don't want anything from you, and if I were having a child, I wouldn't ask you for anything, either."

"Then—you're really not—pregnant?" He truly looked disappointed.

"I'm not," she answered in all sincerity, and for just a fleeting moment she almost wished she were. But her monthly flux had started that very morning, putting to rest any fears that she might be pregnant.

He stared down at her, causing her insides to tremble and flutter like a hummingbird's wings. "Ah, Marlee, Marlee," he breathed. "Why couldn't things have been different for us?"

She didn't understand why he asked this question. Why *couldn't* things be different? What prevented him from admitting that he loved her? Did he love her? Uncertainty ate away at her all of the time now. His very presence intrigued and bewildered her. Her lips ached for his kiss, and she'd have welcomed it. But as always, Lark withdrew from her physically and emotionally when he moved away from her bedside. "I'll send Todd to check on you later," he informed her. "If you need anything, just ask him."

"Thank you," she dispassionately muttered. "You've been very kind to me, Lark, considering— everything."

She didn't think he was going to reply at first, but he seemed to give a moment's reflection before he spoke. "I'd give you the world if I could, if there was only some way that I could make up for what I've done to you, I would. Maybe, someday, I'll get the chance." Turning on his heels, he left the cabin.

Blinking away the tears that pricked her eyelids, Marlee believed him.

Chapter Twelve

"Ship ahoy!" The bellowing from the crow's nest startled Marlee.

Until that moment the morning had been calm with a slight trade wind ruffling the sails overhead. She'd only been on deck for some five minutes with Todd as her companion. The crew had been diligently going about their chores, but more than once she'd noticed someone yawning and stretching from boredom. But now that a ship had been spotted, a surge of energy coursed through the men's bodies, and they craned eagerly forward, their eyes alert.

" 'Tis a pirate ship, I'm thinkin'," Marlee heard one of the men say. He pointed a bony finger in the looming ship's direction. "Aye, I've seen that one before, I think, out of Santo Domingo two years ago."

"Is it a Spanish ship?" Todd asked, breathless with eyes bulging.

"Aye. Someone better fetch Captain Lark."

149

But Lark was already alerted. He'd quietly positioned himself behind Marlee. She felt his hand upon her shoulder before she saw his tense, drawn face. "Go below with Todd and remain in the cabin," he said in a voice that was both a command and a request.

"But, sir, I want to stay up here for the fightin'," Todd adamantly declared. "I don't want to play nursemaid to a finicky female, not when there's goin' to be a real battle."

"Do what I told you." Lark emphasized each word, and Todd reluctantly made a move to escort Marlee from the deck.

For a second, she hesitated and looked directly at Lark, who didn't seem to see her. His concentration was centered on the dark speck in the distance. "Is it Manuel Silva?" she asked him and noticed the high color in his cheeks.

"I hope so!" he answered raggedly. "God in heaven, I hope it is!" Then he was rushing away from her, barking commands to the men, overseeing the loading of the cannons.

Marlee followed behind a very disgruntled Todd.

Booming artillery fire from the pirate ship echoed through the air. Bracing herself for the hit, Marlee was surprised when she found herself still standing in the cabin. She ran to look outside of the porthole just as *Her Ladyship* answered with a resounding boom. "We've scuttled the pirate ship!"

she exclaimed as the white sail was raised in surrender.

Todd nudged her aside to see. "Aye, she's limpin' bad," was his observation. "What a pitiful sea battle this has been. One shot and 'tis over."

Marlee grinned ruefully at the lad. She was sorry for his disappointment yet very relieved that no one on Lark's ship had been injured. "Maybe next time you'll see some real action and not have to watch over a 'finicky female.'"

Todd glanced down at the toes of his boots and had the good grace to flush. "Forgive me, Lady Marlee. I shouldn't have said any such thing."

"Are you sorry you said it or sorry I heard it?"

"Both, I suppose."

She couldn't help chuckling. Todd was such a sweet young boy who yearned for adventure that she felt she'd probably have said the very same thing in his situation. "Well, let's go on deck and see what's happening. I've never been involved in a sea battle with pirates before, even if it has been a small one."

Todd's face brightened but then he dismally shook his head. "Can't go on deck. Captain Lark wouldn't be happy. You're to stay in here and I'm to watch over you."

"Watch over me on deck. We can hide so we won't be in the way, and he won't see us. Anyway, I've never seen a real pirate close up. Have you?"

Shaking his head, Todd was easily persuaded when Marlee left the cabin. Like two thieves, they

151

sneaked up the stairs to the upper deck and concealed themselves behind large water barrels. They observed the bustling crew secure the damaged pirate ship to *Her Ladyship* by grappling hooks. Crewmen jumped to the pirate ship to take charge of the motley prisoners.

Marlee strained to see, craning her neck to get a better view of Lark. He waited on deck with arms akimbo. His dark hair blew about his face, and even at a distance she could tell that each pirate was the object of his withering gaze. She couldn't help but shiver at his fierce stance or the way he assessed each individual man as he was brought aboard. She knew he was looking for Manuel Silva. And she also knew by the slight slumping of his shoulders when the last man had boarded *Her Ladyship* that Silva wasn't among them.

"There's gold on board, Captain," Marlee heard Holcombe tell Lark. "It's a veritable treasure chest we've confiscated. The authorities on New Providence will be pleased."

"Good, good," mumbled Lark who didn't seem to care about the booty. He inspected the pirates, about six of them, who waited in a line. Two of them wore earrings in their ears and one had a woolen cap on his curly head of hair. They were all dressed in what Marlee discerned were clothes which had seen better days, and even from where she was hidden, they smelled in need of a good washing. But there was one man, a man who eyed Lark with utter contempt. Lark seemed well aware

152

of the man's attitude. "What's your name?" Lark demanded of him.

The beady-eyed man regarded Lark in disdain but gave a yowl of pain when one of Lark's crewmen yanked at his arm and brandished a small knife. "Answer the captain," he ordered, "or I'll cut your Spanish throat."

The man gulped and complied. "Pedro Mendoza."

Something like recognition flickered in the depths of Lark's eyes. "I've seen you before, Pedro Mendoza. You were with Manuel Silva when he attacked my ship last year. You were his second-in-command."

Mendoza grinned. "You have a good memory, English dog."

"You have your own ship now," Lark continued, oblivious to the slur. "Did you and Silva have a falling out? Do you know where Silva is now?"

Mendoza's dark eyes glittered with devilment. "You'd like me to tell you, wouldn't you, señor?"

"Yes, I want you to tell me."

"I'll tell you nothing about Silva's whereabouts. But I will tell you that the cargo Silva stole from you has been well used. Very well used, señor, by all of us."

"You bloody bastard!"

Before Marlee's disbelieving eyes, Lark pounced upon Mendoza and started choking the life out of him. If Holcombe wouldn't have intervened, the Spaniard would have died. As it was, after Lark was removed from the man, Mendoza laid on deck and gasped for breath. "Take the bastard to the hole," Lark ordered and tried to compose himself.

One of the crew began to help Mendoza to his feet. The man looked pale and very weak. They headed past the barrels where Marlee and Todd were hiding, out of view from Lark. But Marlee could see every move the man made. In stunned disbelief she watched as Mendoza, in a startling display of strength, knocked the crewman to the floor and stole his knife. Then he turned in Lark's direction.

Lark's back was away from her as he discussed something with Holcombe. Her heart jumped in her chest because she knew what Mendoza had in mind. Todd rose up, realizing what was about to happen but it seemed he couldn't utter a sound. Mendoza rushed toward Lark with the knife pointed in midair, ready to rip into the sinew and muscle. Suddenly Marlee heard her own voice, screaming Lark's name in warning. At that instant, Lark jerked around and the second he saw what was happening, he instinctively reached for his knife at his belt. He seemingly avoided Mendoza's thrust and kicked out at the man. Mendoza fell on the deck floor, and Marlee heard an agonized groan. He lay very still.

Holcombe bent down and turned Mendoza face up. His dark eyes gazed sightlessly at the azure-colored sky, and his unmoving hands clung to the knife on which he'd fallen.

Marlee ran to Lark, a frightened sob died in her throat. "What are you doing here?" he shouted at her and clasped his forearm. "Don't you know you could have been hurt or killed? I told you to stay in the cabin. Where's that Todd?"

The tears she wanted to shed evaporated in the harsh sound of his voice. She'd think the ingrate would have the good sense to thank her for saving his wretched life. "He's over by the barrels, and don't think you're going to punish or yell at him. I wanted to come up here, and it's a good thing I did, otherwise, you'd be dead right now."

"Oh, so you think you've saved my life, do you?"

"Yes, and I'd think you'd be grateful to me instead of shouting."

"I am," he admitted with such sincerity that Marlee felt herself melting. "It's just that I shout when I'm in pain." He removed his hand from his shirtsleeve to show her a large bloody splotch.

She grew a trifle dizzy at the sight of Lark's blood. "You should have told me you were hurt. Mr. Holcombe, Captain Arden has been injured."

Holcombe instantly tore a piece of lace from the collar of his shirt and fastened it tourniquet-style above the gaping knife wound. "My advice is for you to rest," Holcombe advised.

"No need," Lark protested. "I'm not an invalid."

"Stop being ridiculous and come with me to the cabin. I'll tend to your wound and properly bandage it for you," she offered. Marlee hated it when grown men wouldn't admit that they were only hu-

155

man and pretended that pain didn't bother them. She knew Lark's wound must hurt.

Lark shot her a weak grin. "Promise me that you'll stay with me, every moment."

"I'll make no promises to you, Lark Arden." She didn't mean to sound flippant but the very fact that he would say such a suggestive thing to her left her feeling weak-kneed — and it wasn't because of blood any longer.

"I think you'll survive," Marlee observed and finished applying a salve which Holcombe had brought to her. She bandaged Lark's arm and surveyed her handiwork. Despite her trembling fingers and earlier queasiness, she'd done an adequate job.

"Pretty pleased with yourself, aren't you?" Lark asked and leaned against the pillows on the bunk.

She nodded. "Yes. I've never taken care of someone who'd been injured. I've never taken care of anyone. My doctoring skills leave a great deal to be desired, but I believe you'll recover."

"Thanks to you I will."

Marlee shyly glanced down and made a move to get off of the bunk, but Lark grabbed her hand, concealing it within the warmth of his own. She felt him watching her and slowly drew her eyes upward to meet his steady stare. "Is there anything I can get for you?"

"Marlee, stop being so polite. I meant what I said about thanking you. You didn't have to warn me about Mendoza."

"Of course I had to warn you. The man was going to kill you. I didn't do anything out of the ordinary—anybody would have done the same."

"But I didn't deceive just anybody. I deceived *you*."

She wanted to pull her hand away. The memory of what he'd done to her still caused her agonizing moments, but she was beginning to understand why Lark had been so driven. Those horrible pirates were fierce and frightening. Perhaps this Manuel Silva was even worse. "Yes, you did an awful thing to me," she admonished lowly.

"Well, you'll soon be back in Cornwall," he assured her. "You can pursue your life, as if I never happened."

Had she heard a sadness in his voice or had she imagined it? She'd like to think he'd care when she was gone. "But you *did* happen," she found herself admitting. "Do you think me so shallow that I can ever forget? I—I can't forget, yet in some silly portion of my heart, I forgive you." She hadn't meant to say any of that. She'd wanted to remain calm and act surprisingly cool but whenever Lark so much as looked at her, she found herself reverting to a lovesick fool. And to have him touch her was more than unbearable. Sometimes she thought he'd placed her under some sort of an enchanted spell.

This time she pulled her hand away and stood up to restlessly pace the cabin. "Why is going after Manuel Silva so important to you?" she flung at him. "I know he nearly killed you once, but why must you willfully seek him out? If he's such a ter-

157

rible man, he may finally succeed in finishing the job. I can't believe you'd risk your life only to settle a score. You have another ship now, you're starting over again. Material things can be easily replaced. Nothing is more important than life." *Your life,* she silently amended.

Lark stifled a groan and sat on the edge of the bunk. He'd been waiting for her to question him about Silva. Wreaking vengeance for what Silva had done to him was horrible in itself but there was Bettina to consider.

Lark didn't believe Marlee would understand or forgive him for not telling her about Bettina. And he couldn't bring himself to tell her about the woman he planned to marry. He treasured each moment he spent with Marlee, and knew their time was running out. Soon he'd place her on the return ship to England, but he didn't want her to remember him as a mercenary cad, hunting down Silva only because the despicable pirate had destroyed his ship. God, why must he care so much what Marlee thought about him? Why must he feel anything for her? Things would be so much easier if he'd never met her.

But watching her standing defiantly before him, demanding an answer from him, gave him pause. He knew why he felt something for her. Even dressed in man's clothing, she was so incredibly beautiful that he could barely think. Not only was she physically perfect but sweet and trusting—even after what he'd done to her. He felt his loins hardening with need for her and silently cursed his fate.

Bettina needed him, she was the woman whom his dear father had chosen for his wife. Because he hadn't adequately defended her, she'd been used by Silva's pirate crew if what Mendoza had insinuated was true. Lark had to rescue her, he must find Manuel Silva. If Bettina was alive, no matter her condition, he'd bring her home to Williamsburg as his bride. He owed Bettina that much. *And he'd lose Marlee in the process.*

Lark took a deep breath. "Silva kidnapped a— friend of mine from my ship when he attacked it last year. I was penniless after that, as I told you. I needed the money to get a new ship to rescue—this person."

Marlee's face paled. "I'm sorry, Lark. I had no idea." She now understood why he'd needed money so desperately. No matter what deceptive thing he'd done to her, she couldn't deny that his crew respected him and that Simon had fondly regarded him. Perhaps there was a side to him she hadn't wanted to see in her pain. Apparently, Lark was a good friend to have. "Is that why you're going to New Providence?"

"Someone on the island may have information about Silva—and where he took—this person," he admitted, barely able to face her.

"Maybe I can help you somehow when we reach New Providence," she volunteered.

"No!" he burst out and jumped off the bunk. He grabbed her arm. "Stay out of this dangerous

159

business. I don't want anything to happen to you—ever. Anyway, you're going home soon—"

"And you won't have to worry about me any longer, isn't that what you meant to say?" To her own ears she sounded shrewish and she bit down upon her lower lip to keep the tears that suddenly threatened at bay. He was standing so close to her that she could smell the musty male scent of him, could feel his warm breath wafting across her face. Lark's mouth was so dangerously close to hers that she couldn't concentrate. All she wanted was his lips' possession.

"I'll never stop worrying about you, Marlee. You're in my blood like a raging windstorm. I can't stop thinking about you or wanting you. You're driving me insane."

"Oh, Lark!" She threw her arms around his neck, unable to resist. "I hate arguing with you, I hate wanting you when I know I should hate you. But—but I think I know now why you felt forced to do what you've done. Can we make a truce with one another? I can't go on like this another second—"

"Even after all I've done to you?"

"Yes."

"Let's seal our truce," he suggested with a sensuous smile and drew her closer against him.

"How do we do that?" She sounded breathless and waited, poised on the brink of desire.

"With a kiss, my love. I can think of no finer way to seal a truce."

Oh, yes! her mind cried, and her body wantonly dissolved into his when he kissed her. This was what she wanted, what she needed. Nothing mattered to her but Lark. She knew now without a doubt that she loved this man. And though he hadn't admitted he loved her, somehow she trusted that he did.

His kisses stirred her, igniting a fire inside her that burned high and bright. She could feel him touching her breasts, very much aware of the way her nipples hardened beneath his fingertips. Marlee moaned beneath his lips, more than aware of the wet, melting warmth between her thighs. She was ready for him, eager for his rapturous possession of her body, her senses, and her soul.

As for Lark, all conscious thought stopped the second Marlee responded to him. For weeks he'd thought about the night they'd made love the first time, tormenting himself with images of her voluptuous body. He'd remembered every detail of their sweet joining until he feared he was going to end up a babbling idiot. Never had he cherished a memory so much. And now she was in his arms again, she was his for the taking, and being a man who was bewitched, he thought with his heart instead of his good sense. The future ceased to exist for him. There was only this beguiling woman in his arms, this glorious beauty who was now moving toward the bunk with him.

They fell as one onto the covers.

As one, they undressed until nothing but bare,

dew-moistened flesh hotly joined with the other. Lark caressed her body with his wonderful hands, provoking desires inside of Marlee that were so intense she couldn't help but make tiny, mewling sounds of abandoned pleasure. His fingers slipped inside of her with ease and played upon her womanly core like a fine-tuned instrument.

"Oh, Lark, stop," she pleaded between tiny gasps. "I can't stand this torment any longer."

"Do you really want me to stop?" he asked and nipped her earlobe. "Or is there something else you want? Tell me, tell me what you want, Marlee."

In the gloom of the cabin his eyes resembled shining agates. His powerful body rose above hers and with that movement, Marlee's body responded. "I want all of you, Lark, every inch of you."

He smiled down at her, crushing her mouth with his kiss. Marlee instinctively arched upward and parted her thighs for him. She knew exactly what she wanted.

Chapter Thirteen

He entered her with a slow sweetness that took her breath, his name dying on her lips.

Time stood still, reality ceased to exist. There was nothing but the beauty of love, the incredible power of passion. They merged as one, defying the fates that conspired to keep them apart. Marlee's hips gyrated beneath him, her body was controlling her mind. At some point, she had ceased to think but could feel every wonderful thrust as Lark loved her. Like a wind-tossed sea, she was buffeted by passion's tide. Rapture engulfed her.

"Marlee, Marlee, my love," Lark whispered raggedly, and poised above her, not moving. "Are you ready, are you?"

She knew she was unable to stand this sweet torment another second. As it was she could barely speak, but her body spoke to Lark. Her hips rose up to meet him, her velvet sheath expanding to take all of him.

It was his lusty groan that sent her over the edge. Her body exploded just as he thrust into her one last time. Mutual ecstasy inundated their senses, blinding them to everything but the intense bliss they'd found in each other's arms.

Marlee woke to discover that Lark had left the bed and was now sitting by the table. The wavering candlelight illuminated the pinpoints of fire within his obsidian eyes. She couldn't help but smile at him. He was so incredibly handsome and well formed that she felt lucky to be loved by such a man. But she didn't remember Lark admitting that he loved her—he'd never admitted love. Yet, he had to love her, because she loved him so very much.

"Would you care for some port?" he asked and offered his glass to her.

Marlee sat up and instinctively wrapped the bedsheet around her, bringing a delighted chuckle from Lark when she took the glass from him. "You're beguiling even in your modesty, sweetheart," he playfully noted and kissed her forehead.

"Hmm, unlike someone I could name who doesn't mind parading around without a stitch of clothing on," she gently riposted as her eyes drank in Lark's unabashed nudity.

Lark settled beside her, watching her pretty strawberry-tinted mouth sip delicately at the port. He whispered into her ear, "I wish I was that glass right now."

Marlee appeared confused, not understanding what Lark meant until her gaze traveled to his very erect manhood. She couldn't stop her face from turning ten shades of red. "Lark, you're insatiable!"

"Only with you, sweet Marlee, believe me." Without a further word, Lark took the glass from her hand and licked the traces of port from her lips. Marlee was quivering with desire again, unable to resist him.

The next morning, sunshine drenched the cabin and bathed the room in a bright glow. Marlee had wakened to find a note from Lark on her pillow, telling her that he was on watch. Her breakfast plate, consisting of a biscuit and a cup of warm broth, was already on the table waiting for her. She sat down to eat and had taken only a nibble when Holcombe knocked at the door. Wrapping the sheet securely around her, she opened the door and peered hesitantly at the man.

"Begging your pardon, your ladyship, but I've got something you might like to have." He pointed to a large sea chest beside him. "This is part of what we took from the pirate ship, and I think what's inside will suit you more than anyone else on board."

Marlee opened the door to him and he nimbly set the chest beside the bunk. "What is it?" Marlee asked and pulled the sheet tightly around her, most embarrassed to be found in her disheveled state. However, Holcombe was enough of a gentleman that he didn't gawk at her.

"Women's clothing, and from the fancy look of the dresses, I'd say a proper lady owned them." He nodded respectfully at her. "They'll suit a lady like yourself just fine, ma'am." No sooner had Holcombe left the cabin than Marlee opened the chest and practically dove inside.

She eagerly pulled out a number of gowns in a rainbow of colors. Some were day dresses but others were encrusted with jewels and fashioned in velvet and satin. There were chemises, petticoats, and underthings which were trimmed with the most delicate laces Marlee had ever seen. White pillowcases, embroidered with a large pink A surrounded by dainty hearts and pink roses, caused Marlee to decide that this had been a trousseau. Whoever had owned these things had no doubt been quite wealthy. For a fleeting second, Marlee wondered about the woman and what had happened to the ship. Certainly the pirates had destroyed the ship on which she'd been traveling and confiscated the trunk. What had happened to the bride-to-be?

Marlee shivered at the image of the nameless and faceless woman at the mercy of the pirate crew. "I won't think about any of that," she decided and began putting on a lace chemise. After she'd finished pulling on sheer white stockings, she chose a pink silk gown that wasn't too plain or too elaborate. A white lace fichu at the neck and layers of white lace at the elbow-length sleeves made Marlee feel extremely feminine. She couldn't help pirouetting around the cabin, wondering if Lark would find the gown acceptable and somehow she knew he would. He couldn't expect her to wear Todd's clothes forever.

Smiling to herself, she rummaged further through the trunk and discovered a pair of pink kid slippers which she promptly placed on her feet, more than happy to be rid of the ill-fitting boots. Digging deeper, her hand found a black velvet reticule on the trunk's bottom. She opened the drawstrings and emptied the contents on her lap.

"Oh, my!" she gasped aloud when a large diamond ring and a gold locket on a heavy gold chain fell out. From the looks of the ring, she determined that it must be an engagement ring. The stone glittered like a thousand stars and was absolutely the most beautiful ring that Marlee had ever seen, more beautiful than the ring Richard Arden had given her.

She couldn't resist trying on the ring. It was a bit too large for her slender finger, the diamond solitaire overpowered her hand. Once again, she wondered what had happened to the owner, who she had been.

Marlee thought she had learned the answer when she turned her attention to the locket. The initials B.G. were delicately engraved on the front and inside was a miniature portrait of a beautiful woman with auburn hair that fell gently around her shoulders. The artist had done a credible job of capturing the young woman's beauty, even her haughty demeanor in the raising of the left eyebrow.

Had this woman owned the clothes Marlee now wore? Marlee couldn't help but feel a moment's regret for the lady and hoped she had met with a kind fate.

Feeling guilty for wearing the jewelry, she replaced the objects in the velvet reticule and put it in the bottom of the trunk.

Minutes later she was on deck, basking in the morning sun when Todd appeared. "You look mighty pretty, Lady Marlee," he complimented her with a shy grin.

"Why, thank you," she said and held out the skirt of her gown for inspection. "Should I wear dresses or do you think I should change into breeches for the rest of the voyage?"

"Dresses, my lady. Not that you ain't a fetchin' sight in breeches but you're a lady and should dress like one. Besides, we ain't got too much sailin' time left. We'll be at New Providence day after tomorrow."

"Oh, I didn't know that." Lark hadn't told her

that there was so little time left. Soon she'd be returning to England—and leaving Lark behind forever. Marlee felt her stomach sinking at the thought.

"Can I be gettin' you somethin', my lady?" Todd asked and repeated the question when Marlee didn't immediately answer. "You look mighty queer all of a sudden."

"No, thank you. I—I'll go back to the cabin now. The sun is much too warm." She walked past Todd and started down the deck. Lark called to her and waved to her from his perch on the rigging. She waved back, unable to stop watching him. Her heart squeezed painfully in her chest at the sound of his voice, his laughter. There was so little time left to be together, precious moments she'd cherish for the rest of her life. But why must they be parted? She didn't understand why Lark insisted that she return to Cornwall. As far as she could tell, there was no good reason for her to leave him—ever.

"I'm going to stay,—" she decided aloud. "Come hell or high water Lark Arden isn't going to get rid of me. Somehow I'll find a way to make him love me enough so that he'll beg me to stay—beg me to marry him."

And that was the first time Marlee realized how much she wanted to be Lark Arden's wife.

Chapter Fourteen

Marlee stood beside Lark after the ship anchored in New Providence. The soft afternoon breezes wafted over them and slightly ruffled the water's azure surface. Gently waving palm trees, filled with cawing and brightly colored birds, lined the sandy shoreline above small whitewashed houses. The natural beauty of the island enchanted Marlee, and she realized just how much of life she'd missed until she met Lark.

"What a lovely place." She smiled her delight and held Lark's arm. "This is nothing like Cornwall."

"No, it isn't," he amicably agreed. The grin he flashed her was almost as blinding as the sun above them. "But if you'd seen the island just a few years ago, you'd have had a very different opinion. Pirates ran rampant, there wasn't law and order. And you see those little houses nearby, well they weren't there then. Most everybody lived in tents."

"Really? What happened to change all of that?"

"A friend of mine, one Captain Woodes Rogers," he explained. "The Crown appointed him to bring law and order to the island. The pirates tried to run him off, but Rogers and his men prevailed by giving each pirate a piece of land as his own, something no one could take away. Slowly, the pirates began to realize that there was more to life than just raiding ships, that owning land created a permanence in their lives that had been lacking." Lark laughed. "Some of these men were the scurviest lot of knaves you'd ever want to meet. Now, they're gentlemen and even help make laws for the island."

Marlee was fascinated by Lark's tale. "What happened to Captain Rogers?"

"He's Governor Rogers now. I sent word to him that you'll be staying in his home until I can get you return passage to England. It's the safest place for you under the circumstances."

"I see," she told him but didn't really understand why Lark still wanted her to go back to England. They'd been together every moment the last two days, eating together, laughing together—and making love. Her face flushed just to remember the deliciously wanton things they'd done in bed together. They suited each other wonderfully well, so why did he want her to leave him? Why?

She knew it wouldn't do any good to plead with him to allow her to stay. Whenever she asked him why he wanted her to go home all he ever replied was that her leaving was for the best. The best for whom? Certainly, not herself. She knew she loved him and thought he loved her, too. For the life of her she didn't understand him and no longer attempted to try. She was determined to find a way to remain with Lark, to force the bullheaded man to admit that he loved her.

But how?

Marlee's attention was diverted from Lark when he waved at an approaching carriage on a cobblestoned street, stopping just short of the quay. "That's Governor Rogers," he explained and shouted hello to the tall, distinguished looking gentleman who disembarked and headed toward them.

Lark and Rogers shook hands, both smiling genially at the other. "Well, Arden, you're looking fit and chipper," Rogers noted. "I heard about your dispute with Silva and the kidnapping—"

"Yes, well, that's over and done with for now," Lark rudely interrupted the man, his eyes narrowing in Marlee's direction. "I think it's better left forgotten. I want to introduce you to my cousin's widow, Lady Marlee Arden." He brought Marlee forward. She dutifully curtsied to Rogers and extended her hand.

He kissed her hand and patted it in fatherly affection. "How charming and lovely you are, Lady Arden. I'm quite pleased you'll be staying in my

172

humble home until arrangements are made for your passage to England."

"Thank you for having me, sir."

"Ah, I should be thanking you, my lady. It isn't everyday that a member of the aristocracy graces our little island, much less dines at my table. I've arranged a small dinner party for tonight in honor of your arrival. It won't be anything fancy for Lark didn't give me adequate notice, but I've invited a few of our esteemed citizens for the occasion. I hope you'll forgive our less than genteel ways. Some of us are a rowdy bunch still."

Marlee liked Governor Rogers, finding him to be an honest and open person. She wondered what he'd think if he knew she was the daughter of a tin miner. She smiled her thanks. "I'm certain it shall be a most fascinating evening, and I look forward to it with anticipation"

"Good, good." He offered his arm to her. "May I escort you to my home, Lady Arden?"

"That is kind of you, sir." She placed her hand on his arm and followed beside him. After they were settled in the carriage, Marlee realized that Lark wasn't with them. Peering anxiously out of the window, she noticed that he was still on the ship and watching her. "Isn't Captain Arden coming, too?"

"Not at the present time, my lady. He expressed his desire to remain on the ship."

"But—I shall be alone at your home?"

"Oh, no, Lady Arden," Rogers assured her with a horrified expression on his tanned face. "My cousin Beatrix is visiting me. You'll be properly chaperoned, never fear. And no one need know that you were traveling unchaperoned with Lark. That shall be our secret." He patted her hand and pantomimed that he was buttoning his lips.

Marlee nearly laughed aloud at the ludicrous-looking gesture, even though she knew Rogers took her situation seriously. Here she was on an island that had been a haven for pirates only a few years before, and now she had to worry about what these same pirates and their wives would think about her if they learned the truth. And the truth was that she wanted to weep right now because she could feel herself losing Lark— and she wasn't certain why.

"I'm from London, meself," a man who was named Josiah Finch informed Marlee over the conch salad, a tangy dish of raw chopped conch that was spiked with hot peppers and lemon juice. "Me Nora was born in Bristol, weren't you, love?" He peered at the buxomy blonde who sat next to him out of his eye that wasn't covered by a black patch.

"Aye, I'm a Bristol lass," Nora admitted proudly, the bright parrot feathers in her hair

174

bouncing with the effort. "I was on me way to the Carolinas as an indentured servant when I met Josiah. He attacked and robbed the ship I was on. It was a fortunate meeting I always say." Nora laughed out loud and exhibited two blackened front teeth.

Marlee smiled pleasantly but inside she wanted this evening to be over. She found no fault with the bounty at the governor's table. The fare was superb, consisting of an assorted array of seafood, including freshly cooked mackerel and oysters. The governor's home, though small, was clean and neatly tended by his cousin, Beatrix. Marlee found she liked Beatrix, who was small and olive-complexioned and had a few gray streaks in her hair which didn't diminish her prettiness. Beatrix was kind and sweet and tactfully changed the course of the conversation at the supper table when it became too bawdy for Marlee's taste.

Bawdy was an understatement, Marlee decided, to explain the motley assortment of people who surrounded the table. A more dubious bunch of folks she'd never before seen and decided that the men must have been pirates at one time. She'd been introduced to the four women and five men in their colorful attire by the governor himself.

One young man named Sloane Mason was seated next to her and he didn't resemble a pirate at all. Marlee found him to be the most polished and conversant of the group. His clothes were well-made and subdued in color, and any opinion he offered was well received by the governor. At one point when the suggestive talk at the table caused Marlee to blush, Sloane leaned over and whispered in her ear, "I apologize for my friends, your ladyship. Please don't think ill of us or our little island paradise."

Marlee assured him that she didn't, but it wasn't the people or the loose talk that bothered her. Lark wasn't there and she didn't know if she'd ever see him again. For all she knew he may have sailed away after Manuel Silva by now, leaving her to her own devices.

"You mustn't mind our guests," Beatrix said to Marlee when the ladies retired to the sitting room and the men went into the governor's study for rum and cigars. "They don't mean any harm."

"I'm not bothered, really," she said for the second time that evening. "I appreciate your hospitality. You're very kind to worry about me."

"I do, my dear," Beatrix admitted with a frown. "I worried each time Lark Arden's name was mentioned at the table."

"What?" Color rushed to Marlee's face.

Beatrix offered her a small smile. "Pardon me for being blunt, Lady Arden, but you're in love with Captain Lark. Your feelings for him are written on your face for all to see."

Marlee's hands instinctively covered her blushing

cheeks. "I had hoped he'd be here tonight."

"May I give you a word of advice?" Beatrix asked in a motherly tone of voice and continued before Marlee could even nod her head. "Try not to fall under his spell. Lark Arden can only hurt you."

"It's too late for that, ma'am."

Beatrix sighed. "Then do yourself a favor and get far away from him. Woodes told me that Lark is arranging passage for you to England. I think that's very wise on his part, and if I were you, I'd not see the man again before you leave."

"Why? What has he done?"

"Trust me, my dear," was all Beatrix said and joined the women.

Marlee didn't feel like sitting with a group of women. She needed some fresh air and headed outside onto the moon-soaked terrace at the side of the house. She breathed in the sweet perfume of the sea grapes that grew in profusion nearby.

"I'd take Beatrix's advice," came a masculine voice from the shadows.

She turned, the bottom of her emerald satin gown swishing around her calves, to behold Sloane Mason smoking a cheroot and indolently leaning against a palm tree. Silver streaks of moonlight emphasized his dark hair and glittering blue eyes.

"I don't mean to be rude, sir, but I dislike your sneaking up on me."

"I apologize, my lady," he solemnly intoned.

"I also dislike your listening to a private conversation."

She saw the quick glint of a smile. "I won't apologize for that. I learn a great deal by keeping my ears open and my mouth closed. And if I heard correctly, I'd surmise that Beatrix believes that Lark Arden is using you."

Marlee turned away, unable to think of anything else to say to Sloane Mason. In fact, she was horribly embarrassed for the man to have overheard the conversation. And she was seething with indignation not only because of what he'd overheard and said to her but because Lark evidently didn't care enough about her to put in an appearance. No doubt, he was making arrangements to send her to England, eager to be rid of her. But why? Could Beatrix and this Sloane Mason be right about Lark? Had he used her for his own pleasure during the voyage, just as he'd used her fortune? Would he leave and not tell her farewell? He'd done that to her before. She wouldn't believe he'd do it again.

"I don't want your concern, young man," Marlee haughtily pronounced.

Sloane laughed heartily. "You sound like you're fifty years old. I bet you're no more than sixteen."

"I'm nearly eighteen," she declared, vexed for him to think she was a mere child. She was a woman now—Lark had seen to that.

"Again, forgive me." He made a deep bow of apology.

"I think you're making sport of me."

His face softened. "Perhaps a little, my lady."

"Why? I've never done anything to offend you. I don't even know you—or like you, at this point," she admitted in all honesty.

Sloane came closer to her and leaned near to her. "Ah, Lady Marlee, your words wound me. Perhaps I jest with you because you fancy yourself in love with Lark Arden. Perhaps I wish to be as fortunate as Lark in affairs of the heart." He clasped her hand in his. "I own a fine ship and have a beautiful spot on the island to build a fancy house, a house any fine lady would like. I can give a woman whatever Lark can and more—much more. You have only to ask, my sweet, and I will do your bidding." Sloane put her hand to his mouth to kiss but Marlee pulled it away.

"Sir, please, I don't know what you're doing—"

"Yes, you do," he ground out and grabbed her around the waist. "You've enticed me with your beauty and sweetness. I want only to kiss you, please just once I would like to kiss a fine lady—"

His lips barely made contact with hers before Marlee was aware that Sloane Mason had been wrenched away from her. She tottered and clung to the palm tree to keep from falling, suddenly aware that Lark was standing with clenched fists above the prone figure of Sloane who now lay in the sand. "Get up and fight, you bloody cur!" Lark shouted to Sloane. "Get up so I can beat your lying face in."

Marlee had never heard Lark speak like that before, not even to his crew, and there was something frightening about his stance and tone of voice. He looked dark as a black tower in his evening clothes and as wild as a storm as he waited for Sloane to rise to his feet.

"Lark, please, nothing happened!" she cried in fear that he'd kill Sloane Mason.

He shot her the blackest look she'd ever seen and instantly she realized she'd be better off remaining silent. There was something between these two men that she didn't understand, something of which she wasn't a part. "Get up and fight!" Lark cried. "I want you to fight me."

"I know you do, dear brother," Sloane mocked lowly. "And that is why I won't."

Brother? Had Marlee heard Sloane correctly? Lark couldn't possibly be his brother. But as Sloane rose to his feet and she was able to compare the two men together, she quickly saw the resemblance. They were built the same, their hair was the same ebony color but whereas Lark had dark eyes, Sloane's eyes were a startling shade of blue. Yes, they were brothers but bad blood flowed between them.

Sloane dusted himself off, taunting Lark with his nonchalance. "I paid dearly for this suit of clothes, Lark, and now you've made me dirty it. You always were a bully, even when we were children."

"And you were always a hateful bastard," Lark said with such startling calmness that Marlee shivered.

"Aye, you're right, bastard I was and bastard I'll always be in your eyes, big brother." Sloane grinned and looked at Marlee. "I'm the Arden black sheep, the bastard son. Lark detests me as much as I detest him."

"Shut up, Sloane!" Lark commanded and moved near to Marlee to take her arm. "Marlee doesn't want to hear any of your imbecile ravings."

"Hmmm, maybe she should," Sloane mused aloud. "Maybe she should hear all I have to say. I'd think your fine lady might be interested in what I'd tell her."

"Get on your way, you coward, or I'll—" Lark made a move in Sloane's direction, but Sloane nimbly jumped out of the way and chuckled.

"My lips are closed, dear brother, I assure you of that." Sloane made an exaggerated bow in Marlee's direction and said with all sincerity, "Remember what I told you, my lady. If ever you have need of me, I shall help you. I meant every word. Good night to you." He turned and suddenly fixed his sapphire gaze on Lark. "And to you, too, dear brother." Then he headed down the beach and away from the house.

Marlee felt Lark trembling. Apparently the emotions between these two men ran deep. She held onto his hand and looked up at him. "Lark, he wasn't going to hurt me. I would have been able to take care of myself."

"You've no idea what Sloane Mason is capable of," he stated and imploringly sought her eyes. "Stay away from him, Marlee. Promise me you'll stay away from him."

At that second she'd have promised anything to Lark. She was so glad to see him again. "I promise. But you must tell me about Sloane. I didn't know you had a brother."

"As far as I'm concerned, I don't." Lark sounded bitter. "Sloane was a mistake my father made with an indentured servant girl years ago. The girl died in childbirth and my mother took Sloane as her own child. She was determined to raise the boy and believe me when I tell you that Mother loved him like he was her own son. He was my little brother, and I loved him. Father loved him, too. But there was something vicious about Sloane, something not quite right. He was petty and jealous of everything I received, even if he got the exact same thing."

"Maybe he acted that way because he sensed he was different." Marlee empathized with Sloane.

She knew how it felt to be part of a household where you weren't truly wanted.

"Don't feel sorry for him," Lark warned. "Sloane never knew about his mother until he was almost fourteen, but by that time he'd done everything imaginable to turn us away from him. The little bastard would set fires to the stables; once he even started a small fire in the dining room because Mother told him he couldn't have another serving of cobbler. Then valuables would disappear and we learned he'd been selling them in Williamsburg. Father finally had enough when Sloane was sixteen and gotten a neighbor's daughter—" Lark broke off and took a deep, steadying breath. "Sloane refused to marry her and called her a whore to her face. The girl drowned herself. That was when Father ran him off, telling him never to return to Arden's Grove."

"How awful for all of you." Marlee stroked Lark's hand, until he stopped trembling. "How does Sloane happen to be here?"

"An odd quirk of fate, I guess. It seemed Sloane changed his name and joined the men Rogers had picked to clean up the island. I was part of that group. Imagine how I felt to be face to face with my bastard brother again. I've tried to put ill feelings aside, but he always manages to rankle me. Somehow Sloane just seems to know how to upset me."

Marlee slipped into his arms, knowing she be-

183

longed there. She nestled her head against his chest. "Don't think about him anymore," she told him. "I'm happy that you're here. I thought you'd gone off pirate hunting and had left me."

"I wouldn't do that. I had things to do before I could come here tonight."

"Like arranging my passage to England?"

She felt him stiffen and then relax. "Yes."

This time she stiffened and gazed at him through misty eyes. "I don't want to go back. I want to stay with you."

"Marlee, you can't—"

"Why not?" she persisted and clung to the lapels on his jacket. "I love you." She could see the torment on his face and was glad for it. Maybe he'd change his mind.

"You can't stay. Don't make this any harder than it already is. I've got to find Manuel Silva—there are—other—things I've got to do. I don't have room in my life for you now, Marlee. Please understand."

"But I don't understand!" She drew away from him. "I can't understand something if you don't tell me what it is I'm supposed to understand. Why must you torment me?"

"I'm the one who's tormented, Marlee. I'm the one." He swooped down and captured her mouth in a kiss which seared her very soul. Like a captive wanton, she clung to him, reveling in the warmth and desire she felt. Surely he must love

184

her. How could he not when she was bubbling over with love for him?

But the kiss ended as quickly as it had begun when Beatrix suddenly appeared and discreetly cleared her throat. Lark and Marlee guiltily broke away.

"I didn't know you were here, Captain. Please join the gentlemen for a glass of rum. I know Woodes will be pleased to see you," Beatrix invited pleasantly but her worried frown belied the invitation.

"Uh, no, I can't. Please extend my apology to him."

"I shall."

Lark smiled sadly at Marlee. "Good night, my lady. Sleep well." He left her standing on the terrace. She watched him depart from her, her gaze following his dark figure until he vanished into the velvet night.

Chapter Fifteen

Things were different, now that they were in what was loosely termed on New Providence as "polite society," Lark bitterly observed as he stood on the deck of his ship. He'd spent the last three nights alone in his bed, unable to sleep and barely able to eat. Never had a woman had this profound of an effect upon him. Never had he cared for a woman as much as Marlee. To even think he might be in love with her was a thought he couldn't dwell upon. He hadn't loved Bettina, the woman his father had chosen for him. And now, he couldn't face the reality that he might be in love with Marlee only to lose her forever.

He felt it was better for both of them if he didn't see her too often. If he distanced himself from her, then when the time came for her to leave, he'd be emotionally detached and would be able to put on a brave facade. Yet, God only knew how much he'd miss her and nothing could stop the pain he'd experience when she was truly gone.

Lost in his reverie, he didn't notice Holcombe

approaching with a short, overweight man beside him. "Lark," Holcombe said, "this man has news for you about Manuel Silva."

At the mention of the notorious pirate's name, Lark came alert. For the first time he realized the other man's presence and grimaced when he recognized the swarthy little creature in ill-fitting clothes with Holcombe. "Well, well, Lescale, it's been a long time."

"Oui, Monsieur Lark, too long."

"The last time I saw you I think you were jumping ship in Tortuga."

Lescale smiled sheepishly. *"Oui,* I apologize for leaving your ship, but there was this beautiful señorita—"

Lark held up a hand and chuckled. "Enough, don't tell me anymore."

"Then you don't hold a grudge against Lescale?"

Lark sobered. "Not if the information about Manuel Silva is something of value to me."

"Oui, I understand. I've heard you've offered three hundred pounds for this information."

"Only if it turns out to be correct. Do you know where Silva is?"

Lescale moved closer to Lark, his tone conspiratorially low. "I saw him myself only last month, monsieur Lark. I was sailing on a ship bound for Cuba when out of nowhere Silva's black crow of a ship appeared. His flag was raised to attack and he chased us, but to our good fortune, the wind was in our favor and we outran him. But at one point,

187

we were close enough for Silva to be observed on deck. He is a vulture, Captain Lark, a dark, evil man."

Lark knew that only too well. "Where do you think he is, Lescale?"

"There is a group of islands near Bimini. I've heard this is where he anchors his ship, his base when he launches an attack. And Silva doesn't care who he attacks, monsieur, as you well know. He's attacked ships flying the Spanish flag, he's been known to destroy the ships of his own cronies and steal their treasure. No one and nothing is sacred to Silva. He must be destroyed."

"Tell me," Lark asked, his gaze riveted on Lescale, "have you heard anything about a woman he took captive some months ago?"

"Your fiancée," Lescale said bluntly, but his face softened for a moment. "I have heard about her, and the news isn't good, monsieur. I'm not saying the rumors are all true, but—but how can I say this to you without hurting you?"

"Go on," Lark urged and braced himself for the worst.

Lescale sighed. "I've heard that the lady is dead, monsieur. I'm sorry."

A shudder passed through Lark. He'd worried about this very thing and the responsibility for Bettina's death rested with him. If only he'd been able to defend her. He found himself offering his hand to Lescale. "Thank you for the information. If what you've told me turns out to be true, then I'll gladly pay you the three hundred pounds I've promised."

"I know you will, monsieur, for I trust you. But Silva is a slippery fellow and could be anywhere."

Lark realized that very well. Since his offer had been made for information, he'd been contacted by a dozen men with news about Silva, and each man had seen him in a different location. But this was the first time anyone had mentioned that Bettina was dead.

When Lescale left the ship, Holcombe, who had been nearby and heard everything, turned to Lark. "Are you still going after Silva now?"

"Yes, I have to kill the bastard. I have to know the truth."

"Well," Holcombe observed not unkindly, "if what Lescale told you about Lady Bettina turns out to be true, then your—relationship—with Lady Marlee could take a different turn."

Lark nodded but didn't respond, because he'd thought the very same thing.

"Lark Arden's offered three hundred pounds for news about Manuel Silva. I'd say that's quite a handsome sum to catch a bounder like Silva. Wish I knew where the culprit was. I'd like that money myself." A tall, distinguished gentleman had just read aloud to a similarly appearing companion the parchment tacked on the door of the local grog shop.

189

"Arden's daft if you ask me," the companion observed. "No one's been able to capture Silva, though Arden has more reason than others to try."

The two men moved leisurely down the mud-caked street which housed the taverns as well as the only lady's dress shop in the area. Marlee, who'd been waiting in the carriage for Beatrix to finish her purchases in the dress shop, had witnessed the entire exchange between the two men. Curiosity got the best of her and caused her to get out of the carriage under the disapproving eye of Beatrix's driver to read the piece of parchment for herself.

It was as the gentlemen had said. Lark was offering money in exchange for information about Manuel Silva. She shivered in the afternoon heat despite the perspiration which beaded her upper lip to wonder if Lark had finally gotten what he was after. Would he soon be putting her on a ship to England while he pursued Silva? If so, she'd never see him again. She couldn't bear the thought of that, and worst of all, she couldn't imagine Lark not returning from his mission. What if Silva killed him this time?

No matter that he wouldn't admit he loved her or commit himself in anyway to her, she loved him and vowed to help him. But how?

"Marlee, dear, what are you doing outside of the carriage?" Beatrix scolded, her arms loaded down with brightly wrapped packages.

"Nothing but getting a breath of air. It was stuffy inside the carriage."

"Well, you should be more careful. I shouldn't have brought you to this part of the island. You're so young and pretty that anything could have happened to you." Beatrix made a move to get inside with the driver's help when Marlee forestalled her with a hand on her arm.

"Isn't that Sloane Mason?" Marlee asked and pointed to the man at the end of the street who'd just entered a whitewashed two-storied house with a sign that proclaimed it was the Swan Inn.

"What?" Beatrix asked absently and then looked to where Marlee pointed. "Yes, I believe that's him."

"Does he live there?" Marlee asked and settled herself comfortably in the upholstered seat by arranging the flowing skirt of her white calico gown.

"Yes, when he isn't off doing God only knows what on that ship of his. Sloane is a wastrel and a ne'er-do-well, and you'd do yourself a favor by staying away from him."

"I got the impression that Governor Rogers liked him," Marlee observed.

"Woodes tolerates him, that's all," Beatrix said through compressed lips. "Sloane happens to be a good source of information about what's happening on the island and the vicinity, at least Woodes thinks so."

"Then the governor trusts him?"

Beatrix's eyes narrowed. "Yes, to a point, but I don't. He'll do anything for the right price. Marlee, I'm warning you about Sloane Mason, too. Stay away from him. He's more dangerous than Lark Arden." She fanned herself with a delicately painted fan. "I shall be so grateful, my dear, when you're safely in England. Chaperoning such a young and pretty woman is quite draining. I think the best decision Lark Arden has ever made is to send you back to England."

Marlee hid a secret smile. Now that she knew about Sloane Mason, she wouldn't be returning to England after all.

Upon their return to the house, Governor Rogers called her into the study where she found Lark. Her delight at seeing him was tempered by his introduction of another man with him. "This is Captain Neils Lundstrum," Lark introduced Marlee to the gray-haired sea captain with twinkling blue eyes. "Captain Lundstrum is setting sail for England day after tomorrow. I've arranged your passage with him, and I know that you'll be quite safe with him."

"As safe as I was with you?" she bit out before thinking and then blushed. She extended her hand graciously to Lundstrum. "I'm pleased to meet you, sir."

"The pleasure is mine, Lady Arden." Lundstrum smiled at her and kissed her hand. "My little ship is graced by your presence. I look forward to having you aboard."

"How kind of you to say that," she responded to

his compliment but she had no intention of being on board a ship day after tomorrow — at least not Lundstrum's ship. A moment of panic seized her but she brought it under swift control. If what she planned to do was destined to succeed, then she had to speak to Sloane Mason right away.

When Rogers and Lundstrum became engaged in a lively discussion, Lark motioned Marlee outside. "Let's walk," he said, and Marlee noticed his expression was gravely serious. She swallowed hard. This was the moment she'd been dreading. This was the moment of farewell, she could feel it.

They walked the sandy beach with bare feet, a gentle warm breeze at their backs. Not once did Lark reach out to take her hand, and she felt her heart was breaking. Why couldn't he admit that he loved her? she asked herself. Why must she love him so much and hope that they would have a life together once he completed his obsessive mission? And was there reason for such hope?

Finally, Lark stopped on the beach and gazed out at the sun-kissed horizon that stretched in azure waves before them. He turned to her. There were no dancing amber glints in his eyes today, only a profound sadness. "I'm sailing tomorrow at first light," he told her.

She fiddled with a bow at the neckline of her gown. "You're going after Manuel Silva."

"Yes, I think I know where to find him."

"And when you do, what then, Lark? What about us?"

Lark sighed deeply. "There can be no us, Marlee, though I wish to God things could be different."

"Explain to me why they can't be," she persisted and her voice rose a bit over the sea breezes. "You've never given me an adequate explanation for any of this. I understand you're anxious to avenge what Silva did to you, but afterward you could return to me here. I'd be waiting for you. We could have a life together—we could be—married." There she'd said it out loud for the first time. She waited with bated breath for his reaction.

Lark remained silent for a few seconds before he spoke. His dark eyes perused her face as if he'd never looked at her before. "I can't marry you. You're better off without me, Marlee. Once you're in England, you'll forget me, forget everything."

"How am I to forget the man who took my innocence, the man whom I love? And I do love you, Lark. I know you love me, too. Why can't you tell me you love me? Why?"

Her pleading undid him. Without realizing it, he pulled her into his arms and kissed her until his lips ached. Then he broke the kiss and looked deeply into the fathomless depths of her blue eyes. "I'll say this only one time, Marlee, only once." His voice sounded low and husky, almost like music to Marlee's ears. His hands stroked her jawline and stopped at the base of her neck. "I love you. I've never said that to another woman but you, and no matter what happens in the future what I feel for you will never change."

"Oh, Lark, I love you so much," she cried, joyful tears welling in her eyes and threatening to spill onto her cheeks. "I knew you loved me, I knew it. I won't leave you now. I can't."

"But you will."

Marlee blinked at the sudden harshness in his voice, more than dismayed to have him push her away from him. "But you just told me that you loved me—"

"And I meant it, Marlee. But if you love me, you must promise to leave New Providence and pursue your life. You must promise me that you'll forget me. There are things in my past that don't concern you, things you're better off not knowing. I want your promise that you'll leave day after tomorrow. I need to know that you're safe and living at Montclair. Promise me that you'll leave, promise me."

"But you love me—"

"Promise me," he ground out harshly.

She'd promise him the moon if he asked for it. Yet she didn't understand how he could admit he loved her and send her away. Had his vengeful mission against Silva blinded him to everything that made life worthwhile? However, she could see that Lark was struggling within himself, warring with his own demons. Her promise must be made to give him some peace of mind for the moment. "I promise I'll sail away day after tomorrow, just as you ask."

A wrenching sigh wracked his chest. "Thank you, Marlee."

"This is farewell then?" she asked and found her cheeks wet with tears.

Lark gently wiped a tear from her face, and she saw his own eyes were misty. "Yes, my lady. I won't see you again."

"Godspeed, Lark."

Making a wide sweeping bow, Lark didn't take his gaze from her. "You, too, my lady." Despite their sorrow, he managed to flash her a disarming smile that sent a thrill down to Marlee's very toes. And then Lark turned away and walked briskly down the beach. Not once did he look back. But Marlee knew he was thinking about her and wanting her as much as she wanted him.

She wiped the tears from her eyes and remembered the promise she'd made to Lark. That was a promise she intended to keep, too. She'd sail away the day after tomorrow but not on Captain Lundstrum's ship. If ever two people deserved to be together, she and Lark were that pair. And they would be together again with the help of God—and Sloane Mason.

Chapter Sixteen

Marlee walked the distance to the Swan Inn by way of the beach. She didn't use Governor Rogers's driver because she hated Beatrix to know where she was headed. The simple fact was that she didn't wish anyone to know her destination in the event that Sloane was unable to help her. She didn't know if he would help her, but she prayed he'd understand her situation and offer to assist her.

"You be wantin' to see Captain Mason?" the innkeeper asked her and eyed her suspiciously when she was standing inside the inn.

"That's what I said, sir," she answered with a dignified air. "I want to speak to Captain Mason. Is he in?"

"Aye. Room three at the top o' the stairs. You ain't like his other women," the man noted and raked Marlee's petite frame with lecherous eyes.

Goodness! The crude man thought she was one of Sloane Mason's doxies. A flush highlighted her complexion for him to think such a thing though she'd worn a simple blue gown with a modest neckline. "What you think isn't my concern," she replied in a tone which would freeze water. "Please tell Captain Mason that I wish to see him."

The innkeeper was clearly taken aback by her haughtiness. "Tell him yourself, my fine lady! I ain't no lackey. Room three, I told you." In a huff he turned his back on her and left Marlee standing in full view of the diners in the tap room. Some of the men, clearly disreputable-looking creatures, watched her with lecherous eyes. She couldn't stand here all day like she was on exhibit, but she'd never gone to a man's room by herself. However, when one of the men made a motion as if to rise from his chair and come toward her, Marlee scampered up the nearby stairs to seek out Sloane Mason in the belief that he was the lesser of two evils.

Finding Sloane's room, she timidly knocked upon the door. Now that she was finally here she was uncertain that Sloane would help her. She'd been quite rude to him, and he and Lark weren't what one could term "close."

"Who is it?" came Sloane's deep masculine voice when she knocked harder upon the door.

"It's Lady Arden. I must speak to you."

At least a minute passed before he opened the door. When he did she saw that his shirt was opened and he was hastily buttoning his trousers. "Come in, your ladyship," he cordially invited. "It's a rare honor to have you seek me out." Opening the door wider, he gestured her inside.

Marlee hesitated for a moment but went into the room, totally unprepared for the sight of a blond-haired woman who was hurriedly pulling a dress over her voluptuous figure. The true situation of what Sloane and this woman had been doing when she'd interrupted them was clarified by the sight of the rumpled bed sheets. Marlee felt so embarrassed that she immediately put her hands over her blushing cheeks. "Oh, I'm sorry. Forgive me for intruding. I had no idea you had—company—I shall leave at once." She started for the door but Sloane stopped her with a hand on her wrist.

"Addie was just leaving, don't worry about it." Sloane grinned lopsidedly and pulled a gold coin from his trousers pocket and tossed it at Addie. "For services rendered," he told her.

Addie caught the coin and bit down upon it. "Aye, 'tis real."

"Isn't it always?" Sloane winked at her and almost pushed her out of the door.

Addie nodded in Marlee's direction. "Do you want me to come back after she leaves?"

"No, we've finished our transaction for the day."

"What? What you talkin' about?" Addie asked, clearly baffled. "I hate those big words you use sometimes."

"Then maybe I'll have to give you some lessons in proper speech sometime soon," Sloane suggested and began to close the door before Addie was even out of the room.

Addie giggled. "Aye, I like what you teach me."

"Goodbye, pet." Sloane rudely shut the door in Addie's face.

Marlee nervously fiddled with the strings on her silk reticule. "You didn't have to send — your friend — away like that. I could have come back later, Captain Mason."

He waved his hand in a dismissive gesture. "No need to do that, Lady Arden. Addie isn't anyone important to me, whereas you are."

"I don't understand. We barely know one another," Marlee reminded Sloane.

"Then perhaps we should remedy that right now." He escorted her to a chair near a small table and sat opposite her. His heated gaze never left her face and Marlee feared he might be getting the wrong idea about her when his eyes suddenly roamed over the rumpled bed.

"I — I'm here to see you about a business arrangement, Captain Mason."

He leaned closer to her. "Call me Sloane. I insist upon it."

"All right — Sloane. I need to borrow your ship and hope you can help me." Marlee felt incredibly inept. She'd never approached a man of such a dubious reputation, but she realized it was his very penchant for intrigue which might save Lark and their love.

His fingers lightly stroked her hand. "I had hoped you had other things on your mind, my lady."

The suggestive quality of his voice wasn't lost on Marlee.

"I'm here only to ask your help, sir, and will pay your worth. That is all," she snapped and then clamped her mouth closed, wondering if he'd show her the door, too.

Sloane leaned back in his chair and poured a shot of rum for himself. He watched her in speculation. "You have my interest, my lady. What is it you need?"

Marlee took a deep breath, realizing that he wasn't going to send her on her way. "I must have your help in locating Manuel Silva. I've been told that you know a great many things about this area. I hoped you'd be able to tell me where Silva is hiding.

If Sloane was surprised by Marlee's request, he didn't act it. Swallowing the rum, he then smiled. "My sources tell me that Lark has already sailed away in search of Silva."

"Will Lark find him?"

"No, my lady, he won't."

"Do you know where Silva is?"

"Yes."

"Then why didn't you tell Lark? He offered three hundred pounds for the information."

"I don't need my brother's money."

Marlee suddenly understood the enmity between them. "So, you allowed Lark to go on a wild-goose chase, knowing all of the time he'd never find Silva. That's horrible of you."

Sloane poured another rum. "Is it? Lark didn't ask me directly if I knew of Silva's whereabouts, so I saw no reason to tell him. And as I recall, he wasn't too nice to me the last time we met."

"Will you take me to Silva? I have to see him."

Sloane held his glass in midair, clearly shocked by Marlee's request but he said smoothly, "Depends, my lady, on what you'll pay me."

Marlee opened her reticule and took out the diamond ring she'd found in the sea chest. She placed it on the table before Sloane. "This ring is all I have to offer you at the moment, and I'd bet if you have it appraised it will be worth much more than three hundred pounds."

Picking it up, Sloane held it to the light and carefully examined it. "Aye, I'd say it's worth a pretty penny. Where did you get it?"

"It doesn't matter where I got it. Will you accept it in payment for taking me to Silva?"

"Why do you want to go? Silva isn't the nicest of men."

"I must try to help Lark get his friend released. If the poor man is freed, then Lark and I can have a life together."

Sloane looked at the innocent Marlee as if she were addled, then he roared with laughter. She thought Silva's prisoner was a man. "That is rich, my lady! You rushing to Manuel Silva to plead the release of a captive—"

"How dare you laugh at me!" she berated him and suddenly rose to her feet and snatched the ring from him. "I shall not stay here and be treated like an imbecile. I'll find someone else to help me, someone more appreciative of what I offer. I've begun to doubt that you know where Silva is at all, that you even know the man."

"Hold on, Lady Arden." Sloane pulled her down into her chair. "I didn't say I wouldn't help you. And, yes, I do know where Silva is and, believe it or not, I know the scoundrel quite well."

Hope welled within Marlee, brightening her face. "You'll take me to him?"

Sloane considered the pretty, young woman for a long moment. Should he help her? Common sense told him that sailing to Silva's home on St. Augustine was probably foolhardy on his part. He and Silva weren't the best of friends but they respected each other as only two of a kind could. Perhaps Silva had forgotten how he'd left Silva's pirate crew and joined with the English forces to clean up New Providence. After all, years had passed since Sloane had sailed with Silva but he'd not lost track of the pirate. Certain sources had confided to Sloane that Silva was now headquartered on St. Augustine, supposedly living the life of a Spanish gentleman. And if the information was correct, Silva also lived with a beautiful and enchanting English woman, a woman, it was claimed who had been taken from Lark Arden's ship last year—a woman whom Lark Arden planned to marry.

Recently word had circulated that this woman had died, but Sloane knew better. Lark's fiancée was well and very much alive, if Sloane could believe all he'd heard about the auburn-haired vixen.

And now Marlee Arden wanted to beg for the woman's release. The situation would have been highly amusing if not for the fact that Sloane didn't wish to see Marlee hurt. But his desire to see Lark suffer overrode his good judgment. Sloane hated his half brother and anything he could do to add to his suffering was fine with him. He realized that Lark loved the beautiful and innocent Lady Marlee Arden. What better way to gain vengeance upon Lark than through Marlee's discovery of the truth about Silva's captured mistress.

"Will you help me, Captain Mason? Please help me," came Marlee's breathy voice filled with such childish hope that Sloane shivered to think of the dismay she'd feel once she learned the truth.

But anything was worth his brother's suffering. Anything.

"I'll help you," he found himself saying and took the ring back to place on his little finger. "Can you be ready to set sail tonight?"

Marlee quickly nodded. "Thank you for helping me. I appreciate it. I think deep down that you must be a very kind man."

"Ah, my lady, how gullible you are, but if that's

what you wish to think then I won't say differently." He shook his diamond-clad finger at her. "I have a reputation of doing anything for the right price."

By flickering candlelight, Marlee penned a note to Beatrix and Governor Rogers, thanking them for their hospitality. She hoped they wouldn't be upset by her sudden disappearance. Absent from her note was the fact that she was sailing away with Sloane Mason, but she assured her hosts that she was in capable hands and not to worry.

Marlee wasn't the least bit worried. Somehow she knew that she'd see Manuel Silva and would talk him into releasing Lark's friend. The pirate had to listen to her. Her future with Lark depended upon it.

Placing the white parchment atop the bureau drawer in her room, Marlee quietly took two dresses and undergarments from the sea chest and packed them in a small valise. For some odd reason she placed the golden locket with the auburn-haired woman's miniature around her neck, concealing it beneath her bodice. When she was certain she was ready, she blew out the candle and sneaked away from the house. Nearing the beach, she stopped short as a tall, dark figure approached her. For a second she thought the man was Lark, and her heart began an erratic beat as her feet propelled her closer. But when she was within a few yards she slowed her pace. The man was Sloane.

He flashed her a smile that was as bright as the moonlight beaming down upon them. "I decided to escort you to my ship," he told her and took her hand to lead her down the beach. "The crew is on board and all is in readiness."

Suddenly doubt assailed Marlee. Was she doing the right thing by rushing away into the night with a man who was virtually a stranger to her? She could almost hear Clementina's shrill voice, telling her that she had little sense, that Sloane Mason was of dubious reputation.

But so was Lark, the man whom she loved.

"Where are we going?" she asked, hoping that once she knew their destination, she'd stop feeling uneasy.

"Saint Augustine," Sloane unhesitatingly told her. "But you must promise me something."

"What?"

"Don't tell anyone afterward where Silva is hiding."

"I should tell Lark."

"Especially not Lark." Sloane stopped walking and looked directly at her. "Promise me this, otherwise, I won't take you to Silva."

"Are you and Silva friends?"

"Let's just say that we have an agreement of sorts. I respect his privacy and he respects mine."

"Doesn't your crew know our destination? Won't they say anything? What about Lark's friend? He'll undoubtedly tell Lark where Silva has been hiding—"

"Marlee, my crew doesn't divulge what I do or they suffer the consequences. As for Lark's—friend—well, I have a feeling that this friend may not be too quick to leave Saint Augustine."

"I don't understand," Marlee protested but Sloane placed a finger on her lips.

"Just do as I ask, my lady."

Marlee understood there would be no bargaining with Sloane over this, so she nodded. "I promise but I don't care for all this secrecy."

"Keeping secrets makes life all the more interesting, my lady. Didn't you know that?" He smiled roguishly at her and she followed after him until they came to the docks where Sloane stopped before a midsized ship that bobbed gently in the waves beside a larger one. Sloane bowed lowly. "May I present *The Merry Bandit,* my lady. I hope your trip shall be comfortable."

What an odd name for a ship, Marlee mused and couldn't help thinking that the name suited its captain perfectly. Taking her arm to escort her up the boarding plank, Marlee's face was highlighted by a lantern that hung nearby on a post. They were stalled from going further when a voice called Marlee's name from the deck of the larger ship. Immediately Marlee stiffened and pointed her gaze in the caller's direction. It was Captain Lundstrum.

"Lady Arden! Lady Arden, is that you?"

She looked helplessly at Sloane and then at

Lundstrum, realizing that the man had recognized her. "Yes, Captain," she said lowly.

"Wait just a minute, my lady. I wish to speak with you." Captain Lundstrum hurried from the quarterdeck of his ship.

"God, help us, that gossipy Dutchman will have the news of your leaving all over the island within hours," groused Sloane.

Before Marlee was able to reply, Lundstrum came up beside her with a worried and speculative expression. "My lady, I hadn't anticipated seeing you so soon. We're not due to sail until the morrow. And *The Merry Bandit* isn't my ship."

"I-I've changed my plans, Captain. I shall be sailing with Captain Mason."

"For England?" Lundstrum probed and cast a wary eye over Marlee and Sloane.

Marlee was never very good at lying and she could barely drag a "yes" from her lips, however, she was saved from replying when Sloane intervened. "Certainly for England. Where else would Lady Arden be headed?"

"With you captaining the ship, Mason, it could be headed for hell," Lundstrum wryly observed and puffed on his pipe. "Tell me, your ladyship, is Captain Arden aware of your change in plans?"

Marlee shook her head. "Er, no, he isn't."

"Well, I think you should wait here until Lark returns."

"Heavens sakes, man, Arden doesn't own her!"

208

Sloane scornfully exclaimed. "No one's forcing her to sail with me."

Lundstrum could see the truth of that statement. Lady Arden was clutching a small valise which meant that she'd packed and was ready to sail away with Mason. It didn't appear that she was doing anything under duress. But Lundstrum didn't trust Sloane Mason. He'd heard too many unsavory things concerning the man's overall reputation, including his reputation with women. He'd have sworn that Lady Arden was in love with Lark, and he with her. Lark was so worried over her safe return to England, and there was just something about the way she'd looked at Lark on the day he'd gone to Governor Rogers's home to meet the pretty young woman. He'd have sworn the two people were in love. But apparently not. Lundstrum sensed there was something going on between Lady Arden and Sloane Mason, just what he didn't know. However, something wasn't right.

"You are happy to be sailing with Mason?" Lundstrum asked her and gauged her response.

"Of course, sir. I'm sorry I didn't inform you about my change in plans. That was very rude of me. Please forgive me." Marlee spoke in a rush, the words tumbling out of her mouth. She must assure Lundstrum she was all right, otherwise, he might stop her from leaving with Sloane. And nothing was more important to her than finding Manuel Silva.

Lundstrum's gaze moved slowly over them, and, finally, he bowed. "I wish you a fair weather voyage, my lady."

"Thank you, Captain."

"Now that Arden's watchdog is satisfied," Sloane whispered and hurried Marlee up the boarding plank and away from Lundstrum's watchful gaze, "let me show you to your cabin. I think you'll be pleased with it."

At that moment, Marlee didn't care about her cabin. She was worried about what was going to happen once they reached St. Augustine. Everything must be all right, she decided. Nothing was more important than convincing Silva to release Lark's friend. Nothing was more important than proving to Lark that she'd braved a notorious pirate to prove how much she loved him. And once he knew the depths of her feelings for him, then he'd have to marry her. He loved her, he'd told her that. Soon there would be nothing to keep them apart.

Soon they'd be married and their life would begin—together.

Neils Lundstrum watched as *The Merry Bandit* lifted anchor and sailed smoothly out of the harbor. He had a great deal to do before departing in the morning and very little time in which to do it. But he did take the time to write a note to Governor Rogers, informing him that Lady Arden had sailed away with Sloane Mason, and had his cabin boy deliver it to the governor. He'd leave telling Lark Arden about it to Rogers.

Chapter Seventeen

The sun-drenched shore of Anastasia Island beckoned in the distance. From her cabin window, Marlee could see the surf gently kissing the sandy shore as *The Merry Bandit* entered Matanzas Bay. She'd been on Sloane's ship for nearly five days now, having lost a day due to a sudden fierce storm which had seeped terror into her heart. As much as she'd enjoyed her sailing time with Lark, she now couldn't wait to be off of Sloane's ship. Not only had the storm frightened her but Sloane did, too.

There was something disturbing in the lustful way his eyes raked over her when he didn't think she was watching. He hadn't overtly offended her, touching her only when it was necessary, but she sensed he wanted to do more than take her elbow as he guided her about the ship. Her mind replayed Lark's warning about Sloane. She couldn't help remembering the girl who had drowned herself when Sloane refused to marry her. So far, Marlee didn't really have cause to distrust him. He'd been solicitous of her, more than friendly and eager to help. But he was too eager and this disturbed her more than his secretive glances.

"Soon it will be over," she assured herself. As soon as she saw Manuel Silva and pleaded with him to release Lark's friend, she could breathe easier.

A light tap sounded on her cabin door and she knew it was Sloane before he entered at her summons. How very handsome he is, she thought to herself, almost a duplicate of Lark. But again, she felt uneasy with Sloane, finding cause to wonder what secrets he hid behind his mirthful blue eyes.

"We'll be anchoring soon," he informed her and threw himself indolently into a chair. "I'll seek out Silva for you and arrange an interview. It's best if I discover how the wind blows before you come ashore."

"Yes, I suppose it is," Marlee said with worry in her eyes. "What will I do if Silva doesn't agree to see me?"

Sloane stifled a laugh. "My lady, Silva will see you once I tell him how beautiful you are. In fact, Silva's greatest flaw is his weakness for beautiful women. He'll do just about anything for a pretty lady."

Marlee stiffened and regarded Sloane coldly. "Please make it clear to Silva that I have a business proposition to offer him. Releasing Lark's friend is the only reason I've come to St. Augustine. What I look like has no bearing on why I'm here."

"If you say so," Sloane conceded but chuckled as he stood up. His index finger caressed her cheek. "Still it doesn't hurt to be pretty, my lady."

Marlee noticed the lustful gleam in his eyes again and purposely moved herself out of his way. "I'm ready to depart whenever you tell me," she said with a touch of haughtiness in her stance. She hoped to be off of this ship soon.

Manuel Silva rose above the auburn-haired vixen who lay naked and writhing upon his bed. Her fair wrists were tied to the bedposts with strands of silken cord. With each twisting motion of her body, her full breasts quivered and drove Manuel to the brink of climax. She was his prisoner, his captive wanton. Soon he'd spill himself into her, releasing the pent-up lust he could no longer seem to find except in perverse play.

"Ah, *querida,* you drive me insane," he whispered into her ear and stroked her nipples until she mewled in pleasure. "Are you ready for me? Tell me you are ready for I am about to burst."

Her hips arched upward, moving in unison with Silva's. Passion wreathed her face, sparks of desire danced within the depths of her green eyes — eyes which Silva had told her resembled a greedy tigress's. And greedy she was; she wanted all of him and feared losing him. It had been so long since he'd enjoyed her that she wondered if he might be growing bored with her. It had been a stroke of genius on her part that she'd thought of the silk ribbons and told Manuel to tie her up and have his way with her. She found she loved being helpless — and that Manuel enjoyed it, too, made the game all the more delightful. She moaned, feeling him thrusting into her, his largeness filling every crevice of her womanhood until she could stand the pleasure no longer.

"*Si*, Manuel, *si*," she gasped. The moment of release washed over them, leaving them drained and panting.

"You are a wanton witch, Bettina." He nibbled on her ear later and stroked the wet spot between her thighs. "You make me want you again."

"Ah, *si*, my darling, I want you, too." She began writhing again, loving the way her dark-haired pirate stroked her softness. She was ready again, always ready for him because he was her salvation, her life, now.

Manuel lifted himself up, poised to enter her, when a knock sounded on the door. "What is it?" he shouted irritably at the servant.

"There is a gentleman to see you, Señor Manuel. His name is Sloane Mason. He—he will not go away." Doña Carlotta sounded as if she were about to cry.

Manuel lifted his head in bafflement, his eyes narrowed to slits. "I wonder what the bastard wants." He barked at the elderly woman on the opposite side of the door, "Have Mason wait in the dining room for me."

Bettina kissed him, imploring him with her hands on his buttocks, enticing him not to leave her. "Finish, Manuel, please finish," she begged and kneaded the hard flesh with her fingers.

Manuel grinned down at Bettina's flushed face. "You beg so wantonly, *querida,* that I cannot refuse you."

And he didn't. He gave her what she craved, but seconds after he'd found his release, Manuel got up and began to dress. Bettina sat up and pulled the sheet around her voluptuous body. Her mouth formed into a pretty pout. "You treat me like a whore, Manuel."

He finished pulling his white-laced shirt over his head and sat on the bed to pull his boots on. "Bettina, you know what you are to me. I have to see this Sloane Mason."

"I don't care about this person, whoever he may be," Bettina snapped and her eyes sparked fire. "I don't know what I am to you. I'm mistress of your house, Manuel, but what else?"

Manuel stroked his short, dark beard for a second. Should he tell Bettina that he'd grown tired of her, that he grew tired of women very quickly? This one, however, had been different from the others. He'd captured her off of an English ship, and the only reason he'd kept her for so long was because she *was* English. Her beautiful skin was the most translucent and pale he'd ever seen, her hair was the most vivid shade of red, and her lips were the color of rubies — unlike the whores he'd bedded. But her real fascination was that she'd been a pirate hunter's intended bride. She'd belonged to Lark Arden—a man he detested because he tried so hard to capture him. Silva had taken the woman as compensation for the treasures Arden had stolen from him by confiscating other pirate ships and returning the booty to the English on New Providence. The stupid man had attempted to put him out of business until Silva had blown Arden and his ship out of the water.

But Silva had kept Bettina. She belonged to him just as long as he wanted her. The wench thought he treated her like a whore, which is exactly what Silva thought her to be. It turned out she was really no different from the other women he'd known. He'd thought he was taking her virginity the first time he took her, but he discovered she'd faked her "deflowering." She'd known exactly what to do and took an active part in the whole process. He thought he'd heighten his own enjoyment by passing her around to select members of his crew while he watched, but the English beauty had found pleasure with all of them. He'd never forget the way she'd looked after they'd finished with her. *Dios!* she'd been more beautiful and wanton than he'd ever imagined, and it was Bettina's insatiable appetite which made him want her all the more—which caused him to claim her exclusively as his own.

Now she resented that he treated her like a whore. Were all women as silly as this one? Didn't she realize that he would never marry such a one as this? She wasn't pure enough to bear his name or his children. Somehow he would have to be rid of her, but how and when?

He smacked her on the buttocks. "I have business dealings, *querida,* and can't be bothered with your woman's silliness."

"Silliness? I am not silly, you loathsome piece of vermin, I am not—"

Manuel grabbed Bettina by the wrists and pulled her up to him. "Never call me that! You forget that I could have used you and then killed you, throwing your body to be used as fish food, when I took you from that ship. Instead, I brought you here to my home and have pampered you, giving you clothes and jewels and sex, everything you crave."

"What about love?" she asked defiantly, though she shook like mulberry leaves in a tempest. Silva's temper was one thing which she couldn't control. She could ably control his passion, but when he was angry she didn't know what he would do.

He leered at her and whispered hotly against her ear, "You love only yourself, *querida.*" Then he let her go and she dropped to the mattress on her knees and said nothing else, because he was right.

Sloane extended a hand to Silva, finding the swarthy pirate had changed very little since they'd last met. Silva's hair was raven black, his eyes a deep shade of brown that flashed with amusement in his tanned face. The offer of a cup of port was eagerly accepted by Sloane since it was known far and wide that Silva only served the best brew, confiscated from the most prized ships.

"I appreciate your seeing me, Manuel. To be honest, I'm surprised that I arrived in one piece. You've got some very fierce guards at your gate."

"Hmm, *si*," Manuel said and considered Sloane between slow sips of his port. "I pay my men well, so they are loyal to me."

"Loyalty, I find, is something which can't be bought."

A grin split Manuel's lips. *"Si, amigo.* You're proof of that fact. My money didn't sway you to remain with me. Tell me, how is your English friend, Governor Rogers?"

"Very well. To be honest with you, I've brought a friend with me who is eager to meet you and offer you a business proposition."

"Really? Who might this friend be?"

Sloane forged on, not entirely certain he should do this at all, but he needed to settle accounts with Lark. He needed Marlee to meet Silva and see Bettina with her own eyes. "Lady Marlee Arden."

The color left the pirate's face. "Arden? Is she related to Lark Arden?"

"Yes, from what I understand she's the widow of his cousin. And she's very wealthy, willing to part with a fortune to earn your goodwill."

"What could I possibly offer her in exchange for this fortune?"

"Lady Bettina."

Manuel considered Sloane with a jaundiced eye. "I think you better tell me what this is all about, *amigo,* and where you fit into this plan."

Sloane lifted his cup in a tribute to Silva. No wonder Lark hadn't been able to best this crafty sea fox. The man always anticipated another's angle before making any sort of a move.

"There won't be any trouble, will there?" Marlee asked Sloane from the inside of Silva's richly appointed carriage. "I'm so nervous about all of this."

Sloane patted her hand. "If there was going to be trouble, do you think we'd be riding in Silva's very own carriage and going to his home? Do you think I'd place you in danger, Marlee? I swear I wouldn't."

"I hope I can trust you," she said and looked unabashedly into his eyes.

"You can," he assured her in all solemnity. "I won't allow Silva to harm you."

Somehow she believed him.

From the moment Sloane had returned to the ship and told her to dress for her audience with the notorious Manuel Silva, her stomach had been fluttering as if a butterfly had taken up residence. The gown she'd chosen was a deep wine-colored silk with tiny green bows on the sleeves to match the

220

satin underskirt. She'd worn her hair atop her head, threading the curls with a green ribbon. She'd felt she looked fine except for the low bodice of the gown, so she'd worn the gold locket to draw attention away from her breasts. She knew she must hope Silva found her attractive enough to release Lark's friend—but not too attractive.

"Smile, Marlee. You look like you're going to be gobbled up by a troll."

"No," she said, shaking her head at Sloane, "only a pirate."

Marlee found that Manuel Silva wasn't the fearsome dragon she'd expected. He was still a handsome and robust man for his forty years, and though he wore a tiny gold earring in his ear, she wasn't frightened of him. His manners were impeccable, his bearing was kingly. She couldn't believe the horrible stories she'd heard about him from Lark. But she hadn't been on Lark's ship when Silva had blown it to bits and kidnapped Lark's friend. Perhaps there was an evil side to the well-dressed and polite pirate. But at the moment, he was doing his best to be most charming—and succeeding.

He took her hand and politely kissed it. "May I say, Lady Arden, that you are quite beautiful. Sloane didn't lie to me about that."

"Thank you, Señor Silva. I appreciate your taking the time to see me."

"May I offer you a glass of port before supper?" he asked in a honey-smooth voice.

"Er, no, thank you." Marlee glanced quickly at Sloane who leaned against the door frame. Sloane hadn't told her they were invited to supper.

"As you wish, my lady." Manuel poured himself and Sloane a cup of port. He rang a bell and instantly a small, elderly lady appeared. "Please inform Lady Bettina that we shall soon dine," he told the woman who was dressed all in black, even the mantilla she wore on her gray hair was black. "Is she over her pout yet, Doña Carlotta?"

"*Si, señor.* She will soon be dressed and at table."

"*Bueno.*" He waved the woman away with a careless hand and turned his attention upon Marlee. "How do you like my home?" he asked.

Marlee appraised the lavish surroundings, finding everything to be strikingly lovely. The house had only two stories, much smaller than Montclair, but it was set prettily in a garden that was overrun with greenery and the sweet scent of orange trees that were planted outside past the patio doors. The furniture placed in what she'd heard Silva refer to earlier as the *"sala,"* was heavy in appearance. The chairs were covered in a red brocade material with tiny specks of gold and the divan was upholstered in a dark red velvet, so heavy of material that Marlee grew warm just looking at it. The candelabra on the ceiling illuminated the entire room, and though the furnishings were attractive, the walls seemed swathed in dark, dancing shadows.

"Your house is very nice," she complimented Silva. She couldn't help wondering how a pirate could own such a richly appointed house in what seemed to her to be a respectable neighborhood.

"I'm relieved you like it, my lady." His dark eyes roamed familiarly over her. "Very glad you like it. My wish is only to please you."

"Why?"

Silva appeared confused by Marlee's direct question. "I don't understand, my lady."

Marlee placed her hands in her lap and looked probingly at the pirate. "Why do you care what I think? Why should you want to please me? I'm not here for a social call, Señor Silva, as you well know."

"Madre de Dios!" he lowly exclaimed and indicated Sloane with a nod of his head. "Captain Mason was right about you, my lady. You *are* very direct." He stroked his beard, thoughtfully assessing her. "To be honest with you, I'm not used to such directness in a woman."

"I trust you realize why I've come to see you."

"Sí, Sloane told me."

"Did Sloane also tell you that I'm very wealthy, that I'm willing to pay your price to release Lark Arden's friend?"

"He did."

"Then I shall like to negotiate his release as soon as possible."

Silva's eyes danced with merriment, and he took

223

Marlee by the hand and brought her to her feet. "Señora, please dine with me first before we begin such ponderous negotiations. I assure you that the "fellow" you seek to free is quite comfortable and very happy."

"I doubt a prisoner is happy, sir," she replied a bit too heatedly.

"Ah, you wound me with your mistrust, my lady." Silva laid a hand on his chest and heaved a sigh. "Assure Lady Arden," he said to Sloane, "that I am a trustworthy fellow."

"He's trustworthy," Sloane snapped out, but he was scowling darkly.

Those were the first words that Sloane Mason had spoken since she'd been introduced to the wily Silva. Marlee wondered why Sloane had been silent for so long, why suddenly she felt something was amiss. As the pirate led her into the dining room, she was all too aware that the amused smirk on Silva's face bode nothing good.

They were seated at the dining table. The soft glow from the candles lent a softness to the room, a mellowness which Marlee didn't feel. Her insides churned with a slow, steady thread of fear. She tried to convince herself that she was overreacting, that the stories concerning Silva had affected her judgment of the man. There was nothing evil about him, unless one could say the gold earring was daunting, that the way his dark-eyed gaze devoured her was unsettling. But she'd been devoured by another man with ebony eyes and had liked that immensely. This was different and more unnerving than even Sloane's lustful looks.

Sloane. He was no help at all to her. She'd hoped that he'd somehow champion her cause, but now she was under the odd impression that he was in league with Silva. They were too chummy for Marlee's liking. She remembered things Sloane had said about the man—their mutual respect for each other. The old saying "Birds of a feather fly together" came to mind about these two.

Nervously she fingered the locket. Had she placed her trust in the wrong place?

"My lady, you aren't eating your turtle soup," Silva admonished lightly. "My cook shall think you don't like it."

"It's very tasty," she quickly assured Silva. "I just don't seem to have much of an appetite."

"Ah, I think you've been too long among sailors and poor food," he observed with a sly smile. "After you're in Saint Augustine for a while and eat only the best, your appetite will improve."

"But I don't plan to be here for very long—" Marlee began but was cut off by Silva's impatient ringing of a small bell. The summons was immediately answered by the tiny, black-clad woman who'd appeared in the *sala* earlier.

"Doña Carlotta, where is Lady Bettina?" he harshly asked the woman who seemed to cower and grow smaller with each syllable he uttered. "Her soup is growing cold and she has yet to grace us with her presence."

"I don't know, señor. I told her you were expecting her but she—"

"Leave Doña Carlotta alone, Manuel. I'm here." The voice which broke into the old woman's words was lyrical and soft. All eyes turned on the beautiful auburn-haired woman who seemed to glide into the dining room. Dressed in a gold and green satin gown, her brilliant and flawless smile rivaled the diamond and emerald-studded choker at her neck. She was clearly one of the most breathtakingly beautiful women Marlee had ever seen. Apparently Sloane thought so, too, for his enraptured gaze never left the woman. Marlee watched her, too, for a different reason. She couldn't help but wonder why the woman seemed so familiar to her.

Manuel and Sloane rose in unison. As Manuel helped her to her seat, the woman glanced at Marlee for only a second before smiling warmly at Manuel. "You're just too sweet to me, my love," she endearingly murmured and patted the pirate's hand.

The woman was English. Marlee realized it almost immediately. Why was an Englishwoman living under Silva's roof?

"May I present Lady Bettina Gilbert to you." Silva spoke to Marlee and Sloane. He introduced Sloane to Lady Bettina first, something Marlee thought was incredibly rude, but finally he said to Bettina, "And may I present to you, my dear, the

226

Baroness of Montclair, the Lady Marlee Arden."

Bettina's dazzling smile diminished and she played with the choker. "Arden, did you say?"

"Yes, your ladyship," Marlee spoke up.

The woman's face was very pale now, and Marlee wondered if she might be ill. "Are you related to the Ardens of Virginia? I—I knew some of them once—through my father," she hurriedly amended.

"I'm the widow of Lord Richard Arden of Cornwall. He was related to the Arden family of Virginia." Marlee saw no reason to mention her relationship to Lark. Bettina didn't need to know anything about that.

"I see," Bettina said, almost in relief, and placed the napkin in her lap. "Excuse my tardiness. Shall we dine now? I trust Cook has outdone herself this time. The soup smells delicious.

As the four people dined on turtle soup and the most succulent chicken dish Marlee had ever eaten, the room grew quiet, almost too quiet for Marlee's liking. After a brief spell of silence, Manuel lifted his cup of wine in Marlee's direction. "To you, Lady Arden, one of the most beautiful women to grace my humble table. May our business together bring success to both of us."

Bettina's sharp eyes took in the way Silva looked at Marlee and the gracious way she'd acknowledged the toast. Sitting across the table from her, Sloane Mason smirked, and she'd have sworn whatever amused him so much concerned her—and Marlee Arden. She didn't care for the way Silva constantly

227

included the brunette in conversation, taking pains to be gallant. She'd been wooed in the very same way not too long ago. Was Silva about to displace her in his affections and his home with Marlee Arden?

Her mouth hardened into a very unpleasant and hard-looking line. She wouldn't allow this woman to take her place in Silva's bed. Manuel was all that she had. She couldn't return to Bermuda, now that he'd thoroughly debauched her. There would be too much speculation, too many rumors to live down. No one would accept her if the truth of what happened aboard Silva's ship ever was told. Being turned over to a band of pirates was information she never wanted anyone in polite circles to know—but if the news that she'd enjoyed every second of the orgy ever got out, she'd be ruined for life. No one would accept her—not even her own parents or other family members. She had no alternative but to remain on Saint Augustine with Manuel as his mistress—or his wife if he'd consent to wed her.

And no simpering innocent was going to ruin her life.

Chapter Eighteen

"Now we shall discuss the release of Captain Arden's friend," Manuel Silva said and puffed on a cheroot. His sharp-eyed glance encompassed Marlee who demurely sat in the *sala* and sipped a glass of port. The meal had progressed pleasantly enough, but the knots in Marlee's stomach tightened when the pirate had insisted their conversation be a private one. The last time she'd seen Sloane he'd been leading Lady Bettina into the garden for a stroll.

She was alone without a soul to help her. She must keep her wits about her.

"My offer is a generous one." Marlee decided not to mince words or waste time. She wanted this issue settled so she could leave St. Augustine and wait for Lark's return on New Providence.

"I'm certain it is, but what if my price is too high?"

"I trust you'll be reasonable, Señor Silva, and understand that the money will be sent to you as soon as my solicitor in England is notified."

"Ah, that is most disturbing. I had assumed the money was near at hand."

His words upset her. Perhaps he wouldn't release Lark's friend now. "I had hoped you'd understand my situation and would wait for the money to be sent to you. You have my word on this, señor."

"Call me Manuel, please." He grinned wolfishly at her and settled himself familiarly beside her on the divan. "It isn't that I don't trust you," he said and gently stroked the back of her hand which she instantly drew away. He didn't seem upset by her action, seeming to half expect it. "But you must realize that I don't understand your situation, as you say, and I can't be certain that I'll receive the money. You see, I don't trust the English." He blew a smoke ring and leaned against the cushions.

This wasn't going as she'd planned. Nervously, she licked her lips. "You can trust me—Manuel."

"Manuel is it? You may not be as innocent as I thought, *querida,* for you're playing games with me now. But I'm used to such things with women. Now tell me what Lark Arden means to you. Why do you go to such lengths to release a person you don't know? You must realize that I thought I was rid of Arden when I destroyed his ship. Once again, he has surfaced and is obsessed with killing me. I think you don't truly know Lark Arden. Are you in love with him?"

"Yes," she replied, ever honest, perhaps too honest. "I love him and hope we shall be married."

"Hmm, *querida*. I was wrong about you and apologize. You are an innocent, and a very bewitching one."

Marlee grew exasperated with his compliments and leering looks. "Sir, I haven't all night! Do you plan to release Captain Arden's friend?"

Amusement glowed on his face as he took another puff and rose to his feet. "Beauty, innocence, and a temper—an intriguing combination in a woman." He bowed gallantly. "I bend to your will, *querida*. Arden's friend shall be released this night."

"Oh, Señor Silva, thank you!" She knew she was gushing but she didn't care. Finally, she'd convinced Silva to release his prisoner. Lark could stop feeling guilty, he could put the vengeance aside. Now they could be married. Marlee's dearest wish was about to come true.

"You're more than lovely, Lady Arden," he said and kissed her hand. "More than welcome, too."

"Shall Lark's friend come here soon?" Marlee wondered aloud, not the least swayed by his gallantry.

"His friend is here already."

"Here? In the house?"

"*Si*. Just as soon as she can pack her bags, Lady Bettina can leave with Captain Sloane."

Marlee felt as if the wind were knocked out of her. "Lady Bettina is—" She could barely speak the words but Silva finished the sentence for her.

"Lark Arden's friend, my lady, or should I say his fiancée."

"That can't be—I don't be-believe you." She was stammering like an idiot, standing before Manuel Silva in a daze.

Manuel shrugged. "It's the truth. You're surprised to learn of your lover's engagement to Bettina." He made a tsk-tsking sound. "You must be disappointed to learn of it, to realize Arden kept the truth from you. As I said earlier, I don't trust the English." Extending his arm to her, he smiled. "Shall we go tell Bettina the happy news?"

"Leave? You want me to leave?" Bettina's shrill cries echoed from the bedroom while Marlee and Sloane waited on the patio. Silva's monotoned syllables followed the outburst, but the air was again punctuated by Bettina's shrieks. "You bastard! I hate you!"

"It seems Bettina isn't pleased about leaving her captor," Sloane observed wryly and puffed on a cheroot his host had given him.

Marlee barely heard him. Her mind wasn't on Sloane or even Bettina's deafening shouts. All she could think about was what Silva had told her— Bettina was Lark's fiancée. Emotionally, she felt numbed by the news. At first, she was unable to believe him, wouldn't believe him. But then things started to make sense to her. Lark had never told her anything about his captured "friend," not even giving her a name. She'd just assumed the person had been a man, but now she knew the name and felt that a sharp knife had forever etched it upon her heart. Lady Bettina Gilbert.

She found herself fingering the gold locket and looked at it. The engraved letters, B.G. shone ominously in the torchlight. She didn't open the locket—she didn't have to. She knew whose face would be staring at her. A sob threatened to choke her. Lark had hoodwinked her again.

"You knew about Bettina the whole time," she found herself saying to Sloane. "You knew what she is—to Lark."

"I admit that I did."

"And you wanted to hurt me."

"Not hurt you," Sloane hurriedly assured her, "but Lark. I knew his feelings for you and I wanted to hurt him by having you see Bettina and learn the truth for yourself. I hoped you'd turn away from Lark in the process, but I didn't think Silva would agree to release her to us." Sloane frowned worriedly.

"You hate your brother very much, don't you?"

Nodding, Sloane carelessly tossed the cheroot into a fish pond. "I hate him more than anybody in this world."

Marlee didn't hide her resentment or her pain. "Should I be grateful that you hate me less? What I feel now is unbearable, horrible—" She ceased speaking as tears welled in her throat.

Sloane bent down and touched her chin. "I never meant to hurt you so much, only Lark. Please find it in your heart to forgive me. Here, I'm returning this to you." He took the diamond ring that she'd given to him as payment out of his pocket and placed it in her hand.

She gazed in repulsed horror at it, feeling as if the fiery diamond burned her flesh. This was Bettina's ring, the ring Lark had no doubt presented to her to seal their engagement. She didn't want the blasted thing, hated the sight of it. "I don't want this!" she heatedly protested and would have said more except Silva suddenly appeared, dragging a disheveled and defiant Bettina behind him.

"Lady Bettina is ready for her voyage back to the arms of her beloved," he ground out through a mouth that was formed in the shape of a harsh, taut line. He halted his step in midstride, causing Bettina to nearly fall. Sloane reached out and steadied the furious woman who cast a malevolent eye upon Silva.

"Hateful bastard. You know very well that Lark won't want me now!"

Silva leered down at her. "That is your problem, *querida*. Perhaps you should have curbed your amorous appetite, hmmm?"

"God! How I hate you!" Bettina's fingers curled into claws and she went for his face, but he quickly discerned her intention and grabbed her wrists, holding her at arm's length.

"That isn't what you said this morning, my love." He thrust her toward Sloane. "Take the whore to her beloved Lark and be done with it."

Sloane appeared uncertain, but he took Bettina by the arm and quietly urged her toward the wrought-iron gate at the edge of the courtyard. Marlee began to follow suit, but Silva reached out with a hand that could only be deemed ironlike and held her in place. "Dearest Lady Arden, you're not going with them."

"Yes, I am, señor. Our business is settled here."

"Sorry, *querida,* but no. You're staying with me."

Marlee didn't know what was happening, why Silva refused to let her leave, but from the rigid expression on his face she knew he wasn't joking. He meant her to stay. "I'm sorry," she said and gulped, "but I'm returning to *The Merry Bandit* with Captain Mason."

"And I say you're not."

"Manuel, what are you doing? This wasn't part of the plan." Sloane came forward and reached out for Marlee, but Silva bellowed in Spanish and immediately armed guards appeared.

"Touch Lady Arden again, Sloane, and Bettina will be making her voyage alone." The ominous threat wasn't lost on Sloane, and he backed away.

"You can't keep her here," Sloane warned, and there was a frantic, plaintive note in his voice. "Lark will come after her."

"Ah, my friend, I hope he does. I hope he does so I can end his miserable life once and for all."

Marlee made an aborted attempt at struggling, but Silva was far too strong for her. "I won't stay here. You can't keep me here."

"I can and I will, *querida*." Silva leaned down and whispered hotly in her ear, "I decided that I have enough money, that I should like something else for releasing Bettina to her dear fiancé. Let's say I have something more pleasurable in mind for my payment—something so pleasant that you shall swoon from the ecstasy of it."

"You're mad," she proclaimed through pale, trembling lips. "I'll not stay here. I won't."

She started to push against him, but Silva's hands tightened painfully on her arms. "Rail against me, my wild English rose, and Mason is a dead man." His dark eyes glittered with malevolent intent.

Marlee stopped fighting when she noticed two of the armed men circling Sloane with their swords brandished. No matter that Sloane had withheld the truth from her, she didn't want him harmed. Her apparent acquiescence delighted Silva, and he smiled a chillingly lewd smile before he spoke to his minions. "Escort Captain Mason and Lady Gilbert to his ship—and make certain he leaves Saint Augustine and doesn't double back."

Sloane shook off one of the men's hold on his

arm. "You'll pay for this, Manuel. I'll make certain you do."

A malicious smirk turned up the corners of Silva's mouth as he waved his hand toward his men. "Take them to the ship," he ordered. Immediately Sloane and Bettina were led away and Marlee was alone with the leering Manuel Silva. "Well, Lady Arden, the hour grows late. I'll have Doña Carlotta show you to your room."

"I won't be a docile prisoner, I can assure you of that."

"Ah, *querida,* you're my guest, not a prisoner," Silva corrected her. "But I'd advise against trying to escape. My men are everywhere."

"Why are you doing this? I don't understand why—"

Silva cut off Marlee's sentence with an arm around her waist as he pulled her roughly toward him. "You don't need to understand my reasons, you need only to obey me."

"I won't obey you," was her hot declaration. "You don't own me!"

"No? I say I do. From this day onward, I own you body and soul, Marlee." He breathed her name like a warm wind against her cheek, sending ripples of repulsion through her. "And if you believe your beloved Lark shall rescue you, he won't. He shall soon have his Bettina again by his side, and you'll be only a sweet memory. But you'll be more than that to me, *querida,* much more." His hand stroked

237

the side of her breast and he grinned wickedly. "I'll not bother you tonight, but soon, I promise you. Soon you'll belong to me, my innocent English rose."

She couldn't stop the trembling sensations which wracked her as moments later, Doña Carlotta appeared to lead her through a hallway to a bedroom at the back of the house. The old woman lighted a wall sconce and barely glanced at her. "This is your room, señora. I've placed a nightgown on the bed for you. It's one which my lady Bettina never wore."

Marlee barely took in the pretty brocaded coverlet and matching drapes which were closed, barring any moonlight from entering the room. Her eyes burned with unshed tears, and she willed herself not to cry in front of Doña Carlotta. No doubt the woman thought she was Manuel Silva's new mistress, that she'd willingly come here. And God help her, she had come to St. Augustine of her own accord. No one had forced her. Nothing had brought her here but her own foolish heart and dreams.

But no longer would Lark, or any other man, play her for a fool. In her hand she still clutched the diamond ring, a vivid and painful reminder of the woman who'd once worn it and of the man who'd given it to her. She placed it on her trembling finger and peered at the glittering stone for a long time. She'd wear the ring as a reminder of what Lark had done to her. Never would she forget how he'd ruined her life.

"Captain Silva awaits your presence in the dining room," Doña Carlotta informed Marlee the next night.

"Tell him I'm not hungry," she told the elderly woman. In reality, Marlee was starving but she wouldn't give Silva the satisfaction of dining with him.

Doña Carlotta wrung her hands together. "Please, you must come downstairs to table. You didn't eat your midday meal, and I don't wish you to fall ill. He'll be most displeased with me—if you get sick."

For the first time Marlee really looked at the old woman and felt extremely sad for her. Doña Carlotta's thin frame trembled, and Marlee realized that the woman was terrified of Silva's wrath. "How do you come to be here?" she asked her gently.

"Ah, señora, such a tale of woe I could tell you." Doña Carlotta anxiously bit her lip. "In a way, we're both prisoners of Manuel Silva. This house belonged to my late husband, Juan Delgado. He was a powerful and kind man, but he made the mistake of having dealings with a sordid and despicable pirate—"

"Silva," Marlee interrupted.

Doña Carlotta's expression became harsh. "*Sí*. I

had no idea that my husband owed Silva money, a great deal if Silva is to be believed. When Juan died, Silva appeared at my door like a carrion, ready to rip the life out of me in my time of grief. He claimed my home with the governor's knowledge, took all from me. I was distraught, so unhappy." She sniffed into a lace kerchief she took from her pocket.

"How is it that you're a servant? Did Silva take pity upon you?"

Carlotta glanced up in disbelief and scorn. "That one has no heart, señora. Silva is an evil man. The only reason I am here is because he'd captured that red-haired creature and brought her here soon after my Juan died. She was a lady, or so he told me, and she needed someone to look after her. Lady," she spat as if the word tasted vile upon her lips, "the town whore was more of lady than that one!" Calming down, she wiped the tears from her eyes. "I cared for her because it was a way to stay in my home, to keep what was mine, though nothing belongs to me as long as Silva lives here. I do love it when he sails away. Then I can imagine the house is mine, I can relive happy memories—until he returns, which is much too often for my liking. I wish that evil man would sail away and stay away—forever."

Marlee wished that, too. Her heart filled with pity for the old lady. "Does Silva beat you if he is displeased with you?"

240

Carlotta shook her head. "No, but I fear him just the same. His temper is vicious, señora. Horrible." She shuddered and cast a pleading look in Marlee's direction. "Please go downstairs and dine with him and his friends, otherwise, I fear what may happen—to you."

Marlee already feared the very same thing. She had to find a way to escape from the house, she had to seek help in someway, but it seemed there was no way out. The windows on her room were barred, as were the other windows she'd viewed when she'd first entered the house. Besides the bars there were armed men on the grounds. It seemed there was no escape—none whatsoever. Unless Carlotta knew of a way out.

"Are all the windows barred?" Marlee asked and stood up to shake out her gown.

"Si," Doña Carlotta seemed hesitant to continue. "You're not thinking of trying to escape, please don't."

"Then there is a way out."

"Madre de Dios, I shouldn't tell you this," she said, wringing her hands together, "but once Silva has you in his bed, you'd learn the truth. There are no bars on the window of his bedroom, but there is no escape either because the room is upstairs."

Hope blossomed within Marlee's heart. Perhaps this was her way out. Clutching Carlotta's hand, she asked, "What is outside the window?"

"A balcony which overlooks a deserted alleyway,

but please don't try to escape, Señora Arden, please—"

"Do Silva's men patrol this alley?"

"Not often, I think, but don't attempt such foolishness," Doña Carlotta warned and made the sign of the cross. "If that devil of a pirate should discover you'd tried to escape—" Her words were broken off by Silva bellowing from the hallway for Marlee.

A frown marred Marlee's brow at the sound of his voice, calling to her like she was a recalcitrant pet who must obey. She wanted to go to Silva's room and see the balcony that hung across the alley—which very well might be her way to freedom. However, she didn't have time because his footsteps grew closer until he threw open the door to her room and glared at her. "My guests wish to meet you. You've delayed long enough, Lady Arden. Come now."

Gritting her teeth, she took his arm and walked down the hallway with him to the dining room. The only comfort she took was the way he'd formally addressed her by her title, as if he were outdone with her. Perhaps his ardor for her was diminishing, perhaps he realized that he couldn't keep her there and had made a dreadful mistake in judgment. She must keep her distance and act coolly polite for then he wouldn't try to molest her. Her virtue was intact so long as Manuel Silva was displeased with her. He hadn't touched her yet, but for how long would he stay away from her? How long could she keep him at arm's length?

Her only hope was to escape.

A lavish supper was laid out upon the long, mahogany dining table. Upon her entrance into the room, two men who Marlee instantly ascertained must be pirates, stood to kiss her hand. One of the men had long, stringy hair. His suit of clothes which would have fit better on a less corpulent man caused him to appear ill at ease, as if he could barely move for fear of ripping the satin jacket. The other man had curly dark hair and was a bit younger and much thinner. When he smiled, Marlee noticed that his bottom gum was absent two teeth and the top gum had lost three. She wondered how the man could eat at all, but eat he did, and the other man, too. No sooner had she sat at the table than they tore into the pheasant like starving crows.

Silva, however, sipped his wine and took his time with his food. He was totally unlike his friends but as much of a vulture, or more like an eagle-eyed hawk, for he seldom took his gaze from her. His watching her made her horribly uncomfortable but it seemed he took perverse delight in her discomfort. "Domingo," he said to the overweight man, "how do you like my latest possession? Very beautiful, is she not?"

"Huh?" Domingo lifted his head from his plate and caught the tail end of Silva's comment. He grinned broadly and nudged Silva with an elbow. "Ah, *si,* Manuel, she is much pretty."

"Don't you agree, Renaldo?" he queried the other man who heartily quaffed his third cup of wine.

"Very pretty, Manuel," was the quick reply.

"More than pretty, *amigos.* Lady Arden is beautiful, much more beautiful than Bettina, I think."

"*Si, si,*" both men agreed in unison but were more interested in the bountiful fare before them than Marlee.

Marlee felt her insides begin to shake and toyed with the food on her plate to keep from bolting to her feet. She didn't like the way he looked at her, didn't care for the desire which now heated his face and made his eyes glaze with lust. His intentions were obvious, and she feared she'd not last another night in Silva's household unmolested. Escape was her only answer.

"Such a shy thing you are, *querida.* You blush so becomingly." He spoke to her now, seeming to have forgotten his friends who were quite interested in the food on their plates to pay attention to Manuel. Pouring another cup of wine, he grinned and the wicked earring in his ear caught the torchlight and winked at her. "I think you're uneasy with my friends—and me. I wasn't always a pirate, you know."

"Really?" she said, feeling he wanted an excuse to talk. She cared less about what he had to say,

but she'd rather suffer his chatter than his touch.

"Believe it or not, I was the son of a wealthy merchant in Cadiz. My parents gave me everything, a fine education, nice clothes. So, you see, I was meant for grander things than sea-robbing. I was meant to marry a fine lady one day and live an easy life. But my parents died of fever when I was twelve and I learned of all the debts they owed. So, my uncle took me to live with him and when I was sixteen, he told me that I was to be sent to a monastery to train as a priest. A priest of all things!" Silva laughed but it was a hollow sound, even gaining the attention of his two guests—but only momentarily.

"My uncle was crazy. Can you imagine me as a pious and chaste priest, a person who'd had his first woman at—well, I won't tell you how young I was for it would shock you. But can you imagine me as a priest?"

"Definitely not," was her response. She must keep Silva talking all night, if need be. "When did you become a—a—"

"Pirate, you can say it, *querida*. I take no offense from the term, nor do I prettify what I do by pretending to be a privateer. I know what I am." He ran his finger around the rim of the gold cup. "I ran away before I could be sent to the holy fathers and found a sea captain in Cadiz who'd take me on. What else was there for a young boy with no family, no money, but the sea? I learned a great deal from the captain about navigating, but there was little to be earned in the way of monetary rewards. When the ship was captured by a pirate's crew some months later, I saw exactly what treasures could be mine for the taking."

"And now you take whatever you want, without regard for anyone else?"

"Please don't put it so indelicately, but in a word, *si*. Yes, I take what I want."

Silva was staring at her in that familiar and frightening way again. Marlee could barely swallow. She must keep him talking. "Tell me more about your—adventures at sea."

"Oh, some other time. I grow weary of my own musings." He shot her a lecherous smile, almost as if he knew what she were up to. "Go ready yourself for bed, *querida,* while I get rid of our guests. We have a long night ahead of us, and I assure you that we won't do much talking."

Disobedience was out of the question. She couldn't make a scene at the table by protesting. Neither of these men would help her. Escaping Silva was up to her, and if she could manage to find his room and get out of the house while he was still occupied . . .

"Good night, gentlemen," she said with a smile that would have melted even the hardest of hearts. "I enjoyed meeting you very much."

The men barely glanced at her but nodded and kept eating. Marlee hoped they'd never get enough to eat. Perhaps Silva wouldn't be rid of them too soon. Gliding out of the room, she walked down the hallway as if to go to her own room, but instead she sneaked to the back of the house and made her way up the stairs to find Silva's room. The choice wasn't hard since there were only two rooms on the second floor and one of them was a small library without windows.

Silva's room was much tidier than Marlee would have expected, due in part to Doña Carlotta's immaculate housekeeping. Tiptoeing through the room, she couldn't help noticing the large canopied bed with the blankets turned down or the lacy nightrail that rested on the rose-scented sheets. Either Silva wore unusual attire to bed or . . . the gown was meant for her to wear.

Her heart thumped out the words, I've got to get out of here. I must escape.

Escape beckoned to her in the form of a large floor-to-ceiling window. The velvet darkness beyond didn't frighten her as much as the bed beside her. Drawing back the window's thin curtains, Marlee stepped onto the balcony and looked down. She couldn't see very much of the shadowy alley below her because there was very little light reflecting from the full moon directly above her. In the murky blackness she could make out the shape of a number of elephant-ear plants against the stone wall but realized that the rustling of their leaves in the nighttime breeze sounded very far away. The drop to the ground was much farther than she'd anticipated.

But she had to try, she had to escape. But how?

Treading soundlessly on the balcony, she moved her hand on the railing and suddenly her fingers came into contact with a trellis on the side of the house. She glanced at it and then looked down to see that it ran all the way to the ground. She'd found escape at last!

Climbing onto the balcony's railing, she grabbed a handful of skirt in her hand and hoisted herself onto the shaky trellis just as she heard Silva bellowing her name from somewhere in the house.

It was now or never.

Chapter Nineteen

Balancing herself on the trellis with one hand, Marlee lifted her skirts with the other and started her descent. Her heart beat wildly in her ears, its steady thumping mingling with Silva's voice from inside the house. She couldn't stop and think about what would happen if he discovered her hanging outside his bedroom window. All she knew was that she must continue—now that she'd reach the middle portion of the trellis, she felt freedom was within her grasp. Just a few more feet and she'd be on the ground, free to run for help—

"Marlee!"

Silva's shout instantly halted her. A cold, clammy fear rushed over her body when she looked up and saw him on the balcony, reaching out to her as if to rescue her. She refused his hand; he wanted to imprison her and she'd rather die. "Grab onto me," he cajoled in a honey-sweet voice. "You can't escape or run away. All you'll do is fall and harm yourself. I don't want you hurt." He sounded so sincere in his concern for her that she almost believed him. But she didn't believe him, didn't trust him.

"If you cared anything for me, you'd send me back to New Providence," she carelessly flung at him, not worried about offending him. Freedom was a matter of a few feet now, and she'd be damned if she'd pretend something she didn't feel.

"Come, Marlee, *querida*," he crooned. "Please take my hand. I fear the trellis will break."

Resolutely, Marlee ignored him and started back down again. She was going to make it to the ground or die in the trying. Even now, she could hear the sound of running feet as Silva's men came in her direction, could see the flicker of their torches as they rounded the corner and headed into the alley. She swallowed her bitter disappointment that they were going to thwart her escape attempt, but first she was going to prove to Manuel Silva that he didn't own her, that she didn't have to listen to him. "Marlee, stop!" he pleaded with her. "The trellis is not going to hold you! Stop!"

But she wouldn't listen to him, didn't believe him. Even as she stepped on the next laticed rung of the trellis, she felt it pull away from the house before she heard the wood cracking right above her ear.

The trellis broke free of the stone to which it was attached and Marlee could feel herself falling but had convinced herself that she'd somehow land on her feet. Instead, she landed on her backside into a large pot that contained a huge elephant-ear plant. In a daze she looked up from her less than ladylike position to see three of Silva's men above her, their faces sheathed in surprise and grudging admiration.

"Are you all right?" one of the men asked and began to help her to her feet.

Standing up, Marlee slumped and grimaced in pain. Her right ankle hurt unbearably when she put pressure on it, and her backside was so sore she didn't know if she'd be able to sit ever again. "I — I can't walk," she stammered and would have cried, so upset was she over still being in Silva's clutches. And now that her ankle was swollen twice its size, she realized there wouldn't be any escape attempts in the foreseeable future. For the time being she was at Silva's mercy and there wasn't anything she could do about it.

The man was just about to lift her in his arms when Silva suddenly appeared and brushed the man aside. "I'll take care of Lady Arden," was his brusque comment. Before Marlee could do or say anything, he'd picked her up and carried her inside the house to her bedroom. Doña Carlotta bustled about the room, her face was pale and wan.

"I told you not to try anything so foolish," she whispered to Marlee and fluffed the pillow behind her.

"I had to try," was Marlee's less than enthusiastic response.

Her ankle burned with pain when Silva carefully slipped off her shoe. He made a sound of dismay at her swollen ankle that was fast turning black and

251

blue. "Such a headstrong woman you are. You're much less malleable than Bettina."

"I'm not Bettina!" Marlee shot back. "I'll never be like her, nor do I wish to be. I don't want to be here. I hate it here, I hate you! And when I get the chance again, I'm going to escape. Do you hear me? I'm going to run away."

He didn't reply directly to her heated retort. Instead he ordered Doña Carlotta to apply cold compresses to her foot until the swelling went down, to make her as comfortable as possible and see that she received a good night's sleep. Before he left the room, he bent down and whispered so only Marlee could hear. "I'll leave you alone until you've recovered. Believe me, I'm not that much of an animal to force myself upon an injured woman, but"—and here his eyes glowed like two agates and his face darkened—"when you're well, you shall want me. I'll make certain you want me, *querida*. You're a challenge to me and I never turn my back on a challenge. So rest well, Marlee. You shall need it." Kissing her on the forehead, he smiled and then left her to Doña Carlotta's ministrations.

Bettina was bored. She stretched and yawned, greeting the new day with a heavy dose of *ennui* that she expressed with an exasperated sigh. What would she do today? No doubt she'd be forced to accompany Beatrix into town, or what the islanders called a town. Bettina thought it was little more than a

252

cluster of hovels with painted signs on the doors. There was very little that a fashionable lady would want to purchase, certainly nothing like the beautiful clothes which Manuel had bought for her in St. Augustine. She'd already viewed the short supply of materials and patterns that were years' old at the dressmaker's shop. There wasn't anything she wanted to purchase, nothing so fine as the clothes she'd packed when Manuel threw her out of his house.

"Loathsome bastard!" she cursed out loud. She'd gone from absolute luxury to residing in Governor Roger's cramped house in a matter of days. And all because Manuel Silva had taken a fancy to someone new — someone totally unlike herself.

How foolish she'd been to believe that Manuel would marry her. Why should he marry her when he'd had her every way a man could take a woman, when members of his crew had trysted with her, too? She should have known better, should have curbed her own perverted appetites. On Bermuda, her cousin Alastair had told her often enough that she was insatiable — and he should have known since he was the one who'd initiated her into things sexual in the first place.

"I'm going to put Manuel behind me," she lamented aloud in the realization that she had no other choice in the matter. "Maybe when Lark sees me again, he'll realize he still wants to marry me." Lark was her last chance at happiness and must never know about Manuel — and the others. Yet she knew Lark wasn't a stupid man. Certainly he'd reason that the pirate had made love to her, but he didn't need to know she'd enjoyed it. The only recourse was to pretend she would wasn't to blame. If Lark ever probed, she would simply weep that Manuel had raped her and kept her a prisoner, which was true enough in the beginning. She had been his captive but he hadn't raped her and neither had his men. She'd wanted all that had happened to her with a ferocity that had shocked even herself. It was the danger, the forbidden and perverted that had attracted Bettina to Manuel and his way of life. A part of herself would always long for what she'd left behind in St. Augustine.

If only Sloane Mason kept his mouth shut about her activities on St. Augustine, she'd be able to convince Lark that she'd be the perfect wife for him. She'd considered bedding Sloane to gain his silence but had decided against it. No matter how much the men hated each other, she didn't want Sloane to believe she was unworthy of Lark.

Tapping her long, polished nails on her lips, Bettina pondered what she was going to do about Lady Marlee Arden. Bettina sat up and raked her hand through her tousled curls. She considered the strange situation of the meddlesome young woman who'd risked her life to help free someone she'd never met. Bettina didn't need to question why she'd performed such a noble deed for she already knew the answer— Marlee Arden loved Lark and hoped to win his affections by proving herself worthy.

But did Lark love Lady Arden?

Bettina trembled to believe he might. Sloane had already told her that the honorable Lark would rush to free his kinswoman. She expected as much, but she wondered if Lark might prefer this other woman over herself, that he might refuse to marry her.

"He'll marry me," Bettina said out loud and there was true resolve in her voice. "No other woman but myself will marry Lark and live at Arden's Grove. He's promised to me, and if I must prey on his honor to become his wife, then I shall." And she knew she'd do anything to keep Lark. She'd done worse things in her life—things even she dreaded to remember.

Beatrix knocked on her door just then and interrupted Bettina's reverie. Clad in a morning gown of dove gray, Beatrix politely invited her guest for a drive into town. Bettina readily and graciously accepted but she was no longer bored. Lark Arden was on her mind, as well as his thriving plantation along the James River. She convinced herself that she would come out of this just fine indeed. Her future happiness depended upon how well she could convince Lark that she was a true innocent, placed in the hands of a despicable pirate by an unkind fate. So far, she'd convinced Beatrix and Governor Rogers.

Lark was next, and she was up to the challenge. After all, she hadn't lived with the infamous and nasty Manuel Silva for a year and learned nothing about deception.

Chapter Twenty

The search for Silva had proven futile. *Her Lady-ship* dropped anchor at New Providence some two weeks after she'd sailed away, and there was a heaviness which hung about the crew like a yoke. No one laughed or jested, in fact the men were solemn and moved quietly about the ship in fear of riling their moody captain. Some had decided not to sign up again with the somber Captain Arden but would seek a more jovial bunch of seamen with whom to sail.

The only one who truly seemed to understand Lark's frustrations was Holcombe. "We took a good shot at finding Silva. Perhaps next time we'll be luckier," Holcombe expressed his hope to Lark as the late afternoon sun cast a tepid glow over the island.

Lark clutched the rope on one of the riggings and nodded less enthusiastically. "Aye, but I won't have much of a crew. It seems my men are deserting me."

"You can't blame them, Lark. They're not used to idleness and crave the heat of battle."

Lark sighed, his gaze roaming over *The Merry*

Bandit which gently bobbed some yards away. "Maybe I should be more like my half brother who hasn't earned an honest day's wages but is known for giving his crew one hell of a good time."

Holcombe didn't offer a suggestion and Lark was grateful to the man for keeping silent. He'd heard so many gripes and complaints the last two weeks that all he wanted to do was get a good night's sleep for once without worrying about the crew, without having to hear Todd grumbling about what sorry pirate hunters they were. If anyone other than the lad had expressed that sentiment aloud, he'd have chastised the man with a flogging. Todd was only a boy—but an astute one. Lark Arden *was* a sorry pirate hunter where Manuel Silva was concerned. The slimy bastard had eluded him again.

His body craved sleep, but he knew he wouldn't be able to sleep. The last two weeks he'd spent searching for Silva by day but thinking about Marlee at night. Her face was constantly in his thoughts. He noticed that Lundstrum's ship wasn't anchored by the quay, an indication that Marlee had left New Providence for England. An overwhelming sadness filled him, because he'd never see her again.

"Sir, Captain Arden, sir." Lark heard his name being called from the quay and identified Governor Rogers's servant.

"Hello, Cosmos, how are you?" Lark shouted and waved to the black man who was dressed in blue and green livery.

"I've been checking every day for your ship, sir.

I've a message from the guv'nor for you. He wants to see you right away—*right away*. The carriage is waiting for you."

Lark didn't waste time. Immediately he sensed something was wrong for Rogers to have Cosmos, the governor's prized servant, checking on the ship's arrival each day. He didn't change his clothes and bathe as he longed to do but found himself disembarking at the governor's house before ten minutes had passed. Beatrix met him in the foyer.

"Oh, Captain Arden, you're back! Woodes will be so relieved."

Lark thought Beatrix looked relieved, too, as she hurried to fetch Woodes from his study. Woodes, however, appeared with a worried frown on his face as he extended a hand to Lark. "Thank God you're back, Lark. Thank God!"

"I gather something's wrong," Lark burst out, barely breathing as a horrible thought came to mind. "Has something happened to Lundstrum's ship? Has something happened to Marlee—er, Lady Arden?"

Rogers pulled a fine linen handkerchief from out of his sleeve and dabbed his forehead. "No news about Lundstrum's ship, Lark. Lundstrum sailed on time and as far as I know, nothing has happened to his ship."

"Good, good. I've been concerned about Lady Arden."

"Oh, dear!" commented Beatrix who was instantly silenced by the severe expression on Rogers's face.

"Something *has* happened." Lark glanced worriedly at the two people.

"Come into the parlor where it's cooler," Rogers implored. "Beatrix will fix us a nice lemonade."

"Yes, yes, I shall do that instantly." Beatrix scampered away like a frightened house cat for the kitchen.

Lark followed Rogers into the parlor but wasn't up to any amenities. "Tell me what's happened," Lark demanded none too gently.

Rogers wiped his brow. "Something terrible has happened to Lady Arden."

The blood pounded through Lark's temples. "I thought you told me she was safe on Lundstrum's ship."

"No, I didn't say that. I said Lundstrum's ship is safe, as far as I know. I didn't say she was on the ship. The truth is, Lark, Lady Arden didn't leave with Lundstrum at all." Rogers took Lundstrum's note from his pocket and handed it to Lark.

Lark read the note in disbelief before looking at Rogers with a black scowl on his face. "My bastard brother must have kidnapped her!"

"No, he didn't," Rogers protested. "I assure you that Lady Arden left of her own free will, at least that's what Sloane has told me."

"But I saw Sloane's ship by the quay. Is Marlee with him?" Lark crumpled the note in his hand, feeling a tremendous pain to think that Marlee preferred his ne'er-do-well brother to him, to believe she'd led him a merry chase across the Atlantic.

Rogers sadly shook his head, his expression was so serious that Lark shivered. "It seems, Lark, that for some strange reason Lady Arden left with Mason for Saint Augustine. Somehow Mason knew that Manuel Silva is headquartered there and she insisted on being taken to the pirate's den—"

"Sloane took her there!" Lark's shout was deafening, his face had turned a vibrant shade of red.

"It seems he did, but—but," Rogers broke off, sweating profusely, "she didn't return with Captain Mason. Silva is holding her captive, and Sloane doesn't think he'll give her up easily. For some reason, the pirate fancies himself in love with her."

"Dear God!" Lark hoarsely exclaimed, unable to think of anything else to say, unable to fathom why Marlee had left with Sloane to seek out Silva in the first place. She was at Silva's mercy, and his mind couldn't dwell on the horrors his sweet, innocent Marlee must be enduring. He wouldn't think about that now. He had to leave for Saint Augustine and rescue her, but first he had to break his brother's worthless neck. "How do you know all of this?" he asked Rogers.

"Sloane told me in strictest confidence. Beatrix won't say a word to anyone either, because well—the subject is indelicate and Lady Arden's reputation would be ruined." Woodes smiled sadly. "I'm sorry, Lark, truly sorry but something good has come out of this."

"The only good will be strangling my brother with my bare hands."

"I know you're upset, but I have a happy surprise for you."

Rogers must be addled, Lark thought. What happy sort of surprise could come from such a tragedy? His beautiful Marlee was at the mercy of a despicable pirate, the same beast who had kidnapped and murdered Bettina. "I don't have time for surprises, I have to sail to Saint Augustine and rescue Marlee. I have to leave."

"Wait, please!" Rogers's voice halted Lark before he made his way to the door. "Go on the veranda and see your surprise, my boy. Please."

Stifling a curse, Lark strode through the hallway and walked into the bright sunshine. Beatrix was sitting at a wrought-iron table with a woman whose back was to Lark. Beatrix rose at once, smiling broadly. The woman who sat in the shadows followed suit. She turned and faced Lark, and the moment he heard her say his name, he knew it was Bettina.

She came toward him, walking into the dying shafts of sunlight that highlighted her hair. A tender, happy smile rose to her lips but she waited before him, not touching him, only drinking in his face with eyes that he remembered as being incredibly green and a mouth so red and luscious it resembled summer berries. He heard her sigh, her voice breaking with emotion when she spoke. "Oh, Lark, my— darling, how glad I am to see you." Then she threw herself headlong into his arms and wept joyful tears against his shirt.

"Bettina, you're safe," he mumbled, barely aware when the governor and Beatrix withdrew from the veranda. He felt himself to be in a fog. She was alive, very much alive from the way she fit her body snugly against him. He could discern the beating of her heart beneath his hand as she held it against her full breast and spilled warm tears upon it. The rumors about her death were unfounded. He'd spent months in torment over what had happened to this woman, and now she was miraculously in his embrace again. But the joy he'd expected to feel was strangely absent, because the woman in his arms wasn't Marlee.

"I've come back to you, my darling," she crooned up to him and stroked his cheek with a hand which was soft and well polished.

"Are you really all right?" he asked her, wondering why he couldn't summon more enthusiasm, why his own voice sounded wooden to his ears. Gazing down at her, he realized he'd forgotten that she had a tiny beauty spot at the corner of her mouth, or had he ever seen it before? This woman, whom he'd been searching for these last few months, was a stranger to him whereas he could recall every detail on Marlee's face.

Bettina's words caught in her throat as she cast her gaze down, refusing to look at Lark. "I've lived in hell — a veritable hell — with that filthy pirate." She looked up uncertainly, tears misting her eyes. "You do believe that I never — never wanted what happened to me. You will not make me say what I've been through, please, Lark, don't question me about—"

"I won't ask you a thing," he assured her and patted her back. "You're safe, Bettina."

"Yes," she breathed and smiled at him, but her smile was short-lived when he moved away and made a motion to head for the beach. "Where are you going?" she demanded.

"Stay here and gather your things together. We're leaving shortly."

Hope glistened in her eyes. "Are we heading for Bermuda to be married? I would like to see my parents again, to be married there."

"We'll discuss that later," he absently told her, "but first I have to speak to someone."

Bettina appeared uncomfortable for a second. "You're going to speak to Captain Mason, aren't you?" At Lark's nod, she shrugged in what Lark could only term was a hopeless gesture. "He rescued me, you know, but he was forced to leave that other woman with Silva as an exchange for me. I doubt you'll get her back." *I hope you don't,* she thought.

Lark was disbelieving. Could Sloane have been so foolish as to bribe Silva with Marlee for Bettina's release? Something was wrong here, very wrong, and he was determined to learn the truth or kill his brother in the process. "Pack whatever you need, we're leaving just as soon as the tide is favorable," he told her not unkindly and pecked her cheek. As an afterthought, he said, "I'm glad you're safe, Bettina, I truly am."

She clutched at his arm, desperation shone on her face. "We're going to be married on Bermuda. Promise me."

"I promise I'll take you home." His mind wasn't on his wedding to Bettina. It was on Marlee and how to free her from Silva's clutches.

Lark kicked open the door to Sloane's cabin on *The Merry Bandit,* causing Sloane to glance up from the logbook on his desk in an unperturbed fashion which further infuriated Lark.

"I wondered how long it would be before you got around to paying me a visit," Sloane remarked and laid down his quill.

Enraged beyond reason, Lark rushed toward his brother and gripped his brother's throat before Sloane knew what had happened to him. "I should kill you, you despicable bastard!" Lark ground out and at that moment, he meant every word, even tightening his hand to give credence to them. But he noticed Sloane's fear, something he'd never seen on his brother's face. He'd seen cockiness, arrogance, and greed, but never pure fear. Slowly, he released the choke-hold. Sloane fell forward, sputtering and gasping for breath.

"Why don't you kill me? I—I deserve to die."

This unexpected comment from Sloane surprised Lark. "Yes, you do," he agreed, "and I might just oblige you, but I want to hear why you think so."

Sloane groaned, barely able to look at Lark. "I brought Marlee to Silva, as I'm certain you know by now. I'm certain Governor Rogers or Bettina told you."

"Why did you do such a stupid, idiotic thing?" Lark burst out, clenching his fists to stop himself from beating in Sloane's handsome face.

Sloane rubbed his throat. "Hatred for you made me do it, dear brother. But—but I never meant for Marlee to be harmed, or for her to be taken as prisoner by that demented Spaniard. All I wanted was for her to learn about Bettina, to see firsthand the woman you planned to marry. Then Marlee would be forced to turn away from you, and you'd be pining for her, living in abject misery while I wiped away her tears." Sloane heaved a disgruntled sigh. "Nothing happened the way I thought it would."

"Why in the name of heaven did you take her to Saint Augustine anyway?" Lark didn't understand Sloane, and he doubted he ever would.

Sloane gave an anxious little cough. "Because I knew Silva to be hiding there. Because Marlee wanted to rescue your friend, the person whom Silva kidnapped from your ship, as a way of helping you. She thought if she could convince Silva to release this "friend" then you'd see how much she loved you and would consent to marry her."

"Did she tell you that?" Lark felt barely able to breathe.

"She didn't have to," Sloane confessed and his eyes condemned his brother. "I could see how much she loved you and wanted to be your wife. So, I can't take all of the blame. You're partly responsible for never telling her that your friend was really the woman you planned to marry."

Lark barely stifled a groan. Sloane was right, he knew. He hadn't told Marlee about Bettina because he feared hurting her more deeply. He was a coward where she was concerned. Because he conceivably might be in love with Marlee, he'd hidden a part of his life from her. Because of him she was in physical danger, and he must save her by freeing her from Silva, and, in effect, freeing her from himself. "You're going to help me get Marlee away from Silva," he told his brother.

Shaking his head, Sloane grimaced. "Silva's home is surrounded by armed guards. Even the Spanish governor bows to his word. There's no way anyone can get her away from Saint Augustine."

"There's a way," Lark pronounced.

"I doubt that." Sloane was less optimistic. "How many men do you need?"

"I need any men you can gather who'll sail with you on *The Merry Bandit* as defense. I'll take whatever men are left on my crew and head for Matanzas Bay."

"How many men will actually be needed for the assault against Silva's men?"

Lark raised an eyebrow and caressed the saber at his side. "Only one."

"You think you're going to break through Silva's defenses on your own? Lark, you're daft."

"No. I'm just tired of people being hurt because of Manuel Silva. This time, since I know where Silva

266

is"—and he shot a razor-edged look at Sloane—"I can worm my way into the area and get information. This time I'm going to take all of the chances—and win. I've got to win. Marlee's life depends upon it."

"Then this is the first time we'll be working together for a common good," Sloane wryly observed.

Lark bent down to his brother. "Aye, it is, and the last."

Silva's gaudy red carriage clip-clopped along the waterfront and entered the stone city gate of St. Augustine. The carriage meandered through the narrow streets that contained two-story homes whose wrought-iron balconies hung precariously overhead. Finally, the driver stopped at the open-air market and Silva helped Doña Carlotta and then Marlee from the conveyance. He smiled as he kept her small hand in his. "I have great hopes of bringing you to my bed this night, *querida*. I've waited a long time for you, and I grow weary waiting to break down your resistance. Perhaps another bauble or two will cause you to look more appreciatively at me. Besides, your injury has healed. I won't wait forever."

Silva had made a game of wooing her. Within the last three weeks Silva had presented her with elaborate gowns and jewels so breathtakingly beautiful that any other woman would have succumbed and gone willingly to Silva's bed. Marlee, however, wasn't just any woman, and it appeared Silva was beginning to realize she couldn't be bought with trin-

267

kets no matter how beautiful and expensive. She doubted that Silva had paid one peso for any of the items he'd given her, no doubt having pilfered everything from some doomed ship.

"Do what you want," she said without emotion in her voice or color in her cheeks.

"Ah, well, let me tell you what I wish to do, *querida*." Silva whispered something so horribly obscene into her ear that Marlee blushed all of the way to her hairline, delighting Silva with her reaction. "I knew that would make you blush," he delightedly observed, but his face darkened for an instant. "I want more than a blush of embarrassment to cover your body. I want your body to be consumed with the heat of passion—and tonight, tonight it shall be so. Now tell me what you wish and I shall buy it for you."

Marlee hid her trembling hands within the folds of the silk skirt of her gown. "I—I should like an orange."

"That is all?" Silva appeared dumbfounded by her request.

"Yes."

"A strange woman you are, but I suppose that is because you're English." He took her arm and led her to a stall where an old lady with a black mantilla on her head was selling fruits to Doña Carlotta; an old man, who wore a large white-brimmed hat that covered his face, was bending over a crate of the sweet-smelling fruits. The orange was duly purchased and presented to Marlee who bit into the fruit's succulent flesh. When a bit of juice ran down her chin, Manuel hurried to wipe it away with his thumb.

A strange, hot glint enveloped his eyes. *"Si, querida*, tonight you shall be mine at last."

She wanted to die, ached to wither away and die right there. Silva escorted her to the carriage and they headed back to the house with Doña Carlotta.

The old man stood up from his task and sharp eyes would have noticed he wasn't old at all. He glanced at the elderly woman who watched the carriage depart. "Did she take the potion?" the man asked her.

The woman nodded briskly. *"Si,* señor. My former mistress, Doña Carlotta, hates Silva. She'll make certain that he never touches the English lady. Rest easy, señor, your lady is safe for tonight."

Silva watched Marlee like a vulture who waits for its prey to die. He licked his lips at the way she daintily consumed her supper. His loins hardened at the thought of what ecstasy awaited him. And *Dios,* how long he had waited to bed this woman! With his other women, especially with Bettina, there had been no wooing, no waiting. Wooing a woman was something unusual to him, but he found he liked it — to a point. Marlee had been under his roof for three weeks and still he hadn't done more than kiss her a few times. Each time, however, she'd stiffened like a plank and been as responsive as one. He'd grown tired waiting for her reserve to break. Tonight, she'd be his. He'd make her his.

"Is the fish to your liking?" he asked and flashed her a wolfish smile that caused her insides to quake.

"Delicious," she lied. She couldn't taste anything at the moment because she knew what Silva planned for her.

"Did you notice the pretty night thing that Doña Carlotta laid out for you? I hope you like it."

She nodded, because she'd seen the transparent piece of gossamer quite clearly. There was no mistaking the fact that Silva wanted her to model it for him. *"Bueno, querida*, but don't get too attached to it for it won't cover your beautiful body for long, I assure you."

She wanted to retch, literally ached to run to the chamber pot, but she wouldn't allow Silva to see how truly repulsed she was by him and his lewd overtures. "You've thought of everything," she said and her sarcasm wasn't lost on the man.

"Not everything, almost, however. You see, I want to marry you, Marlee. That's why I want you to accept me, to come willingly to me. But since you won't, then I shall force the matter."

Marlee dropped her fork and shook her head. "You can't mean that! I won't marry you or come to you like some chastised puppy with its head bowed. I don't love you!"

"I didn't expect you to, *querida*, but you're the perfect choice for my wife, to bear me sons. Love can come later; for now you're going to let me bed

270

you. To be honest, love doesn't have to enter into it."
He puffed on a cheroot and blew a smoke ring, then
ordered Doña Carlotta to see that his wine cup was
refilled. The woman, who was hovering near the
sideboard, quickly came forward and took the cup.
Neither Marlee nor Silva saw her open the top of the
ring she wore on her index finger and empty a white
powder which quickly dissolved into the wine's contents. Silva hastily downed the wine after she'd
placed it on the table in front of him. With a harsh
voice, he ordered the old lady out of the room and
impaled Marlee with a lascivious expression.

"You're different from that other one," he praised
in a voice which sounded a bit slurred. Marlee knew
he was speaking about Bettina and clutched at the
table's edge. She hated thinking about Bettina, detested her own imaginings about what she and Lark
must be doing, since they'd been so happily reunited.
Were they married now? She felt certain they were.
Lark loved Bettina a great deal to risk masquerading
as another woman's husband to get the money to
outfit a ship to rescue her. Did Bettina know how
lucky she was? Suddenly she was routed from her
torturous memories by the sound of Silva hitting the
table with his fist. "Stop thinking about Lark Arden
when you're with me!" he commanded. "I know
you're thinking about him."

It wouldn't do any good to lie to him. "Yes, I was
thinking about Lark."

"You love him, don't you?" His voice sounded unusually slurred, very unlike Silva, who always

seemed to be in control of his physical faculties.

"What I feel is none of your concern," she said, then wished she hadn't said anything for Silva rose unsteadily to his feet and advanced toward her.

Without a warning, he viciously pushed back her chair until she nearly fell but he grabbed her arm and hauled her against him. "I've given you plenty of time, much more than I've ever given any woman. I've given you clothes and jewels, things you refuse to wear. So, wear nothing then!" He ripped open the front of her dress until her chemise-clad breasts were exposed to him. She pushed at him, clawing at him when he lifted her from her feet. Her pleas fell on deaf ears as Silva carried her toward the bedroom where Bettina had been willingly seduced by him.

But the woman who now cried and fought wasn't Bettina. She was the woman whom Manuel Silva had decided would bear him children, and if on this night, she conceived his son, then so be it.

Tonight was the night when Marlee Arden would become his woman and no tears or she-cat behavior would stop him from having her.

He threw her onto the bed and laid atop her, tearing the very clothes from her body. "Manuel, stop, stop!" But Manuel didn't hear her. All he saw was her beautiful body, the way her full breasts enticed him, the way her shapely thighs kicked out at him. This was a woman worth keeping, no matter how she fought him. In fact, her fighting only made his lust the more potent.

"Quiet, *querida*," he groaned into her ear and began kissing her lips, plunging his tongue into her mouth. Marlee was his now, his to do whatever he wanted. Her struggles beneath him enflamed him further and there was only one thing to do. One way to end his torment.

Silva undid the buttons on his trousers.

Chapter Twenty-one

Marlee pummeled Silva's chest with her clenched fists. "Don't," he growled savagely against her ear and grabbed her wrists. Frustrated tears streamed freely down her cheeks, and she knew it was a matter of seconds before he removed his pants. She was prepared to bite and claw, anything to prevent him from attacking her. "Lie — still," he whispered so quietly that Marlee could barely hear him, but she felt his weight push her deeper into the mattress, making her unable to kick out or further defend herself. His head lowered to hers and she thought he was going to kiss her, but his lips missed their target. His face fell onto her breasts.

She stiffened, waiting for him to continue the assault, but Manuel lay still, so still that she wondered if he had died. But his snores convinced her that he was asleep.

"Manuel?" Her voice sounded hesitant. She was fearful to move, afraid he'd waken, but his weight was crushing her and cutting off her oxygen. Gaining no response, she waited and when his hold upon her grew slack, she freed her hands.

Attempting to push him from her was a hard task. In his stupor he seemed to weigh twice as much, but soon he rolled over of his own accord onto the mattress. She waited and held her breath. When he didn't waken, she hurriedly scampered off of the bed and began to pull on a dressing gown when Doña Carlotta suddenly appeared.

The old woman entered the room and peered closely at the sleeping pirate. When she turned to face Marlee, she was smiling broadly. "The sleeping powder worked well. He should sleep for many hours and when he wakens he'll think it was the wine."

Marlee was disbelieving. "You drugged him?"

"*Si*," the old lady said with pride in her voice. "I did it for you, Marlee."

Marlee impetuously hugged Doña Carlotta. "Thank you so much, so much." She started to cry.

"Now, now, don't take on so, señora. But we must make our plan of escape."

"Yes, yes," she readily agreed and shivered at the sight of the tattered gown on the floor. "I want to get out of here—before—he wakes. I'll escape tonight."

"No, not tonight. You can't get past Silva's guards. Tomorrow night is the agreed-upon time."

"Agreed-upon time? What are you talking about?" Marlee wondered if Doña Carlotta understood how important it was for her to leave Saint Augustine.

The old woman placed a finger to her lips and she took Marlee's hand to lead her out of the bedroom and into the dining room where she poured Marlee a fortifying cup of wine. "Drink this and listen to what I have to say," Doña Carlotta seriously advised her charge. "Someone is helping you. My former servant who works at the fruit stand gave me the powder for Silva's drink. She received it from an Englishman who is here on Saint Augustine and will take you to safety."

Marlee's heart thumped hard. An Englishman? Could it be Lark? She discounted the thought as quickly as it came to her. Lark was busy with his Bettina by now. The Englishman must be Sloane. "When will he free me?"

"Tomorrow night there is a big celebration at the Castillo de San Marcos, given by the governor. Perhaps Silva mentioned this to you."

Marlee nodded. He'd said something about a party and that she must wear her most beautiful gown and the rubies which Silva had given her, but she'd been unconcerned about the whole affair. Now, she listened eagerly to Doña Carlotta who said, "I shall go with you as duenna and I'll make certain you escape. With all of the people and excitement, Silva shall be caught off guard. But you must do exactly as I tell you."

"I'll do anything," Marlee vowed. "I'd even swim

the distance to New Providence to get away from here."

Doña Carlotta laughed, her eyes took on a dreamy quality. "That won't be necessary for a big ship is waiting to spirit you into the arms of your beloved. How romantic for you!"

Marlee didn't reply. She'd do whatever was necessary to escape from Silva, but Doña Carlotta was wrong. No arms were waiting to enfold her, because she had no beloved. He belonged to Lady Bettina Gilbert.

Silva cast an appreciative eye over Marlee as she descended from the carriage in front of the imposing Castillo de San Marcos. The stone walls of the fort had been built one hundred and sixty years before to keep out invaders and was still used for that purpose. But this night there was a glittering celebration in honor of the city's founding and the fort was lit by torches which reflected the dazzling array of jewels worn by the guests. From the corner of his bloodshot eyes, Silva instantly knew that Marlee was the most beautiful of any woman there. She wore an off the shoulder silk gown, a deep ruby red in color, that showed off her alabaster flesh to perfection. The neckline was cut very low in the way Silva preferred, and the ruby pendant that hung between the lush valley of her breasts caused him to lick his lips in anticipation. Somehow he'd passed out the night before—something unusual for he prided himself on holding his liquor—and been unable to finish what his loins ached to do. But tonight when this celebration was over, Marlee would be his, and no amount of fighting on her part would prevent it.

A slight breeze ruffled the white lace mantilla which draped delicately across Marlee's head. She was swathed in rubies, lace, and silk and didn't care. All she worried about was escaping from here and counted the hours until midnight. She wondered if Silva could sense her nervousness and if he did, she hoped he thought it was due to the celebration. Doña Carlotta seemed quite calm and gave not the least hint by look or deed that she was the one who had drugged Manuel Silva into oblivion the night before.

If only this were over, Marlee thought and prayed that all would go as planned.

The governor met them as they entered the fort and any thought of escape was forgotten as the man introduced Marlee to his family members and aristocratic Spaniards who could trace their beginnings back to the early days of the city. Pretending an interest she didn't feel, Marlee smiled brightly. No one made snide comments about her being there with Manuel Silva. It seemed that she was accepted just as Bettina had probably been accepted. No one dared cross Manuel Silva—no one but herself and a poor, defenseless old woman.

The evening passed slowly. Every so often Marlee

would glance in Doña Carlotta's direction, waiting for the sign to begin the escape. As the minutes passed, Marlee's cheeks grew warmer and she tried to hide her agitation, but Manuel made things worse by watching her so closely that she feared he would read her thoughts and know what she planned. His hand resting familiarly on her waist and his tiny kisses on the nape of her neck were enough to make her bolt. But she stayed the impulse — and waited.

Manuel smiled at the tempting array of food which was set on long tables in the courtyard. Numbers of servants hurried to and from the kitchens, loaded down with trays of foods and wines. "The governor has outdone himself tonight. So much food has left me feeling quite sleepy."

"Oh, really?" she asked, not hearing him for her mind was on her escape.

"Si," he said and bent down to nibble the lobe of her ear, "but it won't prevent me from finishing what I started last night, *querida*."

To hide her repulsion, she sipped her wine and was very grateful that a Spanish matron came to speak with her. Silva stayed near, keeping a protective eye over her, but finally as midnight drew nigh, the governor came over and invited them to accompany him to the firing of the cannons to celebrate the founding of St. Augustine. Silva readily agreed, and as he took Marlee's arm to lead her up the stone stairway to the top of the fort, Doña Carlotta caught her eye and nodded. This was the signal.

Marlee stumbled on the second step and her wine sloshed over her gown, soaking into the expensive material and staining it. "Oh, my! I've ruined my dress."

Silva took a handkerchief from his top pocket and began wiping the offending stain away, but Marlee shook her head. "It's only making it worse, Manuel. I'll have to wash it out somehow."

Doña Carlotta came forward from the shadows. "I can take the stain out. Follow me, Lady Arden."

Marlee started after the old lady, but Silva halted her with a clawlike hand on her arm. "I will go with you."

For a moment Marlee thought he would do just that, but suddenly and like a prayer being answered, the governor called to him to hurry and join him. Silva appeared to be in a quandary about what to do, but he didn't want to offend the governor since the man allowed him safe haven in the city. He shot Marlee a warning glance. "I'll be nearby, and if you aren't by my side in ten minutes, I shall come after you and find you. Then I shall drag you away with me." He tilted her face up to his. "Ten minutes, *querida*, no more."

"Yes, ten minutes," she said in a breathy voice that belied her fear. She turned and followed Doña Carlotta through the courtyard and down a hallway into the kitchen area where the food was being prepared and then outside a back door into an area where carts waited, loaded down with fruits and vegetables.

"Over here," Doña Carlotta whispered and hurried to a cart where an old man sat on the wooden seat, his hands on the reins behind a mule. An older woman stood next to the cart and made urgent gestures with her hands. "This is my former servant," Carlotta explained to Marlee. "She is the one who has agreed to help you."

"Thank you," Marlee said. "And is that your husband?" she nodded to the old man who wore the large-brimmed hat that obscured his face.

"No time for introductions now," the woman said and barely glanced at the man. She pointed to a large crate that was on the back of the cart, surrounded by fresh produce of all kinds. "Climb into the box and I'll close the lid," she ordered. "And no matter what happens, señora, remain quiet. When the driver reaches Matanzas Bay, you'll be released to your friends." The woman made the sign of the cross. *"Madre de Dios,* hurry before Silva comes looking for you."

Marlee started to climb onto the cart, but she stopped and smiled at Doña Carlotta. "Are you coming with me?"

"No, no, señora. I'll stay here with my friend."

"But — but what about Silva? He'll know you helped me leave. He might harm you."

Doña Carlotta clasped Marlee's hands in hers. "I shall be safe with my friends. I'll not return to the house. One day, maybe God shall give me back my home, but you mustn't worry about me. I can take care of myself, Señora Marlee."

Marlee kissed the old woman. "I wish you well, and thank you. Thank you and your friend."

"Hurry for time grows short," Doña Carlotta implored.

Not risking another look at either one of the women, Marlee climbed onto the cart and gingerly made her way through the produce before getting into the large crate. The women helped close the lid and Marlee was encased in darkness, except for a bit of light that shone through the wooden slats. A fruity scent like oranges and tangerines wafted over her as the driver clucked lowly to the mule and the cart started across the cobblestoned yard for the street.

She could hear her heart beating, and as each roll of the cart wheels reverberated in her ears, she almost imagined she heard Silva's shouts. But that was impossible, for if he were calling for her, his voice would have been lost in the roar of the cannons which echoed from the Castillo. At any moment she expected the cart to stop and for Silva to wrench open the lid and pull her from the crate. A shiver slid down her backside to imagine his rage. "Dear Lord, please don't let him find me, please let me get away," she prayed out loud.

Finally, the cannon blasts grew so faint that she no longer heard them. It seemed the cart had been moving for a long time when her legs grew numb from maintaining her cramped, fetal position. Soon the quiet of the night gave way to the slight tinkling sound of bells in the distance, and ever alert, Marlee recognized the sound as a ship's bell. They must be near Matanzas Bay!

The cart stopped moving, then three taps on the lid was the signal for which she'd been waiting. She pushed the lid from the crate and stared into the dark night. There wasn't a moon or stars by which to see, but she made out the shadowy figure of the old man as he came to help her off the cart. Extending a hand to him, Marlee was visibly surprised when the old man grasped her around the waist and swung her from the cart to land on her feet with ease. "Thank—thank you, señor." She was so dumbfounded that she couldn't think of anything else to say, didn't know what to say when he pulled her along to the sandy shoreline like a man who was half his age. They came upon a longboat and without saying a word to her, he helped her in the boat and took the seat in front of her. The oars he used to navigate through the dark waters were held firmly in his hands, and he didn't have any trouble cutting through the waves.

Marlee could only marvel at his strength which was surprising for an elderly gentleman. She remembered seeing the man on the day she'd visited the market with Manuel Silva, but she'd only seen him from the back as he bent over the produce. She'd assumed he was advanced in years because of the age of his wife, but she'd never actually seen the man's face and couldn't see it now. The hat's brim obscured her view and the night was so dark that his features were obliterated. But she no longer thought of the man as elderly. His movements were too robust, too certain of where they were headed to be a fruit vendor.

The ship's bell echoed nearby, and suddenly Marlee saw lights on board. In fact, she saw two different sets of lights and realized that there were two ships waiting in the bay. As they grew closer, she saw that one of the ships was Sloane's and she giggled, startling the man in the longboat with her. "For goodness sake, Sloane, why didn't you tell me that you were my rescuer? Your silence is out of character."

The man continued rowing, not responding. Marlee shivered in the warm sea breezes. The man must be Sloane. Who else would have rescued her but Sloane unless—Her face grew horribly warm, her breath dying in her throat. It couldn't *be* Lark. He didn't care a whit about her, he'd never risk life and limb to save her. Or would he?

But she heard another ship's bell; the clear sound struck a familiar chord within her for she'd heard it often enough the last few months when she'd been aboard Lark's ship. Her hands tensed in her lap. "Are you fearful that I'll throw myself overboard if I recognize you, Lark? Is that why you've been so quiet, or is it that you're a coward and can't face me as yourself?" she challenged in a surprisingly steady voice despite the anger which welled within her and threatened to overwhelm her. "Answer me, you coward."

It was then he looked directly at her. Even in the darkness, she could feel his black eyes upon her, familiarizing himself with her face again. She felt stripped to her very soul.

Chapter Twenty-two

"I *am* a coward, where you're concerned." Lark's voice washed over her like a lapping wave in the inky night. "Forgive me, Marlee. There's so much I need for you to forgive—"

"Never! I'll never forgive you for what you've done to me." A sob rose in her throat, nearly choking her.

"I understand how you must feel," he said and continued rowing to the ship but his gaze was riveted upon her. "But first, I need to know if you're all right. Did—Silva touch you?"

"Do you care if he did?" she blurted out, not wishing to answer Lark, wanting to hurt him for the pain she'd forever carry in her heart.

"I care very much, Marlee. Tell me if you're all right." His voice sounded like a caress, and she shivered from the perverted wanting which suddenly consumed her.

"Please—don't question me now. I don't want to talk." He probably thought that her silence was a way of punishing him, but she could barely speak as memories assailed her, precious memories of the moments she'd spent in Lark's arms. Never again would she experience passion, because no man but Lark could inflame her. And he was no longer hers but Bettina's.

Lark anchored the longboat beside *Her Ladyship*. With his help she managed to climb the rope ladder to the deck of the ship. The whole time she was very much aware of Lark behind her, how he was there to catch her if she stumbled. The warm pressure of his hand on her waist as she made her way up the ladder was a sensation she couldn't shake even after he'd removed it. Holcombe appeared and helped her over the edge of the railing. He smiled at her and told her how glad he was that she was safe.

Sloane was the next person she saw. He rushed forward and took her in his arms. "I've been worried sick about you, Marlee. Did that bastard hurt you? God, I'll never be able to make any of this up to you—never. I never dreamed Silva would hold you against your will. I'm so sorry, so very sorry."

His apology was sincere. Marlee could see the worried frown that marred his brow, his fear that she'd not forgive him for being unable to protect her from Silva. But in his own way, Sloane was as much to blame for her situation as Lark. Because of his hatred for Lark, she'd been left at the mercy of a despicable pirate. "I'll be all right in time," she told him but wouldn't absolve him for what he'd done. Maybe one day she could forget and put all that had happened behind her—but not now—not when she was on Lark's ship and in his very disturbing presence.

Lark removed his hat and pushed his hand through his thick hair. Even dressed like a Spanish peasant, he looked magnificent. Her foolish heart speeded up its beat when his gaze met hers, but he spoke to Sloane. "Marlee needs her rest. I think you better get back to your ship before Silva discovers what happened and decides to come looking for her." He held out a hand to his brother. "Thank you for sailing alongside of me. I appreciate your offer of help."

Taking Lark's hand, Sloane almost smiled. "I owed it to Marlee. I did it for her, not for you. You'll see that she's safely returned to England?"

Lark nodded. "I'll protect her with my life."

"You better," Sloane observed wryly, "otherwise, it won't be worth a tinker's dam if anything happens to her. You'll answer to me, I promise you."

Lark made a mocking bow. "I wouldn't have it any other way."

Planting a gentle kiss on Marlee's cheek, Sloane squeezed her hand. "I wish you only the best of luck, my lady. If you ever have need of a strong shoulder, you'll know where to find me."

"Thank you," she mumbled and did her best to smile gratefully but was so weary from the night's happenings that her eyelids started to close. Suddenly she felt herself being lifted from her feet and discovered that Lark was carrying her down the stairs to the rooms below. Her dismay and embarrassment was witnessed by Todd who stood quietly in the hallway and two other crew members who watched with eyes agog. "What in the name of heaven are you doing?" she asked and struggled to be put down but found herself held firmly in Lark's arms.

"You need to go to bed and rest."

"I don't need for you to carry me like an invalid. What will your crew think? Put me down, I insist that you do!"

"God, I hate it when you sound like a haughty dowager." He kicked open the door to his cabin and placed Marlee on his bunk from which she quickly bolted.

"I won't stay in your bed! I refuse to sleep—here!" She pointed to the bunk like it was a loathsome reptile and whirled around to face him. All of the pent-up fury was there for him to see. "I'd rather sleep in the galley with the potatoes for company than you!"

"I never intended to sleep in here with you, Marlee. I have another place to sleep. The cabin is yours."

He spoke so quietly that she strained her ears to hear him, very much aware of a sadness that tinged his words. In the candlelight from the wall-sconce she noticed, too, that his face seemed lined in places where there had been no lines before. Since she'd last seen him, Lark appeared to have aged five years. Was it because of her? She didn't dare think so, wouldn't allow herself to wonder if he'd missed her. But she felt a part of herself softening to think that maybe, just maybe, he might still care for her. He had risked his life by coming after her. There was so much she wanted to say to him, so many things which ate away at her heart. She needed to thank him for rescuing her, and nearly made the effort, but the words locked in her throat because at that second she noticed Bettina standing in the doorway. The woman was dressed in a green silk gown and looking absolutely beautiful.

"Dearest Lady Arden, you're safe! I've been beside myself with worry." Bettina came into the cabin and placed a proprietary hand on Lark's arm, which he didn't shrug off. Her ruby colored lips turned upward into a self-satisfied smile, and a defiant spark shone in her sly, green eyes. "Did that beastly pirate harm you, my dear? I sympathize with you entirely for I know what an ordeal you've lived through."

Marlee nearly laughed aloud. The woman was so obvious that she wondered if Lark didn't notice, but apparently he didn't. No doubt Bettina had wormed her way into Lark's affections again and convinced him that her relationship with Silva had been one-sided. Marlee knew differently, but she didn't care to tell Lark about Bettina. What good would it do anyway? Let him learn on his own about the whore he planned to wed, she decided. It would do him good to marry a woman who planned to use him, to drain him dry in the same way he'd drained all of the dreams and longings out of Marlee herself.

Clementina's self-righteous voice echoed in her mind, "An eye for an eye," she'd always said, and perhaps that's how things would be for Lark. But Marlee didn't take any pleasure in the suffering Lark would experience when married to such a wanton, greedy creature as Bettina. She felt unbearably sorry for him — and for herself.

"I'm perfectly all right, Lady Gilbert. Thank you for your concern," was Marlee's only comment.

"Please call me Bettina, I insist that you do. And since we'll be sharing this cabin until we reach Bermuda, I hope we'll become good friends."

"We'll be sharing the cabin —"

"Uh, yes," Lark interrupted Marlee. "I'm bunking with Holcombe. You two ladies can sleep in here. Marlee will take the bunk and I've arranged for a cot for you, Bettina."

"A cot? I have to sleep on a cot? But I've slept on the bunk for the last few days, why must anything change —"

"Because I say so," Lark snapped irritably and strode into the passageway to shout for Todd to bring in the cot.

Bettina grew sullenly silent and waited for the makeshift cot to be delivered by Todd. Before Todd arrived, there was a strained atmosphere in the cabin, and Lark appeared so ill at ease that Marlee nearly felt sorry for him. When Todd finally came and set up the cot, he doffed his cap to Marlee and beamed a smile of pure pleasure. " 'Tis good to see you safe and sound, my lady. If there's anything you want, anything at all, just call for me. I'll be nearby." Todd's heartfelt offer touched Marlee. He was such a sweet young boy. She thanked him profusely before he departed.

"Hmph! That lad never bowed and scraped to me, and I'm the captain's fiancée." Bettina didn't bother to hide her jealousy but was only quieted by a raised eyebrow from Lark.

"Now, ladies, I'll leave you for the night. Rest well." Lark watched Marlee through troubled eyes and was unprepared for Bettina suddenly lifting her lips to his for a good-night kiss.

"Sleep well, my darling," she whispered into his ear and suggestively leaned against him. "Soon, we'll be married and won't be parted again."

"Er, well—good night." He started for the door and halted when Marlee called to him. His expression was almost one of hope as she walked toward him.

"I have here something I think you need," she said and before he could ask her what that might be, she took off the diamond engagement ring and placed it in his hand. "This doesn't belong to me."

"What is that, what is that?" Bettina rushed forward and saw the ring. "Why, it's my ring. How wonderful! Wherever did you find it? I thought it was gone forever." Grabbing it out of Lark's hand, she placed it on her finger. The diamond flashed blue fire in the candlelight.

So engrossed in the ring's return, Bettina failed to see the pain that crossed Lark's handsome countenance but Marlee saw it and shivered. He mouthed "good night" and then disappeared into the darkened hallway.

"Lark always did have the most wonderful taste in jewelry," Bettina declared with a wicked grin. Her emerald eyes appraised Marlee's attire, her gaze resting on the ruby necklace at Marlee's throat for a number of seconds. "My, my, Lady Arden, it seems Manuel has an eye for pretty baubles, too. I underestimated you. You've managed to prosper from your captivity. Apparently, you warmed up a great deal to Manuel after my—hasty departure. And to think I thought you were a sweet innocent."

Marlee clenched her teeth. She refused to be baited by Bettina, aware that Bettina was jealous of what she believed had happened with Silva but also because of Lark. She must have deduced by now that Marlee loved Lark—or had loved him. She didn't dare to think of that love in the present tense any longer. No matter what she felt for Lark now or in the past, she wouldn't allow Bettina to get the upper hand with her. "You're quite right about looks being deceptive, Bettina, and I'll call you Bettina. I do feel I know you so well. Manuel was always speaking about you." She didn't fail to notice Bettina wince and continued, "I wonder just how long it shall take Lark to see beneath your deceptively innocent facade."

"Whatever do you mean by that? Are you threatening me?" Bettina placed her hands on her hips and arched an eyebrow.

"Heavens, no! Why should I threaten you? I was only wondering how long Lark is going to be duped

293

by you. He must realize that Silva didn't release you in the same pure, untouched state he found you. But to be quite honest, I doubt you were lily white even then. However, that's something with which Lark must deal." Marlee stretched out on the bunk.

Bettina's hands trembled as she began to pull the pins from her hair and get ready for bed. As Marlee was drifting into sleep, she heard Bettina and opened her eyes to find the woman was standing menacingly over her. Her eyes glittered dangerously. "I refuse to be left out in the cold again, Lady Arden. I'd advise you to keep your mouth closed about what you think you know about me and Manuel Silva. I can make things horrid for you. I didn't live with Silva for a year and not learn something about torture."

"Piddle!" Marlee burst out and sat up to stare her down. "Don't try to intimidate me. Your life with Silva was far from torturous. And I'd advise you to consider what he may have taught me in the time I was with him. Your threats don't bother me, not after what I've lived through the last few weeks."

Seeing that Marlee wasn't about to quiver in fear, Bettina presented a stony face and went to lay on her cot. Before Bettina blew out the candle on the table beside her, she looked at Marlee with a sly glint in her eyes. "No doubt you're right about Lark. I'm sure he realizes that Silva made love to me, but I never loved Manuel. Lark is the man I'm going to marry, he is the man who'll love me night after night for years to come. In fact, my time with Manuel hasn't dimmed my ardent response to Lark. Why, just last night we laid in the very bed you're on now and—"

Marlee faced the wall, placing her hands over her ears. She didn't want to hear the details about how Lark had made love to Bettina. Bettina, seeing that Marlee was trying to ignore her, laughed out loud and settled herself down for the night. Bitter tears slipped down Marlee's cheeks, tears she'd sworn not to cry. But she couldn't help herself. Lark was lost to her and she'd have to get over him.

But how?

Lark reclined on a cot in Holcombe's cabin. Another night spent away from his own bunk. Not that he missed sleeping in his cabin, because he'd had precious little sleep the past few weeks. But Marlee was sleeping in his bed and that made wanting to sleep there all the more unbearable. He knew he should be worried about Bettina. She'd slept alone in the cabin since he'd brought her on board and he hadn't cared a whit. Yet now Marlee was there. His Marlee was safe and he couldn't go to her. He had no right to her.

On the other side of the room Lark heard Holcombe clear his throat. "Captain, you've certainly got your hands full with those two ladies aboard. I don't envy you one bit."

"Get to sleep!" was Lark's swift and less than pleasant rejoinder.

"Aye, aye, sir," came Holcombe's voice. Lark swore the man sounded amused. Lark, however, wasn't amused and groaned his dismay. Would this voyage ever end and did he want it to end? Once they reached Bermuda, Marlee was forever lost to him. He'd be forced to place her on a ship to England and never see her again. Once more, he'd have to tell her goodbye and he didn't think he could.

In fact, he knew he couldn't.

Chapter Twenty-three

"We'll throw a party, a huge party for you, Bettina, so that all of your friends and our neighbors can welcome you home. I can think of no other way to celebrate your return to us, my dearest daughter." Lord Cyrus Gilbert affectionately placed a kiss on Bettina's forehead and patted her hand. Lady Olivia, Bettina's mother, smiled brilliantly though her eyes were misted with tears. The Gilbert family had been reunited, and Lark's part in the affair was not overlooked.

Lord Gilbert came to stand beside Lark who woodenly waited alongside the open parlor window. Once again, as he'd done when Lark returned Bettina to her parents just the day before, Lord Gilbert enfolded Lark in a fond embrace. "Thank you, lad, thank you for bringing our only child back to us. I can't tell you how much this means to her mother and I. We've been beset with worries, horrible imaginings, since that heathen took our girl."

"I had to find her, sir," Lark simply said, finding

Gilbert's gratitude embarrassing. Because of Lark, Bettina had been lost in the first place. He had to go after her, and now that she'd been safely returned, he was no longer in their debt. Soon all of them would know this.

From across the room, Lady Olivia gave a tiny sob and wiped her eyes with the hem of her lace handkerchief. "Are you really all right?" she asked Bettina. "I've been beside myself—"

"Mother, I'm fine, don't I look all right to you?" Bettina said and hugged her mother.

Lady Olivia smiled. "Yes, you're beautiful, but—but did that filthy pirate—touch you in anyway?"

"Olivia! please don't badger Bettina about any of that—not with Lark here," Lord Gilbert interrupted and cast a sideways glance at Lark. "That pirate didn't molest her, you can see how healthy she is. Assure your mother about that, Bettina."

"I'm well in every way," Bettina smoothly lied. "Do you think Lark would want to marry me if I weren't untouched?"

Lady Olivia fanned herself with the handkerchief. "Please don't think ill of us, Lark, but you must realize what would happen to Bettina if malicious gossip was started about her virtue. As Bettina's fiancé, you will make it clear if anyone has the audacity to ask that Bettina wasn't molested by that filthy man."

"I shall, Lady Olivia." Lark nodded but looked guiltily away. What a lie that would be!

Lady Olivia appeared satisfied and Bettina smiled in triumph. Her reputation was safe.

298

"How long shall Lady Arden be staying with us?" Olivia questioned Lark and poured a cup of tea from the silver tea service.

Before Lark could reply, Bettina readily jumped in. "Until a ship can be secured for her return passage to England, Mother, I told you that yesterday."

"Oh, yes, I'd forgotten in the happiness of your return. She's such a charming and quiet person. Will she stay for the wedding, do you think?"

"I doubt it," Bettina commented dryly, aware of Lark's continued silence.

Lord Gilbert chuckled. "That's one event I do so look forward to. It's always been my fondest wish for Bettina to marry my best friend's son, and now it really is going to happen." He bent and kissed the top of Bettina's head again and smiled affectionately at Lark.

"Really, you must excuse me," Lark blurted out, feeling as if he were suffocating. He had to get away from this talk of marriage. "I need to see to some things on the ship."

"I do wish you'd consider staying here, Lark. Will you return for supper?" Olivia called but Lark was already striding away and didn't hear. Bettina hurriedly rose to her feet and followed after Lark.

"That really was very rude," she scolded him when she caught up to him on the beach. "My parents will wonder why you're acting like this. Whatever is the matter with you, Lark? You're outrageously grumpy, I can't say a civil word to you. Either you're shouting at me or not paying me one bit of attention."

Bettina pouted and Lark was too exasperated to pretend any longer.

"I don't want to marry you, Bettina! I won't marry you."

Her mouth dropped open. "What?"

Taking a deep breath, he took her hands in his and his face softened as did his voice. "I hadn't meant to tell you like this, but I don't love you. There is no way that I'll marry you, even if I lose my honor in refusing."

"But—but my parents are planning the wedding, they believe we'll be married. My father expects you to marry me," she said harshly.

"I don't care what your father expects. I don't love you and I'd be doing all of us a disservice by marrying you."

"Damn you, Lark! How do you think this will appear to everybody if you refuse to marry me? People will assume that Silva ill-used me."

"Dear God, Bettina, what a choice of words. You know perfectly well that you were his willing mistress. Do you think I'm so dense that I didn't realize your true situation with the man?"

She bit nervously down on her lower lip. "I—I admit that I was his mistress, but only because I had no other choice."

"Did you try to fight him off? I heard that you didn't." His penetrating eyes found hers and she couldn't look at him. "You've answered my question." Lark began to move away from her, but she grabbed his hand.

300

"I suppose you fancy yourself in love with Marlee, the virtuous and innocent Lady Arden," she shrewishly jeered.

"Yes, I love her."

Bettina grimaced and her hold tightened on his fingers. "You'll have to live without her love, dear Lark, for I'll never release you from your promise to marry me. Because you didn't adequately defend me, I was captured by Manuel Silva, and I'll never let you forget it. Who'll marry me if you don't? People will think the worst. I'll never be able to hold up my head around here again. The shame will kill my parents."

"You should have thought about all of that, Bettina, before you shamed yourself with Silva and his pirate crew."

She dropped his hand and sucked in her breath. She turned a pale shade of white. "That's—a lie. I suppose Lady Arden told you what Silva said about me. She wants to make me look bad in your eyes, Lark. She's lying to you."

"Marlee never mentioned anything to me, but one of Silva's crew members did."

She shrugged her shoulders, seeing he already knew the truth. "None of that can be proven, and besides, what difference would it make if I'd had one man or ten before you? You're going to marry me, you have to marry me."

Lark had one last way to reason with Bettina. He felt so sorry for her, he truly did, but he didn't love her. She was a beautiful woman standing there on the beach with her auburn hair blowing wildly about her face. He should have confronted her sooner but while on the ship, they'd encountered days of fierce storms and he hadn't been able to speak to her or to Marlee. Now that he had told her how he felt, his conscience was clear. Bettina must be made to understand that he wouldn't marry her. "I'm going to speak to your father about breaking the engagement."

"No—please." She clutched at his arm and looked up at him with tears in her eyes. "Mother told me that Father has been unwell since my kidnapping. I don't want him to suffer a shock. Could you wait until after my homecoming party? I do so love seeing him happy. I mean, I don't know how much time he may have—" Her voice drifted away and she dissolved into tears.

Lark hated to see a woman cry. He wondered if Bettina's tears were genuine but he hadn't any reason to doubt what she told him about her father's health. The least he could do for her was to wait until after the party to speak with Lord Gilbert. "All right," he said and handed her his handkerchief. "I'll wait until then."

Bettina dabbed prettily at her eyes. "Thank you, Lark."

Lark left her a few moments later. Once he was a distance down the beach, she heaved a sigh of relief. Thank goodness that he'd fallen for her lie about her father's health, something she regretted doing but the ends justified the means. And in the end, Lark would be forced to marry her and he better get used to the idea.

The night air was perfumed with the scent of roses which grew wild along a thin strip of path that led to the beach. A carpet of moonlight, dazzling as silver, danced upon the seafoamed waves of St. George's Harbor. Marlee found her way to the beach easily enough for it was nearly impossible to get lost on the small island of Bermuda. The place enchanted her with its lush, tropical vegetation, and the romantic spell it weaved over her wasn't to be denied. However, there wasn't anyone with whom she wanted to share the moonlit night but Lark. And he belonged to Bettina.

A ragged sigh split her lips. Only half an hour ago, she'd left Lord Gilbert's large stone house to wander aimlessly by herself. Lark had eaten supper with them, and she'd forced herself to politely listen to the conversation at table and answer any questions placed by Bettina's parents and Alastair Caine, a young man who'd been introduced as Bettina's cousin.

Somehow she'd made it through the meal, attempting unsuccessfully not to meet Lark's gaze or notice how Bettina monopolized Lark and hung on his every syllable. When Lady Olivia turned the conversation to the wedding plans, Marlee excused herself on the pretext of being so weary that she needed to rest. Instead of going to her room, she went outside. She simply couldn't stand seeing Lark and Bettina together. She prayed a ship would soon be ready to transport her to England. Lord Gilbert had told her one would be arriving from the colonies within a matter of days, days which passed interminably slow.

The skirts of her blue silk gown billowed about her like a summer sky when she sat on the sand. A warm breeze caressed her face and neck, and she closed her eyes to breathe in the sea air. She thought that she'd like it here very much if not for Lark's and Bettina's impending nuptials. If only things could be different, if only —

"A rose for your thoughts, my lady."

Marlee opened her eyes and settled her startled gaze upon Lark who knelt in the sand beside her. He held out one of the wild roses she'd seen earlier. What was he doing here? Did the man live only to torment her? "I don't think you want to know what I'm thinking," she proclaimed more crisply than she'd intended.

"Hmm, I think your tone is sharper than the thorns on this rose, but I'd like to know what you're thinking, Marlee. Indulge me, please."

"Hah! I'd rather not do anything to please you. Why don't you go back to your fiancée? I'm certain Bettina is eager to discuss wedding plans."

Lark sensuously traced the rose across the bridge of her nose and then her mouth. "Bettina isn't my fiancée any longer. I've called off our wedding, because I can't marry her when I love you."

"Don't you dare trifle with me, Lark! Not again!" Marlee rose to her feet, nearly knocking him down in her haste to get away. How could he tease her like this again? Did he possess no decency? She got no further than one foot away before Lark imprisoned her in his heated embrace and they toppled in the sand. "Leave me alone, let me be," Marlee pleaded, so close to tears that her eyes burned.

"I'm telling you the truth, Marlee. I've told Bettina that I won't marry her. I love you, my darling, only you." He captured her face between his hands so she was forced to look at him. Her heart beat so hard that she didn't hear the ocean's swelling crescendo. Was Lark telling her the truth? Could she finally believe he loved her?

His kiss told her she could.

It was a bewitching kiss, passionate yet gentle. Marlee found herself trembling and clinging to him, unable to stem the mounting desire which flowed through every artery and nerve in her body. "I love you, Marlee, say that you'll marry me. Say it," he pleaded and held her so tightly that she could barely draw breath.

"I'll marry you," was her husky whisper and pure joy exploded within her for this was what she'd wanted for so long. Her arms went trustingly around his neck.

Lark groaned. "Ah, I want to make love to you, now, Marlee, but not here on the beach. Maybe we should wait—"

"No, no," she protested and molded herself into

305

him. "I want you, too, Lark. Isn't there someplace we can go and be totally alone?"

He stared at her, his eyes alive and dancing with wickedly bright flames. "I know just the place, a perfect place." Lark lifted her to her feet and took her hand.

They ran joyously down the beach, their footsteps sinking into the sand and blending together in spots. Five minutes or five hours might have passed because Marlee lost track of time when Lark halted before a rocky cove. Pulling her along with him, they followed a winding path of sparkling water that lazily meandered away from the aqua-colored ocean and beach to a secluded garden of oleander and hibiscus hedges.

"How pretty this is!" Marlee exclaimed. "Where are we?"

"This property belonged to my mother's sister. She willed it to me, but I've never had any use for it — until now." Lark grinned seductively at her and began a tantalizing exploration of her throat with his tongue.

"Oh, Lark, what if someone sees us?" Marlee asked but her worry was tempered by her desire.

"No one ever comes this way, my love," he whispered. "We're totally and completely alone." His lips moved wantonly over her shoulders as he pushed the sleeves of her dress and chemise down her arms.

"Isn't this wicked to be out here like this, letting you undress me?"

"Hmm, yes," he said and his tongue slithered

across the tops of her breasts, "very wicked."

"Lark?"

"Yes, Marlee?"

"I suppose I'm a wicked woman because I find I like this very much."

His lusty chuckle was lost in the valley of her breasts when he pulled her gown to her waist. The warm night air wafted over Marlee's nakedness as she allowed Lark free rein to feast upon her nipples. A warm wetness filled the spot between her legs; she moaned with pleasure and anticipation the moment Lark's fingers snaked up her thigh to stroke the pulsating bud of her femininity.

Sheer ecstasy washed over her the second he touched her. She clung to him, her small cry of fulfillment filled the night. Her pleasure quickly gave way to embarrassment for he'd barely started before she'd finished. "Oh, forgive me, Lark," she said, her voice sounded thick and husky. "I—never meant—"

"I know," he said and grinned wolfishly, "but I'm glad you respond so easily to me. I adore hearing your gasps of pleasure, to know you're enjoying yourself."

Marlee smiled and began unbuttoning his shirt. "Can we undress now? I want to feel you against me—every part of you."

He nipped at her ear. "Any part in particular, my love?"

"That's a difficult question to answer," she pondered with mock seriousness when he shrugged out of his shirt. "I suppose I shall have to thoroughly examine you and tell you my decision later."

"And what sort of examination do you have in mind?" Lark could barely speak he was so aroused.

"You'll need to remove your breeches. I must see all of you."

With a sure hand, Lark undid the buttons on his breeches and removed them, kicking them out of the way. He stood shamelessly naked before Marlee. The moonlight emphasized the broadness of his shoulders, the rippling muscles in his upper arms that could expertly brandish a sword or tenderly hold a woman in his embrace. She found herself reaching out to trace her hands upon his fur-planed chest, re-acquainting herself with the way his flesh tautly fit across the sinew and muscle. Lark was beautifully made.

"Are you happy with me so far?" he asked through clenched teeth. He ached to throw Marlee on the ground and enter her velvet softness. His arousal was all too evident, and the wicked wench was biding her time, making him so hard that he literally hurt.

"So far, so good. Now for the rest of you."

"Oh, God," he groaned when her hands slid down each side of his buttocks and then his thighs.

"You're extremely—strong," she whispered, the words dying in her throat. She knelt on the ground, her fingers following the lines of his powerful legs and ending at his calves. "And very hairy."

Lark looked down. The top of her head was visible in the moonlight and he could feel the wanton way her hands moved over him, massaging him and leaving a trail of fire in their wake. He'd made love to many women in his life, but none of them had ever made him feel the way he did when he was with Marlee. He felt powerful and vulnerable at the same time and certain that he'd never love another woman as much as he loved her.

"Have you finished with me yet? You seem to be taking your sweet time."

"Are you in a hurry, my lord?" She lifted her head and looked at him with wide, innocent eyes. "I'm not through inspecting you. There's one part I need to examine before I can give an unbiased opinion on which part of your anatomy I find most appealing."

"As you wish, madam," was his husky response.

A cloud skittered across the sky and blacked out the moon just then. Lark saw nothing in the darkness, but he felt her hands moving upward to his aroused manhood. Stiffening his stance, he dug his feet hard into the ground. He feared he'd fall when she touched him, that the very pressure of her fingertips could topple him to the earth like a landslide. Never before had he experienced such desire, this heavy ache within him that was pleasure and pain. And he knew now with certainty that he loved her beyond caring, beyond life. Without Marlee, he had no life.

Her fingers lazily trailed up his inner thighs to the pulsing manhood. If only she'd hurry and touch him, if only she'd enfold her hands over him — it would be heaven. And it was the instant her hand sheathed him. Just having her seductively stroke him felt wonderful.

"Oh — Marlee — Marlee —" He sounded like a drowning man, he was unable to breathe. His heart beat so fast and so hard that he feared he might die from the ecstasy of what she was doing to him. "Stop, stop." Stopping was the last thing he wanted, but he didn't think he could last much longer and he wanted to spill himself inside of her.

Lark lowered himself and knelt beside her. His kiss upon her lips was so fiery that the flames which had laid dormant inside of her the last few minutes flared anew. Lifting her onto his haunches, Lark positioned her legs around his waist and fitted her buttocks against him before entering her with a swift thrust.

Sheathing him with her warmth, she welcomed him into her body and moved urgently against him. Their lovemaking was instinctive, raw, and heated. Nothing kept them apart now. They belonged only to each other and gave fully of themselves. In perfect unison, their bodies exploded into ecstasy at the same moment.

Later, after the flush of passion had disappeared, Lark dipped his hand into the stream of water to spread sensuously across her chest and breasts. "To cool you off," he said but Marlee knew he was washing her because he couldn't stop touching her. She felt the very same way and their earlier passions ignited again, leaving them drained and deliriously contented.

The moon had risen higher by the time they dressed. Lark and Marlee walked arm in arm down the beach to the Gilbert home. "Do you think anyone missed you?" he asked and kissed her.

Marlee shook her head. "No. Lady Olivia allows me a great deal of freedom since I'm her guest. She's been taken up with Bettina, which is as it should be." Her voice broke, and she gazed at Lark with hope in her eyes. "You've really called off the engagement?"

"Yes, yes." He assured her with another kiss. "I'll never be dishonest with you again, Marlee. I swear on my father's grave."

Could she believe him? She must believe Lark and trust in him. He was her whole life. They stopped on the beach in front of the Gilbert home. When Lark took her in his arms, a mischievous spark emanated from his eyes. "You never did say which part of my anatomy you preferred most of all?"

"Which part do you think?" she teased and kissed the tip of his nose before breaking away and rushing into the house. Lark chuckled heartily for he now knew the answer to that question very well.

"What are you looking at, Bettina?" came Alastair's voice from Bettina's bed. "Are you going to stand by that window all night?"

"Hush or you'll wake my parents," Bettina commanded in a hoarse whisper.

"Hah! Your father was so tipsy that I helped put

311

him to bed. No sooner had he rested his head on the pillow than he was snoring away. Your mother was already sound asleep, courtesy of the seven generous glasses of sherry she imbibed this evening. The house could tumble to bits around their ears and they'd never know it. Now what is so fascinating outside the window?"

Alastair rose nude from the bed and came to stand behind Bettina. He parted the lacy curtain and saw Marlee running back to the house, her figure and Lark's were clearly visible in the moonlight. "Lady Arden is out quite late," he noted with a sly grin, "and it seems she's been strolling with none other than your faithful fiancé."

"Be quiet, Alastair! You're obnoxious."

"Why? Because I tell the truth, dear Bettina? Admit to yourself that you don't love Lark Arden and never did." He turned her face to his. "You've always been in love with me, and you know it."

She brushed aside his hand on her face and paced about the room, not the least bothered by her naked state. "I can't let Lark cast me aside like an ill-fitting slipper, Alastair. I have to marry him. I want to be mistress of Arden's Grove."

"Damn, Bettina! Arden's Grove is nothing in comparison to what I'll be able to offer you one day. Some day I'll be so wealthy that you'll kick yourself in your pretty behind for not accepting my proposal."

"Oh, yes." She sniffed the air and placed her hands on her curvy hips. "You're going to make a fortune, literally prosper from selling straw. Gold only comes from straw in fairy tales."

"Then I shall offer you a fairy-tale life, my love."

Shaking her head in disbelief, Bettina decided that she didn't understand Alastair's empty dreams. Straw, indeed! All it was good for was feeding live-stock, and now some aristocrats decided to wear it upon their heads in the form of hats. Alastair thought his fortune was secured because he was ex-porting straw by the shipload to England. He hadn't changed one bit since she'd been gone. Alastair had always pined after that which he couldn't have—like herself, for instance. He was ten years older than she and ever since she could remember, he'd lived with her family. His parents had died when he was quite young and Bettina's parents had raised him. They had doted upon him and treated him as if he were their own son. She wondered what they'd think about Alastair if they learned just how long ago he'd started sneaking into her room each night.

Bettina had been thirteen years old when she woke one night to the most exquisite sensations she'd ever experienced between her slim thighs. She'd groggily opened her eyes and discovered Alastair between her legs. His head was bent over her, his mouth doing something unbelievably wicked to her, something she didn't understand but wouldn't protest because it felt so wonderful. They never spoke about this strange occurrence—and she never locked her door on the nights she wanted him to come to her again. For al-most two years, she'd lain in her bed and waited for him, eagerly and wantonly parting her legs the moment she heard her door open.

When she was fifteen, Alastair taught her other things about sex, because now she was old enough to accept him inside of her. That was when he confessed that he loved her and had only been waiting for her to physically mature. The young Bettina had cherished every forbidden act, and Alastair had joked that she was insatiable. But she never intended to marry him, though she knew they were well suited. He wasn't wealthy enough; he had no prospects of attaining that wealth. The day she'd left Bermuda with Lark, she had shed tears. Lark had thought that she was crying because she didn't wish to leave her parents. She cried because she didn't want to leave Alastair—ever.

But she must leave him when Lark married her. She found Lark to be a very attractive man, but why couldn't she break this spell that Alastair had woven over her? Why must her perverted body ache for his possession? Things would be so much easier if Alastair would only leave her alone. But from the second she saw him again she knew she'd be unable to stay away from him. That first night on her return home, she didn't lock her door. He had come to her, as she'd known he would. It was almost dawn before he sneaked back to his room, and once again, she was his willing slave. She'd not felt the least bit of guilt about their lovemaking even though Lark hadn't broken the engagement at that time.

Now he had and discarded her for another

woman. She didn't know if her pride was hurt because of Marlee or the fact that if Lark didn't marry her, she'd appear unworthy in the eyes of her family and friends. Everyone would wonder what had actually happened with Silva. Already she'd seen people whispering behind their hands about her. The servants even whispered about her when they thought she wasn't in hearing distance. Lark had to marry her and save her reputation, she had to become mistress of Arden's Grove. Nothing and no one would prevent that from happening, not even her twisted love for Alastair.

Alastair reclined on the bed and observed her with a lustful and hungry look. He never tired of this woman, he doubted he ever would. To Alastair's eyes, Bettina was the most beautiful and perfectly formed woman in the world, and Lark Arden didn't deserve her. Arden would never understand her as he did. The very fact that he'd broken the engagement was proof. Though Bettina hadn't confessed the reason for the broken betrothal, Alastair guessed that it had something to do with the pirate who'd kidnapped her. Apparently Lark couldn't accept that Bettina wasn't pure—that she might not have been virginal in any case. Alastair would stake his life that the virtuous Lark Arden hadn't bedded Bettina before her kidnapping. Maybe if he had, the bastard wouldn't be so swift to break the engagement. Bettina was a lot of woman for a man to handle. And Alastair knew just how to handle her. They shared the same heritage and blood, a perfect match. Somehow he was going to marry her, even if the little vixen protested the whole way down the aisle.

"Quit being so childish and start acting like a woman. You're nearly twenty, time to stop your pouting and posturing." Alastair didn't smile at her like he longed to do. Bettina needed some sort of scolding to make her see reason. It was too bad that her father never took a paddle to her pretty rear. She'd been so spoiled and coddled that she couldn't comprehend why Lark didn't want her. But Alastair wanted her desperately.

"I'm a woman," she persisted and formed her mouth into a moue. "You know how much of a woman I am."

"Yes, me and how many others, my dear?"

"Oh! You're as horrid as Lark!"

"No, I'm not like Lark," he insisted. "I want you, faults and all. Come here, my pet, and be quiet." Holding out his arms to her, Bettina hesitated only a second before settling into his familiar embrace. Minutes later Alastair thrust deeply inside her, stifling her wanton cries with his lips.

If only things could always be like this, she later thought before drifting off to sleep.

Things will always be like this, Alastair decided, and didn't fall asleep.

Chapter Twenty-four

Black servants dressed in their finest livery waited in attendance upon the large flock of people who descended upon Lord Gilbert's home for Bettina's welcome-home party. Trays of meats, seafoods, and fruits were passed among the guests, the wineglasses filled with only the best of Lord Gilbert's personal stock.

The candelabras had been lit, and the house glowed brilliantly. Happy chatter drifted throughout the dining room and ballroom, and there was no one happier than Marlee. After tonight, she and Lark would be free to leave Bermuda for Virginia. He'd promised her that he was going to tell Bettina's parents that he and their daughter had mutually decided against marrying. After all the months of heartache, finally Marlee's dream was becoming reality.

She'd just taken a sip of French champagne when Alastair Caine walked over to her. Though she thought the fair-haired Alastair was handsome, there was something about him that caused her flesh to crawl. Perhaps it was his smarmy smile that seemed to be continually in place, almost as if he were afraid to relax his guard around people. "Lady Arden, may I say that you are especially lovely tonight?"

Marlee inclined her head in acceptance of his compliment, a bit disturbed by the way his eyes swept over her. Suddenly she felt uncomfortable in the violet satin gown she'd recently purchased at the town dressmaker when his gaze remained glued to her bosom. To gain his attention to her face, she cleared her throat. "Bettina mentioned that you export straw to England." At the mention of his cousin's name, his gaze moved upward to her face and he smiled warmly.

"Yes. The straw is used to make hats—a very lucrative venture. Straw hats are the rage in London. I've turned a pretty profit recently. Strange how some people will buy something so common to perch on their heads. But as an astute gentleman of commerce, I'll supply the necessary straw as long as its needed," Alastair grinned at her. "I'm boring you, aren't I?"

He was boring but she wasn't bored. There was too much activity at the Gilbert home, too many people to meet and converse with. But it was the thought of seeing Lark that night, of sneaking away to be alone. She existed for the moment when they would strip naked and make love for the rest of the night.

318

"Lady Arden, have you heard me?"

"What did you say? I'm sorry, Mr. Caine, my mind was wandering."

"I said that Bettina seems to be having a merry time. "She's a bit of a flirt, you know."

"Really? I wouldn't have guessed," Marlee replied but her sarcasm was lost on Alastair.

"She looks well despite her tribulations, don't you agree?"

"Most definitely." Marlee realized that Bettina looked better than well, she was incredibly beautiful in a gold gown which showed off her ample bosom and creamy skin to perfection. From the moment the unattached gentlemen had arrived, many of them military friends of Lord Gilbert's, Bettina had been surrounded and admired. Her laughter drifted across the ballroom, her face glowed with excitement as one of the young officers led her onto the dance floor. Marlee couldn't help but feel that Bettina's attitude was quite odd for a young woman whose engagement had recently been broken. She appeared not to have a care in the world, not in the least crestfallen.

"Where is Lark?" asked Alastair. "He should be squiring his fiancée instead of these sea swains."

"I believe he had things to look after on the ship," she said and attempted to keep her expression blank. "He'll be along, I'm certain."

"Hmph! If Bettina were my fiancée, I wouldn't let .

such a beautiful creature out of my sight for a moment."

Marlee stole a glance at Alastair, her interest peaked. Could he be in love with Bettina? Or were these the outraged ramblings of a possessive relative?

Marlee was mercifully saved from any more of Alastair's scathing comments by Holcombe who appeared at her elbow and asked if she'd care to dance. She gratefully accepted and was whisked onto the dance floor. "You should be dancing with a pretty young woman," she told him.

"But I am, my lady," he replied with a broad smile.

"Thank you, sir, but there are plenty of young ladies here who would love to dance with you, I'm certain. In fact, I'd wager that the young woman in the pink dress, speaking to Lord Gilbert, would like you to ask her. I've noticed that she's cast more than an interested eye in your direction."

Holcombe blushed and grinned. "I hope you're right. I've been watching her all evening and I'd like to be introduced to her. Do you know her name?"

"Her name's Arabella Landower and her mother is a great friend of Lady Olivia. I had tea with them just the other day. I think an introduction can be arranged," Marlee assured the smitten young man.

When the dance ended, Marlee strolled with Holcombe over to where the shy Arabella stood with Lord Gilbert. After the introductions, Holcombe escorted Arabella Landower onto the dance floor.

"They make such a nice couple," Lord Gilbert commented and patted his protruding abdomen. "Why, they're as handsome a pair as my Bettina and Lark."

Marlee couldn't nod her head in agreement. She felt almost like a traitor to be a guest of Lord Gilbert and his wife when she knew that Lark didn't love Bettina and would soon break the news to this kindly gentleman. If only this night were over. Lark had assured her that he'd tell Gilbert in the morning about the broken engagement, and then they'd be on their way to Virginia where she'd finally become Lark's wife.

"I'd invite you to dance, Lady Arden, but I can't. I do apologize."

"That's perfectly all right, sir, I heard you'd been ill and mustn't overdo," Marlee said.

"Ill? Me?" Gilbert appeared confused and a bit annoyed with Marlee. "My dear, I've never been better. Just yesterday Doctor Manley said I shall live to be one hundred. However, I do have some joint pain, and that is all that precludes me from dancing. Wherever did you hear such an absurd rumor?"

Marlee stammered for words. She felt like a fool. Lark had told her that Gilbert wasn't well, that he couldn't speak to the man until after the party as not to upset him, to allow him to enjoy himself before he heard the distressing news. Where had Lark gotten such an erroneous idea? She floundered around for a way to extricate herself from this embarrassing situation when Lark suddenly appeared in the ballroom. Suddenly she felt light-headed and lighthearted.

As always he looked magnificent but even more so in a wine-colored jacket and black satin trousers. The high sheen of his black boots caught the reflections from the lights. His dark gaze scanned the room for Marlee. When he found her watching him, his lips turned up in a slow, sensual grin that she recognized so well. Without words, he was telling her that he looked forward to their time alone after this party, to the moment he possessed her body and soul.

Reaching Marlee and Lord Gilbert, Lark bowed and kissed Marlee's hand before shaking the older man's hand. Marlee wondered if Gilbert heard the heavy beating of her heart but apparently not. He pounded Lark heavily on the back in a friendly gesture. "Lady Olivia and I wondered what had happened to you, Lark," Gilbert said and laughed. "I thought perhaps you'd decided not to join the party."

"I'm sorry I was late," Lark apologized, "but there were rumors of pirates being spotted offshore and I took out the ship to see if there might be a pirate vessel nearby."

"Good heavens! Did you find one?"

"No, sir."

Gilbert breathed a relieved sigh. "Ah, that's good

since most of the military men are here—and dancing with Bettina, I might add. You should be jealous, Lark. They've monopolized her every dance. But I think it's your turn now for here comes Bettina on the arm of young Lieutenant Bainbridge."

Bettina's delighted laugh echoed throughout the ballroom when the music ended. She dashed toward Lark, young Bainbridge barely able to keep up with her. "Lark, my darling," she cried and flashed a radiant smile. She grabbed his arm, hanging onto his satin sleeve like a leech. "You were naughty to leave me at the mercy of such handsome young men. I was beginning to think you weren't coming to the party."

"I'm certain you did very well without me," Lark said and acknowledged young Bainbridge before the man went to join the other officers.

"Well, I feel hurt just the same. Mother and Father have gone to such trouble and expense for this party."

"And a lovely party it is, too," Lark agreed politely but appeared uncomfortable with Bettina's clutching fingers digging into the material of his jacket.

Bettina narrowed her eyes at Marlee and asked her, "Are you enjoying yourself, Lady Arden? You seem to have lost the color in your cheeks. Are you well?"

"The party is wonderful and I'm quite well," Marlee assured with a false smile. She didn't feel well, not well at all with Bettina pawing Lark. What was wrong with the woman? Why was she so blatantly showy when she knew Lark wasn't going to marry her? Was it only for appearances' sake?

"I'm so glad. I shouldn't like you to become ill." Bettina dismissed Marlee with a less than concerned smile as people came over to greet Lark. Marlee found herself pushed aside by the crowd, almost buried in a corner behind a potted palm, as pleasantries were exchanged. More than once she heard Bettina's shrill voice introducing Lark as her "fiancé." She gritted her teeth to keep from screaming. Why would Bettina keep referring to him in that fashion? Why did she suddenly feel so sick to her stomach when Lord Gilbert, flanked by his wife, daughter, and Lark, lifted his glass high in the air.

"A toast to my Bettina and Lark Arden," Gilbert proclaimed in a loud, proud voice. "May the course of their lives run smoothly. And may God grant them children who are as beautiful as my daughter and as intelligent as her future husband." Everyone clapped politely and toasted the couple. Gilbert's voice rang out again. "All of you are invited to the wedding in a week's time!"

A week's time? Marlee heard this news as in a dream, and she noticed that Bettina took the congratulations from the guests in good stride. She didn't look the least bit disturbed, as would a woman who knew she wasn't going to be married. Either Bettina was a good actress or there really was going to be a wedding! Marlee glanced at Lark for confirmation that this was all a mistake. But he only shook the hands of the people that surrounded him, totally oblivious to Marlee's shocked expression.

This was more than Marlee could bear. Tears streamed down her cheeks as she fled the ballroom, nearly bumping into the stalwart chest of Alastair Caine. Something indefinably sad in his face told her that he was less than thrilled with this announcement—that his pain was as great as hers.

Lifting her skirts, Marlee ran outside onto the beach. She ran until her legs ached and she couldn't take another step. Stopping, she tried to catch her breath but the sobs choked her until she wanted to retch. It was only when she glanced around did she realize that she'd stopped at the spot where Lark had made love to her. Groaning her agony, she slipped to the ground.

Lark had lied to her again! All of the things he'd told her were lies. Lark never intended to marry her, he hadn't broken off with Bettina. No wonder Bettina had gone about as if she hadn't a care in the world. Lark hadn't broken the engagement, otherwise, Bettina wouldn't have allowed her parents to plan a wedding when there wasn't going to be a groom. And there wasn't anything wrong with Lord Gilbert's health as Lark had told her. Lark had lied to her about that, too!

When would she ever learn?

Wiping away her tears with her fists, Marlee took

deep gulps of air into her lungs. She refused to cry anymore—so tired of shedding tears that her eyes burned and were probably so puffy she looked a mess. And all because she happened to love a rogue like Lark.

"Marlee! Marlee, are you here?"

Lark's frantic cries sounded from the pathway and intruded into her misery. At first, she refused to answer him, cowering behind an oleander hedge like a frightened rabbit that had been hunted by a ferocious dog until it was trembling and weak with fear, and now only waited for the kill. She didn't want to speak to him or see him again. But she hated acting like a coward—she was no fearful, little animal. Sooner or later, she'd be forced to confront the bounder and now was as good a time as any other. But what did he want with her? Hadn't he hurt her enough?

Rising to her feet a bit unsteadily, she straightened the bodice of her gown and shook the skirt free of sand. All the while he was coming closer and calling for her. "I'm over here!" she peevishly snapped.

Moonlight streamed over him when he came into view. There was something frantic in his movements at first, but a great wave of relief rushed over his countenance when he saw her. "You gave me a start, running out of the house like that, darling. What happened?"

She blinked in utter bafflement at Lark's inane question. Was he daft as well as treacherous? "How dare you come after me like this and insult me with your stupid question. I'd almost believe you loved me if I didn't know any better."

"What are you talking about?" His face darkened at the bitter tone in her voice. "You know that I love you."

"Oh, yes, I know how much that is. A tumble in the sand every night is love to you. Deception is love to you. Sweet lies are love — to — you." Despite her resolve not to cry, her sobs choked her words.

Instantly he was near and holding her in his arms. "Let me go, you no good bounder! Don't touch me!" She pushed at him with all of her strength, but she wasn't a match for Lark. All of the fight went out of her. She fell limp against him like a doll whose sawdust stuffing was draining away.

His embrace tormented her. Hot, anguished tears slipped down her cheeks. She heard his voice, soft as silk, caressing her in the darkness. "Marlee, look at me. Tell me what's wrong."

She didn't know whether to laugh or continue crying. Was Lark so dense that he didn't realize what he'd done to her, or didn't he care? She stared up at him in haughty disdain. "I think you should go back to your fiancée," she coldly said. "I'm certain you must have a great many things to do since your wedding is only a week away. Please don't allow me to keep you."

"Marlee, stop this nonsense. You know there isn't

going to be a wedding. How many times must I tell you?"

"Until I believe it!" she blurted out.

"Is that what this is about? You don't believe I've broken with Bettina."

"Exactly, my lord. I don't believe one damn thing you've told me. And neither does Bettina. If you'd broken off with her, then why is she still planning a wedding? Why is she acting as your fiancée? That party tonight wasn't just a welcome-home party, Lark, it was an engagement party, too."

"I didn't know about that. I was caught off guard, in fact I didn't know that the wedding was planned for next week. That news took me by surprise."

She didn't believe him. "Of course it did, Lark. After all, the groom is always the last to know these things. I'd wager the news didn't come as a surprise to Bettina."

"Bettina knows I'm going to tell her father tomorrow. I was waiting until after the party because of his health. Really, Marlee, I didn't realize the wedding plans had progressed this far so fast." Such honesty was reflected in his voice and on his face that Marlee nearly believed him, but she knew he was lying. Lord Gilbert was in perfect health.

"I happen to know that Bettina's father isn't sick. He told me tonight that there's not a thing wrong with him, he's in good spirits and good health. Either you're a liar, Lark, or you've been royally duped."

Lark's face turned an ashen color. "The little bitch lied to me! She played me for a fool."

"Then you know how horrible it feels."

He loosened his grip on her waist, allowing her the freedom to push away, if she wished. "I haven't lied to you," he insisted in all sincerity. "What's happened here is that Bettina intends to force the marriage, believing that I won't back out because of the love I bear for my father. But I will speak to Lord Gilbert—I'll speak to him tonight."

Marlee's head swam. Could she believe Lark? Had he been telling her the truth all along? She didn't know what to believe.

Very gently, he tilted her chin upward and gazed lovingly down at her. No matter what she thought in her confusion, Lark's eyes spoke of love. "If we're going to have any sort of a life together," he said lowly, "then you're going to have to trust me. You must trust me. Allow me to prove myself to you. Come back to the house with me and pack your things. Tonight, you'll stay on the ship with me for I doubt you'll be welcome after I tell Lord Gilbert that you're the woman I'm going to marry."

"Oh—Lark." She bit down on her lower lip in indecision.

He flashed her a grin that was dazzling in his tanned face. "You have nothing to lose, my love, but the world to gain by placing your trust in me. More than anything in the universe, I want to win your trust, Marlee."

Was she a fool for wanting this, too? Should she give him this one last chance to prove himself? It was almost ironic, she thought, that to win her trust Lark must throw away his honor by refusing to wed Bettina. "Will you trust me?" he asked, and his voice trembled, almost as if he counted upon her answer.

She sighed heavily and leaned into him. She very nearly smiled at the anxiety she saw on his face. "I trust you, Lark." And the second she murmured the words, she knew that she did.

"Sir, I'm sorry to drag you away from your guests, but we must talk." Lark waited solemnly in the center of Gilbert's study while the man offered him a freshly rolled cheroot, which Lark refused.

"Yes, yes, lad," Gilbert amiably agreed. "It's always good for the bride's father to have a talk with the groom. You know, to arrange for the dowry. And I'll be very generous, I can assure you."

"I'm not here about the dowry, sir."

Lord Gilbert puffed on his cheroot and smiled knowingly. "Ah, you're worried about being a good husband to my little girl. I know you'll do fine, son. Your father was my best friend—a most honorable man. You're just like him."

"No, sir, I'm afraid that I'm not," Lark retorted and was immediately sorry for sounding harshly abrupt. He softened his tone of voice. "I always tried to do as Father wished, and he wished that I marry Bettina. But unforseen circumstances prevented that."

"I know, I know, lad. But that's all past now. Don't worry about any of it. Just be happy and take care of my daughter."

"I sailed after her and rescued her—it was my duty to find her. You understand that I had to find her, sir."

Gilbert smiled warily. "Yes, and Lady Olivia and I are forever grateful."

"I'm glad to hear of your gratitude, sir, because I've come to tell you that I'm not marrying Bettina. I told her this already, but she told me that you were ill and I didn't want to distress you with this news—"

"What did you say!" Gilbert stopped puffing on the cheroot and held it in midair. His face was the same red color as the lighted tip. "You better be joking, boy!"

"I'm not joking, and I'm a man, not a boy or a lad." The lines in Lark's forehead deepened into furrows. "My father wished this marriage, I agreed only to please him and intended to marry Bettina. But I don't love her."

"Love? What a bunch of nonsense! No one loves their future spouse before the wedding. Love comes with time," insisted Gilbert.

"Even in fifty years' time, sir, I regret to say that I'll never love Bettina. She deserves a man who shall cherish her and love her. Unfortunately, I won't."

Lark's honesty left Lord Gilbert agog. The older

man's jaw dropped open in mute surprise. He shook his head in what could only be disbelief. "How dare you not want my daughter! Your nerve is surpassed only by your lack of honor."

"Yes, you're right," admitted Lark with a grim face, "but what good is honor that forces two people to live unhappily for the rest of their lives? I'm not going to spend my life with a woman whom I never shall love."

"You're turning Bettina down because of that blasted pirate!"

"No, sir. I don't love her."

"Damn you, Arden, for your lack of honor toward my daughter, for my family. Your father must be rolling over in his grave. Now *he* was an honorable man."

"I agree with you. He was, and in my own way so am I. If I possessed no honor, I'd marry Bettina and subject her to an unhappy life as my wife. With your permission, Lord Gilbert, I would appreciate being released from the betrothal agreement."

"Hellfire and damnation! I won't release you," blustered Gilbert whose face was now so red that it looked ready to burst. "I know why you won't marry Bettina. You've got an itch for another woman. Tell me that I'm wrong."

"You're not wrong. I'm going to marry Lady Arden whether you release me from the agreement or not."

"Despicable cad! I won't release you. You'll marry

332

my girl in one week's time — you owe her that much. Because of you, my innocent child was kidnapped by that accursed pirate."

"And because of me, she was returned to you. Don't forget *I* was the one who brought her back." Lark didn't mention that Bettina was no innocent to her father. The man should be allowed to retain some illusions about his daughter. "If you loved Bettina as much as you say, then you'd do well by releasing me from the agreement. Either way, whether you formally do it or I refuse to marry her, there won't be a wedding next week."

"Then you tell her that to her face!" demanded Gilbert and he rushed to open the study door.

"Bettina knows I don't want to marry her. I've told her."

"Tell her again!" Gilbert cried, losing control in the wake of Lark's calm, earnest demeanor. He rushed into the foyer and bellowed for Bettina above the music coming from the ballroom. Some of the remaining guests ceased dancing and stared at the irate Lord Gilbert. "Where's Bettina?" he shouted when it was apparent that she wasn't mingling with the guests. Lady Olivia dashed over to her husband in alarm.

"Cyrus, Bettina is upstairs changing her gown. She spilled champagne upon it. What's wrong?" she asked.

Pointing to Lark, he hissed under his breath, "The cad refuses to marry our girl."

"Oh, my!" Lady Olivia's exclamation was uttered lowly. "There shall be a scandal. Bettina's reputation shall be ruined—everyone shall believe the worst."

"I'm sorry, my lady, but I won't marry Bettina when I don't love her."

"Oh, I didn't realize—perhaps it would be better if the wedding is called off."

"Olivia! How can you say such a thing!" Cyrus Gilbert was outraged.

"Love is important. I thought Lark loved Bettina, but if not, then he shouldn't marry her and make her life miserable."

"Well, he will find her and tell her to her face why not, and I shall be there when he breaks her heart. And I shall call him out afterward," declared Gilbert who even now was moving toward the staircase.

"I won't duel with you, sir." Lark followed behind him. "You're making all of this quite difficult."

Gilbert huffed and puffed his way up the stairs, his rage blinding him to reality and what was best for his daughter. He thought that Bettina loved Lark, that she was pure and innocent. Since the day she was born, he'd doted upon her, and as she grew up, he believed anything she told him. He believed her when she'd told him that Manuel Silva hadn't molested her. If she told him that the sun rose in the west, he wouldn't doubt her.

On the second-floor landing, they ran into Marlee. Her worried expression was met by a hostile glare from Gilbert and a half smile from Lark.

334

Without stopping, the two men headed down the hallway to Bettina's bedroom.

"Now you shall tell my daughter to her face with me as witness that you won't marry her, Lark Arden." So angered was Gilbert that he did something he'd never done before. He entered his daughter's bedroom without knocking. And was so horrified by what he saw that he vowed that for the rest of his life, he'd never lose his temper again.

"Bettina! Alastair!" The names were ripped from Gilbert's throat in absolute agony. He stood frozen in the doorway and watched as his daughter and her cousin jumped from the bed as naked as the day they were born. From the disheveled looks of them and the rumpled sheets, he'd arrived too late. Or was he years too late?

Alastair gallantly took a sheet from the bed and wrapped it around Bettina while he wound a coverlet around his waist. Calmly, he surveyed the two men who watched them, but Bettina was clearly flustered and broke out in a gale of tears. "Father, Father— don't hate—me—"

"Get dressed! I want to see the both of you downstairs immediately." Lord Gilbert slammed the door closed behind him and took deep drafts of air. He was dazed by what he'd just witnessed and so distressed that Lark worried the man might fall ill.

"Are you all right, Lord Gilbert?" Lark inquired and was joined by Marlee.

Focusing his gaze on them, Gilbert nodded and it

335

was some seconds before he found the power to speak. "There will be—a wedding—next week but Bettina won't be marrying you, Lark. I release you from the betrothal agreement. Go on, take Lady Arden with you, marry her. I wish you both a happy life."

Lark extended his hand to Gilbert who took it as in a trance. "Thank you, my lord."

Marlee smiled gratefully but Lord Gilbert didn't notice. She and Lark left the man, waiting outside of Bettina's door. They left the Gilbert home and when they were a good distance down the beach, Lark lifted her from her feet and twirled her around and around. The only sounds that could be distinguished under the star-filled sky were the pounding waves and their delighted laughter.

Chapter Twenty-five

Marlee snuggled against Lark's warm body and sighed contentedly. She hated to wake up. Nothing was more wonderful than to sleep in Lark's embrace, to feel his arms around her, pulling her close against him. And soon they'd be sailing to Virginia where they'd be married. For the rest of her life, Lark would hold her in his arms each night, and nothing would separate them again.

Lark stirred, and she opened her eyes to find him staring at her with a lazy smile that speeded up her heartbeat. "We've overslept," he told her. "My men must be wondering what sort of ship I'm running for the captain to sleep so late."

Stretching like a well-fed feline, Marlee could only nod in agreement. A mischievous grin turned up the corners of her mouth. "Tell them that I've kept you a prisoner, that I refused to let you leave your bed. Maybe they'll forgive you."

"I rather think they'd envy me instead." Lark leaned down and kissed her gently on the lips. Her ardent response immediately caused his eyes to flame. "But I'm captain of this ship and Holcombe is capable of seeing to things. Why should I get up when I have a willing, warm wench in my bed?"

Marlee wrapped her arms around his neck and whispered, "Why indeed, my lord?"

It was high noon before they emerged from the cabin.

Ships continually docked at Bermuda's busy harbor. The king's navy logged in each new arrival and patrolled the seas in the vicinity, ever on the lookout for pirate ships. Sometimes a pirate ship wouldn't be spotted, seeking safe haven in isolated coves. Such was the case only the day before. Word had reached the island about a possible pirate sighting and Lark, well known for pirate hunting, had taken out his ship to search and found nothing. No pirate vessels were sighted on the open seas for the small sloop had already successfully slipped into its hideaway.

The military men of his majesty's navy were more than a bit worried about pirates. A large frigate was due to arrive at Bermuda any time now from England. Its eventual destination was Virginia, and the cargo was gold bullion, being sent from a London countinghouse to the governor's palace in Williamsburg. The ship would dock in Bermuda for a day before sailing to Virginia. All of this information was supposed to be a well-guarded secret, but three pirates had already learned about the bullion and even now were prepared to report back to Manuel Silva, their captain, with the information.

But the gold bullion wasn't the only thing they'd bring back to Silva.

"There she is," the pirate named Renaldo nudged his companion, Domingo, from their hiding place behind wooden crates on the dock. "She is Silva's woman, I remember her well from the night we dined with her."

"I don't know," Domingo said, carefully considering the beautiful young woman who walked on the deck of an English ship. "Maybe."

"She is the one. You don't remember too well because you didn't take your face out of your plate that evening for more than a second."

"*Si,* Manuel does have the best food —"

"Shut up about food and pay attention," Renaldo insisted. "If we take her back with us, then Silva will be most appreciative. Perhaps our reward will be a larger share of the gold."

"*Si.* Much gold will buy much food."

Renaldo scathingly glanced at his companion's more than amply shaped stomach. "We'll go back to the sloop. Diego is waiting for us there. He might be needed when we kidnap the señorita tonight."

Like silent birds of prey, the two men slipped quietly away from the harbor.

It was the smell of smoke coming from the galley which alerted Lark and his crew. He and Marlee had been dining in his cabin when they'd heard the excited cries of "Fire!"

"Get off the ship and wait on the quay until the fire's out," was the only thing he said to Marlee after he'd grabbed her hand and rushed her up the stairs to the upper deck.

"But Lark—" she began to protest but thought better of it. Lark knew what was best, and she trusted his judgment.

The crew dashed past her, many of them formed a line from the quay to the ship where they passed buckets of water to douse the flames in the galley. She decided to help, too, for the ship was important to Lark and he couldn't lose another one.

She found a place in line beside Todd on the quay; they were soon joined by sailors from other ships and passersby who eagerly offered to help. The buckets brimmed over with water and were passed along the line as quickly as possible. A large group of people had gathered to watch, and Marlee found herself being pushed backward into an alley by two staggering men, apparently drunk, who broke through the line.

"Stop!" she cried when her backside smacked into a wall. The wind was knocked out of her and she dazedly viewed the two men converging as one against her. They rammed into her, the musty scent of their sweating bodies filled her nostrils and then a large hand was placed over her mouth. Her fingers curled into claws to defend herself, but one of the men grabbed her wrists and painfully pulled her arms behind her back, swiftly tying them with a piece of leather. What was happening to her?

One piercing scream was torn from her throat before a dirty cloth was thrust into her mouth, nearly choking her. She was hauled from her feet and slung over Renaldo's shoulder and no amount of kicking on her part could free her.

"She's a spirited one, Manuel will be pleased with us," declared the pudgy Domingo as he tried to keep up with Renaldo. A third man, Diego, suddenly appeared at the end of the alley. He clutched a burning torch in his hand and waved them forward.

The three men bolted down a side street with their kicking captive. Domingo, however, grew winded and his pace started to slow. "Keep up," urged Renaldo when they neared the moonlit beach and headed for the cove at the other end of the island where the sloop was hidden.

Though Domingo tried his best, he couldn't keep up. His breathing was labored and his legs weakened with each step until he'd fallen far behind his comrades. "Wait—please—" he called but his friends didn't heed him. Finally, he fell onto the sand and gasped for air.

Renaldo turned and saw his comrade. He stopped with his kicking burden. "Domingo needs our help," he shouted to Diego who was sprinting ahead. Diego halted in midstride and might have offered assistance to his fellow pirate, but in the clear, quiet night he heard the distant shouts and could see flickers from the torchlights that were headed in their direction.

"We're being pursued. Let the ton of blubber fend

341

for himself. I've no use for him anyway, neither does Manuel. Hurry, we're near the sloop!" he cried to Renaldo and started running.

Renaldo's indecision was etched upon his face. He hated not helping Domingo, but the thought of being captured by a group of English dogs made up his mind. He left his friend to face the fury of the English.

Lark's heart threatened to burst from his chest. He'd never ran so hard in his entire life, he'd never experienced such unbridled cold fear before, either. The beach was as familiar to him as the back of his hand, but tonight the moon ominously glowed and everything looked foreign. Not even the torches that he, Todd, and Holcombe brandished provided any comfort. If not for Todd, who had witnessed two men dragging Marlee away and who now ran furiously beside him, he'd never have known of Marlee's kidnapping. At first, he'd felt fortunate that *Her Ladyship* was saved from total destruction. Only a small portion of the galley had burned. But now, Marlee was being spirited away from him, and if anything happened to her, he wished to die.

Holcombe ran a bit ahead of Lark and suddenly halted to a grinding stop on the beach. "I've found one of them, Captain!"

Seconds later, Lark was upon the cowering and out-of-breath Domingo. The pudgy pirate held out his hands in supplication. "Have pity, señors, have— mercy—upon—me."

Lark instantly recognized Domingo as one of

342

Silva's men. "Where is the woman?" Lark grasped the collar of Domingo's shirt, squeezing the rest of the breath from him. He'd have gladly choked the white-faced man, but he needed to know about Marlee, so he released the pressure when he saw Domingo's eyes bug.

"Aaagh!" Domingo drew breath at last. His friends had left him, and at that second he hated Renaldo and Diego more than the cruel Englishman. He hoped the Englishman found them and killed them for leaving him here to be captured.

"Tell me where she's been taken?" Lark persisted in a voice that cut through the night like the cold blade of a rapier.

"The cove—that way." Domingo weakly pointed in the direction. "There's a sloop—"

Before Domingo could finish, Lark bounded away, kicking up the sand in his feverish haste. His heart wildly thumped inside his rib cage. This couldn't be happening again to him! Bettina had been taken away—and now Marlee, the only woman he'd ever loved. And once again, he had Manuel Silva to thank.

His legs swiftly carried him to the cove. With the moonlight sparkling across the water, he clearly made out the dark-shaped silhouette of the sloop. And then he saw the two men rushing toward it and Marlee who was slung over the back of one of the men. Rage and pain flared within him. He dropped his torch and reached for the knife at his side in one motion, but for the first time in his life, he was without a strategy. He didn't think about his next move. Instead, a sound of pure agony and anger was ripped from his throat and he hurdled carelessly toward one of the men.

Knocking Diego from his feet, Lark straddled him and lost his knife in the process. Diego had heard Lark's anguished cry. Aware of pursuit, he was prepared for an attack. Whereas, Lark had acted on instinct, Diego acted out of cunning. Within his hand was a sharp, little knife with a jagged edge that not only inflicted immense misery but was also coated with a poison that left even the strongest of men burning with pain. No sooner had Lark tackled him than Diego's blade struck into Lark's right shoulder.

"Son of a bitch!" Lark cursed and attempted to wrest the knife from Diego, but he didn't anticipate the searing pain which left his arm and shoulder area suddenly weak and powerless. Diego pushed Lark from him, though Lark valiantly tried to control him with his left hand. It was then Diego had the advantage for Lark fell backward onto the sand. Once again, he viciously thrust the knife, targeting Lark's abdomen. Lark moved just as the knife jutted into his side. A shaft of scorching pain, unlike anything Lark had ever experienced, ate through him and incapacitated him.

"English dog, I shall end your pitiful life." Diego's malevolent hand rose up but the sound of Holcombe's shouts stalled him.

"Diego, hurry!" yelled Renaldo from the sloop.

"You're lucky I'm in a hurry," Diego said and

344

smirked before rushing to the waiting sloop. Just as Holcombe came into view, the sloop sailed swiftly away.

Dawn was breaking upon the horizon when the sloop met up with Manuel's brigantine. Marlee was hauled aboard by Renaldo and brought to Silva's cabin. Renaldo unceremoniously placed her on the floor bound and trussed like an offering of thanksgiving before Silva, who had just finished dressing.

"Diego and I have brought back your woman, Captain." Renaldo flashed a proud smile.

Silva glanced down at her in disinterest. "*Si,* you have done well. Now go."

"But I've information about the frigate—"

"Go now!"

Renaldo quickly left the cabin.

Silva stood over Marlee, daunting in his physical strength and height. Dressed all in black, he resembled a crow. His dark eyes appraised her, seeming to strip her of the pink and white calico gown she wore. His malicious smile chilled her, but she refused to cower. In an outward show of defiance, she straightened her shoulders and impaled him with a dark, hate-filled gaze. Yet inside, Marlee quivered with fear.

"So, *querida,* you've been returned to me, and much worse for wear, I think. What happened to the pretty red silk gown I bought you? It seems your beloved Lark doesn't outfit you as well as I. How foolish of you to have run away from me." Bending down, he met her at face level. "I trust that when I remove the gag from your mouth that you won't scream. Not that it would do you any good. Still, I prefer you to be quiet."

Silva took the gag away and then to her surprise, he cut the leather tie that bound her wrists. He caught her hands in his. "Tsk, tsk, Marlee, your wrists are marked. I shall take my men to task for this carelessness." His mouth was only an inch away from hers. "I know how to tie a cord and not leave any markings on the skin. Soon I shall show you exactly how it's done and you'll experience the pleasure with the pain."

"I hate you!" she hoarsely whispered, her throat dry and aching.

Touching her face with his fingers, he traced a path from her earlobe to her chin and stopped at her lips. "You may hate me as much as you choose, *querida*. I have no use for your love. Once, I would have welcomed it but no longer. You're a treacherous bitch but a beautiful one. All I want from you is your sex, the pleasure which your body shall give to me. As long as you're on this ship, you belong only to me and will service me in any way I wish. And perhaps if you're a very good mistress, I'll buy you a present when we reach Saint Augustine."

She spat, hitting him squarely on the cheek. Barely flickering an eyelash, he calmly took out a handkerchief and wiped his face. However, he tightened his grip on her wrist, hurting her with his iron grasp. "You English have no manners, but soon you'll be bowing and scraping to me. I'm master of your body and soul now, Marlee, so stop fighting me."

Dropping her wrist, Silva strode from the cabin and shut the door. The bar fell into place with a heavy thud, but Marlee didn't bother to get up and try the latch. She knew she was trapped.

Chapter Twenty-six

"Lucky, that's what you are, Captain. A less robust man wouldn't have survived your wounds. And you're more than fortunate that whatever substance covered the knife resulted in only a temporary paralysis. With a few days' rest, you'll be hale and hearty again." The physician closed his bag and peered through his spectacles at Lark, instantly realizing this was no docile patient.

"I don't have the time to lie abed," objected Lark and lifted himself to a sitting position on his bunk. For a few seconds, the cabin spun dizzily before him then righted itself. He still felt weak from loss of blood yet was more than grateful to have regained physical sensation in his arm and hip. For nearly three hours after his attack, he'd been unable to move. His worst fear was that he'd be paralyzed and unable to go after Marlee, but suddenly the numbness had started wearing away. Evidently whatever substance that had coated the pirate's knife caused only a temporary paralysis. The next time he ran across the pirate who'd stabbed him, he'd be prepared. And next time was swiftly approaching.

The doctor shook his head. "You need your rest, sir."

"I'll mend faster if I'm on the open seas," Lark insisted and rose unsteadily to show the man to the door.

"I won't be responsible for your health," the kindly, gray-haired physician solemnly uttered.

"Thank you for your help, sir, but I can take care of myself now." With a weakened gait, Lark pulled himself up the stairs to the deck where he bade the doctor farewell. He called to Holcombe, who instantly scampered down from the rigging. "Have you spoken to the admiral of the fleet yet?"

"Aye, aye, sir. Even as we speak, the navy is organizing the men. A crew of the king's finest will accompany us on board while four other ships sail beside us. We lift anchor at dawn."

"Good job, Holcombe. Thank you for speaking for me when I couldn't."

"I'm pleased to help you. That Spaniard, Domingo, was also a help. Because of him, we now know that Silva has set his sights on the frigate's cargo."

"Damn the cargo! I don't care if the bullion is lost at sea, all I want is to find Marlee—and finally rid myself of Manuel Silva forever."

"This time we'll find him, sir." Holcombe smiled optimistically.

Lark nodded in grim determination. "Yes, and when I have that mangy cur in my hands, I'm going to end his miserable life."

Manuel's brigantine was buffeted by the strong winds which rose out of the west. The sky turned an ashen gray before shading to a deep, malevolent purple. Huge waves struck the ship's hull, lifting it out of the water then dropping back again with a jarring motion. A storm was fast approaching, the smell of imminent rain filled Silva's cabin. Marlee tensed in her chair each time the ship heaved upward, and it seemed her stomach followed suit.

She hadn't seen Silva since she came on board and prayed never to lay eyes upon the man again. But she knew that soon he'd return to the cabin and she lived in dread of that moment. If only Lark would find her.

Where was Lark? Would she ever see him again? Had that horrid Diego, whom she'd heard boasting to Renaldo on the sloop about stabbing an Englishman, been speaking about Lark? Not Lark, she prayed, please don't let the man have been Lark.

The bar lifted on the cabin door, startling Marlee out of her seat. With her heart thumping out a wild staccato rhythm, she expected to see Manuel. Instead, a thin woman whose dark hair reached to the middle of her calves entered Silva's cabin while outside, a burly pirate stood guard. She wore a thin red skirt and white peasant blouse, and her feet were bare. Swinging her hips from side to side, she carried a tray that contained a bowl of broth, a piece of hard cheese, and a slice of freshly baked bread which she placed on a table.

Her dark eyes contemptuously roamed over Marlee. "Captain Silva has sent your supper. He asked me to tell you that he'll join you when the storm ends. For now, you must eat and wait. He has more to do on his ship than pine after you, English *puta*." She spoke with so much vehemence that Marlee flinched. The woman noticed and cackled. "I don't know why Manuel wants you when he can have me."

"Take him, please, for I don't want him at all." Marlee recovered herself and stared defiantly at the woman.

"Bah! You have no taste, *puta*. Now I, Rosalina Torres, know what a man like Manuel wants from a woman."

"Give it to him then."

Rosalina placed her hands on her hips and circled Marlee. "You think you're grander than me with your fancy dress and talk. But you're the same as me—no better, no worse than a *puta*."

"Enlighten me, Rosalina. What is a *puta*?" Marlee didn't really care what it was. She was gauging Rosalina, attempting to determine if she might be able to help her escape somehow whenever they docked.

An amused grin turned up the edges of Rosalina's scarlet mouth. "A *puta* is what you'd call a whore in your language. Manuel says you're his mistress, but I know better. There's no need to use a fancy word. Maybe you bed Manuel for a while, but soon, he'll grow tired of his fancy English lady like he did that other one. And then, well, you'll be turned over to his men. You'll be just like me."

"No, I won't. I'd kill myself first." Marlee grew queasy. Perspiration droplets broke out upon her forehead. Suddenly she felt horribly and unaccountably ill when the ship gave a violent lurch. Falling to her knees, she held onto the table leg. "Please help me," she begged Rosalina through pale lips.

"You've nothing but the seasickness," was Rosalina's adept diagnosis.

"No, no, I need your help to escape Manuel Silva."

Rosalina looked dumbstruck. "Escape from Manuel? But why would you want to?" she asked, shaking her head in bafflement. "Manuel is a good lover. Maybe you'll be fortunate and he'll keep you for himself for a long time before sharing you with his men. Maybe you'll even come to like opening your legs for the crew, eh? That red-haired English *puta* liked it." Rosalina threw back her head and burst out laughing. "You English are a crazy people," she observed and shut the door behind her.

Once more, the bar slipped into place.

Marlee's fingers clutched the table leg, holding on in abject fear and misery. A short time ago everything had been wonderful, her future with Lark gleamed bright as gold. Now, darkness claimed her soul.

"Lark, Lark," she mouthed his name over and over again, offering a silent prayer that he'd find her soon and deliver her from this pit of hell and the devilish Manuel Silva.

"Sir, the storm has ended," Lieutenant Monroe, one of the English navy's finest young officers, reported to Lark. "Holcombe requests you go above deck. He believes he's sighted the frigate, *Morning Star,* and her companion vessel."

Glancing up from the maps he perused, Lark nodded and took a small swig of whiskey to dull the ache in his shoulder. "Any sign of Silva yet?"

"No, sir."

"Where can that blasted swine be!" Lark burst out, his frustration and fear showed in his weary, lined face. "We've been sailing for more than a day—and nothing. One would think that his majesty's finest would be able to rout out the bastard before now."

"The storm threw us off course for a while, sir," Monroe defensively explained, "but now that the frigate is in view, Silva can't be far behind."

Lark stood up from behind the table and grabbed his saber, tying it to the loop on his waistband. Then he opened the sea chest and took out a pistol. "I wonder which way that bastard prefers to die," he said, referring to Silva in a chilling voice. "Pass the word to the men that if Silva is captured, he is to be brought to me — and only to me."

"I doubt the admiralty will approve, sir."

"Damn the admiralty! This is *my* ship and I'm in charge."

Lieutenant Monroe saluted but appeared a bit stunned by Lark's outburst. "Yes, sir!"

"You may go," Lark said. Monroe hurriedly left the cabin.

The man most probably thought he was demented, and maybe he was right, Lark decided when he caught sight of his reflection in the wall mirror. His unshaven face stared back at him from dark-circled eyes. He hadn't combed his hair in days; in fact, he hadn't slept in days, either — not since Marlee had been kidnapped. The clothes he wore were clean at least, having changed after the stabbing, but they were rumpled. The stab wounds still pained him some but nothing hurt as much as the pernicious ache in his heart. Sometimes he wondered if he was already mad and didn't know it.

Every moment of the day was passed in agony. When Bettina had been taken, Lark hadn't dwelled

354

upon what might have happened to her. But now that Marlee was gone, he couldn't concentrate on anything other than what Silva might be doing to her. Was the bastard touching her, forcing himself upon her? He hated to think about Marlee in Silva's bed, or being used by Silva's men. The sordid images revolved in his mind like a windmill. To counteract the images, he began to concentrate on how he'd kill Manuel Silva with his bare hands and this is what saved him from insanity.

"Marlee, my sweet love, I'm coming for you," he whispered and left the cabin to join the men on deck.

After a long, dreadful night of wind-tossed seas and violent rain, all was now calm. A timid sunbeam slid into Silva's cabin to bathe the interior in a yellow glow. Marlee laid on the velvet-cushioned window seat which allowed a sweeping view of the ocean and sky. But she wasn't concerned with the view, instead she'd placed her arm over her eyes to block out the light. Her head hurt, and her stomach felt as if she'd heaved up the sea, having spent hours during the storm bent over the chamber pot. Never had she been so ill, not even on Lark's ship where she'd spent weeks. She wished to die.

But death didn't come. Manuel Silva did.

She was too ill even to steal a glance when she heard the bar being lifted, the creak of the door opening and closing. But she knew Manuel was in the room, she sensed him watching her and shivered beneath the blanket.

"Rosalina told me you were sick," he said with a heavy dose of annoyance in his voice. "Don't attempt to fake illness, Marlee. I realize you're playing a game with me."

She slowly removed her arm so he could see the pallor of her complexion, the blue eyes which stared dully at him. "Do I look like I'm playing a game?" she asked weakly, dismayed to discover that he hovered over her like a vulture.

"*Madre de Dios,* you look wretched!"

"Thank you—so much."

Silva sighed raggedly, disturbed and frustrated by Marlee's condition. He'd been on deck for hours, fighting the storm, keeping his men under control. All he wanted was to return to his cabin and possess the English beauty who had captured his heart—if it could be said that Manuel Silva had a heart, and many people believed he didn't. But he did have one. He felt pain and love as much as any man, lust, too, and that was the main reason he'd wanted Marlee in the beginning. Her delicate loveliness overpowered him, and he wasn't used to being denied anything he wanted, much less endure being scorned by a woman.

This woman had scorned him and hurt his pride. Even now, lying sick and weak before him, she scorned him. Where was the justice? He'd offered her marriage and would be a good father to the children she'd bear. Instead, she'd turned loathsome eyes upon him, cringing each time he touched her. Didn't she realize that he loved her? What more could he do to make her want him?

Her escape with Lark Arden had stung and humiliated him. Never would he forget the way he'd searched frantically for her at the ball when she didn't return with Doña Carlotta. But Doña Carlotta was gone, too, and he'd never seen her again. It was hours later, after he'd suffered the humiliation of Marlee's abandonment in front of the governor and his friends, that he learned two ships had been spotted in Matanzas Bay. One belonged to Sloane Mason and the other to Lark Arden, his enemy. His anger knew no bounds.

A part of him was now pleased to see Marlee in physical distress, feeling that she deserved to suffer for what she'd done to him. Yet he wanted her well again very soon. His loins ached to possess her and make her truly his. Somehow he'd have to free her of Arden's memory. His only alternative was to hunt down the English dog in the same way Arden had hunted him and to finally kill the bastard. Such a black thought immediately lightened Silva's disposition.

"You know, *querida*, I could take you here and now. You'd be much too weak to fight me off." Silva didn't intend to touch her while she was ill, but he was unwilling to give her the satisfaction of

357

knowing she was safe from him for the moment.

A wave of fear flashed across her face only for an instant, but she bravely hid her terror behind a forced smile. "Yes, I suppose—you could. But if I'm not suffering from seasickness, you might catch whatever ails me. Then you'd be the one retching into the chamber pot all night. Not a—pretty picture, is it?"

Damn! he cursed under his breath. The wily wench had turned the tables on him, causing him again to look and feel foolish. "I'll send Rosalina to tend to you," he muttered and scowled blackly. "But I warn you, *querida*, that soon I'll have my way with you, whether it's here or in Saint Augustine."

"Lark will hunt you down like the swine you are," she hissed.

"No, I shall hunt him instead. Time and cunning are on my side. No one has ever outwitted me. No one ever shall. Rest and regain your strength, Marlee. I think I'll go on deck and search for Arden's ship, and when I find it, I shall dispose of it and Arden."

She stared at him in haughty disdain until her glower forced him to turn and leave.

"Captain Silva, there's the English frigate and her companion vessel." Renaldo gazed through the spyglass and pointed to two dark specks on the distant horizon.

"Let me see." Manuel took the spyglass and smiled at what he saw. He stroked his short beard. *"Bueno.* There shouldn't be a problem taking both ships. Diego is captaining the sloop and will back us up. Renaldo, order the square sails opened, the cannons readied for firing. This shall be an easy victory." Manuel was certain the frigate would fall without too much trouble. The ship was large but slow moving. He determined that the other ship wasn't as big as the frigate but moved at the same speed. His own brigantine was quick and sturdy as a workhorse, never failing him in a battle; the sloop that traveled alongside was smaller but equally as swift—a perfect escape vessel if the brigantine was incapacitated.

With all his senses alerted, a surge of energy rushed through him, reviving his tired body. He lived not for the plunder but the challenge and a good fight. May it now be so.

The sound of a cannon's boom echoed in the distance. Lark grabbed his spyglass and shouted to Lieutenant Monroe, "Silva's brigantine is attacking the *Morning Star!* All men to their posts!"

"Aye, aye, sir!" Monroe rushed away, leaving Lark alone on the bridge. Men ran hither and yon below him, readying their swords and muskets while the gunners stood at attention behind the large, formidable cannons. The men on the four navy ships followed similar orders. With their sails

359

at full mast, the ships pressed solidly forward as one body. So many men and so much firepower almost certainly spelled doom for Manuel Silva, however, Lark had learned never to underestimate the cunning pirate. And he wouldn't do so now.

Another boom exploded, this one was from the *Morning Star* and seconds later, the smaller ship protecting the frigate struck back with cannon fire. "Men, hold your fire until we're closer!" Lark commanded from the bridge. "Aim only to cripple the brigantine, not destroy it!"

"But, sir," Monroe protested from the deck, "our orders are to wipe out Silva and his crew."

"You're on my ship and will follow my orders! There's a woman on board Silva's brigantine. Under no circumstances do I want her harmed!"

Monroe opened his mouth to speak but evidently thought better of it so he clamped it shut. With a disgruntled air, he returned to his post.

"Damn military men!" muttered Lark under his breath and scanned the horizon through the spyglass. From what he could see and the cannon explosions he heard, Lark determined that Silva's crew had turned their attention to the smaller ship that acted as a buffer for the *Morning Star*. Evidently, the pirate decided that it was better to be rid of the companion vessel before using full force against the frigate. Lark didn't doubt for a second that Silva would be successful. His sleek-hulled brigantine could maneuver the ocean currents swiftly and easily. The frigate wouldn't stand a chance any other time. But he doubted very much that Silva anticipated five ships bearing down upon him. An easy victory appeared likely because Silva's brigantine was outnumbered. But Lark knew Silva well enough to realize that he'd never be captured so easily. It wasn't the promised booty that drove Manuel Silva but the chase, the smell of gunpowder and burning timbers that stirred his soul. He'd always survive to fight another day.

By now, Silva must have seen the four navy ships and *Her Ladyship* quickly approaching the brigantine to realize his inevitable defeat. But Silva wasn't the type to surrender or be taken prisoner. What would he do?

It was then Lark spied the small sloop following behind the brigantine. "Good, God!" he exclaimed as a shudder of apprehension raced through him. He knew exactly what Silva planned to do. "Break away from the formation and head south!" Lark shouted to Holcombe who steered the ship. Holcombe nodded, instantly obeying.

Lieutenant Monroe broke away from the gunners he'd been commanding upon hearing Lark's order. His young face was livid with rage. "Captain, sir, breaking formation is against the admiral's orders. I won't allow this to happen. Such a course is foolhardy and will lead us wide open to attack."

Lark had had enough of Monroe and his men. They'd boarded his ship only to offer assistance, but he'd made it earlier understood to the admiral that his orders were to be implicitly followed. Marlee's life might very well depend upon breaking formation and sailing south. No one was going to disobey him, especially not a young, wet-behind-the-ears officer. He glanced down at Monroe from his higher position on the bridge, the bridled anger in his voice was sharper than finely edged steel. "Are you threatening mutiny, Lieutenant Monroe?"

Very much aware of the gazes of his men upon him and not wishing to appear cowardly before the daunting pirate hunter, Monroe defiantly thrust out his chest. "If need be, sir, yes, I am. The concerns of my men must be placed before the fate of one woman."

"How very ungallant of you, Lieutenant." Lark grasped the pistol that was tucked in his waistband and shot an ominously black look over the assembled military men. Then he whistled shrilly and his own crew broke away from their posts to silently surround Monroe and his men. The men who'd sailed and remained with Lark since New Providence were seasoned fighters. They were few in number compared to the navy men, not as polished—a motley assortment, to be certain—but they were tough as old shoe leather and would fight to the death, if the need arose. Every one was loyal to their captain, more so than to any admiral or king. And Lark knew this was the deciding factor in avoiding a mutiny. "My crew is not cowardly; they'll fight with me and do what I command without question. If there is to be a mutiny aboard my ship I won't be the one thrown overboard, I assure you, Lieutenant. I trust you and your men can swim."

Monroe's pale face flushed in humiliation. There was nothing to do but follow Lark's instructions. "You're the captain, sir." Turning on his heels, he fled to the opposite end of the deck.

"Well-handled," complimented Holcombe.

Lark sighed, stroking his hand through his dark hair. "I hope I can handle Silva as well." *And bring Marlee home.*

The battle was going badly.

The brigantine had fired a number of volleys in the direction of the frigate's companion, even hitting it broadside. But the small ship continued firing, and then the frigate, too. None of this bothered Silva—he knew he'd be able to wear down the English sailors in time. But then he saw the five ships approaching and realized he couldn't defend himself against so much collective artillery. *"Madre de Dios,"* he lowly declared. "The English will sink us." When a cannonball from the *Morning Star* hit the brigantine's hull and caused extensive damage, Manuel realized the doomed outcome. Yet he felt immense pride because five ships, the frigate, and its smaller companion ship

363

were needed to capture his one. The sloop, however, wouldn't be captured.

From the formation of the five English ships, they were headed straight for the brigantine. The frigate was no longer his main interest—self-survival was. Manuel stood on the quarter deck and waved a green flag at the sloop, following a short distance behind the brigantine. Immediately, Diego signaled back with a matching flag.

Time was of the essence, he knew, and must act quickly. The brigantine would be used as a decoy while he made his escape with Marlee. Rushing down the deck and past his men, some of whom loaded the cannons to point at the English ships which loomed ever closer, Manuel ceased to be calm. Usually during a battle he never expressed nervousness—in fact, never was afraid. But now he was and he wasn't certain why. A strange, clawing sensation in his chest which he'd never before experienced threatened to suffocate him. He must escape so he could breathe freely again.

Marlee watched the five ships approaching from the window seat. She'd stayed in place even when the brigantine took the cannonball. The impact rocked the ship with such force that she nearly rolled off the cushion. Their flags proclaimed them as belonging to the English navy, and she guessed they'd been sent from Bermuda. But there was one ship that broke away from the other four and appeared to be sailing as to go around the brigantine instead of straight toward it. She couldn't stop staring at it, almost transfixed by it, before she recognized the flag on the mast that blew wildly in the stiff sea breezes as belonging to *Her Ladyship*.

"Lark!" Her jubilant cry echoed in the cabin. For the first time she truly felt she was going to be rescued. Lark was coming for her, really and truly coming to take her away from Silva. "Hurry, my darling, hurry, please," she whispered as a warm, happy glow filled her.

So engrossed was she in the stirring scene before her, she didn't hear Manuel releasing the bar on the door or entering the room until he was upon her and scooping her into his arms like a demented fiend. "What are you doing!" she cried but was still so weak she didn't have the strength to push at him.

Manuel didn't reply. He looked nothing like the polished pirate she'd come to know and hate. His hair was wildly tousled, his black shirt was torn and smelled of gunpowder from the fray above deck. There was something feral and vicious in the way he looked at her, almost as if he were a hunted animal that was now trapped. Stark and vivid fear swept through her. "Leave me here, Manuel. Where are you taking me?"

"Quiet!" His shout sounded like a growl.

With Marlee in his arms, Manuel ran out of the

cabin like a man possessed by inner demons. In the dark passageway, they nearly collided with Rosalina whose dark eyes were round and flecked with terror. She clutched at Silva's arm. "Are you boarding the sloop, Manuel? Take me with you, *si,* take me with you! I don't want to be at the mercy of the English. They'll kill me, I know they will!"

Another volley hit the brigantine, knocking Manuel against the wall. Rosalina fell to the floor, her frightened screams sliced the air. Her hands grabbed him around the ankle, nearly tripping him. "Take me with you, Manuel! Please don't leave me here to die!"

Manuel shook her hands off of him. He deliberately kicked out at her and his booted foot hit her squarely in the face. She squealed in pain and doubled over. "Never touch me, *puta!* I don't care what happens to you. Get out of my way!"

Marlee's horrified gaze saw the blood seeping from between the fingers Rosalina held against her face. And that was the last time she ever laid eyes upon the woman.

They burst through the door that led onto the deck. A dark, ghostly haze covered everything, obscuring visibility. The acrid smell of gunpowder wafted over them. The pirate crew ran in uncontrolled abandon, no longer able to douse the small fires that had started in different portions of the ship. Bright flames wantonly slithered like an orange snake toward the powder room door. *Madre de Dios,* we've got to get to the sloop before this ship blows up." Manuel coughed hoarsely and hurried along the deck, dodging the panicked members of his crew.

Marlee's eyes burned, her throat felt raw, and the smoke hung so heavily in the air that she was unable to draw a good breath. Out of the black mist, the sloop appeared.

The men on the sloop stood near the railing and ran a boarding plank between the sloop and the brigantine. The pirates pressed forward in fear of being left aboard the burning brigantine. A pistol shot deafeningly rang out, stalling the brigantine's crew. "The captain and his lady board first!" shouted Diego from the sloop. "I'll shoot any man who tries to go before them."

"Si, si, hurry before the ship explodes!" Renaldo hysterically cried. The other pirates raised their voices in panic but moved aside for Manuel. He was, after all, their trusted captain.

Manuel nimbly spanned the distance with Marlee in his arms. Before she was aware of it, they were safely on the sloop. "Push the boarding plank into the ocean, even if someone is trying to come across," he commanded Diego and the sloop's crewmen who clustered around him for instructions. "There's no time to save anyone. Set sail now!"

Marlee heard the enraged shouts from the brigantine, followed by pleading cries. Manuel sat her on a crate while he took over as captain of the sloop. In no time they were a distance away from the brigantine but she could still make out the figures of people running on deck, jumping into the ocean to escape the searing flames.

Her heart contracted in pity for them. No matter that they were scurvy pirates, they were still human beings, and Manuel had abandoned them. "You should have helped them," she coldly proclaimed to Manuel when he came to stand beside her. "You're a hateful monster—"

Marlee's words were interrupted by the distressingly loud explosion of the brigantine. Scarlet and orange flames turned the ocean into a furnace and lit the sky with golden drops of fire. Debris flew in every direction and haphazardly tumbled to litter the water's surface.

"Oh, God!" was all Marlee could say and clutched her throat in absolute horror.

"Marlee, you're wrong about me," he said with such control over his facial features that he might have been a statue. "If I were a monster, as you said, then I'd have left you to burn in that inferno. Regard yourself as lucky that I love you."

Tears sparkled in her eyes when she steeled herself to remove her gaze from the ocean and look at this spawn of the devil. "Because of your—perverted love—I was taken on board the brigantine in the first place. You don't know anything about love, Manuel, nothing about love."

"And I suppose you'll tell me that Arden knew a great deal about love," he vindictively snapped at her. "In time you'll forget the bastard."

"No, I won't. Lark's coming to rescue me."

"And how can you be so certain of that, *querida?* We've outrun the English navy ships, soon we'll be home in Saint Augustine."

"I doubt that," she said softly as she riveted her sapphire gaze on the swelling ocean and the familiar ship coming toward them at an angle, "because Lark is already here."

Chapter Twenty-seven

Manuel screamed at the top of his lungs to his crew, "Man the cannons! Blow that son of a bitch out of the water!" The pirates quickly took their positions, their steady gazes trained on the oncoming ship. Taking a spot on the bridge, Manuel shouted, "Fire!"

The deafening roar from three cannons reverberated in Marlee's ears. Rising to her feet, she went to the railing and breathed a relieved sigh to see that *Her Ladyship* hadn't been hit but was still slicing rapidly through the silver-tipped waves. Unexpectedly a cannonball from *Her Ladyship* ripped through the sloop's rigging. Two more volleys quickly followed, one finding its mark in the square topsail that gave the sloop an extra measure of speed; the force of the other volley struck the mast, causing it to break in two and tumble into the churning waters. Without sails to catch the wind, Manuel's sloop was doomed.

Manuel roughly grabbed her arm and dragged her away from the railing. He pulled her along the deck and through a doorway which led to the cabins below. Though she struggled, Marlee was still too weak and soon found herself thrust into a dark room without a window of any kind. "You'll remain here until the fight is over," Manuel proclaimed and before she could open her mouth to protest, the door was slammed shut. As on the brigantine, the bar was slipped into place. God, how she hated that hollow, clanking sound!

"Open the door!" she yelled but to no avail. No one would help her. She'd be forced to stay in this dark room, listening to the fracas above, until someone let her out. But who would it be— Manuel—or Lark?

Destroying the sloop's rigging presented Lark with the opportunity he needed to capture Manuel Silva. Without the sails for wind power, the sloop slowed to a crawl. Still, the pirates fired, but *Her Ladyship* steered by Holcombe, eluded the volleys. *Her Ladyship* finally docked beside the sloop, and within moments, the military crew had laid out the running planks and swarmed aboard Manuel's sloop.

A bloody battle ensued between Manuel's pirates and the navy personnel with Lark's crew fighting alongside. The Spanish pirates were clearly outnumbered but fought like wounded tigers. Lark was bending over a pirate whom he'd just knifed when Diego loomed over him. "Ah, English dog, I shall now finish you off," Diego espoused with a wicked grin and brandished the jagged-edged knife that Lark would never forget. Diego came at him, but Lark threw himself away from the blade's thrust. Lark kicked out with his right foot and purposely tripped Diego. The pirate landed on the deck, dropping his knife. In blind panic, Diego reached for it, but Lark was quicker. Within the space of two heartbeats, Lark had retrieved the knife and stuck it into Diego's chest, instantly killing him.

Lark's gaze swept over the deck. His crew and the military had successfully captured or killed all of Silva's men. But where was Manuel Silva?

"The sloop is ours," Lieutenant Monroe boasted to Lark. "I'd say we've a done a damn good job! The admiral will be well pleased. I wouldn't be surprised if I received a promotion."

Lark felt certain that Monroe would take all of the credit for the mission himself, but Lark didn't care. He was worried about Marlee. And Silva. Where was that infernal blackguard?

"Arden!" Lark heard his name being shouted from the bridge and looked up to find the answer to his question. Manuel Silva stood with a sword in his hand and stared down at him in what could only be amusement. "The time has come to end our differences, señor. Just you and I. No one else."

372

"Why don't you just surrender, Silva!" Monroe cried. "You're outnumbered and haven't a chance at escape."

"Ah, but that would take the enjoyment out of things, señor."

Lark understood what Silva was doing. The man knew the battle was lost, that he'd be tried and hung in an English court as a pirate. Silva, for all his evil doings, was a proud man and wished to die the way he had lived—by the sword. Lark felt that even a person as despicable as Silva deserved to die valiantly. Lark withdrew his sword from the sheath at his side. "Just the two of us, Silva."

"*Bueno,* señor." Silva flexed his sword and jumped from the bridge to land on his feet before Lark and flashed a grin. "Now the real battle begins."

Silva circled Lark, thrusting then withdrawing, almost as if he toyed with Lark. When he again thrust forward, their swords met in a hollow, clanking sound. Silva retreated then sidestepped Lark's parry. Lark drew back to wait for Silva's next thrust. So far, they'd been barely contacting each other, but suddenly Silva thrust viciously forward, engaging Lark's sword. All of the pirate's strength flowed into the sword, causing Lark to use equal force to hold him off. In a sudden movement Silva pushed Lark against the railing, forcing Lark to push back with all of his strength. But instead of Silva continuing the assault, he dropped his sword and purposely impaled himself upon Lark's weapon.

Staggering backward, Silva fell onto the deck. The sword protruded from his abdomen, his face was contorted in agony. Lark bent over him when he saw Manuel's mouth move, each whispered syllable further depleted his strength. "I—placed—Marlee—in a—cabin. I did not want her to—see me—die. You have won—señor." He said nothing else, his eyes stared unseeingly at the sky.

Lark wasted no time after that. Striding quickly away, he went below deck and kicked open every door in his search for Marlee. Finally, he came to a door that was barred.

Marlee froze in the darkness, hearing the unyielding bar give way. Her heart thumped hard and fast, her pulses raced. God, what if Lark had been killed? What if Manuel opened the door? She'd rather die than be at Silva's mercy again.

The door flew opened. She blinked, unable to determine who was silhouetted in the doorway. "Marlee, are you in here?"

"Lark!"

Rushing toward him, she found herself enfolded in his loving embrace. Happy tears fell onto her cheeks as she threw her arms around his neck. "I knew you'd come!" she cried.

Lark squeezed her tightly to him and tenderly kissed her. "And how did you know that?"

"Because I trust you, I'll trust you forever."

Out of all the things she could have said to Lark, that meant the most to him and for a few seconds, he was unable to speak. Finally, he whispered huskily in her ear, "Come on, love, we're going home."

Chapter Twenty-eight

Arden's Grove Plantation
along the James River

"You're the most beautiful bride, my dear, I'm so pleased that Lark is marrying you. Already I love you like a daughter." Emma Arden, Lark's mother, wiped the joyful tears from her eyes with the edge of her handkerchief and embraced Marlee. "I wish you every happiness."

Marlee kissed Emma's unlined cheek and offered a tremulous smile. "I'm happy already. Thank you so much for accepting me into your home—"

"This is your home, too," Emma kindly reminded Marlee. "Now take a look in the mirror and see how perfectly beautiful you are."

Marlee faced the cheval mirror and surveyed her reflection. The yellow-ribbed silk gown in which she'd chosen to be married was embroidered with bright blue flowers, the underskirt was white satin. The square bodice fit tightly but was modestly cut; the elbow-length sleeves were edged in layers of white lace that ended at her wrists. Sapphire combs to match her eye color pulled up the sides of her hair while long dark tresses flowed down her back in a riot of soft curls. She silently marveled at how elaborate was this wedding gown from the one she'd worn the day she'd married Richard Arden. Lark had commissioned Williamburg's finest seamstress to design this dress especially for her, and the gown fit perfectly—almost perfectly—she decided and realized that the bodice and waist were a bit snug. Smiling a secret smile, she turned to Emma. "I'm a bit nervous."

Emma laughed, her blondish curls bobbing in her enthusiasm. "No more so than Lark. I've never seen him so worked up. All morning he's been checking the clock in the entrance hall, counting the hours until you walk down the staircase to become his wife. He loves you so much, Marlee, so very much."

"I know, and I love him," Marlee dreamily declared.

A light tap sounded on Marlee's bedroom door which was partly ajar. Marlee gasped in surprise to see Barbara poking her head into the room. "May I come in?" she asked.

"Barbara! My goodness, what are you doing here?" Marlee rushed to her cousin and the two young women embraced, both laughing and crying at the same time.

"Simon and I arrived yesterday morning," Barbara explained through the laughter and tears. "We've been staying at his father's home. Mrs. Arden was visiting when we arrived, so she already knew I was here and wanted to surprise you. You've no idea how thrilled I was to learn you were all right and going to marry Lord Arden. I've been so worried about you."

"I can keep a secret, Marlee, so you see what a good mother-in-law I shall be." Emma chuckled and smoothed down the satin stomacher on the front of her gown. "Now, ladies, I'll leave you two alone while I see to our guests, but don't be too long up here," she advised Marlee with a merry wink "because I've got an eager son downstairs who can't wait to marry you."

After Emma had gone, Marlee confided to Barbara, "It's odd but I already feel married to Lark. I've felt that way from the first moment I saw him—probably because I thought he was my husband already."

"I understand, you believed yourself to be married. When Simon told me how Lark Arden had deceived you, I was beside myself," confessed Barbara. "I thought Arden was a horrible person, but Simon assured me that you'd be safe in Arden's care and it seems he was right. We didn't know if you'd be here in Virginia. Simon wanted me to meet his father, but imagine our surprise when we arrived at Mr. Oliver's and Mrs. Arden told us that you and Lark were being married. I was stunned to say the least, but Simon said you and Lark owe your happiness to him."

378

Marlee nodded and clasped Barbara's hand. "Yes, we do. If not for Simon putting me on Lark's ship after I'd fallen, I wouldn't be marrying him at all. It's strange how things work out sometimes."

Barbara giggled. "Speaking of marriage, I've some news about Daphne. She and Mr. Carpenter are betrothed."

"Daphne — and Hollins Carpenter!"

"Yes. It seems that Mr. Carpenter has always been in love with her. When Daphne and my parents arrived at Montclair for my wedding, Mr. Carpenter was still in residence at the time. Well," Barbara animatedly continued, "Daphne suddenly discovered she cared for him. It's really charming to see them together, they have eyes for only each other, and believe it or not, Daphne is so sweet to be around now. She's like a different person, never has an unkind thing to say to anyone."

"I don't believe it."

"I swear it's the truth. Mother is thrilled about the engagement, especially since she and Father have temporarily moved into Montclair with Hollins overseeing the estate while Simon and I are visiting his family in Virginia."

"I'm pleased for all of you. My marriage did profit my family but in ways I least expected." Marlee didn't mind if the McBrides stayed on at Montclair forever. Since the estate legally belonged to her, she had already decided to write and ask Simon if he'd live permanently at Montclair and run the place. Since he was now in Virginia, she'd personally speak to him about the matter. She wanted to keep the estate in a trust for the children she and Lark would have one day—a day not too far off.

The clock in the foyer chimed the hour. She clutched Barbara's arm. "It's time and—I just realized I don't have someone to stand up for me. Oh, Barbara, will you please—"

"I'd be honored, Marlee," was Barbara's calm response.

Minutes later, Marlee floated down the wide, walnut staircase to the entrance hall and then into the large parlor that faced the swiftly moving James River outside. The invited guests consisted of family members and longtime friends of the Ardens. Out of the corner of Marlee's eyes, she spotted Simon, who looked more handsome than ever. But once again, when she laid eyes on Lark who wore a burnished-colored jacket and trousers that matched the autumn leaves which even now drifted to the ground, she knew no man could ever be as handsome or hold a place so dear in her heart. She loved him with her whole soul.

With their hands clasped in each other's, Lark and Marlee stood before the minister and were married.

That evening they were alone in the house. Emma had accompanied Barbara and Simon to the Olivers' plantation where she'd visit for a few days. The servants discreetly stayed away, but were in answering distance of a bell that was connected from the house to the servant quarters.

Lark and Marlee stood on the front veranda of the red brick mansion. Their gazes followed the autumn-hued landscape that softly swept down to the James River. The setting sun reflected various shades of oranges, reds, and lavenders onto the watery surface. "It's beautiful here," she whispered and put her arms around his waist. "For the rest of my life I'll remember this moment. I'll remember how cool the wind feels upon my face, how the river looks right now, and how much I love you." She lifted her hand and gently pushed a wayward lock from his forehead.

Dark desire smoldered in the depths of his eyes. Crushing her to him, he kissed her until her head swam and she was forced to hold onto his jacket to keep from buckling at the knees. "Let's go to bed," he thickly whispered. His words were barely uttered before she took his hand to enter the house. When they were passing through the dining room, she noticed the windowpane with four sets of initials engraved in the wavy glass.

"Wait," she said and pulled off the large diamond wedding ring that Lark had given to her and smiled mischievously. "I want to see if this stone cuts glass."

Lark stared at her in disbelief. "Now, Marlee? Can't this wait until morning? I assure you that it's real."

She shook her head. "No. If I'm to belong to this family, I want to know that you're worthy of my affections, otherwise—" She didn't need to say anything else. Lark was more than ready to strip her of the wedding gown and he'd have done anything to appease her.

He gave a great fake sigh and took the ring. "The things a husband must do to keep his wife happy." Near the etched initials of his parents and those of his grandparents, Lark scratched his and Marlee's initials into the glass. Tenderly, he placed the ring on her finger. "Are you satisfied now?"

"No, not satisfied at all." She seductively leaned into him and placed her arms around his neck. "I'd like you to carry me upstairs and satisfy my every wanton wish."

Lark easily lifted her into his arms and carried her up the staircase to the bedroom they'd share as husband and wife for the rest of their lives. With practiced ease, they undressed each other until fiery passion won out. Tumbling onto the bed, their bodies melded in a consuming heat. Ecstasy was a heartbeat away, and together they claimed it for their own.

Lark cradled Marlee in his arms after their passion had given way to sleepy fulfillment. The night's stillness was broken only by the gentle lapping of the river against the shore, the plaintive cry of a dove taking wing. Never in Lark's life had he experienced such peace of mind—and he owed his new found contentment to the woman lying in his arms. Kissing the top of her head, he asked, "Are you asleep?

"Not yet," came her breathy whisper in the darkness. "I was just thinking."

"About what?"

"About the things I'm going to remember in years to come."

"That again." He couldn't help smiling. He'd never known anyone so sentimental as Marlee. "What else are you going to remember? None of the bad things, I hope, like how I came to England and deceived you—"

"Especially that," she insisted and reclined on her elbow to look at him. Her fingers lightly skimmed across his chest. "My life began because you came to England. Before I met you I had no life at all to speak of, Lark. I shall always be forever grateful that you fell in love with me."

Marlee's innocence and honesty struck a chord in his heart. Was there ever a woman like her? Lark didn't believe so. "I'm grateful that you saw fit to love me in return, sweetheart."

She snuggled closer against him. "Another thing I'll always remember is that you married me and made an honest woman of me just in time."

"Just in time for what?" he asked, clearly perplexed.

Strands of moonlight beamed through the window and illuminated her beautiful face and bewitching blue eyes. "Remember I told you how sick I was on

Silva's ship and thought it was seasickness. Well, seasickness wasn't the only reason I was sick, and that reason should probably be born in the early spring."

"Marlee, are you saying that you're—having—a baby?"

"Of course, silly, what else would I have but a baby?"

A large delighted smile split his lips and he kissed her perfectly pretty mouth. "You've made me a happy man, Marlee. I'll never want for anything else as long as I have you and our children."

"Children?" she sputtered. "So far, I'm only having one."

"You never know, twins run in my mother's family. Now be quiet and kiss me back or I'll return that diamond ring to the jeweler in Williamsburg," he teased.

"Oh, dear, the things a wife has to do to please her husband." Returning his kiss, she found every one of those things very pleasant indeed.